KJ BURRAGE

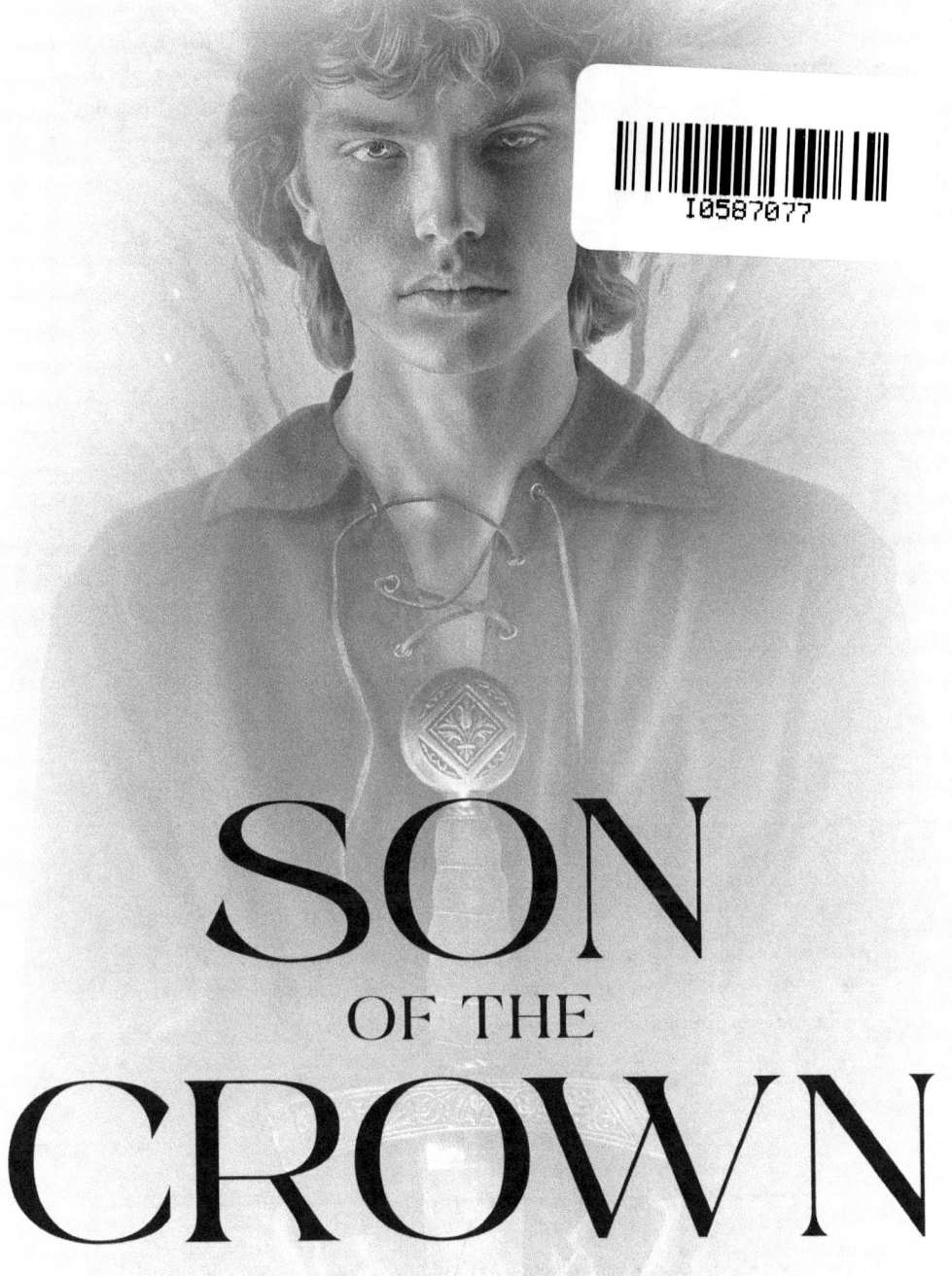

SON
OF THE
CROWN

BOOK 1
THE DRAGON'S HEIR

ISBN: 978 -0-6454001-0 -6

Published by Valiant Heart Publications

VALIANT HEART
PUBLICATIONS

Cover designed by MiblArt

Son of the Crown is written from multiple character points of view. Each chapter begins with the character's name and their location.

At the back of this book, you will find character, location and language indexes for your convenience. Please use them to reference new characters and learn how to pronounce and translate some words you may find difficult to articulate. This book is written using UK English.

Themes and Warnings

Son of the Crown includes themes and discussions including alcohol consumption, animal death, anxiety and depression, blood and corpses, branding, death, mentions of executions, mentions of grief, mentions of past poisoning, physical abuse, kidnapping, mentions of past infant loss, slavery, violence and torture.

For my daughters Jasmine, Alana and Esther.
May you find your own path to live valiantly.

To my husband Scott, who always believed I could. I love you more!

Dedicated to those searching for their own voice and destiny.
You can do it! I know you can!

Contents

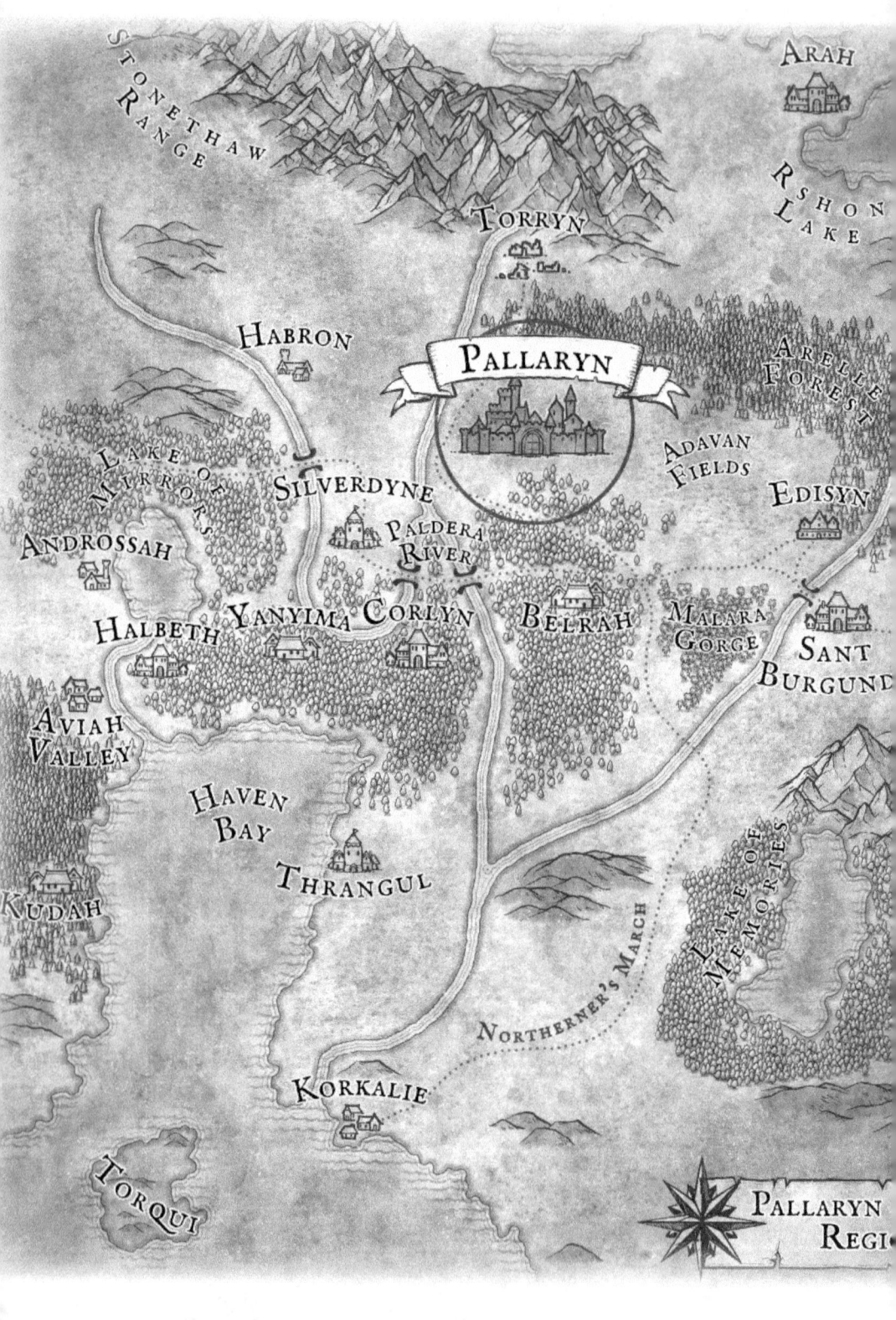

Chapter One

Jodathyn

The Citadel of Pallaryn

"I could end up on the streets for doing this. The stable masters are pretty handy with the dog whips."

Repressing a flinch, Jodathyn ignored the unkind reference to his disfigurement. All of Rama knew how he had sheltered a cowering pup with his own body. His pleas for mercy went unheeded as the dog whip sliced open his exposed back. Although he had been only six summers at the time, he still bore the scars.

Lifting his chin, Jodathyn studied the worn, tatty cloak the stable hand was offering him. Without a word, he took it, wrinkling his nose at the unfamiliar pungent smell. If he was honest, he was curious as to where his requested items had come from.

"It's nearly midnight," Jodathyn hissed, pressing two silver coins into the servant's hand. "I have been waiting in this dingy stable for over an hour!"

"If you want to escape the palace unseen, you won't find better than this here cloak." The stable boy thrust out his hand again for another coin. His long bony fingers beckoned Jodathyn to pay the bribe.

Jodathyn scowled. He had a strong suspicion he was being swindled. If he didn't pay the grinning servant, he was sure his disappearance would be discovered. Instead of arguing he removed the silver clasp from his cloak. He took a moment to study the royal insignia of the flaming crown and sword. Then he pressed the cloak pin into the servant's hand.

"I hope you understand I am purchasing your silence."

The stable hand gave a mocking bow. "A wise investment," he declared. "I serve the lordly types like you all day long. I am a master of discretion."

"I am not like them," Jodathyn snarled.

"O' course not," the stable hand replied as he bent down to inspect the clasp. "It's raining."

Jodathyn turned his face skywards and cursed his ill luck. Warm, heavy droplets ran down his cheeks. The tepid rain would not cool the heat of the Ramian high summer.

By the time he looked back, the servant had disappeared into the gloom of the night.

"Pitiless Otherworld!" Jodathyn swore as he shrugged off his dark grey cloak, which was trimmed with silver thread. He brought his new acquisition to his nose and sniffed. The cloak reeked and he had to wonder if it belonged to someone who slept in the stables.

Shrugging, Jodathyn swept the old cloak around his shoulders, before tucking his own cloak behind a row of scraggly bushes. He would need to return for it later. Pulling up his hood, he strode from the stables in the direction of the guards' gate.

Escaping unseen was the first obstacle Jodathyn faced on his quest to leave the confines of his palace prison. He rarely left the palace grounds, so he would have to rely on his instincts to find his way through the citadel of Pallaryn.

As Jodathyn made his way through the outer parts of the palace, the common guards paid him little attention. He was amazed at how easy it was to slip through unnoticed. It was almost as if the dreadful cloak had granted him invisibility.

Two young King's Guardsmen, identifiable by their black and silver uniforms, lounged against a stone wall. Jodathyn hesitated. Unlike the palace guards, the King's Guardsmen were his brother's elite force. As they lifted their gaze Jodathyn waved, suppressing his fluttering anxiety. Seeing no threat, they nodded, and resumed their conversation. Relieved, Jodathyn continued his journey towards the gate.

"Evenin'," Jodathyn rasped, approaching the guards stationed by the gate.

"Take care, it's a bit wet tonight," one guard murmured, glaring up at the sky.

"Of course," Jodathyn replied.

"Wish I was inside," the other muttered.

Chuckling, Jodathyn stepped out from the safety of the palace. The rain made it difficult to see ahead. At least it gave him an excuse to conceal his face.

Jodathyn drew himself to his full height to evoke a sense of confidence. He ignored the uneasy feeling that the stable hand might be tempted to betray him. It was an established fact that many of the common people in the palace spied for the nobles. It occurred to him that his brother, the High King might also have spies.

He shuddered, imagining the High King's fury if he found out about his illicit excursion.

The desire to prove himself worthy had always beat in Jodathyn's heart. His dreams seemed to hold knowledge of what might happen in the future, as if he had lived the moment before. His tutors had always scoffed and rebuked him when he asked questions about his Sight. They dismissed his predictions as a child's fancy. He knew they were afraid of his talents.

Jodathyn reasoned that his Sight had been given to him for a purpose. It seemed foolish to ignore his dreams and do nothing. He needed his forbidden power to accomplish greatness.

Of late, his dreams spoke of an unfortunate soul in Pallaryn who would be sold. This was his opportunity to be a hero, even if only for one person.

Jodathyn paused, cursing, as he sloshed into an invisible puddle. He was thankful he had kept his leather boots; at least his feet would stay dry. His gait became more cautious lest he slip on the cobblestones. It was with some dismay that he noticed the crowd had become sparse. Those out in the rain were walking with their heads down, as if to make themselves smaller.

Pallaryn, the southern shining citadel of Rama, was different to how Jodathyn imagined. He knew, of course, that most people didn't live in the palace. Dark and imposing, the ramshackle homes of the ordinary people of Rama towered over him. An uncomfortable feeling settled in the pit of his stomach; this was a completely different world to his gilded cage. He was a stranger in his own city.

Jodathyn exhaled with relief as he reached what his Sight had been showing him these past sleepless nights. He had found the tavern that featured in his recurring dreams. Above his head was a painted sign: *Whytehorse Ale House.* He was comforted by the yellow glow coming from the window. It would be warm and dry inside.

Jodathyn dithered as he heard raucous voices singing a rather vulgar song about a dragon queen seducing an enemy king. He considered translating it into the ancient tongue. It would be fun to rile Donatein, his servant who had been with him since boyhood, with a few musical lines. He memorised the chorus, tucking it away in his memory for later.

According to palace gossip, *Whytehorse Ale House* was the black underbelly of the slave trade in Pallaryn. Arturyn Pallarus, the first King of Rama, had outlawed the trade, and those caught engaging in slavery were put to death either by the noose or the axe. Jodathyn shivered at the thought – executions were often messy affairs. But as with any lucrative trade, the threat of death was not enough to deter criminal types. Especially those with money.

Jodathyn opened the door, puffing up his chest as he swaggered inside. The smell of sweaty bodies crowded into a small space was overwhelming. From under the shadow of his hood he studied the dim room with a curious gaze.

Around the fireplace was a company of arguing drunks. Opposite them was a bar serviced by a rotund barkeep who was watching his customers with small, greedy eyes. Jodathyn's Sight had been clear – the slave was outside in the rain. He needed to get an invitation to step into the tavern's courtyard.

Sauntering towards the bar, Jodathyn ignored the curious stares of the patrons, who paused in their conversations to study the stranger in their midst.

"Beer," Jodathyn snapped imperiously at the barkeep, hoping he sounded like he belonged in a rundown tavern. Palace life had taught him that it was always wise to pretend you were more confident than you felt. He leant on the bar, pinning the barkeep with the glare he had modelled from his personal guard.

The barman's cloudy eyes narrowed in irritation. "Your gold first, pup," he replied in a deep guttural voice. There was a threatening undertone in his words.

Jodathyn fumbled through his borrowed cloak, fishing out a gold coin. "Will this do?"

Snarling through yellow teeth, the barkeep snatched the coin from Jodathyn's fingers. He held it up to the gloomy light. "It'll do. You'll not be staying the night."

"I'll have a drink and move on." Jodathyn stole another look around the room. He had no experience of taverns and wondered if this was the type of establishment the palace guards would frequent. He leaned closer to the barkeep, trying to hold his breath at the man's unusual odour. "I hear there is an interesting sale ..."

"You already been drinking, pup?" the barman barked as he slopped beer all over the counter. "*Sales* are for invited guests and yer not worth my spit."

Jodathyn took his beer from the counter, muttering an apology. There was a sale here, he reflected as he made his way over to an unoccupied table. The barkeep's surly response had told him as much.

While he considered what to do, Jodathyn stared at what apparently passed for beer. It seemed vastly different to the tart wine his brother favoured. He took a concealed sniff and recoiled in horror. Did the palace guards truly drink this poison? He lifted the cup to his lips and took a tentative sip.

Jodathyn choked and pushed his cup away. It was undoubtedly the most horrible thing he had ever tasted. And that included the herbal tonics Donatein was fond of. His servant had a herbal remedy for every need.

As Jodathyn stood to leave, the barman growled at him, "Yer not finished your drink."

"I am aware, thank you."

The barkeep snorted in disdain, turning away to clean some dishes with his dirty rag.

Jodathyn stepped out into the warm rain. To the left of the tavern, he remembered spying a small laneway. He glanced over his shoulder, then without pondering the wisdom of his actions, he slipped into the shadows. As he'd guessed, the alley took him around the back of the tavern. Obscured by the darkness, he crept forward.

Jodathyn heard the hum of men's voices before he saw their black cloaks. He held his breath. It was as his Sight had shown him. Thirteen men with their hoods over their faces were gathered in a tight semi-circle around a small stage. The stage was fashioned after a set of gallows and held a cage with a prisoner.

Jodathyn could almost count the ribs on the slave. He was shocked by the poor condition of the young woman. Rags hung off her scrawny hips and shoulders. Wincing in sympathy he studied the dark shadows under her eyes. If the bruises on the slave's skeletal hands were any indication, she had some fight left within her. For this Jodathyn was glad.

"Gentleman, this one is interesting." A tall, thin man stepped up onto the platform. The slave leered at him, baring her teeth, snarling.

"This piece of merchandise has been mostly broken in." The tall man's voice rang out as he addressed the crowd. "This one has an unusual talent, which I am sure many of you will find useful. With a supernatural ability to tell truth from lies, gentleman, this slave can ensure you will never be cheated."

"Can the slave lie?" one of the cloaked figures shouted.

The thin man crossed his arms against his chest. "Alas for our slave, she does not seem able to tell a lie. Barkeep Grul thoroughly tested her."

"Twenty gold coins!" a man shouted from the crowd. "I'll take her now."

"Twenty-two!"

Jodathyn skirted the edge of the wall and approached the back of the stage. As if sensing his presence, the slave glared down at him. She shook her head in warning. Long curly strands of black, matted hair flicked from side to side. Now that he was closer, Jodathyn could see more bruising on her deep copper skin. From her complexion, he concluded she was from the west of Rama. She was a long way from home. He brought a finger to his lips to hush her.

The bidding continued. Jodathyn knew from his dream that the price would go to forty-five gold coins; after that, his Sight had shown him no more.

"Fifty!" Jodathyn cried.

Like an angry nest of hornets, the crowd thrummed. Their eyes sought out Jodathyn in his hiding place.

"Fifty!" Jodathyn called again, this time feeling more confident. He stood up.

"You do not have fifty gold coins," the thin man sneered.

"I most certainly do!" Jodathyn protested, thinking about the gold he had pilfered from the palace. Lifting his chin, he faced the crowd and stepped forward.

"A truth," the slave intoned.

"You're a common thief."

"I am not!"

"A truth and a lie," the slave murmured. Despite her unfortunate circumstances, her lips twitched in amusement.

"Look! I have fifty gold coins." Jodathyn pulled out a heavy purse from the folds of his cloak. "It's good money either way."

The words were barely out of Jodathyn's mouth when he was grabbed from behind and his purse was snatched from his hands. Shaking himself free, Jodathyn pivoted to punch whoever had dared lay a hand on him. The man grunted as he stepped back. After a moment's pause Jodathyn heard him grinding his teeth. Hard, cruel eyes studied him through narrowed slits.

"Fight!"

A cheer went up from the other patrons as Jodathyn came to his senses and realised the magnitude of his idiocy. The man he had attacked towered over him; his shoulders were broad. Anxious, Jodathyn stepped back, studying the sea of ferocious faces pressing down on him. He glanced about, looking for an escape. Many of the cloaked figures had already moved to surround him.

Jodathyn stretched out his hands, shaking his head, as the man grabbed the front of his cloak in his calloused hands. A gasp of pain escaped Jodathyn's lungs as he was thrown against the brick wall of the tavern. The men crowded around him, jeering, as he fought to catch his breath.

There was a brief respite as the crowd took the chance to spit on him. Jodathyn considered his first mark. Fist fighting among courtiers was frowned upon. That didn't mean he had to go down without a fight.

Not wanting to give his tormentors any more time to think, Jodathyn lashed out with his fist and connected to a smaller man's face. An ominous crack told him he may have broken the hapless man's nose. Twisting, Jodathyn managed to knee another in the groin, laughing at the man's satisfying howl of pain.

A dozen men against one highborn was not an even match. Moments later a large meaty fist collided with Jodathyn's temple. Stars exploded behind his eyes as he reeled and dropped to the ground, stunned. Strong hands wrenched his arms behind his back and pinned them.

Crying out in agony, Jodathyn kicked his feet. In the space of a few heartbeats, he was dragged forwards to a large barrel. He bit and struggled, but there was nothing he could do to free himself.

"Time to give you your fill, boy!"

The crowd cackled with glee.

"Please, no," Jodathyn cried. He didn't care if he disgraced himself; he knew he did not want to go into the barrel. His pleas were ignored as he was pushed onto his knees.

"Do you know what happens to thieves and beggars, boy?"

CHAPTER TWO

Jodathyn

The Citadel of Pallaryn

"Please, no! I'm highborn." Jodathyn held up his hand and scrambled to his feet, hoping to ward off his attackers. If he revealed himself, he knew they would let him be. Only a fool would harm a highborn.

"Don't care, pup," growled the man Jodathyn had punched. "How about we give you a collar, eh?"

With an ugly leer he began to circle Jodathyn. Between his clenched fists he coiled a length of rope. The crowd pressed in closer, shouting taunts. In the confusion Jodathyn lost sight of the man circling him. Before he could register the danger, the rope was around his neck. Thick, muscled arms tugged him close in an unforgiving embrace.

The rope constricted. In a desperate attempt to free himself, Jodathyn moved his hands to his throat. Terror blinded him as he flailed, gasping for breath. He thought he could hear war drums in the distance, only to realise it was his own heartbeat. Bright lights danced behind his eyelids as he battled to stay conscious.

Mocking Jodathyn's tears, his attacker propelled him forward towards the barrel. Jodathyn pushed out his hands, but the force behind him was unrelenting. Fingers clutched at his neck, plunging his face into the beer. Warm liquid flooded his nostrils and stung his eyes. Jodathyn screamed.

As he was hurled out of the barrel, he could hear the crowd's laughter. He coughed, his chest heaving.

"Drink up, lad, time for a man's fill."

Jodathyn used the side of the barrel to steady himself. Twisting, he grabbed one of his assailants, kneeing him in his nether regions. He spat in the face of another.

"Off to the Otherworld with you!" Jodathyn croaked, his voice little more than a whisper.

The rope around Jodathyn's neck tightened, cutting off his cries. Once more he was dunked into the barrel. His struggling slowed to feeble movements as he was held under. In defeat, he closed his eyes.

Jodathyn felt himself falling into a strange, fearful blackness, before suddenly being yanked upwards. Shivering, he lay at the feet of his attackers. He vomited over the stones.

"Come now, pup, don't you wanna play?"

"Not so bold now, are you, lad?"

Humiliated, Jodathyn made no attempt to answer. Much to his tormentors' delight, he retched again until there was nothing left in his stomach. He tasted bile mixed with the rich gravy he had slathered on his venison earlier that evening.

"Now, what's this behind your ear?" enquired the barkeep, who had waddled into the courtyard to witness the entertainment. He pulled down the high collar of Jodathyn's shirt.

"It's a scar."

"Get away, you dog," Jodathyn rasped. He shook his head, pushing the barkeep's hand away. He stood, trying to maintain what was left of his dignity, and glared.

Another patron grabbed Jodathyn's collar, forcing him off balance. "It's a scar ... runs from his right ear down 'is neck."

A lit torch was brought to Jodathyn's face. Wrenching his chin towards the light, the tall, thin man swore. "Otherworld Dragons! He has the grey eyes of Vadroil! It's him!"

Jodathyn growled, pushing himself against the wall. His attackers scrutinised him with varying degrees of horror. Some even took steps backwards, as if to separate themselves from what had happened. If Jodathyn hadn't been so disoriented, he would have found the situation amusing.

"You're Jodathyn ..."

"Monster!" one man snarled, spitting in Jodathyn's face.

"Dragon Dung!" another cried.

"Vadroil's whore-seed."

Jodathyn stared in open-mouthed dismay, bewildered by the vehemence of their hatred. Was this what the ordinary folk thought of him?

"It seems like you gents have caught a rather fancy highborn fish tonight."

The men jumped at the sound of a new voice entering their conversation.

"You and yours ain't welcome here, Will Hartcurt," said the barkeep.

Jodathyn pursed his lips, staring at his unexpected rescuer. Will, a few years his senior, had arrived in Pallaryn five years ago. The rumours at court said that he had run away from his father's house after a terrible argument. Whatever the truth, Will had been disowned. The gossip among the Ramian courtiers could be brutal – Will's rivals called him the court seducer, a man of ill repute. The talk of the court didn't seem to phase Will Hartcurt, he continued to hold himself with a quiet dignity. He had a natural confidence and striking deep ochre complexion that was the envy of many a young lord.

A teasing smile flitted across Will's comely features as he studied the tall man first, then the barkeep. There was a strange intensity in his expression as he turned towards Jodathyn.

"He's the very image of the late king," Will murmured, his grin widening as he shook his head. He seemed to be amused by Jodathyn's predicament. "How you didn't immediately recognise him is baffling."

Jodathyn flinched as Will unsheathed a simple hunting knife from the belt at his waist.

"I'll not harm you," Will said, striding towards Jodathyn. He cut the rope, setting him free. "The Son of the Crown doesn't belong out here in the squalid part of town."

"Neither does a lord from my brother's court."

Will snorted, pressing the knife into Jodathyn's hands. He took Jodathyn's upper arm in a surprisingly strong grip, sweeping his imperious gaze across the gathered crowd.

He spoke again, lowering his voice. "You've certainly complicated matters for me tonight, Jodathyn."

Attempting to shrug the lord off him, Jodathyn stilled as Will's patronising eyes searched his face. Then he growled under his breath at the audacity with which Will steered him through the parting crowd.

"He's seen our faces," one of the men grumbled. "Do you know what the punishment is for attending a slave auction?"

Will paused. "The hangman's noose is too good for the likes of you. Turn your captive free and I won't speak of this incident."

"You're not in a position to bargain, Will Hartcurt. We could just slit Jodathyn's throat. I hear they don't really want 'im anyway."

Jodathyn tensed, ready to flee.

Will's grip on his arm tightened. "And have Pallarus blood on your hands? Do you know the punishment for slaying a royalborn? Give me the girl."

"She is expensive merchandise."

"A truth," the slave whispered, her head lowering.

"How much is your life worth?" Will continued, ignoring the slave's interruption.

"You'll not breathe a word?"

"I will not speak of tonight's unfortunate incident with the King or any of his men."

The crowd turned towards the slave to hear what she had to say.

"A truth."

At the slave's declaration, the cage was opened and she was ushered out. Will gave Jodathyn's shoulder a harsh shake as he escorted him through the tavern and out to the cobblestone streets. The slave followed them out, her shoulders hunched.

"But ..." Jodathyn hated the way his voice sounded so husky. Otherworlds, it hurt to talk. "They can't get away with it."

"If you had any brains, you wouldn't have wandered into Pallaryn this time of night," Will snapped, as his fingers pressed into Jodathyn's shoulder. There would be bruises come morning. "Mark my words, if your father was still alive you would be getting a thrashing."

Jodathyn was shocked. Who was Will to tell him his father would have given him a thrashing?

"The King is going to be furious," said Will.

Despite himself, Jodathyn hung his head. A wave of dizziness overcame him and Will had to pause to hold him up.

"How did you find me?"

"You're not the only one with a talent," Will muttered.

"A truth. We all have a gifting."

"You don't have to do that now," Will said with a sigh, turning to the rescued girl. "You're free. I'll help you get out of the citadel if that is your wish."

The young woman's head shot up. Large eyes speared Will with a longing that was almost painful. "I sense what you say is true. This is unexpected from a highborn."

Will nodded, as if expecting her disbelief.

"I can go home?"

Again, Will nodded.

"What is it you want from me?" The woman's eyes hardened in suspicion. "Those in lofty places are always after something."

"I would like to call you by your name." Will's gaze didn't waver from her face. He looked at her as if she was his equal. "Are you hungry? I have a healer, a west countryman like us, who can look at any injuries you might have."

Puzzled, Jodathyn stood to the side – his companions seemed to have forgotten his presence. Everyone at court knew Will was a vain, selfish man who lived only for pleasure. His interaction with the girl seemed to defy the rumours.

"Fydellah," she whispered.

"Let's get our royalborn fish back to the palace. Then I will take you somewhere safe for the night."

Jodathyn shook his head in disbelief. "I don't understand."

Will rolled his eyes. "Is it so unbelievable that a narcissistic run-away might do some good in this world? I thought you were more charitable than that, Jodathyn Pallarus."

Jodathyn swallowed through the painful lump in his throat. "If I have offended you, my apologies."

Will didn't reply; he continued to lead them through the dark shadows of Pallaryn. He walked with such confidence, Jodathyn had to wonder how often he ventured out into the citadel at night.

"They knew you," Jodathyn gasped.

"Not the first time I have freed a slave," Will muttered. "I do it to annoy the great lords who are behind the trading of human souls."

"A truth that you have freed slaves," Fydellah said. She wasn't taking too much interest in the conversation; her chin was raised to the sky as she studied the stars. Jodathyn could only assume she was enjoying her freedom. "Your reason is a lie ... but you have not yet discovered the truth."

Jodathyn smirked as Will opened his mouth to reply, but then clicked his jaw shut. It seemed that Fydellah had rendered him speechless.

"Will isn't the name your mother gave you," Fydellah continued. Jodathyn found her all-knowing eyes unsettling.

"How about we arrange some new clothes and some shoes, hm?" Will said, his shoulders stiffening at the mention of his mother.

"What's your birth name?" Jodathyn rasped. It was most unusual for a highborn to ignore the name they were given at birth. Everyone knew names were important. They held power. To reject one's birth name was like denying part of oneself.

Will shrugged.

"A lie. It's Willyrd."

Jodathyn snorted back a laugh. He studied Fydellah, his curiosity getting the better of him. "You're braver for a slave than I thought," he admitted.

Fydellah stared back at Jodathyn with something between surprise and contempt. "I wasn't always a slave. Once I was free."

"And you're free once more," Will said.

As they approached the outer walls of the palace, Jodathyn huffed in defeat. Everything from the palace's striking towers to the thick walls spoke of the might of Rama and her High Kings. Its imposing shadow loomed over the citadel. Inside his ancestral home, Jodathyn lacked for nothing and yet he wanted something more.

"Are we going to let those men get away with what they did?" Jodathyn asked.

Will smirked. "I promised that I wouldn't speak … *you* made no such promise."

"Pardon?"

"If you want to play hero, Jodathyn Pallarus, this is your chance. Tell your brother you were assaulted."

"*Confess?*" Jodathyn couldn't believe what Will was saying. Did he not know about the King's legendary temper?

"Good King Kieryn is going to find out you left the palace," Will said, a self-satisfied smile lighting up his handsome features. "You might as well direct his fury to some other sinners."

Jodathyn's shoulders slumped. He knew Will was right. He might be able to sneak back into the palace unseen, but come morning his injuries would be noticed and his brother notified. Jodathyn resolved to seek an audience with his brother once he'd had some sleep. He was not looking forward to divulging his wrong-doings.

"When you speak with the King, don't mention me," Will continued. "I want to keep my involvement in freeing slaves quiet."

Jodathyn nodded.

"If you ever have need," Will said, "there's an abandoned house near the Paldera River, near Edisyn. It's a safe house I use to hide slaves and other merchandise. It's stocked with food."

"I don't get to leave the palace," Jodathyn said with a sigh.

"It's always good to have a little bit of information tucked away," Will replied. "It's late. You'd better go."

"Wait!" Jodathyn cried as Will and Fydellah turned to go. Tugging a ring off his finger, he studied it briefly. It had belonged to his maternal grandfather, a man he felt no connection to. Stepping forward he offered it to Fydellah, who shook her head. He took her hand and pressed the ring into her palm. Then he closed her fingers over it. "Please take it. I wasn't able to help you tonight … do with this what you will."

CHAPTER THREE

Kieryn

The Citadel of Pallaryn

High King Kieryn was proud of his imposing presence. The great nobles of Rama quivered in their boots when faced with his stern stare. He had been a boy when he took the throne; trapped by the wiles of the rich and powerful. But he was Pallarus. Before he came of age, he fought to retain his birth right and took his rightful place. The same great lords who sought to manipulate him as a boy king, now bent to his unyielding will.

All of Rama praised him for how he had taken the kingship with grace and dignity. And then there was his half-brother, Jodathyn, who didn't seem to care for his sovereignty.

"Otherworld Jodathyn!" Kieryn swore. He picked up a full goblet of wine and threw it against the flagstone wall of his chamber. It hit the stone with a deafening clatter, spilling the wine before rolling along the floor. "Of all the imprudent ...!"

"My King ... my husband, your temper solves no problem."

Kieryn turned to his wife, who was watching his tantrum with the serenity that never failed to calm his rage. He felt his face relax as she tightened her night robe around her waist and padded across the room.

"Odelle, my sweet, you should be asleep." Kieryn could almost see his King's Guardsmen sigh in relief as he lowered his voice. "Jodathyn's misadventure does not concern you."

Smiling, Odelle tilted her head. "My marriage oath was to stand by you when you are troubled."

Kieryn grunted in reply. He was a High King of a mighty nation. There was always something to worry about.

"I shall not sleep until I know that our little brother is back where he belongs." Odelle's small hands touched his bearded cheek. Kieryn clasped her fingers, bringing them to his lips. She seemed to possess a strange ability to understand the inner workings of Jodathyn's mind. From the day they had married she had called Jodathyn their 'brother'. Jodathyn was fond of Odelle.

"Send guardsmen to search for my wayward brother."

"I have already done so, Your Majesty." Captain Tiernan, of his King's Guard, straightened to a salute. Kieryn was ever thankful for his own elite soldiers, who were honour bound to serve him above all others. Under Captain Tiernan's leadership, Kieryn never feared betrayal would come from their ranks.

"Where is Jodathyn's personal guard?"

"Valt has been searching low and high through the palace, Majesty. He hopes to intercept his master when he returns."

"Forgive me for being blunt, Your Majesty."

Kieryn turned to look at the second King's Guardsmen, who had been tasked to inform him of Jodathyn's disappearance. Quieter than his comrades, Jael only spoke when he felt it was necessary.

"Continue, Guardsman Jael."

"There is a possibility of Jodathyn returning injured." Jael touched the leaf motif upon his shoulder, signifying his rank of troop medic.

Kieryn shook his head and swore again. "Go, find Jodathyn. Make sure he's safe and well. Then I will see him in my audience chamber. Bring also Jodathyn's servants."

"Oh, Kieryn," Odelle burst out, as Jael retreated. "Is that necessary? Must you sit in judgement of your own brother? You know the lords will not be kind to him."

"Jodathyn must learn that there are consequences to his misdeeds," Kieryn said. Out of the corner of his eye, he saw the approval on Captain Tiernan's face. "The court's unkindness will only injure his pride, not cause him to die."

"He's outgrowing the small world of the palace," Odelle warned him. Kieryn regarded the tapestries of his chambers to hide his growing irritation. He had heard this argument before. "He is no longer a child. Your brother is almost a man and he's hurting, Kieryn."

"Am I not enough?" Kieryn snapped. "Do you think it's easy, Odelle, to navigate between being that boy's High King, brother and father?"

"You are good for him, my King. Never doubt that."

"His damnable mother has made it nigh impossible to protect him as a brother. The only way to safeguard Jodathyn is to use my power as the High King."

"There are other ways."

"Odelle, when my father died, Lord Solan and his men tore a screaming Jodathyn from my arms. They took him from Pallaryn for my 'own good'. He was three summers old, my dear. And no matter how much I argued with the council, no matter how much I begged ... I couldn't save him. Only when I consolidated my power was I able to move against Solan and retrieve my brother ... and then it was too late. I will never forgive myself for what happed to Jod at Solan's summer house. *Never.*"

"The actions of Solan's drunken liegeman wasn't your fault."

"Jodathyn is my responsibility, Odelle. When he was born I made a vow to protect him from the evils of this world."

"You were fourteen."

"Old enough to make an oath."

"My King, what matters is that you still look after your brother, even now."

For a long moment Kieryn didn't answer his Queen's observations. The weight of his kingship often had him at the edge of despair. If it wasn't for his Queen and his small son, he would have gone mad years ago. He often wondered if this was why his father, King Hadryn, had married Jodathyn's mother so quickly.

While Kieryn was still reeling from the sudden loss of his beloved mother, his father had married the beautiful Consort Ammerie. He had been angry and petulant. In turn she became a source of torment. When she announced her pregnancy, her taunts had grown to include predictions of his violent death. How such a vile woman could birth such a child as Jodathyn was beyond him.

"Perhaps you should send Jodathyn to live with my father in Arah," Odelle suggested quietly. "Far up north among the mountains there is no court."

Kieryn had considered this option. The northerners would be more accepting of Jodathyn and his gifting, but there would be no guarantee that once Jodathyn left Pallaryn he would be able to return. Perhaps it was selfish. Kieryn wanted his brother close by, where he could oversee his safety.

Striding towards his desk, Kieryn stared down at the evidence of Jodathyn's misadventure.

When Lord Hallidyn Whitoak had come to his chambers and requested an audience, he had not hesitated to admit him.

Clever, ambitious, but with a strict moral code, Hallidyn had been invaluable to him during his rise to power. It was Whitoak that orchestrated Solan's disgrace and brought Jodathyn home. To him, Kieryn had entrusted his brother for a year while he recovered from his ordeal.

Snarling, Kieryn clenched his fist. He had gifted the cloak pin to Jodathyn at the last High Winter Festival, to celebrate his birth. It infuriated him that one of Hallidyn's palace spies had been in possession of it. No doubt Hallidyn rewarded his man for his service.

"Whatever Jodathyn is up to, it meant a lot to him," Odelle whispered. "He wouldn't have relinquished your gift otherwise."

Kieryn brought the cloak pin close to his heart. "If he returns to us hurt ... I would bring him home by the ear if I could."

Odelle sighed. "We have to trust your King's Guard."

Kieryn brushed a hand through his hair. He slipped out of his night robe and searched the chamber for his heavy ceremonial robes. As he dressed, Odelle went to fetch his crown and his gold rings.

"You are handsome, my King," Odelle said, as Kieryn slipped on his last ring. "Why did you also send for Jodathyn's servants for judgement?"

"Perhaps if Jodathyn realises that his misbehaviour affects other people, he will think twice. He loves his servants dearly. Me punishing them will sting."

"You aren't going to dismiss them?"

Kieryn didn't like the way Odelle had looked up at him in horror.

"No. Of course not," Kieryn assured her, laying his hands upon her shoulders. "Jodathyn needs his servants. But he also needs a harsh lesson. One I intend to teach him."

"Be kind to the servants."

Kieryn tilted his head, feeling the weight of his crown. "My dear, I am the wise, benevolent High King Kieryn of Rama. The servants have no reason to fear me."

CHAPTER FOUR

Jodathyn

The Citadel of Pallaryn

Humbled Jodathyn returned to his gilded cage. His stomach churned with a mix of envy and defeat. What had started out as a mission to liberate a fellow Ramian ended with Will Hartcurt saving him. Come morning, he would fall at his brother's feet and plead for forgiveness. He could only hope his brother was in a merciful mood.

Jodathyn listened to the guards high above his head as they exchanged pleasantries. Any palace guard would be certain to question a man who had been injured. Jodathyn had to come up with a more covert way to enter the castle.

Silent and still he waited, until he heard the clipped sound of boots moving away. Then as soon as they rounded the bend, he dropped to a crouch and scuttled along the wall. Blind in the dark he used his hands to feel for the hole he'd discovered during his exploration the previous summer. As far as he was aware, no one else knew of its existence.

Ignoring the sharp sting of spindly branches, Jodathyn pushed his way through the bush. He pressed his body close to the wet earth, slithering on his belly. In moments he had made his way inside the palace walls.

Jodathyn stood, brushing away the blood beading on his cheek. The garden was in such disrepair that he doubted many ventured here. Whenever he needed to escape the suffocation of palace life, this was where he hid.

Creeping forward, he patted the trunk of his favourite climbing tree as he passed it. When he had been just shy of thirteen summers, he had fallen from its branches, breaking his arm. Much to Donatein's exasperation, Jodathyn had been reading a forbidden text about the Dragon Lords at the time.

Keeping close to the shadows, Jodathyn stalked towards the bushes where he had hidden his cloak. He was dismayed to find that his dark grey cloak with the silver threads was gone.

"Dragon Dung!" Jodathyn hissed. The stable hand must have watched him tuck away his cloak. Donatein would be angry.

Seething, Jodathyn returned to the forgotten courtyard. From here he could enter the palace corridors unnoticed from the laundry rooms.

On tiptoes, Jodathyn pushed opened a door. As anticipated, the laundry was quiet. Like a wraith he skulked up the stairs.

Even as a boy Jodathyn had watched the palace guards. It paid to be aware of their movements and which guards were likely to be antagonistic. He noted with some amusement that the roster was still the same as when he was a child. No one ever bothered to watch the laundry doors at night.

Jodathyn edged forward, trying to ignore the pain in his back. He felt suddenly disorientated. As a wave of dizziness overcame him, he leant against the wall. Blinking, he was shocked to realise he couldn't work out where in the palace he was.

His breathing was laboured. He opened his mouth to call for help, only to discover his voice seemed to have failed him. Slumping to the floor, he clutched his chest.

So, this is what it is like to die. Jodathyn lay his head down on the cold floor. Alone and afraid, he shivered, concentrating on taking his next breath.

He nearly cried in relief as he heard the muffled sounds of boots running towards him. Desperate, he tried to move, but his body remained feeble and unresponsive.

"Prop him up," a clipped voice demanded.

He was pulled against a warm, broad chest. His hair was brushed out of his face. "Otherworlds! He's ashen! Jodathyn – breathe. Breathe!"

Jodathyn's head lolled forward. *It's alright,* he thought, *Valt's here. Everything will be alright.*

"No, you don't!" A hand came out of nowhere, cracking against his cheek.

Startled he reared back.

"Carew! Not helpful."

Jodathyn tried to suck in air. His lungs burned with the effort.

"What's wrong?" Valt's voice rumbled.

"Judging by the state he's in – soaking wet, breathing difficulties and a blue tinge – he's experiencing second drowning."

"Pardon?"

His wet cloak was peeled from his shoulders. A warm hand untucked his shirt from his breeches and slipped up to his chest.

"He's had a near-drowning experience. There's liquid in his lungs."

"Get it out!" Valt sounded like he was in a panic.

"You two secure the corridors. I don't want anyone seeing what I'm going to do. Valt Axtin, you are never to reveal to anyone what's about to happen."

"You have my word," Valt answered.

Exhausted, Jodathyn closed his eyes. A warm glow blossomed in his chest. The hand under his shirt was searing hot. Breathing became easier, his airways seemed to open of their own accord. Jodathyn gulped in air. He coughed and spluttered, before vomiting.

It was like the world had snapped back into focus. A King's Guardsman was kneeling before him, the torches in the dark corridor lit his golden-brown skin and grim expression. Jodathyn had met this guardsman before ... although he was too confused to remember how.

"You're a magic healer ..." Valt's voice shook.

"I kindly ask you to keep that to yourself."

"You're a good man, Jael Aryk, you don't need to worry about me blabbering," Valt replied. "Jod won't either."

"I know you," Jodathyn mumbled, feeling like a fool.

Guardsman Jael glanced over at him with deep brown eyes full of concern. "When the King dismisses him, make sure your master gets his rest."

"I am well," Jodathyn grumbled. "I am no child."

Valt shook his head. Against Jael his pale skin looked sallow; his hands were still shaking. "Master, you foolish boy, you nearly died!"

"Shall I inform the others?" A young King's Guardsman with sandy hair and a ready smile approached. He clapped Jael on the back.

"Yes. But let them know I'm providing some healer's assistance."

"The King knows?" Jodathyn rasped.

"Our orders are to detain you and escort you to the King's audience chamber." The younger guardsman regarded him with a cool expression. Jodathyn hated it when young men not much older than him looked upon him as if he were a foolish child.

Jael waited until his companion had left before turning to Jodathyn. "I will speak with the King about your other injuries. It is best that you learn from the natural consequences of your actions."

Jodathyn nodded, trying to seem unconcerned.

"Good. Let's get you on your feet."

Valt grabbed Jodathyn's elbows and hauled him to stand. Then, sandwiched between his personal guard and the King's Guardsman, he was ushered to the audience chamber.

As they reached it, Jodathyn balked. One of Kieryn's manservants was by the ornate doors, watching for them. It was a sure sign that the King was already waiting to make judgement.

Seeing Jodathyn's dishevelled appearance, the servant pursed his lips. Jodathyn winced. This old man had seen many of his scrapes. He had been serving Kieryn for as long as Jodathyn could remember.

"It is the King's pleasure that you do not under any circumstances mention any of your 'dreams' or 'visions'," the servant said in an undertone.

Nervous, Jodathyn looked about him. The great lords of the council were spooked by those who held powers. For the time being, the High King's influence was enough to protect him.

"No mention of your power, is that understood?"

Jodathyn nodded his head.

"Must you take such frivolous liberties with your master, Valt Axtin?" Some of Kieryn's servants had a strange disliking of Valt. Jodathyn could never understand why.

"I'm propping him up so he doesn't collapse," Valt grunted.

"Wait here."

Jodathyn breathed in through his nose, counted to five and released his breath through his mouth. He wriggled his fingers and tapped his thighs. It was a technique Donatein had taught him to stay calm in stressful situations.

Valt reached out and placed a firm hand on Jodathyn's shoulders. "Courage."

Jodathyn could see Jael watching him closely from the corner of his eye.

The King's servant returned, frowning at Valt's familiarity with Jodathyn. Valt returned the stern stare with an unconcerned gaze, as if daring the man to reprimand him. He gave Jodathyn's shoulder a slow, deliberate squeeze. Jodathyn had to bite his lip to contain his nervous giggle.

"Come now." The servant ushered Jodathyn forward, shaking his head in disgust. Valt leered at him.

The great doors were opened and Jodathyn was met with the sight of his brother dressed in the finery of the High King of Rama.

High on his throne, King Kieryn surveyed Jodathyn with solemn, dark eyes. Broad shouldered, with a bronzed complexion and perfectly trimmed black beard, Kieryn was the very image of the Pallarus dynasty's dignity and prestige. Where Ramians regarded King Kieryn with reverence, Jodathyn was treated with scorn.

Jodathyn tore his gaze from his brother as he felt the familiar, unwelcome feeling of envy. Donatein always said jealousy was an ugly trait that did not become him.

Along the columns stood a few dozen King's Guardsmen, the elite guards who had earned the King's trust. His unfortunate servants, Donatein and Orion, were already standing before the King. They looked wretched. The lords and ladies that formed the king's council were seated in a semi-circle around the High King's throne.

Valt nudged Jodathyn forward so that he stumbled. He steadied himself and concentrated on stepping one foot in front of the other. His footsteps echoed in the great expanse of the audience chamber. Once he was directly before the King, Jodathyn knelt. He lowered his head in submission, wincing as his abused knees pressed against the stone floor.

"My King. My sovereign lord; I bow in surrender to your judgement." Jodathyn intoned the traditional words of a man who was summoned before the High King. He cringed at how sore and irritated his throat sounded. He swallowed. Kieryn would have noticed.

CHAPTER FIVE

Jodathyn

The Citadel of Pallaryn

"You can be of no doubt, Jodathyn Pallarus, son of Hadryn, as to why we have summoned you."

Jodathyn cringed as his brother's voice resonated through the audience chamber. He slumped his shoulders as he lowered his head; his wet wavy hair brushed against his face.

"Your behaviour tonight, Son of the Crown, can only be described as atrocious," a lady to the King's right barked.

Jodathyn stole a glance up at her through his eyelashes. Unlike some, he was well aware that the King loathed the bolstering and manipulation of many of the lords. Kieryn was more likely to trust the opinions of the female members of his council. Jodathyn had hoped he could garner some sympathy from a lady or two. If he could do that, his brother may be persuaded to be lenient.

"Perhaps we should question Jodathyn's red ogre as to how his charge managed to escape his notice?" Lord Solan stole a haughty glance at Valt.

Jodathyn flinched, turning his face in time to see his personal guard recoil at the rebuke. "How was it that Jodathyn was able to leave without being questioned?"

"I eluded Valt, the palace guards and some King's Guardsmen, my Lord," Jodathyn pointed out. Two captains of the King's Guard exchanged a glance. They would be interrogating him later in regards to the identity of the men he had slipped past.

Jodathyn felt queasy, hearing the discontented murmurs of the King's council at his last statement. He did not like the way some were eyeing Valt. Not wanting the council to dismiss another of his personal guards, he continued, "Valt's hardly to blame. And I would rather you kept your tongue civil, Lord Solan."

Behind him, Jodathyn heard the quiet, strangled sound of Valt catching a laugh in his throat. He bit his tongue. Valt was always saying his brazen speech would get him in trouble one day.

"Indeed, perhaps, Lord Solan, we should concentrate on the matter of the stolen coin?" Lord Frayn's eyes shone with malicious light. A self-contented smile curled on his lips as he watched Jodathyn squirm. Lord Frayn was the youngest member of the King's council and had much to prove. Jodathyn was an easy target.

Scowling at him, Jodathyn felt a stirring of resentment. It infuriated him that the old rumour that King Hadryn had loved the young Frayn more than him was still circulating.

"Jodathyn's lack of respect is hardly Lord Solan's fault," Lord Kamoore retorted. All of Rama knew he was a weak-willed man who aligned himself with Solan to maintain power. He was an egotistical fool.

An older lady rolled her eyes before addressing Jodathyn. "First, Jodathyn Pallarus. You returned to us drunk and battered."

From his position on the floor, Jodathyn lifted his head so that he could look Kieryn full in the face. "Your Majesty, I'm not drunk!"

Lord Kamoore scoffed, fingering a thick gold chain around his neck. "That seems unlikely."

"I'm not!" Jodathyn cried. He started to stand.

King Kieryn raised an elegant eyebrow. "Look where you are, Jodathyn! You are not before me as my brother but as my subject. I am your High King. I am your sovereign lord who has protected you. Another king may not love his half-brother as much as I have you."

"Please, my King, I wasn't drunk. I–"

"Kneel, Son of the Crown! I did not give you leave to stand before me!"

Flinching as if he had been struck, Jodathyn knelt, face to the floor. "My King."

"Are you going to explain yourself, Jod?"

"I got into a fight, Your Majesty," Jodathyn murmured, shamefaced. He hated it when Kieryn used his moniker to convey his disappointment.

"How does that explain your stench?" Lord Kamoore hissed.

Jodathyn had never felt more humiliated. "I was stuffed into a beer barrel."

"A *beer barrel*?"

"A full barrel." Kieryn always had the ability to hear what Jodathyn hadn't said. "Were you held under?"

Jodathyn nodded.

"Have you sustained any other injuries?"

Jodathyn's eyes darted towards Donatein, his favourite manservant. If Kieryn found out how close he had come to being murdered, would he dismiss all his household servants? He couldn't bear to lose Donatein.

"Kieryn, please, let my servants go. This isn't their fault."

"Silence, brother!" the King snapped. "You will do well to remember I am King. Now, are you injured?"

The council remained still; the seconds seemed to slow. They were waiting for Jodathyn to speak, but he seemed at a loss for words.

"Very well – stand and disrobe."

Jodathyn tilted his head up, staring at his brother in shock. Surely, he hadn't heard right.

"Majesty, please."

"Clearly there is more that you do not wish me to see," Kieryn said. A bejewelled hand urged him to stand. "Kindly rise and disrobe."

"But ... Your Majesty ..." Jodathyn glanced around the council, his eyes wide, pleading for mercy. He rose to his feet as his brother had commanded.

Valt had also risen. The big man took a few steps forward, laying a gentle hand on Jodathyn's shoulder, his eyes enquiring if Jodathyn needed his help. Jodathyn shooed him away, sending a plaintive glance towards his brother, who responded with a scowl.

The King raised a hand to stop the council from commanding Valt to back down. He would at least allow Jodathyn the comfort of his familiar guard.

With shaking hands, Jodathyn removed his tunic, handing it to Valt.

"Kieryn, my King ... Please." Jodathyn tried once more.

The King remained impassive.

Swallowing, Jodathyn lifted his hands to the laces on his shirt.

"Master Jodathyn, you must obey your King." Seeing Jodathyn's discomfort, Jael had come alongside him. The healer took the hem of his shirt, and in the next instant he was standing vulnerable before the High King and his council.

Jodathyn refused to look in the King's direction. Kieryn knew he preferred to keep the humiliation of his scarring to himself. As a boy he had avoided swimming with children his age.

Even with his gaze diverted, Jodathyn saw his brother's pained expression. He swallowed, feeling the tight pain in his throat.

The King stood from his throne and descended the stairs. Moments later the King was before him, running gloved fingers over the angry welts that adorned Jodathyn's neck.

"Oh Jod, what's this?" The firm lines around Kieryn's mouth softened. "How can I protect you, if you do not allow me to?"

"Majesty." Shamefaced, Jodathyn bowed his head. His anger was dissipating.

"Jodathyn, these marks ... someone tried to strangle you."

As the memory of his struggle to survive resurfaced, Jodathyn's breathing hitched. His mouth felt dry.

"Where can I find this man?"

He could feel the warmth of Kieryn's palm on his cheek. His brother was trying to keep him grounded. It would not do for the council to see his panic. Jodathyn was grateful for the King's small kindness. "I don't know."

"You might have spared a thought what burying another family member would do to your Queen."

"Odelle knows?"

"Your Queen has been beside herself." Kieryn drew Jodathyn's forehead to his own. "My foolish little brother, what am I going to do with you?"

"I'm sorry."

"Yes, you will be." There was a sharp tone of dark amusement in the King's voice. He released Jodathyn to return once more to his throne. "I am assuming the fight took place in a tavern. The name of the establishment, brother?"

"Whytehorse Ale House," Jodathyn muttered. His brother's last whispered comment only gave fuel to his nervousness. "I had heard rumours of a slave auction. Kieryn – if you had only seen what I saw tonight ..."

"Silence!" Solan barked. "We're not here to discuss criminals."

"She wasn't a criminal, Lord Solan," Jodathyn burst. "She was suffering all for what ... her talent?"

"Filth," Kamoore harrumphed. "She's better off dead."

"I will deal with those men in due course ..."

"How can you sit there and allow these atrocities to happen?" Jodathyn cried. "If you won't do something. I will! I will end the trade!"

The council stilled.

"It is not your place, brother." Kieryn's face tightened with fury.

"Am I to stay imprisoned?"

"You will stay where you are safe," Kieryn snapped. "And where I can keep an eye on you."

"Because you're all afraid of me," Jodathyn said.

"Enough! On your knees, Son of the Crown."

Jodathyn knew he had gone too far and sunk to his knees. Kieryn was now establishing his dominance over him. The council seemed pleased by his obedience. Angry, Jodathyn ground his teeth together. If only Kieryn would listen to him.

Ignoring those around him, Jodathyn didn't hear the question that was addressed to the King. But he heard his brother's clipped reply. "I assure you, Jodathyn's gift is under control. It is rudimentary at best. My lord has no reason to fear ..."

"What I would like to know is why a fight broke out?" Lord Frayn asked. He seemed eager to see Jodathyn put in his place.

"I tried to buy the slave freedom," Jodathyn mumbled. "They stole the coin purse ... and I punched a man."

"How many men attacked you?"

Jodathyn shook his head. "A dozen or so."

"Did you not tell them who you were?" one lord enquired.

"I tried," Jodathyn said. "I told them I was highborn, then they placed the rope around my neck, and I couldn't ... breathe ..."

The King indicated to a pair of his Guardsmen. "Burn the establishment to the ground. Arrest the landlord and all who were present; bring them to me. They will all face my wrath at the edge of the axe."

Jodathyn jolted, taken aback by the King's command. While Kieryn didn't use executions to bend people to his will, he did not hesitate to do so when the death penalty was required. Never before had Kieryn ordered a mass execution with so little debate. And why send his own King's Guard to arrest the wrongdoers when ordinary palace guards would suffice?

"You were also robbed of a considerable sum," Kieryn continued, as if he hadn't just commanded a mass execution.

"That is true, my King."

"How do you plan on paying that money back?"

"You know I have no way to pay it back, Majesty," Jodathyn replied, doing his best to keep his tone respectful. He was the Son of the Crown; he had no coin or land of his own. He lived by the King's good graces.

King Kieryn leant back on his throne and pierced Jodathyn with a hard stare. "In the matter of stealing from the Crown ... the Autumn Festival is approaching; you shall not be roaming about enjoying yourself. You will content yourself serving others. I think you'll make a fine cup bearer for myself and the council for the duration."

Jodathyn froze in disbelief. The Autumn Festival was one of the largest festivals of the year. It was one of his few opportunities to leave the sanctuary of the palace and spend a few carefree hours feasting and dancing.

"Majesty," Jodathyn acquiesced.

"I would also like to introduce Captain Tiernan Candyde. He will be joining Valt in watching your every move. You are forthwith under heavy guard."

Captain Tiernan bowed to the High King and the council before he approached Jodathyn, appraising him. Jodathyn visibly flinched when the captain studied the scar behind his ear.

Jodathyn groaned. Both Tiernan and Valt were well over six feet tall. He would be surrounded by two muscly mountains. In comparison, he was a grasshopper.

"While I do believe Donatein Manideep is a gifted apothecary, Your Majesty, perhaps our own troop healer should examine your brother." Captain Tiernan's voice carried across the audience chamber.

"A waste of the Kings Guard's resources," Lord Kamoore snarled, tugging on his opulent lace sleeves. "Let the impertinent whelp bruise."

Captain Tiernan quirked an eyebrow. "The fight was brutal. Not all damage in fights is visible. I wouldn't expect a gracious lord like yourself to know about such things."

"Your request is granted." The King sighed, looking in Kamoore's direction. The lord was still preening, a sly smile playing on his lips. "Captain, seems like my little brother could do with your expert training. You have of course my *full permission* and blessing to make him one very sore, very tired and very sorry young man."

CHAPTER SIX

Jodathyn

The Citadel of Pallaryn

Jodathyn returned to his rooms with his three servants at his side. Frowning, he turned to face them. If he looked suitably chastised, maybe Donatein would forgo the tongue lashing.

"I am sorry, all of you," he whispered.

"If only I was your natural-born papa," Donatein growled. "Don't you dare apologise and hope a remorseful face will ease my ire at you."

"I didn't intend to get into trouble!" Jodathyn blurted. "I was trying to save a slave's life."

The concerned lines on Donatein's aged face deepened as he stalked past. He grabbed a thick woollen towel, draping it over Jodathyn's shoulders. "You'd better dry yourself, Master. You're cranky when you are ill."

Jodathyn hummed at the luxurious touch of the Sionian wool. His comfortable feather bed beckoned him with its promise of plush cushions and clean sheets. But first he needed to make things right with his manservants.

"What if Jael hadn't been with me when we found you? You would have died in my arms." Valt's blue eyes glinted. "If you are too afraid to trust me with your plans then chances are you're about to do something reckless."

Orion stifled a chortle, which turned into a cough at Valt's angry stare.

"It's strange how you two feel comfortable talking to a royalborn like that," he said, shrugging his shoulders.

"Comes with the privilege of raising the boy," Donatein muttered.

"You should all go to bed," Jodathyn sighed. "Otherworlds, Orion! You look like you could fall asleep where you stand."

Orion, a country lad who was unused to palace life, had recently come into Jodathyn's service. He indeed looked like he had a terrible night. It must have been a harrowing experience to be summoned to stand before the King.

Stunned at being acknowledged, Orion jumped back. His heel bumped into Jodathyn's small hunting dogs who were napping on the floor. Their sleep interrupted, the dogs started to wag their tails. Bear growled, waddling over to Jodathyn's feet to beg for attention. Jodathyn bent to pick him up, stroking his silky brown ears. Parrie, his younger black and white dog, rolled over onto Orion's feet to expose his belly. Orion looked like he was contemplating whether he should pick up the dog or ignore it.

"Leave the dog, boy."

Jodathyn stiffened. It was unusual for Kieryn to enter his personal chambers unannounced. He paused before turning to face his brother.

Dreading another bout of scolding, Jodathyn released Bear as he knelt. The dog, delighted by the royal visitor, padded over to the King's side where he waited for a pat.

"At least he has returned to us safe," Orion said, his voice sounding uncertain. His face flushed as the King's reproachful stare swept over him. Chastised, Orion fell silent.

"Come here, boy," the King commanded.

Startled, Orion moved forward, a blush seeping through his deep olive skin. He averted his gaze, kneeling before the King.

"Your name."

"Orion Maysden, born of Silverdyne, my King."

"Pray tell me, boy, why are you in my halls as a servant, when you ought to be about the stables?" The King reached down and grasped Orion's chin, forcing him to look into his eyes. "I see you have the Silverdyne horseman's lock on your left temple. You are military trained."

"If it so pleases you, Sire, my parents have died and so I have lost my place among my peers."

"Yes, good evening, Bear." King Kieryn bent and picked up Jodathyn's old dog, who was still begging for attention. The little dog wagged his tail in delight and licked his fingers. Bear had always loved the King. "It does not please me to hear of your parents' death. In what manner did they serve?"

"Your Majesty, my father was among the ranks of the horsemen of Silverdyne. My mother was a Sionian woman who specialised in leather work."

"Tell me, were they given a respectful Ramian burial? Or perhaps farewelled in the Sionian fashion?"

Orion tilted his chin downwards and stared at the flagstone floor. Shame washed over Jodathyn – he should have thought to enquire about Orion's most peculiar appointment.

"I do not know what happened to them, my King," Orion murmured. "I would have liked to honour them as a good son ought."

"Perhaps I shall make some enquiries for you," Kieryn replied. "It is indeed a sad day when those who have served Rama are scorned."

Jodathyn could see the hope shining in Orion's eyes as his head shot up.

"Well, Master Maysden, one day you may have the chance to prove yourself. Fortunately, I hear that Valt Axtin is a marvellous sparring partner." The King glanced towards Valt with something akin to a smile.

His eyes then slid to Jodathyn and his expression softened further. "Jael had a private word with me. Are you in pain, brother?"

Jodathyn shook his head. "I will recover, my King."

Kieryn studied Jodathyn for a long moment. "Donatein, my brother requires a bath ... something for the swelling around his neck wouldn't go amiss."

Jodathyn sighed as Donatein ushered the other two servants to fetch water. "Your Majesty, I just want to go to bed."

"You're having a bath first, Jod. You quite frankly reek."

"It's very late. A few more hours won't hurt."

"For Merciful Otherworld, Jodathyn, stop being so reticent and disrobe at once. I'll not have you ill because you didn't have the sense to strip off," the King chided.

Petulant, Jodathyn obeyed, undressing and wrapping the towel about his nakedness. The King had seen him in various stages of undress, but he was never comfortable with being so vulnerable in the presence of his great and noble brother. Whenever Kieryn caught sight of his scars, his eyes took on a guilt-ridden expression. Jodathyn hated seeing that look on his brother's face.

"Jodathyn, this high winter you will be nineteen." The King took Jodathyn's shoulders, steering him to the fire to warm himself. "Do you know why you are the Son of the Crown and denied the title of prince?"

Jodathyn's station in life had been explained to him many times before. "My mother was consort only, unworthy of the title Queen."

"That is correct – you are the son of Ammerie, the consort of the King. Your mother proved to be a danger to Rama. She was a traitor, brother."

Jodathyn stared up into Kieryn's face. He had heard it argued before that King Hadryn should have executed his second wife. Fortunately for her, she had been pregnant with Jodathyn at the time. Ramian law forbade the execution of a woman carrying a child.

"My King, I am loyal."

"I know, Jod," Kieryn replied. "You, my brother, were born of the wrong bloodline. Many fear that you are Vadroil's Heir."

Jodathyn scoffed. "People think I'm descended from a great dragon? You've always told me they were fairy tales."

"You must not give anyone a reason to doubt your loyalty."

"The men tonight. They called me a monster. Is that what you are afraid of, Kieryn? That I'm a monster?"

Kieryn shook his head. "I am not afraid of you, brother. I am afraid *for* you. Making such grand statements about your destiny ... don't ever do that again in front of the great lords."

"What is wrong with wanting a purpose? Is wanting to end the underground slave trade so terrible?"

"Challenging the great lords openly when you don't have a speck of evidence is dangerous."

"You didn't see what I saw!" Jodathyn cried. "The slave trade is evil!"

"Which is why it is punishable by death," Kieryn snarled. "There are others working in the shadows to discredit the great lords. We must be patient."

"*Patient?*"

"I am but a servant to this kingdom, Jodathyn. What happens when you take too much power from the great lords too quickly?"

Jodathyn remained silent.

"Civil war."

"Just cut Solan's head off. You didn't think twice about those you condemned tonight."

Kieryn snorted. "You cut off one dragon's head and another appears, Jodathyn. Solan is powerful. He has many allies. Besides, I cannot execute a man from a ruling house without sufficient evidence."

Jodathyn crossed his arms against his chest. "Then I'll find some."

"You will not."

Jodathyn huffed. "What am I supposed to do, then?'

"Study your languages, grow into a man with good character and stay out of trouble."

"I don't want to be mediocre. I was born for something more. I know it!"

"It is the best way you can serve your nation, Jodathyn. Above all else, House Pallarus must endure."

"I am forever your servant, my King." Jodathyn bowed his head, knowing he could not argue with his brother and win.

Kieryn closed the gap between them. "In this moment, I am a man begging his brother to be careful. Goodnight, Jodathyn. Captain Tiernan will join you tomorrow afternoon."

Jodathyn reached out to touch Kieryn's arm as he turned to leave. "Please give Odelle my apologies for worrying her."

At the mention of his wife's name a small, fond smile lit Kieryn's face. "She would be pleased to know you are safe. Goodnight, little brother."

The King slipped into the corridor.

"Bath, young man. Now." His arms laden with herbs and ointments, Donatein entered from the shadows. Jodathyn knew that the old servant had been waiting for the King to leave before making his presence known. He twisted the towelling around his body, moving to Donatein to assist him. Tired, aggravated eyes stared up at him.

"Go clean yourself up so we can both get to bed."

"Don't be angry with me," Jodathyn pleaded. He reached over to arrange the ointments into perfect order, knowing full well how finicky Donatein could be about such things.

"Merciful Otherworld." Donatein swept his hands through his hair in irritation. "You were nearly murdered tonight. None of us knew your whereabouts. This may come as a shock to you, but common folk don't wander about starting brawls. No responsible father would allow it."

"Ahh, but you're not my father."

Ashamed by his response, Jodathyn turned away. Donatein didn't deserve his disrespect. He yelped when his servant smacked him on the back of his head, which wasn't an unexpected reaction from Donatein. When he was younger his servant often clipped him round the ear.

"I may not be your father," Donatein commented, "but I raised you."

Jodathyn half-heartedly glared at him. "I want to go to bed, Donatein, and forget this ever happened."

Donatein pointed at the forgotten tub. "In. Wash well or I will have to do that for you. I don't want the stench of cheap beer on your bed sheets."

Grumbling unflattering comments under his breath, Jodathyn slunk into the bath chamber. He dropped the towel on the floor before slipping into the tub. Knowing Donatein would make good on his threat to wash him, Jodathyn lathered a generous amount of soap. He scrubbed at his skin in a bid to remove the stench of the beer. Leaving his curls to last, Jodathyn braced himself before submerging his head under the water. Since entering this bath chamber he had been attempting to keep the memories of drowning at bay. Now, under water, he felt the tendrils of panic creeping into his mind. He resurfaced, gasping.

"Master Jodathyn, are you well?"

Hearing Donatein's footsteps coming closer, Jodathyn felt foolish for his vivid imagination. He was in his own rooms, not in the ale house, surrounded by men who wanted to hurt him. "I'm well, Donatein."

Donatein appeared at the door, his eyes saying he didn't believe Jodathyn. "I will prepare a sleeping tonic."

"I'm not a child, Donatein."

"A strong dose will do you wonders," Donatein murmured, nodding to himself as he retreated back to his herbs.

Jodathyn sighed, knowing it was useless to argue with his overprotective manservant. Stepping out of the bath, he retrieved his towel and patted himself dry. He made a cursory effort to dry his hair, before padding into his bed chamber.

The familiar scent of Donatein's tonics welcomed him. The old man's back was to him as he lit a herbal candle, meant to coax the body into a deep slumber. Jodathyn stared into the small, flickering flame; the candles were Donatein's creations. He had spent many hours crafting them for Jodathyn's use.

"A good sleep is what you need, after your ordeal."

Without comment, Jodathyn took the tonic Donatein pressed into his hand. He downed it in one swallow, grimacing at the strong aftertaste.

"Come by the fire," Donatein said, ushering Jodathyn to a velvet chair that had been placed by the hearth. "Let's see what we can do with your bumps and bruises, hmm?"

Kneeling beside his master, Donatein uncapped the first jar. Jodathyn watched as he worked with deft, nimble fingers. He knew, thanks to Donatein's ointments, the bruising would soon be just a terrible memory.

When Donatein rose on creaking knees, Jodathyn reached out to grasp his hand.

"I was lucky tonight," Jodathyn admitted, his voice no more than a whisper. "If it hadn't been for a stranger, I would be dead."

Donatein shooed him to his bed. "You don't belong out there."

"I don't belong here, either."

"You have a place here."

Jodathyn shifted. "A place that is resented."

"Is it, Jod?" Donatein replied.

"I am not a child, Donatein, you can't protect me from court gossip anymore."

"Well, then, let's agree that your place is here … with me," Donatein conceded.

"You're being improper, Donatein."

"I suppose I am," Donatein agreed. The creases around his eyes betrayed the old man's mirth. "It was improper to allow a small Son of the Crown to sleep in my bed. It was improper of me to take the responsibility of raising you and it was most improper of me to strike you as you so richly deserved. I don't think I'm terribly worried about being *proper*, Master Jodathyn."

As Donatein moved around his chambers, Jodathyn helped his dogs onto his bed. He kissed each in turn. He placed old Bear on his own pillow. Parrie would sleep in his arms.

At the door, Donatein paused. "Would it be terribly improper if I told you your dogs are spoilt?"

The scent of autumn fruits and earth was heavy in the air. Oranges, yellows and reds danced across Jodathyn's vision. Strands of taunting festival music joined with the sound of a child's laugh.

"The dragon is stirring..."

Jodathyn turned about, looking for the bodiless voice. But he was blind. Lifting a hand to his eyes, he touched something warm and wet. He wiped at his face until he could see blurry shapes.

"Hello?"

"More wine," Kieryn's voice answered in the distance.

"Kieryn, help me!"

Jodathyn continued to wipe at his face. A curling feeling of dread in his stomach fed into his desperation. Even though he could not see well, he glanced down at his hands. They were covered in blood.

Lord Frayn stood before him, leering. In his hand a letter written on thick parchment. Jodathyn could see the wax seal of House Frayn. "The dragon is stirring... thrice covered in blood..."

Frayn's face distorted into that of Illeanah's, his cherished childhood friend. She was glaring at him.

"Don't I mean anything to you?" She stormed away, her long auburn hair glinting in the sun. "Your words are cruel. Shall they be the last words I will remember you uttering to me?"

Breath caught in Jodathyn's throat. He flung up a hand to stop her retreat. But it was too late. She was gone.

Kieryn's only child, Prince Carvelle, danced about Jodathyn's feet. "Play with me!" the Prince cried, prancing about. "Come and find me."

Jodathyn felt a longing to follow his nephew, but was intercepted by Lord Kamoore and Solan. His eyes were drawn to the large red jewel on Kamoore's fingers.

About them, oddly shaped leaves of green and red rained from the sky. The world tilted on its axis. He was alone in the forest.

Jodathyn screamed.

Jodathyn woke with a sudden shout. The remnants of the dream lingered at the edges of his memory as he glanced around looking for what had woken him.

"I'm sorry, Master!"

With one hand Orion held a tray of food, his other was clutching his side. Under a chair, Parrie was cowering. Jodathyn huffed – the little dog had a habit of getting under the servants' feet. Orion would just have to get used to moving around the stubborn dog.

The light in Jodathyn's room indicated that it was nearly mid-morning. He marvelled that Donatein had let him sleep so long.

"Master, what's the matter?" Donatein's clipped steps came closer. He entered Jodathyn's rooms, eyeing a cringing Orion, the nervous dog and his master still abed.

Jodathyn threw off his blankets, sliding out of the warmth of his covers. He plucked a protesting Bear off the pillow and set the old dog on his feet. "It's nothing, Donatein. Just a strange dream ... I need some parchment, ink and a quill."

He heard Donatein's long-suffering sigh as he took the food tray from Orion. The old man set it down on his desk. Paying no attention to the food, Jodathyn rummaged through his desk compartments for his favourite quill.

"What's the master up to now?" Valt had appeared at the door of Jodathyn's chamber.

"My apologies. I had the strangest dream ... I'm writing down the details," Jodathyn muttered, his eyes fixated on his quill racing along the parchment he had found. To appease Donatein, he absently plucked a piece of fruit off the tray, which the old man had been nudging closer.

"Go to my rooms and grab me my herbs ... Master needs to relax."

"I don't need a herbal tonic or ointment for every little complaint," Jodathyn responded, refusing to glance up at Donatein's pointed stare.

The herbal tonics seemed to interfere with his Sight ability. He had decided to stop taking so many of them. It would need to be done covertly. He didn't want to arouse Donatein's suspicions.

CHAPTER SEVEN

Jodathyn

The Citadel of Pallaryn

Defeated, Jodathyn sat bare chested doing his best to ignore the curious gazes of the guardsmen. When Jael had summoned him to the tiltyards, he had been tempted to refuse. But Valt's threat to throw him over his shoulder to escort him convinced Jodathyn to meet with the medic without complaint.

Jael was astute to his patient's feelings. Upon seeing Jodathyn's discomfort the troop medic removed his shirt so that he was bare chested as well.

"Now we are equals," Jael said. "Now you can see my scars too."

"You have nothing to be ashamed of," Jodathyn replied. He glanced over the star-shaped scar on Jael's shoulder and the light brown scar line along his belly. Not wanting to be rude, Jodathyn averted his gaze.

"Neither do you," Jael replied. "You'll find the only thing guardsmen find disturbing is that someone would maim a child. The excuse of drunkenness was indeed a poor defence."

Uncomfortable with the topic of conversation, Jodathyn stared at the black and silver banner of the King's Guard.

"*Araae helphelwyn. Teirini gorthorawyn,*" Jael said, seeing where Jodathyn's attention was. "They are our ancient words. *Live Valiantly. Die Honourably.*"

"How does an ordinary man do that?" Jodathyn exhaled, fiddling with the sleeves of his shirt, which lay on his lap.

"You are no ordinary man."

"I am less," Jodathyn griped. "I am a man adrift with no purpose."

"We all have a purpose." The healer's fingers brushed behind Jodathyn's right ear. "You are stronger than you think, Master Jodathyn."

"Good afternoon, Jael, how is Joddie today?" asked a younger King's Guardsman, who threw himself on the bench beside Jodathyn. "He's certainly looking a little less wet."

"Master Jodathyn, this is Guardsman Carew. You may remember meeting him last night." Jael turned to his comrade. "Honestly, Carew, you have not been given leave to use any moniker of Jodathyn's. Remember your manners or I'll have Captain Candyde make you muck out the stables."

Wanting to distract the guardsmen before they started arguing, Jodathyn asked the question that had made sleep impossible last night. "You don't think the King means to execute every man who was at the ale house? He is bluffing, yes?"

"Surely you jest, Master Jodathyn? His Majesty will have them gutted like fish!"

"Carew!" Jael barked. Jodathyn hissed as the healer prodded his ribs a little harder than necessary. "That's quite enough of that talk."

"His Majesty will have their entrails left to roast in the high summer sun."

"Carew, really!"

Looking not at all apologetic, Carew shrugged.

Jodathyn snorted at his antics. "How many do you think will be caught?"

"All of them." Carew's eyes glinted; all traces of laughter had vanished from his cheery face. "Men like that tend to turn on one another easy enough. My father has a gift for making scum like them sing like little birdies."

Jodathyn glanced up at Carew in confusion. "Whatever do you mean?"

"I said, enough of that talk," Jael growled.

Carew had the decency to look abashed. "Prisoners seem to tell my father everything, that's all, Master Jodathyn."

Satisfied with Carew's answer, Jael continued to prod Jodathyn's bruised ribs. "Guardsman Carew is one of the King's Guards' rising stars. Perhaps you will be lucky enough to spar with him."

Jodathyn made a face. "I don't spar."

In response, Carew beamed up at Jodathyn, showing rows of straight white teeth. Leaning closer, as if he was about to tell a secret, he whispered, "You do today."

Captain Tiernan was stalking towards them across the tiltyards. Seeing the sword in his hand, Jodathyn swore under his breath. Carew's grin widened.

Captain Tiernan halted by Jael's side, peering down at Jodathyn. Seated at the mercy of the troop medic, Jodathyn thought Tiernan looked taller than he had last night. He gulped, and Carew chuckled.

"Don't you have somewhere to be, Guardsman Carew?" Tiernan barked. His stern gaze turned to the younger guardsman.

"Yes, sir." Carew blanched. He saluted, and without a backwards glance fled the tiltyards. He looked like he was in a hurry to get away from the captain.

"I am done here," Jael said standing. There was a hint of laughter in his tone. "Captain, he's all yours."

Wanting to escape the stern lines on Tiernan's face, Jodathyn threw his shirt over his head. Fastening the laces, he refused to lock eyes with the giant.

"Take up your sword."

Incredulous that Tiernan intended to spar with him, Jodathyn angled his face to study the captain's powerful frame. He had been hoping that if he must spar, it would be with someone physically less impressive. "To what purpose? What could I possibly do against a mountain?"

The captain raised an eyebrow. "Tell me, is your plan to flop your fancy backside down anytime you're intimidated?"

Jodathyn crossed his arms against his chest. "I'm not intimidated."

"It is the King's pleasure that we should attempt to train you," Jael remarked.

"But not my pleasure," Jodathyn grumbled.

"Oh, but I'm sure *I* will find this pleasurable." Tiernan shot Jodathyn a smirk. "Sword now!"

Jodathyn's attention was drawn to where his servant, Orion, was observing the proceedings. The familiar look of disgruntled envy was easy to read on the other boy's face. Flushing, Orion bent his head down as he continued to polish Jodathyn's boots.

Tiernan charged with a snarl and, panicked, Jodathyn scrambled to his feet. The captain's abrupt attack forced Jodathyn to grab the first sword in his arm's reach. Growling, he lifted his sword and parried Tiernan's next blow.

The training Jodathyn had received in swordsmanship was rudimentary. As a child his appointed swordmaster had no patience for a gangly youth who preferred quieter pursuits. Jodathyn had become the swordmaster's favourite target. He had come to loathe the tiltyards and weaponry so much that Donatein had to drag him to his lessons. Jodathyn's reluctance fuelled the swordmaster's dislike of him.

It had been some time since Jodathyn had taken up a blade in the tiltyard. He did his best to fall into step and answer each of Tiernan's attacks.

"Don't insult me, fight back!" Tiernan barked, changing direction and slapping the flat of his blade across Jodathyn's rear. The gathering onlookers hooted with laughter as Jodathyn howled in shock.

Captain Tiernan paused to give Jodathyn a few precious seconds to gather his wits. There was a half-hearted apology in the curl of his lips, but the mirth in his eyes told Jodathyn the captain was enjoying himself. "I'm not here to play ... Fight back."

Rolling his shoulders, Jodathyn snuck a quick look towards the gathering of guards. Among the sea of faces he locked eyes with Valt. Jodathyn's personal guard had edged himself to the forefront to watch the action. He was grinning. Jodathyn groaned, hoping Valt would not want to duel him as well.

"Don't look at him, you are duelling me. Fight!" Tiernan darted to the side to aim at Jodathyn's backside again. Ready for the trick, Jodathyn dodged, aiming his sword to whack the captain. He missed, but the crowd cheered in appreciation.

In a burst of speed Jodathyn stepped forward, trying as many movements as he could remember. Sweat dripped from his forehead, plastering his curls to his skin. His shirt clung to his chest and he almost wished he had kept it off.

A grim line of satisfaction was set on Tiernan's face as he manoeuvred himself out of Jodathyn's reach. He started to call out stances and encouragement, forcing Jodathyn to work hard to keep up with him. Finally, Tiernan had enough of the duel. He grabbed Jodathyn's arm, shaking the sword right out of his grip while dropping the younger man to his knees.

"Next time I command you to pick up a sword, you obey. You fight hard and fast."

Panting where he lay in the dirt, Jodathyn felt his face flush with embarrassment.

"An assailant will not have pity on you." Tiernan bent, offering Jodathyn his hand. His stern eyes pierced two palace guards. "Stop sniggering, you two. You're only marginally more proficient than Jodathyn."

The gathered King's Guardsmen guffawed at the clipped remark and the indigent look the palace guards shot their captain. There had always been a rivalry between the ordinary guards and the King's Guardsmen.

Valt left his vantage point and joined Jodathyn in the ring. The wrinkles around his eyes gave away that he was holding back his laughter. "Come, Master. I think you have earned a rest."

Jodathyn opened his mouth to reply. The guards' friendly banter ceased, trickling to low murmurs of discontent. Confused, Jodathyn turned to see what had caused the change of mood.

He wasn't prepared to see the barkeep from last night being escorted by two of Kieryn's finest. Seeing the chains around the man's wrists and the look of misery on his face, Jodathyn felt a mixture of relief and guilt.

"It's his own actions that condemn him."

Valt knew him well, Jodathyn thought as the red giant lay a steadying hand on his shoulder.

The barkeep attempted to lunge out of the guard's grip as he caught sight of Jodathyn. "Dragon whore's whelp!"

One of the guardsmen rammed his fist into the struggling man's gut. Jodathyn could almost hear the whoosh of air as the barkeep hunched over. Valt's protective grip on his shoulder tightened.

"Keep your tongue civil or we'll cut it out for you!" the other guard barked.

"I think it's time to show young Master Jod some hand-to-hand combat. And look – we have a volunteer," Tiernan said, eyeing the unfortunate prisoner.

There was an answering cheer from the guardsmen.

"Shall I get some rope?" Carew asked with a vicious smirk.

"Shouldn't you be in the stables, Guardsman Carew?"

Carew merely smiled and shrugged good-naturedly. "I wanted to see how Jodathyn would cope with being under your expert care."

Despite himself, Tiernan chuckled and shook his head. "Go. Get the rope." The captain's gaze never wavered off the barkeep. "All we need now is a beer barrel."

Valt scoffed. "Waste of beer. We could use a horse trough with the water for the horses. Come this way, Master, let's get you a grand seat to watch the entertainment."

"Shouldn't you take him to the King?" Jodathyn was perplexed.

"Sometimes, Master, a man needs to take what he can, when he can," Valt said. "The prisoner will face the King when we are ready for him to."

"I don't think the King will mind waiting to exact his kingly vengeance." Carew grinned. He had returned with a length of rope.

The moment Captain Tiernan had finished punishing the barkeep, Jodathyn turned upon his heel to leave the tiltyards. He knew he was supposed to wait for the captain, but he didn't feel like being shadowed by two men.

Used to Jodathyn's habits, Valt followed shaking his head. "Don't antagonise the captain, Master."

"I have better things to do with my time than watch grown men pummel each other."

Valt scoffed. "You enjoyed watching."

Jodathyn drew in a deep breath. The truth was, he did delight in watching the barkeep's punishment. As he listened to the man's howls of pain and pleading, he felt an excitement in his belly. With the disgust he felt for himself and the embarrassment of his spar still fresh, Jodathyn was unsure if he wanted to face the captain.

Any hope of avoiding the captain for the afternoon was short lived. Like a foreboding shadow, Tiernan appeared from nowhere.

"Master Jodathyn, His Majesty was quite–"

Valt held up a hand to forestall whatever Captain Tiernan was going to say. "I have reprimanded the master already. He will behave himself."

The captain grunted and stepped back in line with Valt.

Sighing Jodathyn nodded an apology and continued his search of the gardens for his childhood friend, Illeanah. He couldn't help overhearing the whispered conversation of the two guards behind him.

"Master Maysden, how long has he been in service?"

"A season or two," Valt replied. "Did you cross paths with him?"

"Aye, he assisted me in tracking the master."

Outraged, Jodathyn stopped short. Valt shook his head at him and waggled his finger. "You'll not have words with Orion," the red-haired giant said. He turned back to Tiernan. "You'll find him a good sort of lad. Wasn't his choice of appointment, I'm afraid."

"He's still a little too young for a guardsman for my liking." Tiernan hummed. "I can only assume that is what a boy like that wants. We'll see how he takes to his current appointment. Hardships build character."

Valt grunted. "He's had his share."

"Do you not think you were a little too severe on the prisoner, Captain?" Jodathyn asked. He peered over his shoulder to regard Tiernan, who had stopped, staring at him in surprise. Most highborns did not like to engage their guards in conversation. He wasn't like most highborns.

"Not at all," Tiernan gruffly replied. "I spoke with Jael at length last night about the catalogue of injuries you sustained, in the hope I would have an opportunity for revenge."

"You were thorough," Jodathyn conceded. He couldn't help but shiver at the memory of how the barkeep's eyes had bulged when Tiernan had tied a rope around his neck and cut off his air supply. "I hope you won't be in trouble with the King because of me."

Behind him Tiernan sniffed. "Don't you fret. Speaking of trouble, who were the King's Guardsmen you snuck past?"

Jodathyn glanced over his shoulder and gave the captain his most winsome smile. "It was dark. I couldn't possibly identify them."

Tiernan ground his teeth together.

"Master, you know very well I can tell when you're lying," Valt replied. "We ought to know our own weaknesses."

Valt was right. He had the uncanny ability to tell when he was lying. From the moment Guardsman Carew introduced himself, Jodathyn had recognised him.

"I saw them as I neared the guards' gate," Jodathyn admitted. "Guardsman Carew was in conversation with another guard. They looked up and saw me. I waved and walked past."

"You walked past ..." Valt looked stunned. *"Waving?"*

"In their defence, I don't look threatening and I left from inside the palace walls."

"Oh, Carew." Tiernan shook his head with a groan. "We've talked about your inattention before, son. What am I going to do with you?"

"Son?"

"My second-born," Tiernan growled. "The most gifted and most infuriating."

Jodathyn felt a stab of guilt for dobbing poor Carew in. He hoped that Captain Tiernan would not be harsh with him on his account.

CHAPTER EIGHT

Jodathyn

The Citadel of Pallaryn

Jodathyn found Illeanah sitting on one of her favourite garden seats. By the rigid set of her shoulders and the blank stare directed at the mathematics journal, she had been waiting for him.

After the scandal at Solan's summer house, his brother had been at a loss as what to do with him. Jodathyn always surmised Kieryn felt Pallaryn wasn't the best place for a traumatised child to recover. So, Illeanah's father, Lord Hallidyn Whitoak, had taken Jodathyn from Aviah Valley into his own home. Jodathyn had spent a happy year with Illeanah living in Androssah.

Lord Hallidyn had encouraged his daughter's fascination with mathematics, and Jodathyn's in foreign languages. Eager to please, they had both excelled. In fact, Jodathyn was fluent in several languages and dialects. He had hoped that if he continued his studies, Kieryn might use his skills as an emissary and he might be able to leave the citadel. But after his argument with the King last night, that future looked less likely.

"Good afternoon, Lady."

As Jodathyn interrupted her daydream, Illeanah jumped, snapping her book shut. "I have been hearing the most outrageous rumours, Jodathyn. Were you hurt badly? I heard there was a brawl?"

"I am unhurt," Jodathyn replied, disregarding Valt's snort.

"Hello, Valt," Illeanah said, greeting Jodathyn's regular guard. "I see you do not agree with Jodathyn's statement."

Jodathyn winced, glancing over his shoulder. Valt lifted a hand to greet Illeanah. "Indeed, I do not."

"I also heard you were to enjoy the company of the King's Guard, Master Pallarus," Illeanah continued. Her keen eyes pierced Captain Tiernan. "Are you not going to introduce me?"

Jodathyn gestured to the captain as if he didn't care one whit what the man thought. "Lady Illeanah, this is Captain Tiernan of the King's Guard."

"You've been assigned a captain; your brother is mighty serious," Illeanah commented. She looked pleased.

"Spare me further lecture, Illeanah." Jodathyn regarded her with his solemn grey eyes, which then flicked back to his guards in annoyance. "I'm never going to leave the suffocating confines of the palace."

"Do you think that life in a summer house would be any different?"

"I want to see more of Rama and beyond her borders. The King of Sion invited me to visit his Silk Palace. King Kieryn, in all his regal wisdom, declined the invitation." Jodathyn scowled at the memory of the argument.

"That is a shame. It would have been a lovely experience to see the Silk Palace. I hear it is magnificent, their commerce and trade systems are intricate." Illeanah sighed. Jodathyn knew she was thinking about the missed opportunity to witness the famous traders in person. "You have lived in other places, Jod."

"Androssah and Aviah Valley." Jodathyn laughed bitterly. "When I was living at Lord Solan's summer house in Aviah Valley, there was a horrible knight who used to look after me."

"I've heard of him."

"I used to sneak into his chambers with my friend Ruevyn, to steal copper coins."

Illeanah stared at Jodathyn in wide-eyed astonishment. "Shouldn't a son of a royal house know better than to steal? What would you want with copper coins?"

Jodathyn shook his head with a frown. "The servants were starving and I couldn't bear to see them suffer. So, we stole the newest, shiniest coins we could. But only copper, so the old knight would never find us out ... I miss Ruevyn."

Illeanah stared. "Did you get caught?"

Jodathyn smirked. "Not once."

Jodathyn and Illeanah headed to the gardens that were more popular among the courtiers.

"How did you manage to get out?" Illeanah asked after a few minutes of silence.

"*Pardon?*"

Illeanah leaned forward and whispered in Jodathyn's ear. "How did you get out?"

A slow smile curved on Jodathyn's lips. He peered over at Valt who was only a few paces behind him. Captain Tiernan seemed preoccupied with his own thoughts.

"Come, Jod, we are friends are we not?" Illeanah teased, tossing her long auburn braids over her shoulder. "Won't you please confide in me?"

Jodathyn leant towards Illeanah so that his lips were almost touching her ear. She shivered at his closeness. "The outer wall is horrendously unkempt in the unused gardens by the laundry exit. There's a hole one can wriggle through ... The guards never watch the laundry."

"I'll be watching the laundry," Valt muttered darkly, sharing a significant look with Tiernan.

"Ri rshon hanoch!" Jodathyn muttered a curse using the ancient tongue, locking gazes with Valt. Beyond Valt he could see that Captain Tiernan's stern façade had crumbled in disbelief.

Turning his attention back to Illeanah, he could see she was mortified by his outburst.

"I do apologise to current company for my language," Jodathyn said, ashamed of speaking so crudely. "I'm sorry, Illeanah. I had forgotten I had taught you so much of the ancient tongue. You could translate that, no?"

Illeanah pressed her lips together and laughed. "Where did you learn *that* expression?"

"My most gracious brother, High King Kieryn of Rama."

"No?" Illeanah's eyes widened in shock.

Jodathyn smirked. "In retribution, Queen Odelle stabbed an embroidery needle into our King's arm. She said he should not utter such foul profanities in front of his little brother."

"Surely not!" Illeanah laughed again, and Jodathyn knew she was trying to imagine the serene Queen Odelle sticking her husband with the pointed end of her needle. In response to her disbelief, Jodathyn's lips curled into a sly grin before he sauntered off down the path. Once Illeanah had gathered her wits she was forced to hurry after him.

She caught up with him when he stopped to study a group of young courtiers socialising by one of the fountains.

Will Hartcurt was reclining, his dark gaze fixed on two of his female companions. The expression on his face was one of polite boredom as he listened to the two sisters prattling on. After last night, Jodathyn had to wonder what other secrets Will was hiding. He seemed to be more than just a notorious court seducer.

"Don't you ever feel lonely?" Jodathyn asked.

"You want a lady wife?" Illeanah's voice sounded a little strained.

Jodathyn started, and stared at her as if she had said something outrageous. "A *wife* ...?" he stammered. "*No.* Should I be looking for a wife?"

"Look at the enthralling way her hips sway, Milord. Her elegant raven tresses around her perfect oval face, her large alluring eyes, dainty nose and inviting ruby red lips. Look how tight her purple dress is around those delectable bosoms. She's the vision of feminine charm."

Jodathyn shook his head at Illeanah's teasing. "It looks like those bosoms could eat me."

Jodathyn heard the amused intake of breath from Valt as Illeanah chuckled at his inappropriate observation.

"It isn't nice to make fun," Jodathyn continued in a stern tone. "Thankfully, Will Hartcurt serendipitously saved me from being consumed by bosoms last week. I shall ever be in his debt."

Illeanah giggled. "How do my bosoms compare?"

Her comment had its desired effect; Jodathyn's face flushed.

"Jodathyn! A word!"

Jodathyn spun on his heel to see that his brother, the King, and the King's favourite, Lord Whitoak, were quickly approaching. Not wanting to provoke his brother, Jodathyn knelt. Illeanah and his guards followed suit.

Lord Whitoak was staring at Jodathyn. But when he spoke it was to Illeanah. "Perhaps, daughter, you should attend to your studies."

Illeanah bobbed and left Jodathyn to the mercy of the King and her father.

"Greetings, Your Majesty," Jodathyn murmured, then he turned to greet Lord Whitoak. The lord's jaw was clenched and his fists were by his side. "Have I offended you, Lord Whitoak?"

Lord Whitoak's expression hardened. "Keep your unwholesome talk off your tongue when addressing my daughter."

"Yes, my Lord." Jodathyn dipped his head. "You have my sincerest apologies, Lord Whitoak."

It stung to think that Whitoak, a man Jodathyn admired, was angry with him. Jodathyn had always been grateful for the man's patronage. It had been Lord Whitoak who had gifted Bear to him.

Lips drawn into a thin line, Lord Whitoak studied him in silence. "My daughter will not be contemplating marriage with you."

Jodathyn schooled his features into what he hoped conveyed a polite indifference. It was no secret that he admired Illeanah. He valued his friendship with her and he would do nothing to jeopardise it.

The lord stepped closer, closing the gap between them. "You're better than Will Hartcurt and those brazen sisters ... act like it."

In the distance, Will Hartcurt looked up and caught Jodathyn's eye. The young lord glanced to Lord Whitoak, and his carefree expression melted into gloom. Will stalked away.

"Perhaps kinder words would benefit Will Hartcurt more than scorn, Hallidyn," King Kieryn commented; he had also stopped to watch Will's retreat.

Jodathyn was confused. Kieryn seemed to think Will knew what had been said. That was impossible.

"Scorn never hurt anyone," Lord Whitoak replied.

"Will has known enough heartache, Lord Whitoak. Don't add to it." Kieryn seemed to be impatient with his favourite. "If you would be so kind, I would like a private word with my brother."

Looking angry with the world, Lord Whitoak left the King's presence.

"Have I done something wrong, Your Majesty?" Jodathyn asked, perplexed.

"Keep your distance from his daughter, brother," Kieryn suggested.

"Illeanah is my only friend in this world, my King."

"You are becoming a man and you know what that means."

"Illeanah is my friend."

Kieryn raised his eyebrow. "It is only natural you would want more, Jodathyn. However, aligning yourself with the Whitoaks brings complications."

"Such as, Lord Whitoak does not approve of the match?"

Kieryn inclined his head, then pressed something small and metallic into Jodathyn's hand. "Whatever trouble this world may bring, I am on your side, brother."

Jodathyn glanced down to see what the King had given him. It was the cloak pin that he had used to bribe the stable hand.

"Before you were born, the royal historians confirmed that you are indeed descended from Vadroil, through your mother."

Shocked, Jodathyn stared into his brother's grim face. Why had Kieryn never told him that the rumours of his ancestry had been verified?

Kieryn placed his hand on Jodathyn's shoulder as he continued. "You are also Pallarus through our father's bloodline. Remember that."

Jodathyn curled his fingers around the pin, bringing it to his chest. One day he would prove himself worthy of his heritage to his brother, and the court.

CHAPTER NINE

Kieryn

The King's Orchards

Much to the frustration of the King's council, Kieryn had announced that morning that he wished for some respite. During the weeks leading up to high autumn, the King's Orchards were his favourite place to find solitude. Only a few short miles from the walls of the citadel, it was a place Kieryn felt he could relax. Breathing in the heady perfumes of ripening fruit, he strolled through the trees, enjoying a rare moment of peace.

"Your latest decree has created some division." Lord Whitoak, kept pace with Kieryn, his harsh eyes watching for eavesdroppers. As a young king, Kieryn had learnt the hard way that there were those willing to risk spying on him. It paid to be vigilant.

"Let the fools talk."

"They blame Jodathyn."

"As I said. They are fools."

"Well, at least your brother was happy to join us today."

Kieryn chuckled. When Jodathyn had heard that he was allowed to join the King's party, his face had lit up. He'd raced his guards to the stables and had his horse saddled before any of the stable hands could offer their assistance. Kieryn had also heard how Jodathyn then saddled Captain Tiernan's mount, much to the guardsman's annoyance.

Jodathyn's joyful countenance did not last long. As they passed under the outer gate, Kieryn had seen Jodathyn's gaze stray to the outer wall of the palace. His eyes were transfixed on the bodies of executed criminals. For a moment he was puzzled by Jodathyn's shiver, then one of his King's Guardsman had leant over and whispered that the dead were those who had attended the slave auction.

Thinking Jodathyn afraid, Kieryn had wheeled his horse around. But his brother's grip on his reins tightened so that his knuckles were white. Grey eyes darkened. His black stallion danced to the side, sensing his rider's rage.

Captain Tiernan had put out a gloved hand to settle the prancing horse. "Master?"

Jodathyn took a great shuddering breath, blinking in clear confusion at Tiernan's concern.

Jodathyn's out of character anger and confusion worried Kieryn. But he thought it unwise to give attention to his brother's strange reaction to the corpses. So, he resisted the urge to approach Jodathyn. Tiernan would look after his brother.

Kieryn halted his stroll as he spotted the object of his thoughts. Jodathyn was huddled with Illeanah Whitoak under a tree. Their heads were bent together as they whispered over a shared text. Illeanah shifted closer to touch Jodathyn's hand. Jodathyn looked up with a tender smile and her porcelain skin blushed under his brother's attention. The pair made a pretty little picture.

Beside Kieryn, Lord Whitoak made an irritated sound in the back of his throat.

"Uncle Jodathyn!"

Jodathyn and Illeanah's moment of quiet was shattered by Kieryn's only child, Prince Carvelle. The little prince sprinted across the grass, tackling his unsuspecting uncle. He wrapped his arms around Jodathyn's neck, pressing their foreheads together. Even at a distance, Kieryn thought he could see his brother's wince.

Jodathyn lifted Carvelle and spun him about until the little Prince squealed in delight. Illeanah also stood, brushing the leaves from her emerald dress. Pausing his game with Carvelle, Jodathyn watched Illeanah leave. The soft, contented smile on his brother's face spoke volumes. Kieryn knew if he wasn't careful, Jodathyn might find himself infatuated. It was a match which would only cause them heartache. Perhaps it was already too late.

"Is it wise to allow Jodathyn, your brother, such close access to the Crown Prince, Your Majesty?" Lord Whitoak's stare was trained upon his daughter.

"Jod means no harm," Kieryn replied. "He loves my son and when the time comes, he will make an excellent father."

"Perhaps it would be wise not to entertain the thought of a wife and child for Jodathyn, Sire." There was an edge of warning in Whitoak's voice.

Kieryn decided to ignore the comment, instead he continued to observe Jodathyn and his son. Carvelle was chattering away; Jodathyn, ever attentive, was listening, his head tilted to the side. The smile on Jodathyn's face was genuine, open and relaxed.

"If Jodathyn fathers a child, the threat to your crown increases."

"For now, let him have what little happiness we can give him," the King huffed. "As yet he has done nothing wrong. Our own spies are watching and waiting."

"Your Majesty cannot afford to be moved by your feelings for him."

"He is my brother. My flesh. Despite the so-called dangers to my throne, I have come to care for him."

Lord Whitoak regarded him in silence. The King returned the solemn gaze with ill-concealed impatience. He didn't need Hallidyn Whitoak's approval.

"You would have me eliminate the threat to my throne."

Lord Whitoak conceded with a curt nod of his head. "It would be wise."

"My brother is not to be harmed."

"It may seem brutal, Majesty ..."

"He is not yet a full-grown man."

"In two years, he will be."

Kieryn turned to regard his brother once again. Lord Whitoak was right; with Jodathyn's coming of age, new dangers would emerge.

"That's the crux of the problem, Hallidyn, isn't it?" said Kieryn. "Jodathyn is a young man, now. A young man who may naturally show your daughter some interest."

"The blood of Vadroil runs through his veins. His eyes are proof enough of the curse within him."

Kieryn sniffed. It was true that Ramian legend spoke fiercely against those born with grey eyes. But not all legends were true. "As a father, you would do anything to protect your daughter. You would not have her bearing a child for my brother ... for Vadroil's bloodline."

"Rumours that the dragon is stirring are starting to emerge."

"Who told you that?" Kieryn demanded. "Your wicked little stable hand?"

"Majesty, if I may be so bold to say, you are blinded by your affection for your brother. Steps need to be made to protect you. To protect Prince Carvelle."

"Enough! My brother is under my protection unless I state otherwise. Jodathyn respects you, Lord Whitoak."

"Majesty ..."

"I will personally assure you that Jodathyn will not make any unwanted advances on your daughter."

"Majesty ..."

"I am the only father figure Jodathyn has ever known. To betray my own brother ... He isn't one of your unwanted pups for you to drown."

"As your Majesty commands." Lord Whitoak dipped into a bow, his tone indicating he did not understand his sovereign's reluctance in the matter. "You would not have to do the deed yourself. Any number of your guards could humanely ... Tiernan, perhaps, while Jodathyn is sleeping ..."

"Not another word!" Kieryn snarled.

Across the path, unaware of the argument, Jodathyn pretended to faint. Carvelle clambered all over him, cackling as his uncle tickled his belly. Any outsider could have been forgiven for thinking they were brothers. Both Jodathyn and Carvelle had the same brown curls, olive complexion and adventurous spirit. Bile rose in Kieryn's throat at the mere suggestion of ridding himself of his brother.

Extracting himself from Carvelle's grip, Jodathyn lifted his head, realising he had an audience. He struggled to his feet, brushing dirt and grass from his trousers.

"My King." In an attempt to hide his flushed cheeks, Jodathyn swept into a deep bow. He was still grinning as Kieryn approached him. "The Prince and I thought to have a spot of sport."

"Rise, brother." Kieryn indicated with a simple gesture that Jodathyn was to come closer. "I'm surprised not to find you and my son up a tree again."

Jodathyn drew near, kneeling at his brother's feet. Prince Carvelle tore across the garden, barrelling into his side. With one hand Jodathyn fumbled with the Prince, while trying to maintain his posture. He failed, finding himself sprawled on the green grass.

"The chastisement of the Prince's tutors was enough for Carvelle and I not to consider the matter," Jodathyn replied with feigned innocence.

"At least, not in their presence," Prince Carvelle admitted.

The King shook his head. "You were always such a proficient climber, Jod. I will never forget the time you scrambled up the palace walls."

"You soundly punished my backside." Jodathyn snorted. "My bottom never forgot the incident."

"Papa, did you really chastise Uncle Jodathyn?"

"It was a dangerous stunt, my son," Kieryn replied with a hint of teasing. "Your uncle almost fell and broke his neck."

Jodathyn snickered. "That wasn't the first time I scaled those walls, my King."

"But it was the last," Kieryn retorted.

An expression of guilt flitted across Jodathyn's face.

"Do we need to *talk* about climbing walls again, Jodathyn?" Fixing his brother with a stern, dark gaze, Kieryn delighted in Jodathyn's discomfort.

"No, Your Majesty, the walls are safe from me. I assure you."

Kieryn smiled in amusement. "Carvelle, leave your uncle alone."

The young prince tumbled out of Jodathyn's arms then sprinted through the gardens once more.

"Come, perhaps it is time I rewarded your guards," said Kieryn. "Lord Whitoak and I have *finished* our conversation. Let us ride out."

The King took the crook of his brother's elbow, steering him towards their impatient mounts.

When Lord Whitoak went to follow them at a respectful distance, Kieryn turned and eyed his favourite.

"You should enjoy the day, Hallidyn," the King said. "You're sour today and make poor company."

"As Your Majesty commands," Lord Whitoak replied. His inscrutable glance brushed over Jodathyn, before he left the King's side.

Jodathyn seemed to shrug off Lord Whitoak's animosity. He swung himself into the saddle and waited for the King and the rest of the riding party to mount.

"So, we are heading north on the Northerners' March," Jodathyn said aloud, when Kieryn urged his entourage to take the less-taken road.

"Must we have a destination in mind in order to enjoy the day?"

Jodathyn seemed to consider Kieryn's response. "I dare say we're not hunting in the Arelle Forest."

"I'm not such a talented hunter as our Papa was," Kieryn replied.

"So, I must conclude you intend for us to ride in circles."

"Perhaps we shall."

"Don't you ever get the urge to explore the nation you rule over? Why not go to Torryn?"

"Torryn?"

Jodathyn sighed. "It was the first place that came to mind. The capital of ancient Rama, the crown jewel of Arturyn the Unifier."

Kieryn turned to Jodathyn, watching the muscles in his brother's face relax as he closed his eyes. Undoubtedly, Jodathyn was imagining the fortress of Torryn rising up from the road. As a child, he was fascinated with the legends of his ancestors.

"Can you imagine him? Arturyn, the escaped slave, transforming into our warrior king."

Kieryn had been right. Jodathyn's mind had wandered off to his history books.

"It is such a shame we don't know more details about his many battles … and how he vanquished Vadroil on the day of the Autumn feast."

"Not many men are born with the valour of Arturyn," Kieryn agreed. "Can you imagine the task of unifying many different groups to fight a common enemy? He must have been quite the statesman."

"I was thinking about the dragon battles," Jodathyn confessed.

"It's best not to speak about dragons, little brother."

"But do you think Vadroil was a real dragon? Like some of the stories say?"

"All we can really know is this: there are *no* dragons in Rama," Kieryn replied.

"I had always ..."

Kieryn needed to distract Jodathyn, and change the tone of their conversation. He trusted the King's Guard, but he didn't want any talk that his brother was discussing dragons and battles.

"These roads King Arturyn built his army are safe. How about a race?" The King had barely finished speaking when he goaded his stallion into a gallop. A guardsman taken by surprise uttered a curse. The sound of Jodathyn's mount thundered close behind him.

Checking on his brother's progress was Kieryn's undoing. Jodathyn took advantage of his inattention, and his stallion passed him on the inside.

"I am the King!" Kieryn cried. "You can't let me lose, brother!"

Jodathyn laughed into the wind. "Catch me if you can!"

The brothers' enjoyment of the race did not last. Jodathyn suddenly stiffened and pulled back on his reins. Before his stallion had stopped, he jumped from the saddle.

Terrified that a guardsman might knock Jodathyn over, Kieryn shouted out in alarm. His mount snorted in frustration as he pulled the reins tight, halting the beast's gallop. Kieryn guided his horse around and breathed a sigh of relief seeing that all the guardsmen had been able to stop before they reached Jodathyn.

Jodathyn stood on the dirt road, his eyes darting about, as if seeking something that wasn't there.

"Tiernan!"

Tiernan had already dismounted and was striding towards Jodathyn. Before he could reach him, Jodathyn darted to the side of the road and disappeared into the scrub.

"Master!"

Jodathyn gave no sign he'd seen or heard Tiernan.

"Jodathyn!" Kieryn bellowed, handing his reins to the closest guardsman as he dismounted. "Come back here this instant!"

Leaving his horse on the road, Kieryn pressed into the bushes. His hands trembled as he recalled what Whitoak had told him. Surely if the dragon was stirring, he would have noticed the signs.

"Jod!" Kieryn yelled, he tripped on his cloak and tumbled down. The moist smell of the forest floor filled his nostrils. He paused cursing, taking in a deep breath. Another smell mingled with the scent of the foliage. He gagged.

Pushing himself to his feet, Kieryn was glad that none of the guardsman had seen him fall. He covered his mouth and nose, taking a few steps forward. "Otherworld, Jod. Please!"

"Here, Sire."

Only a few paces further in, Kieryn caught sight of Jodathyn's ashen face. Tiernan was standing close to his brother, his hand wrapped around his wrist. Together they were staring down at the rotting carcass of a man.

Taking a closer look, Kieryn could see that it was the body of an ordinary soldier. Flies buzzed around the dead man's unseeing eyes, making their homes in his nose and mouth. From the unnatural angle of the unfortunate's neck, he guessed it was broken. Whoever had killed him had been strong.

Pivoting, Jodathyn vomited, gasping for breath. His brother was no stranger to how cruel and violent the world could be, so his reaction puzzled Kieryn.

"This wasn't an accident." Jodathyn's eyes glazed over. He fell silent, his expression was one of guilt.

"The house insignia had been removed from his uniform. The murderer had not wanted his victim's employer known." Tiernan's voice was a low rumble as he sent Jodathyn a sharp glare which clearly said, *keep silent*.

Kieryn knew then and there that Captain Tiernan, known for his trustworthiness, had asked his brother not to speak. Ignoring a flash of boiling rage, he strode forward, taking Jodathyn's shoulders in his grasp. He could guess what it was that Tiernan didn't want Jodathyn saying aloud. The captain was only trying to protect him. "Brother, are you well?"

Jodathyn nodded, his movements jerky. His eyes shot to the other King's Guardsmen, who had assembled behind them.

Tiernan knelt down to examine the corpse. "Well, the murderer didn't check the body too closely."

"What is it?"

Tiernan twisted the corpse's arm over to reveal a tattoo on the left wrist. It was a red fox. "This is Lord Kamoore's house insignia."

Paling, Jodathyn jolted as if he'd been struck; his lips parted. A second sharp gaze from the captain was enough to stop him from uttering a sound.

Turning on his heel, Kieryn looked at his guardsmen. He knew they would only speak the narrative he chose to tell. He could not allow the council to discover Jodathyn's strange behaviour.

"My brother fell from his horse. He is dazed and confused. Escort him back to the citadel."

Jael, the troop medic, stepped forward to guide Jodathyn back to the road. Hearing the King's command, Jodathyn shook Jael's hands off his shoulders. He opened his mouth to protest, but Jael caught Jodathyn's sleeve.

"Your King has given a command. Silence."

CHAPTER TEN

Jodathyn

The Autumn Festival - The Fields of Adavan

Jodathyn stood petulant at the King's side, his back rigid, his face blank. He observed the grand celebrations that ushered in high autumn with a sense of longing. Oh, how he wished to walk in the shade of the forest, its canopy a crown of yellow, red and bronze. Instead, he was on display serving his brother and his nobles.

Jodathyn suppressed a sigh as he watched the younger members of court enjoying themselves among the golden pavilions. Will Hartcurt, who hadn't spoken a word to him since the incident at the ale house, was laughing with a company of King's Guardsmen. Illeanah was dancing barefoot, her hair flowing behind her like a copper river.

He returned his attention to the royal pavilion.

"Wine, brother," King Kieryn said, lifting his goblet. Unaffected by Jodathyn's mood, the King reclined, surrounded by his council. His heavy, traditional crown of Rama had been exchanged for a garland of autumn leaves. At his side, Queen Odelle looked cheerful with her painted red lips.

Delicate autumn berries were woven into her golden hair and her fair face glowed with joy.

"Jod, wine," Kieryn repeated, lifting his goblet higher.

Mumbling his apologies, Jodathyn stepped forward to refill his brother's goblet. As he did so he stole a quick glance at Captain Tiernan. Since the day he had found the corpse, the big man had been a near constant companion. The captain had been adamant that Jodathyn should forget his vision. But Jodathyn worried about the lie of omission. Lying to the High King of Rama was a serious offence. Why would a man known to adhere to a strict honour code request him to remain silent? Jodathyn had a niggling feeling that Kieryn knew something was wrong, so why hadn't he punished him?

"Uncle Jodathyn has a black eye." Prince Carvelle galloped into the royal pavilion. He grasped Jodathyn's hand and swung on his arm. The small boy looked up at him with a cheeky grin before he addressed Captain Tiernan. "How did it happen?"

"Pray, entertain us with how you got this bruise, brother." King Kieryn demanded; his attention was on his Queen as he raised her hand for a kiss.

Jodathyn opened his mouth, but clenched his jaw shut when he couldn't find words that wouldn't make him sound like a clumsy dolt.

"Captain Tiernan wanted to teach our master how to handle multiple opponents in a fist fight. He stepped right into Guardsmen Carew's swinging fist."

Valt had no compunction about embarrassing him, Jodathyn thought sourly as he glared at his unrepentant guard.

Kieryn chuckled, lifting his goblet in mock salute to Captain Tiernan. "Well, as long as you gents make sure he is properly tired and sore at the end of each spar, he's learning a lesson."

Jodathyn glowered at Valt and Tiernan who were sniggering at his expense.

"Play with me, Uncle." Prince Carvelle tugged on Jodathyn's sleeve, looking up at him with wide, hopeful eyes.

"He may not," Kieryn answered, without glancing in Jodathyn's direction. "Your Uncle Jodathyn is working off a debt."

Prince Carvelle pouted and flopped into his father's lap. "Can I play with his dogs then, Father?"

The Queen smiled indulgently and smoothed her son's hair from his face. "Perhaps that is a question for your uncle."

Carvelle's large, pleading eyes looked up at Jodathyn. Feeling he had very little choice in the matter, Jodathyn nodded.

Prince Carvelle whooped. He bounded up from his father's lap and whistled for Jodathyn's dogs. Off they capered, the small princeling and two hairy hunting dogs. With a peculiar sense of foreboding, Jodathyn wanted to call them back. He didn't.

"The trade of prisoners in the south has decreased alarmingly, Majesty," Lord Solan said. Sneering, he indicated with an imperious wave that he wanted more wine. Jodathyn stepped around the gathered nobles to fill his goblet to the brim.

"The transport of prisoners to Artroth has been happening since King Arturyn's great victory," Kamoore added. "Their trade is essential to Rama's economy, my King."

Confused, Jodathyn looked around at the nobles. Many were frowning at Kieryn with cold expressions. They were unhappy and they were blaming the King. Why had he not heard rumours of discontent earlier?

Kieryn lowered his goblet. "Don't you mean the selling of prisoners into slavery is essential to your own purse, Kamoore?"

"If you don't like the consequence, don't do the crime," Frayn continued, thrusting his half-full goblet at Jodathyn.

Jodathyn spluttered as he refilled the goblet. Frayn seemed unapologetic; instead he curled his lip at Jodathyn. "Most are criminals, or malcontents with terrible secret talents. Why should their lords not profit?"

Outraged, Jodathyn felt a warm tingling spreading through his body. Donatein had warned him that today he was a servant and should remain silent. But Frayn's self-assured blather infuriated him.

"It was also compulsory during King Arturyn's time that fathers give the village chieftains and rulers their firstborn, to serve in the army. Luckily for you, my Lord Frayn, that practice was abolished many centuries ago, along with slavery," Jodathyn replied.

"You are here to serve," Lord Solan growled, smoothing his beard. "Not to lecture your betters. We of the great houses know and understand our history. The selling of prisoners to Artroth is not slavery."

Queen Odelle offered Jodathyn a delicate hanky, which he took, dabbing his face dry. "Just because the Crown did something in the past, that does not make it right, fair or just."

"You are but a boy ..." Frayn continued.

Jodathyn ignored his brother's warning look. "Your behaviour is not much better than a child's, Lord Frayn. To hear Lady Illeanah speak, you threw the most spectacular tantrum when Lord Whitoak refused you her hand in marriage."

Hearing the titters of laughter, Jodathyn enjoyed the furious look of embarrassment on his rival's face.

"At least you will never breed," Frayn snarled through clenched teeth. Ignoring the plaintive expressions of his supporters, he stormed from the pavilion. "His Majesty has given assurance that you will never take a wife or sire a child."

Shocked, Jodathyn looked towards his brother for confirmation.

Kieryn's face was neutral, frozen as if he were afraid to show emotion.

"My Lords," Kieryn sighed almost in defeat. "I have merely placed a hold on the types of criminals the magistrates are sending over to Artroth. Indeed, it is distressing to see how many southern magistrates are condemning those whose crimes are petty." The King pierced Solan and

Kamoore with a grim stare. "The consequences of continuing this practice will be dire for any that ignore my royal decree."

"You're listening to that whelp, my King," Kamoore insisted.

"I assure you, my Lord, I am my own man," Kieryn said. His voice was soft. "I make decisions for the good of my realm. Not to soothe bloated egos or to fatten purses."

"Perhaps we should send the magistrates to Artroth in chains," Jodathyn said, feeling a little reckless. "I am sure the Artrothian markets would welcome them."

The King's bitter laugh had a cruel edge to it. "A fine solution indeed. What do you think to that, Lord Whitoak?"

"Jodathyn could learn some tact, Sire." Hallidyn Whitoak examined Jodathyn with a sombre expression. Unlike the other lords he was not partaking of the wine. Jodathyn knew Whitoak preferred to keep his mind agile and his tongue sharp.

"Abuse of power is serious," Jodathyn replied. "Is it not the role of the King's council to protect the people of our nation?"

"Ah, but my brother, the Son of the Crown, occasionally has some interesting and wise opinions. He is passionate."

"Indeed." There was a strange light in Hallidyn Whitoak's eyes. He turned away, searching for his daughter. Jodathyn followed his gaze.

"Perhaps you should remove all thoughts of friendship with my daughter."

Jodathyn flinched, taken aback by the lord's abruptness. He stole a second glance at Illeanah, who was laughing, surrounded by other young courtiers. She was one of the few Jodathyn counted among his friends. He felt his mood further sour. Kieryn had warned him about paying Illeanah too much attention.

"If that is what your lordship wishes." Jodathyn tore his eyes away from Illeanah's form and stared straight ahead.

Queen Odelle stood, smoothing out her skirts. "Come husband, we should make ourselves available to our court." As the royal couple passed him, the Queen squeezed Jodathyn's hand.

Jodathyn watched as the King left the royal pavilion. Try as he might, he could never quash the feelings of bitterness. Kieryn had everything: the love of the people, a wife who adored him, and a strong healthy boy. The greatest to the least in Rama paid him tribute. Jodathyn was left with contempt and loneliness. If only he had been born to a poor farmer ... he might have a family of his own to cherish.

"Perhaps you would be happier if you accepted your place," Lord Solan said. He lifted his goblet to drink. His eyes were cold.

"Whatever do you mean, Lord Solan?" Jodathyn asked, his brow furrowed.

"You were born under three ill omens," Lord Kamoore said, rubbing his gold rings. "Whatever could a Son of the Crown amount to?"

Jodathyn flinched. It was not the first time he had heard that his birth coincided with three bad omens. The peoples of ancient Rama had been superstitious.

"I have heard about the omens," Jodathyn confirmed, proud of how steady his voice seemed.

"And then there is your mother ..."

Flushing, Jodathyn clenched his fists around the silver jug he was holding. There was a slight tremor in his hands as he replied, "I never knew her."

"Of course not," Kamoore said with a feral grin. "Your birth killed her. Your ill omen was fatal for your whore of a mother."

"Lords," a noble lady cut in. "You're being cruel."

Jodathyn gave the lady a sad smile in thanks. She was an older woman who had never spoken to him. He understood. It was rumoured she had been a lady-in-waiting to Jodathyn's mother. When King Hadryn refused his consort a physician, it was this woman who had delivered Jodathyn, unassisted. Her political prowess helped her maintain her rank during his mother's downfall.

"He is the image of his departed father," another aged lady chimed in. "If you wish to talk about omens, then that is a fair sign."

Jodathyn blinked, wishing he was anywhere other than the royal pavilion. He would rather be back at the palace, mucking out the stables, than here under the scrutiny of the courtiers.

"His mother didn't name him, as is tradition. Old King Hadryn had the right idea. He didn't want to bother with a name for his inconvenient son. King Kieryn named the whelp."

Jodathyn had known, of course, that his mother had passed from the mortal world before she had the opportunity to name him. He hadn't known that his father had refused to gift him with a name.

"King Hadryn brought the squalling piece of flesh before the council," Solan confirmed. "We voted on what to do with him."

"What to do with me?" Jodathyn felt the blood drain from his face; a sense of dread washed over him.

"We voted on whether you should live or die," Lord Solan replied.

"Prince Kieryn pleaded with your father to show you mercy," Lord Whitoak said. His voice was soft, as if he wanted to soothe Jodathyn's hurt.

Jodathyn jutted his chin forward, refusing to look at him.

"Hallidyn!" someone cried. "The King did not want Jodathyn to know this."

"There's a great deal King Kieryn does not want Jodathyn to know. Better he hears this now," Lord Whitoak continued. He sent a warning glance at Lord Solan to silence him. "Jodathyn, King Kieryn spoke well on your behalf."

Jodathyn sucked in a deep breath, forcing air into his burning lungs. The ground beneath him tilted. He stumbled. His father, the great Hadryn, had not cared if he lived or died. If Kieryn hadn't intervened ...

Jodathyn searched his memories for any presence of the man many Ramians still admired. What he thought he knew of the benevolent King Hadryn now seemed like an empty husk.

Tears pricked Jodathyn's grey eyes. His body trembled – he didn't know if it was from frustration, sadness or anger. Turning his face away, Jodathyn slammed his heavy jug down onto a nearby table with a loud crash. No one moved to stop him as he stormed away.

CHAPTER ELEVEN

Jodathyn

The Fields of Adavan

Dashing between dancing ladies and servers, Jodathyn made his way through the festivities. Behind him he could hear his two shadows muttering apologies for any upsets he had caused. Jodathyn didn't care who he offended.

"Master!" Valt called out.

Jodathyn continued to charge forward. He was so flustered he didn't notice Will until it was too late.

Will, holding an overflowing goblet, nearly knocked Jodathyn off his feet. For the second time that day, Jodathyn found himself covered in festival wine. He spluttered as Will attempted to mop up the mess.

"Oh! Begging your pardon!"

Angry words were about to burst from Jodathyn's lips, but Will had the gall to shush him. Shocked at the young lord's audacity, Jodathyn looked up into his smiling face.

"A thousand apologies!" Will cried. He lowered his voice as he made a pretence of drunkenly straightening Jodathyn's tunic. "Empty pavilion on the far side of the clearing. Go."

Will's eyes glinted with mischief as he winked. Staggering past, he took a moment to bump into Captain Tiernan.

Jodathyn shook his head. Will wasn't as drunk as he wanted people to think. Without questioning why the lord would want to help him, Jodathyn pressed on towards the empty pavilion.

By the time Jodathyn reached it, he was almost gasping for breath in an attempt to rein in his temper. He entered the privacy of the tent and gave a frustrated yell.

Jodathyn heard Tiernan's voice from outside. "Be with him. I'll stand watch here."

He wanted to scream at his guards that he didn't want company. He swallowed his fury. It wouldn't do for him to be observed fighting with his minders. He'd made enough of a scene already. Shame washed over him.

Valt entered the pavilion, striding quickly towards Jodathyn. He took his master's shoulders in his firm grip. "Calm breaths, Jod, like Donatein has taught you."

Valt used his moniker on the rare occasions where he felt Jodathyn needed comforting. The last time, Jodathyn had still been a boy, bruised and humiliated by his unforgiving swordmaster. The use of it now annoyed him.

"I am not panicking!" Jodathyn snapped, rounding onto him. "I am ..."

"... needing to calm down."

Jodathyn snorted, snatching up a pitcher of wine and a goblet. He poured himself a drink and downed it in one go, not taking the time to savour the sharp aroma. Pouring himself a second, he brought the rim of the goblet to his nose to smell the richness of the King's favourite wine. He drank it under Valt's disapproving gaze.

"Master, I don't think drinking to excess is wise."

"When have I ever been wise?" Jodathyn spat. He felt the familiar stirring of uncontrollable anger building within his belly. His insides felt hot.

Valt took a step back, as if he didn't like what he saw in Jodathyn's face. "Jod, calm down. I can't protect you if you lose control."

"Control of what?" Jodathyn snapped, pouring yet another drink.

"Jodathyn! Please stop!" Valt begged. "I will hold you down if you continue to behave like this."

Jodathyn jutted out his chest and brought the goblet to his lips. "Really? *Hold me down.*"

Valt frowned at him. "Jodathyn, please."

Illeanah stepped into the tent. "It would be prudent to listen to your guard."

Jodathyn's goblet paused at his lips as he appraised her cream gown, accented with bronze leaves. She looked divine. Remembering her father's request to end their friendship, he tore his eyes away from her face. He wished he was already drunk.

Ignoring Jodathyn's pained expression, Illeanah glided into the pavilion and plucked the goblet from Jodathyn's limp fingers. She set it down with a clink.

Like the morning mist, Jodathyn's anger dissipated.

"My father sent me. You are understandably distressed."

"Your father has made it known he is my enemy." Jodathyn's words were clipped. Had Lord Whitoak sent Illeanah to him so that he must break their friendship that very day?

"Your accusation has no founding," Illeanah retorted. "What has gotten into you?"

"It's over."

"I'm afraid I don't understand."

"Our friendship is over."

Illeanah brought her hand to her chest. She stared up at Jodathyn wide eyed. "If this is a marriage proposal, it is a strange one, Jodathyn Pallarus."

Sucking in a deep breath, Jodathyn turned so that Illeanah couldn't see his expression. He'd hoped she might harbour feelings for him that went beyond brotherly. If he was to do as Lord Whitoak wanted, he would have to do it quickly.

"This isn't a marriage proposal."

"Then what is this about?"

"I am a dangerous man."

Scoffing, Illeanah glared at Jodathyn.

"We are no longer children. You are an eligible young woman and I am a man. A man the court cannot accept. It would not do for nobles to think that House Whitoak is aligning itself with someone like me."

Infuriated, Illeanah slapped Jodathyn's cheek. Jodathyn let her, his eyes shooting to Valt, to tell him to do and say nothing.

"I came here to say your father may have been a great and powerful king, but as a father he was a pig. Now I am standing before you I can see you are no different than he. You're a pig, Jodathyn Pallarus. A pig!"

Swallowing past the lump in his throat, Jodathyn tried to dispel feelings of guilt as Illeanah's big brown eyes filled with tears. He forced himself to bite his tongue and say nothing. It hurt to see the hope in Illeanah's face.

Jodathyn lowered his head and whispered, "Please, stay close to the Queen. I foresee she will need you in the days to come."

Illeanah shook her head, unblinking, as if bidding Jodathyn to say more to her. "The Queen?" she choked through her tears. "Don't I mean anything to you?"

Jodathyn fought the urge to tell Illeanah that her father had demanded the end of their friendship. In this world, she had only her father. Her mother had died birthing her. He would not see her lose her close bond with him because of his own hurt.

"So that's it?" Illeanah turned, storming to the pavilion's entrance, where she faced him one more time. "Your words are cruel. Shall they be the last words I will remember you uttering to me?"

Resisting the call to run after her, Jodathyn turned his gaze to Valt who stood motionless, watching him with piercing blue eyes.

"You're going to tell me that was ill done," Jodathyn declared to the stillness of the tent. "Lord Whitoak would have expected nothing less."

"That girl loves you," Valt rumbled.

"Do you think I do not hurt?" Jodathyn was crumbling. "But I have Donatein, as I have you. I do not need the love of a woman."

"We should leave and make for the citadel, hm?"

Jodathyn nodded.

Valt moved forward, wrapping Jodathyn in a rare, quick embrace. "Life will not always be so cruel. I'll ask Tiernan to inform some of the guardsmen we are leaving."

Jodathyn nodded, not trusting himself to answer. Together they left the pavilion. He did his utmost to ignore the pointed gazes of servants and nobles alike. As Valt stood shoulder to shoulder with Tiernan, he let the low sounds of their voices wash over him.

Jodathyn took some calming breaths. He closed his eyes, wishing the darkness would swallow him up. Everyone would be much better off if he were to disappear. The world would continue on without him.

"I wonder how many of my father's council wanted me dead," Jodathyn murmured, as Valt's heavy hand landed on his shoulder.

"The King loves you," Valt replied softly. He led Jodathyn to where the horses were left during the festival. "Let's find our horses and go home."

Jodathyn scoffed "I have nothing and no one in this world. My own father ..."

"You are angry." Valt's voice was low and filled with unnecessary pity. "It's perfectly human to be furious. Master, please listen, you must stay in control."

Jodathyn paused. "My own father contemplated *killing* me ... What crime did I commit?"

"Your father was a fiend for even thinking of taking his own child before the council for judgement."

"You shouldn't speak of a High King of Rama like that," Jodathyn whispered.

"Why not?" Valt replied. He took a few long, angry steps forward, so that Jodathyn had to hurry to keep up with him. "I am only speaking truth."

"Something is wrong with me, Valt."

"I don't think there's anything wrong with you. There's something wrong with this world in which we live."

"I know you were offered a better rank among the King's Guard ... even the Sionian King wanted you to join his ranks. Why didn't you go?"

"I couldn't leave you," Valt replied. His voice sounded gruff. "It was a matter of honour."

"I have always wanted to ask you – did you know the personal guard you replaced? You share a family name ..."

The muscles in Valt's face twitched. "He sent me to pay off his debt to you."

"He never said goodbye."

"He would have stayed if he could."

"It was my fault."

Valt shook his head. "He should not have left his post."

"So, you stayed because of another man's mistakes?"

"In the beginning," Valt confessed. "Then I stayed because of you."

They reached the horses, and Valt went to find their mounts, leaving Jodathyn to stare into the woods.

When Will had tried to straighten Jodathyn's tunic, he'd left it lopsided. While he waited for Valt, Jodathyn adjusted it, and noticed Will had tucked something inside. Curious, Jodathyn dug out a tiny piece of parchment. Unrolling it, he read a scrawled message: *Danger. You're being watched. Be careful of Lord Solan.*

Amused, Jodathyn slipped the piece of parchment back into his tunic. Will was trying his hand at palace spy, was he? His message didn't contain anything Jodathyn didn't already know.

Jodathyn was still puzzling over why Will would bother warning him about Solan, when he caught a glimpse of something moving into the forest. Curious, he took a few steps away from the horses and closer to the tree line.

"Master?"

Jodathyn lifted his hand for silence. If he strained his ears, he could almost hear the sounds of dogs barking. It struck him seconds later, that he was the only one whose dogs accompanied him everywhere. It took a few more moments to realise that the last time he had seen his dogs was with his nephew. A thrill of unease tingled up Jodathyn's spine.

"Carvelle!"

The woods were cool and quiet as Jodathyn stepped into the shade of the trees. There was no sign of the Prince or Jodathyn's dogs. Jodathyn pressed further into the forest.

"Carvelle!"

"Master, we should turn back," Valt said.

Jodathyn jumped – he hadn't heard his personal guard following him into the forest. Looking back, he stared at the red giant. "Something isn't right."

"The princeling is not here."

Jodathyn shook his head and slunk further into the woods. Behind him, Valt growled, threatening to pick him up and sling him over his shoulder.

Jodathyn wasn't listening; he caught the sound of a dog's yelp. A few paces to his right, on the forest floor, was a child's rumpled cloak.

"Carvelle!" Jodathyn yelled. "Come out this instant!"

Valt muttered a dark curse, drawing his sword. "Get behind me."

"Uncle!"

Not caring about his own safety, Jodathyn darted forward. Valt was quicker; his fingers caught Jodathyn's sleeve. In one swift action, his master was behind him. "Stay behind me, do you hear?"

Scowling, Jodathyn nodded as he glanced back in the direction they had come. It was considered ill-advised for a servant to have a weapon, so he was unarmed. Jodathyn's eyes bore into Valt's glacial-blue ones. Even if he did have a weapon, he wouldn't be much use. Satisfied, Valt returned Jodathyn's nod, his body taut, ready for whatever danger lay ahead. There was no time to return to the clearing.

"Uncle! Help!"

"Steady," Valt growled under his breath. "Charging into danger is not going to help Prince Carvelle."

Valt's cautious advance towards danger was almost enough to drive Jodathyn to madness. Inch by careful inch they stepped forward.

A twig snapped behind Jodathyn. Before he could turn, he was grabbed from behind. A sharp blade kissed the exposed skin of his neck.

"You weren't supposed to bring the red barbarian."

Snarling, Valt brandished his weapon at the unkempt man who had dared to lay hands on Jodathyn.

Beads of sweat blinded Jodathyn, his limbs trembled as his attacker lifted a blade under his chin. "Are you afraid, boy? There's worse to come."

"Lay down your weapon and I'll promise you a quick death." Valt's voice was a quiet growl. He was not playing.

Jodathyn tensed as the blade pressed a little harder into his flesh. He could almost see his attacker's answering grin.

"We have the princeling. Jodathyn is volunteering to take the blame for his kidnapping. The King will have no choice ..."

"Is Carvelle alive?" Jodathyn bit out. He could feel the build-up of heat in his insides as his fear gave way to fury.

"Our employer bid us to kill him," the attacker said. "But he's worth more alive."

"Good." Jodathyn didn't know what had come over him. He felt his hand twisting of its own accord. "That's all I needed to know."

One afternoon, after Tiernan had finished training him in the tiltyards, Guardsman Carew had taken Jodathyn aside. Carew had whispered some unconventional tactics in his ear, in case he found himself in a brawl.

Taking a deep breath, Jodathyn steadied himself, then quick as a flash he grabbed his attacker's manhood and twisted his wrist. As the man hollered in pain, Jodathyn spun and punched him in the face.

"Run!" Valt said, leering as he stepped towards the hunched man.

"Valt?"

"Run," Valt repeated. His voice took on a flinty edge. "I'll come for you."

Jodathyn swallowed, but as he turned to flee, a second intruder blocked his escape. In his hand his would-be attacker wielded a nasty-looking dagger. Without hesitation Jodathyn charged, pushing the unsuspecting man off his feet.

"Good lad." Jodathyn heard Valt's deep rumble as he jumped over the prone attacker. He turned his head in time to see two more assailants appearing from behind the first attacker, who was still clutching his privates.

"Go!" Valt shouted, baring his teeth in a ferocious sneer. "I'll find you."

CHAPTER TWELVE

Kieryn

The Fields of Adavan

The first thing Kieryn noticed was the stony expression on Captain Tiernan's face, as he came stalking from the far pavilions. There was an imperceptible tick in the man's temple. His captain was upset. Frowning, Kieryn noticed that Jodathyn and his personal guard were not by Tiernan's side. His stomach dropped. What trouble had Jodathyn gotten into now?

The captain stopped by some of his younger guardsmen. He exchanged some clipped words with his underlings before one of them lifted a hand to gesture in Kieryn's direction. The captain nodded to his men and approached.

"You wish an audience, Captain?"

Tiernan bowed his head in deference. "My King, Valt and I have judged it wise to return to Pallaryn with Jodathyn."

"Why might that be?" Kieryn asked. "Are you keen to see my brother dismissed from his punishment?"

"That is not so, Your Majesty," Tiernan replied. "I have worked him hard in the tiltyards as I promised. A firm hand will curb his rebellious tendencies."

Kieryn chuckled. "Yes, Jodathyn has been subdued of late."

"My King, it is in your brother's best interest to leave. He is distressed. Some thought it was a good idea to discuss the trial your father put him through as a babe."

"I had hoped this day would never come." His brow furrowing, Kieryn's countenance changed. "Are these the same instincts that had Jodathyn withholding information?"

Tiernan shifted, straightening his shoulders. "Your Majesty, you tasked me to do whatever it takes to keep your brother safe. As long it doesn't compromise your wife, your son or yourself, I will do what I feel is necessary."

"You should have told me," Kieryn sniped.

"I was hoping to gain his trust. Jodathyn ..."

"Are you going to tell me?"

Inclining his head, Tiernan exhaled. "He *saw* nothing that I couldn't have worked out myself."

"Jodathyn had a *vision*?" Kieryn clarified, lowering his voice.

"I am sure you suspected as much, Your Majesty. Jodathyn saw a battle between a horse and a fox amidst falling green and red leaves. He also saw the soldier being engulfed in a dark red shadow. From my investigation it was simple to interpret. The leaves were the changing of seasons, the red shadow speaks of death and the man was one of Kamoore's household guards, murdered by one of Solan's men. The horse and the fox. The murderer has been punished."

Kieryn removed the crown of leaves from his head and brushed his hand through his hair. He looked down at the festival garland, biting his bottom lip. "His visions are getting stronger."

Tiernan frowned. "Jodathyn also confessed he can feel 'unnatural anger'. It may be only a matter of time before the dragon truly stirs."

"Unnatural anger?"

"Your Majesty, from my observations, he is able to gain control. Even when ropable. Solan pushed Jodathyn too hard today; Valt saw the dragon stirring in your brother's eyes."

"Otherworld."

"For now, my King, he is in control. However, I think the safest choice for Jodathyn is to send him to Sion or another foreign power who would give him sanctuary in exchange for Ramian favour."

"Are you suggesting I banish my own brother?"

"He would live, my King."

Kieryn turned away from his most trusted captain. If he, as High King, proclaimed a banishment, the one exiled would never again stand before him. To send Jodathyn to Sion would mean he would never see his brother again.

"Your Majesty, sometimes painful solutions are required to protect the ones we love."

"When we return to Pallaryn, I will make contact with the King of Sion. He was quite taken with Jodathyn. We will need to find a way to destroy …"

"Kieryn!"

Odelle, his Queen, was running through the revellers, her skirts held up at her knees. Kieryn could only imagine what catastrophe prompted her unladylike behaviour. Panting, she reached Kieryn's side and grasped his elbow. She gave him a shake, looking up at him with large, panicked eyes.

"Kieryn," she whispered urgently. "Carvelle is missing. He can't be found."

Kieryn snapped his jaw shut. "Were not the Prince's attendants watching him?"

Odelle shook her head. "They were enjoying the feasting and Carvelle snuck away."

"Bring them to me."

A nearby servant bobbed and dashed away to do his bidding.

Captain Tiernan waved some of his men closer. Confusion wrinkled across the guardsmen's brows, but they thrust their goblets at a passing server and hastened to obey.

"If it pleases Your Majesties, I will go with some of my men to search for the Prince at once."

The King did not respond. His eyes were fixed on something over the captain's shoulder.

Seeing her husband's preoccupied expression, the Queen uttered a horrified cry.

Kieryn could not believe his eyes. One of the servers was making their way through the festivities with a bloody, furry bundle in his hands.

Excusing himself he met the server halfway. "Oh, Bear! Otherworld – no!" Kieryn groaned. Taking the small whimpering dog, he cradled him close to his chest. He didn't care about the blood and dirt. Bear had served his brother well and he was fond of the old dog. Quivering in fright, Bear nudged the King with his snout and licked his hands.

"Where did you find him?"

The server, who had prostrated himself at the King's feet, looked up. "He came crying out of the woods. Near where the horses are tethered, my King."

"Hush, Bear, you're alright." Kieryn gave the dog one last pat. When he spoke again, it was to the server. "Find King's Guardsman Jael, ask him to give this poor creature a fast-acting poison. Stay with the dog until it is over."

The server's eyebrows shot up at the bizarre instructions. Kieryn knew the man was thinking that Jael's poisons were wasted on the dog. But he didn't want Bear's suffering to be prolonged. The dog was a beloved companion.

"Tiernan!"

Kieryn needn't have shouted, the captain was already waiting, standing a few paces behind. "Have your men escort my Queen back to the citadel. You come with me."

"No, Kieryn! I would rather stay." Odelle grabbed at Kieryn's robes. Her eyes pleaded with him to allow her to search for her child.

Kieryn always had trouble saying no to his Queen. Today he would have to be resolute in his decision. Patting her hand in comfort, Kieryn shook his head. "Go to the palace and wait for me there."

"Kieryn ... Carvelle is too little to be out there alone." Odelle waved in the general direction of the forest, her bottom lip trembling. "What if he is lost or hurt or scared? He needs me."

"Odelle, I am going after our boy. I need to know you are safe." Kieryn reached out and touched his wife's soft cheek. "Come now, sweets, I'll escort you to the horses."

Bowing her head, Odelle took Kieryn's offered elbow. Not wanting to waste any more time, he ploughed through the celebrations.

The forest was silent and still. The hushed atmosphere almost drove Kieryn insane. It was as if all the woodland creatures were holding their breath, waiting for him to discover a terrible secret.

Ever since the fated day the King's Guardsmen returned to Pallaryn without his father, Kieryn had hated the forests. King Hadryn had been an avid hunter with a reputation for slipping past his bodyguards. It proved to be his undoing.

The day his father went missing, Kieryn had been trying to teach Jodathyn his letters. At first, he wasn't concerned. His father often returned without his guards. By midnight, the palace was in panic.

Lord Solan's men found the late king dead three days later, his body ravaged by wild animals. Kieryn had not been permitted to view his father's corpse as per the usual traditions. The king's council had decided that it would be too distressing for their new boy-king.

"Majesty."

Kieryn jolted. He had almost forgot that Tiernan was only a few paces behind him, making a swift search of the area.

Tiernan waited until Kieryn made his way over.

"Cursed Otherworlds! Parrie!"

At Tiernan's feet lay Jodathyn's second dog. The poor beast was already dead. Beside the dog was the imprint of a child's foot.

Kieryn didn't know he had swayed until Tiernan's strong hands kept him from stumbling. He told himself that an accident had killed Jodathyn's dogs, and Carvelle had hidden himself, fearing he was in trouble.

"Carvelle!" Kieryn bellowed, turning from his guardsman. "Come out, son, Papa isn't mad."

Tiernan bent, inspecting the indentation. He scanned the area looking for any other sign of the Prince. He found none.

"Captain! Boot prints!"

Kieryn strode past his captain, in search of the guardsman who had called out.

Guardsman Carew crouched, studying the ground. "There's two set of boot prints. A big, heavy man and a lighter individual. Father, who had any reason to be out here?"

Kieryn shook his head, unable to answer. He could already feel himself falling apart. If anything happened to Carvelle, he would never be able to forgive himself.

Neither of the guardsman attempted to comfort him.

Tiernan spared Kieryn a concerned glance as he unsheathed his sword. He thrust out his chin to indicate that Carew should follow the trail.

Soft, wet, gasping sounds halted their search. Kieryn watched father and son listening. Exchanging weary glances, the guardsmen kept along the path, creeping forward. In a small clearing, they made a disquieting discovery.

Valt Axtin, Jodathyn's personal guard, was sprawled in the mud. Beside him lay two slain men. Valt's eyes stared beyond. Small desperate gasps indicated he was still fighting to cling to life as he lay helpless in his own blood. His large hand fluttered over a gaping wound in his side. Blood bubbled from his lips.

Captain Tiernan slunk forward, kneeling before the red-haired giant. Valt blinked, trying to form a word.

"I'm sorry," Tiernan murmured, pressing his hand to Valt's side.

Valt's eyes searched Tiernan's face. He rallied his strength, his lips trembling to whisper one last word. "Jodathyn ..."

"You have my word; we will do everything possible to protect him. Rest, friend, you have fought well."

Valt's lips twitched in a parody of a smile. His duty complete, he released his last, sighing breath. The light of his eyes dimmed as he slipped into the Otherworld.

"*Araae helphelwyn,*" Carew said.

"*Terini gorthorwyn,*" Tiernan murmured, his head bowed. "You might not have been a King's Guard but you certainly held our respect. Peace go with you, friend."

When Kieryn finally emerged from the forest, the royal pavilion was in an uproar.

"Foul play if I ever did see it," said Solan, sweeping his hard gaze across the gathered nobles.

"Milord, we are not sure of that," Tiernan replied.

"You should be silent before your betters," Lord Frayn snarled. He glanced around, keen to see who had noticed him put the captain in his place.

"Oh, stop," snapped an older lady, pinching the bridge of her nose. "You do give me such a terrible headache, pup."

Frayn scowled at the reprimand, turning his shoulders to regard the rest of the pavilion in sullen silence.

"What was my brother up to?" Kieryn muttered.

"No good," was Kamoore's grumbled reply. "The fact he was gallivanting around in the forest is suspicious."

"Perhaps if my lords and ladies kept their forked tongues idle, Jodathyn would not have had the need to venture." The King's eyes flashed in warning. "I did not give the council leave to gossip like milkmaids in front of my brother."

"Apologies, Your Majesty," Lord Whitoak said, glancing at his crestfallen daughter. Kieryn had heard about Jodathyn's squabble with Illeanah Whitoak. "I thought it best to say something gently rather than have some other lords get too excitable."

"The situation remains, however," Lord Solan commented, ignoring the fact that Lord Whitoak's pointed remark was referring to his behaviour. "Prince Carvelle is missing, a personal guard has been murdered and the whelp has scampered away."

Guardsman Jael snorted in amusement. When he returned to the pavilion, he gave Kieryn an almost imperceptible nod; he had done his duty in regards to Jodathyn's dog. "If you are insinuating that Jodathyn lured his man into the woods, murdered him and made off with the Prince, you must be mad."

Lord Solan's face turned puce, but it did not stop Jael from continuing. "Jodathyn does not have the skill to successfully attack and kill Valt Axtin."

"Besides, Jodathyn was carrying no weapons," Tiernan pointed out. He lowered his voice slightly. "The fact that Valt felled two men before he was cut down would suggest this was a planned attack."

"There is also a third point, which should be made," Jael commented. "That boy does not have what it takes to kill a man."

Kieryn nodded in agreement. Jodathyn did not possess the qualities that made a good soldier. He was more suited to his history books and languages than the physical art of fighting.

"His mother predicted this very betrayal," Solan continued with a look of contempt. "She predicted her child would herald the coming of the dragon king to topple the Pallarus Dynasty. She predicted King Kieryn's death. The predictions—"

"Milord," Kieryn cut in. He found if he remained silent and listened to the lords fighting, he could learn more about their motivations and scheming. However, there was only so much of Lord Solan that he could stomach. "You are wrong. The Consort Ammerie predicted the death of a Pallarus King. The king in question was not named."

"The dragon has stirred," Lord Frayn said, his eye flickering over to Lord Solan for a moment, as if to gain the older man's approval. "Mark my words. The dragon is coming. He's plotting with outsiders."

"Nor did Ammerie ever name the dragon," Kieryn said.

"It is clear what that woman thought," Lord Solan argued. "Your brother is the last of Vadroil's bloodline. She saw it as Jodathyn's birth right to take your throne. Your father had enough sense ..."

"To what – to leave his youngest son defenceless against the wiles of the council?" Kieryn sneered, feeling the remainder of his patience slip through his grasp. He sighed, brushing his hand through his hair. "Give me proof that Jodathyn is disloyal first, before you make accusations."

"My King."

Kieryn did not like the dangerous gleam in Lord Solan's eyes. He had always had a sense that his brother's life was precariously in the hands of the king's council. His discussion with Tiernan had him remembering the day he laid his eyes on his newborn brother.

Kieryn had been at first shocked and then confused by his father's decision to bring the small squealing babe before the council to decide his fate. Jodathyn had been a tiny, noisy little one, with a shock of dark fluff adorning his head. A strong son, despite being born early.

"If your lordships would kindly remember that we have restricted Jodathyn's access to the world. He has no connections outside of the palace. Those who he has been allowed to socialise with have been strictly monitored," Kieryn said firmly. "All of you leave. Except you, Hallidyn. A word."

Lord Whitoak bowed as the other nobles left the King's presence, muttering and grumbling. Kieryn ignored their complaints. The richer and more powerful the man, the louder he whined. Sometimes they were no better than spoilt children.

"Jodathyn's dogs were slain," Kieryn said, once he was sure the last courtier had left and he was alone with his favourite.

"They are friendly hounds from my kennels, my King," Lord Hallidyn replied. "Perhaps someone lured the dogs into the woods and the young one followed."

"Perhaps." Kieryn stared past Lord Hallidyn, as if by sheer will alone he could bring his son home.

"The fact that Jodathyn is also missing is a concern, Your Majesty."

"Perhaps." The King turned slowly to look his favourite lord in the eyes. "Maybe Jodathyn saw his man cut down and was frightened. What if he is lost? What skills or experience does my brother have with life outside the palace?"

Taking up a goblet and a pitcher, Kieryn poured himself a glass. He offered the wine to Hallidyn, who shook his head.

"I promised to protect them both. Now I find myself helpless to do anything." The King took a deep drink before he continued. "Before accusations start ... I knew about Jodathyn experiencing some visions ... just like Vadroil. I had my eye on him."

"You *knew* of his visions, Your Majesty?"

"I would be a fool not to know," Kieryn laughed, thinking it was ironic he had just learned how strong Jodathyn's visions were becoming. "He doesn't comprehend what it means. I have sheltered him too much from the cruelty of this world. There is so much he still doesn't understand."

"The council will not like this revelation," Hallidyn warned.

"That's why I'm asking you, despite your reservations, to keep this secret."

Hallidyn stood silent.

"When you first laid eyes on Jodathyn, what condition did you find him in?" Kieryn asked.

"He was small, undernourished ... he was bleeding from where he had been struck with a dog whip. The wound running down his back and behind his ear."

"Why was Jodathyn struck?"

"He was trying to protect a pup and got in the way of a drunk knight. Your Majesty, why are we discussing this? These are well-established facts."

"Facts. Exactly. My brother was beaten, resulting in permanent scarring. All over a little pup." Kieryn shook his head. "Do you remember how you described Jodathyn's demeanour to me all those years ago?"

"I told you he was afraid of the world, my King."

Kieryn was leading Lord Whitoak on a merry verbal dance.

"Of course he was afraid," Kieryn commented, stroking his beard. "He was six summers old. The same age as my Carvelle is now. Poor little Jodathyn's crippling fear of the world is why you gifted him a pup to comfort him."

"It is as Your Majesty says."

"At one stage, Lord Hallidyn Whitoak, you felt a stirring of compassion for my brother. Perhaps, in future, you should remember that scared little boy before you open your mouth to speak."

Hallidyn dipped his head in silent assent.

Kieryn's smile didn't reach his eyes. "Tell me this. How is it that so many who claim to be wise believe so rigidly that a child who was willing to sacrifice himself for a dog will grow up to be the ruin of an entire nation! It is *ludicrous.* Then, even I sometimes in the dead of the night wonder, is it my fault the dragon is stirring in Jodathyn? Maybe the mistreatment Jod suffered has angered the dragon."

"What are you saying, Your Majesty?"

"I need you to use your network and get a message to the King of Sion. I raised my brother, Lord Whitoak. Help me protect him."

CHAPTER THIRTEEN

Jodathyn

The Arelle Forest

Jodathyn felt abandoned, even though the forest was alive with the haunting calls of nocturnal birds. When he'd made his escape, he'd run in the direction of where he thought Carvelle's voice had originated from. He reasoned that if Valt was only detained for a little while, his personal guard would escort both Carvelle and himself back to safety.

But midnight was approaching and there was no sign of Valt. He was alone and incredibly, helplessly lost.

All that time Jodathyn had spent poring over maps was of no value now. He knew he was in the Arelle Forest, but there was no way for him to work out where in the forest he was. To him, the forests of Rama were green masses on the palace maps.

Worse, Tiernan had decided that yesterday was a good time to teach him to spar with his fists. Much to the delight of onlookers the captain had shown him no mercy. When he lamented that the muscles in his backside were protesting, Captain Tiernan smirked and declared the session a success.

Jodathyn had also spent most of the day serving his brother. The servants had been so ecstatic about the King's punishment, they had run him ragged from dawn. This meant he hadn't eaten.

Jodathyn was tired. His eyes stung with phantom grit, but he dared not rest. Were there animals in the woods who ate unwary travellers? Jodathyn couldn't be sure. He had heard guards talking about making a camp and drinking beer around a campfire. But he had no idea how to make a fire.

Being the Son of the Crown had some dreadful pitfalls, Jodathyn decided – one being he was uneducated on how to look after himself. He had no weapons, no food and no coin.

"Merciful Otherworlds," Jodathyn murmured, taking a rest on a fallen stump. He hung his head in despair. "Which way do I go?"

Fatigue won, and Jodathyn's eyes closed. As he dozed, unbidden pictures came to his mind. Beyond the stump he could see half a dozen men stamping their way through the forest. Carvelle was being carried under one burly man's arms. Little crystal tears dripped from the end of his nose. Jodathyn's Sight was showing him he was moving in the right direction. Afraid that if he opened his eyes he would lose an important piece of information, Jodathyn squeezed his eyes tighter. Through the forest his Sight showed him the path he should follow. The vision concluded with a campsite and Jodathyn's fingers caressing his leather belt.

"We need to move."

Jodathyn sprung to his feet, instantly aware of his surroundings. His eyes searched the forest around him, even as his instincts told him he would find no apparition.

"Where are you?" Jodathyn commanded the darkness. "I demand you make yourself known."

"You demand, human?" the voice chuckled. *"I am within you ... I am the half that you have denied."*

"Go away!" Jodathyn called. He withheld a shiver as a foreign sensation rippled beneath his skin.

"Follow the Sight. When you have need, I am near."

While hoping the voice was a symptom of hunger, fatigue and desperation, Jodathyn decided to obey its commands. He lurched to his feet.

Stumbling through the hushed forest, he couldn't help but wonder who was behind the plot to discredit him. The man who assaulted him said he was working for someone. Why such a reckless plan? Everyone knew it was treason to harm anyone born of the Pallarus bloodline. There was little doubt that if caught, the kidnappers could expect a swift end at the blade of the executioner's axe. Kieryn would not be inclined to show mercy.

"Who's playing on the puppet strings?" Jodathyn murmured.

"They're scared of us," the voice replied. *"They always have been. Quiet. We are getting close."*

Crouched low to the ground, Jodathyn had no idea how the voice inside his mind knew where they were. But he concluded it was wise to stop and listen. Hidden, he could hear the deep, guttural voice of a man.

Jodathyn slithered forward on his belly so that he could peer through the gloom. Beyond the glowing embers of a dying fire, he could see the fuzzy outlines of sleeping men. By the fire stood a sentry who was muttering to himself. Jodathyn sighed in relief when he noticed Carvelle at the man's feet, asleep and unharmed.

"Should have slit the Prince's throat ... Jodathyn should have been the scapegoat."

Sweeping his gaze through the campsite, Jodathyn observed the sentry closely. He bit his lip; the guard needed to be encouraged to leave the campsite.

Slipping his hands down his side, Jodathyn felt the intricate etching on his belt. The memory of his fingers brushing along the leather during his vision gave him an idea. He could only hope that he was strong enough to execute his plan. Taking a deep breath, he unbuckled his belt and stood in the shadows. He took a few more breaths, stepping further into the dark. Before he could change his mind, he knelt to grab a stone and threw it into a tree.

"Who goes there?"

Jodathyn closed his eyes, counting in his head. When he felt the sentry was starting to relax, he picked up a sizable twig and snapped it between his fingers.

Holding his breath Jodathyn counted the sentry's footsteps as he came closer. He slipped around the trunk of the tree, so that he was further out of sight.

Jodathyn was surprised by the sharp, jerky shaking of his hands. He wasn't sure if it was fear or excitement. He tightened his grip on his belt as he waited for the sentry to step level with him.

With one slow, deliberate step forward the sentry made his mistake. Jodathyn leapt from his hiding spot and before the man could cry out in alarm, he had wrapped his belt around his neck.

The sentry's eyes bulged and his face twisted in terror as Jodathyn squeezed with all his might. He gritted his teeth, bringing the man to his knees. Pressing his body against his victim, Jodathyn caught the glint of a hunting knife in his boot. He slid it free with his left hand. Being armed would only increase his chances of survival.

Pressing the blade into the sentry's lower back, Jodathyn hissed into his ear, "Scream and I will kill you. When I release you, you are going to tell me what your plan is and why. Do you understand?"

Desperate for air, the sentry nodded.

"Good." Jodathyn loosened the belt. "Speak."

"Kill the Prince and place the blame for his murder on Jodathyn." The sentry's voice was low and husky.

"Why?"

"Jodathyn is growing to be a threat ... and we get rid of the heir to the throne."

"Why wasn't Carvelle killed?"

"Byrant thought we could get more gold for a Prince rescued. There, I have told you. Let me go."

"I never said I was going to let you live," Jodathyn whispered. Gritting his teeth, Jodathyn forced himself to finish his task. This was no time for mercy. Carvelle's life depended on him.

Before his intended victim could cry out, Jodathyn tightened the belt around his throat once more. The man's body jerked. Detached, Jodathyn watched his hands wringing the life out of the kidnapper.

The man's face contorted in silent agony. Looking up, so he didn't have to look at the man he was murdering, Jodathyn started to recite the ancient alphabet. Backwards.

The sentry slumped.

Jodathyn swallowed down the bile in his mouth. He knew if he relented and released the sentry now, he would regain consciousness. He had come too far.

Closing his eyes against the sight of the dying man, Jodathyn held onto the belt like it was a lifeline and continued muttering the ancient alphabet. In order to save his nephew's life, this man had to die.

Once he was sure his evil deed was done, Jodathyn knelt, choking back vomit. The dead man's face was frozen, twisted to forever tell the tale of his final moments. Blinking, Jodathyn forced himself to close the sentry's eyes. He didn't want to see the silent accusation.

"Dragon Dung and Otherworld! What have I done?"

Jodathyn had been taught from a young age that respect for the dead was expected. He had no idea what region of Rama his victim was from. The provinces surrounding Pallaryn were known for the Shredding of Flowers ceremony. He grasped at some leaves, tore them and sprinkled them over his victim's face. It was a pathetic attempt at upholding Ramian values. But he had done his duty. The sentry's friends would find him in the morning. A respectful burial for the dead was not his concern.

Numb, Jodathyn stumbled towards the camp. He shook his head to try and make the dizziness dissolve. Moments later he came back to awareness, standing over Prince Carvelle. Somehow, he hadn't woken any of the kidnappers.

"It's Uncle, be still," Jodathyn whispered, touching his nephew's shoulder.

The Prince stirred, rubbing his eyes and blinking up at Jodathyn. "Uncle?"

Holding up his hand for silence, Jodathyn helped his nephew to his feet. Carvelle's keen, honey-brown gaze shone with admiration. He huddled close to Jodathyn's side, taking his uncle's hand in his own. With a gentle tug Jodathyn led him away from his kidnappers.

Jodathyn knew they would not get far before the men discovered the Prince was missing. As soon as they passed the dead sentry, he motioned for Carvelle to jog.

"Uncle, where is my father?" Carvelle asked. "I'm scared and tired."

"I don't know," Jodathyn replied, his throat constricting. "We will find him together."

Carvelle surveyed Jodathyn with eyes that seemed too wise for his tender six summers. "Uncle, why was the bad man asleep so far away from the fire?"

Jodathyn sighed, leaning against a tree in exhaustion. He tried to erase the image of the sentry's panicked face from his memory. A bubble of revulsion overpowered him. This time he couldn't stop feeling sick. With a mumbled apology he turned away from his nephew and was violently ill.

He should have stolen some water from the kidnappers, Jodathyn thought, wiping the stinging bile from his lips.

"Are you well, Uncle?" Carvelle asked. He blinked up at Jodathyn with wide, innocent eyes.

"I'm well," Jodathyn replied. "We need to find somewhere safe to hide. It'll be just like one of our games."

This was not a game they could afford to lose. This was a matter of life and death for them both. He hoped that Kieryn was on his way with a rescue. He didn't know how long he could outrun the kidnappers.

"We need to find water, food and shelter," Jodathyn murmured.

"The river is that way." Carvelle pointed into the dark.

"Are you sure?"

"Ah-ha. One of the men went to fetch some water earlier."

Jodathyn patted his nephew's shoulder. The river was an obvious place for the kidnappers to look for them. On the other hand, Jodathyn was dehydrated. And if he could use the river to work out where they were, he was reasonably sure he could get Carvelle to safety.

"Come, then. In this game we need to work out a strategy. Do you understand?"

"Strategy, Uncle?"

Jodathyn's brain was abuzz trying to puzzle out what to do. "We need to move quickly and quietly. It is also important that we listen for those men. We need to keep moving until we reach the river and safety."

"Okay. I can do that."

"Good."

Jodathyn's heart twisted, seeing the look of hope and faith in Carvelle's eyes. The question was, was he worthy of such confidence or would he let his nephew and the King down?

CHAPTER FOURTEEN

Jodathyn

The Arelle Forest

The forest floor was shrouded in the early morning mist. Since leaving the kidnapper's campsite, Jodathyn and Carvelle hadn't stopped moving. Jodathyn stumbled and glanced down at his nephew. Even though he was exhausted, the Prince had not protested when Jodathyn coaxed him to keep walking.

"Uncle, I hear voices." Carvelle looked up at him. "What do we do?"

Shaking his head to clear the fog of sleepiness from his mind, Jodathyn was suddenly alert. Whatever he was going to do, he needed to do fast. The dagger he had stolen from the sentry was no match for armed men. He could not risk a fight. Instead, he would need to outmanoeuvre the kidnappers using his wits. Carvelle's survival depended on him.

"We hide," Jodathyn replied, glad that his voice sounded steady and calm. "This is another game we are going to play. Let's find a tree to climb. When we are high in the branches we will be still and quiet. We will win the game if they don't find us."

"Will they find us, Uncle?"

"No. Not many people think to look up." Jodathyn ushered Carvelle to a tree.

Carvelle studied his uncle with a regal air reminiscent of his father. "Where did you learn this?"

"Quickly," Jodathyn hissed. "Up you go!"

Jodathyn marvelled as the Prince scampered up the tree. He had taught him well. When Carvelle was safely hidden among the branches, Jodathyn began to climb. He may not be a talented brawler, but he was a proficient climber.

Just wait until I return to the palace, Jodathyn thought. *I can finally tell Kieryn exactly how useful my skulking is.*

Hiding himself where he had a clear view, Jodathyn watched the forest floor for any signs of movement. He took in deep breaths to forestall a panic attack.

The kidnappers were approaching – Jodathyn could hear their voices and the swish of swords slashing at the undergrowth. He didn't claim to know much about tracking, but he didn't think making such a racket was intelligent. Hopefully this was a sign that these men were inept. If he was clever, Jodathyn could use this to his advantage.

Carvelle's small fingers tapped on Jodathyn's hands, but his frightened eyes remained on the kidnappers down below. His chin wobbled and Jodathyn hushed him with a quick gesture. Reaching up, Jodathyn gripped Carvelle's hand in his own and gave his fingers a tight, comforting squeeze.

Jodathyn held Carvelle's hand until the men disappeared and their sounds faded away. He indicated for Carvelle to stay put and quiet. Something wasn't quite right.

Jodathyn was glad his instincts had kept them ensconced in the tree. Below them, another man stalked. His footfalls made no sound. They weren't so stupid, after all. It had been a trap.

Jodathyn felt sweat beading on his brow as the man moved stealthily underneath him. He watched, not daring to even blink. His hand was upon the dagger.

"What I wouldn't give to tear him apart."

Jodathyn's lips parted in surprise, and he leant against the trunk of the tree.

"You did well with the sentry," the voice purred. *"You need to be strong for a little longer until we can find a place to rest."*

For almost an hour, Jodathyn remained hidden within the tree.

"Uncle, is it safe?"

Jodathyn reached up and squeezed Carvelle's fingers. "Well done, Prince. We have won the game."

"I miss Papa," Carvelle replied. His large, deer-like eyes filled with tears. "I'm scared."

"I'm sure he is looking for you," Jodathyn soothed. "I need you to keep being brave."

"I can be brave, Uncle," Carvelle said, pushing out his little chest. "I can!"

"I know you can," Jodathyn assured him. "Let's climb down. We should go in the opposite direction to those men."

"Where shall we go?"

"We still need water – don't you worry. We'll find your river." Jodathyn licked his dry, chapped lips. He hadn't had a drink since the wine he'd guzzled at the festival and he felt weak with thirst. Carvelle had been mistaken as to the river's direction.

It was by pure chance that Jodathyn spotted a plump rabbit caught in a trap.

"Food," Carvelle cried. He danced about Jodathyn's legs in glee. "That was one thing on your list."

"Do you think it's stealing to take the rabbit from the trap?" Jodathyn thought aloud. Who knew that living outside of the palace would be full of so many moral conundrums? How did common people learn right from wrong?

"Honestly, Uncle!" Carvelle exclaimed. "We're desperate. No one will ever know."

Jodathyn took a step towards the rabbit and frowned. His education at the palace didn't include how to prepare an animal in order to eat it. Once he broke its neck, what was he to do with it? "We don't have a fire; how will we cook it?"

Carvelle blinked and then stamped his little foot. "We need to eat. I'm hungry. I command you to build me a fire."

"Lighting a fire here would be most unwise if you are in trouble and wanting to hide." A young woman stood silhouetted against the trees. "And yes, taking my rabbit from my trap is stealing."

Jodathyn jumped, pushing Carvelle behind him. "We meant no disrespect!"

"Ah, Jodathyn Pallarus ... the King's brother, the Son of the Crown, we meet once again."

Jodathyn had never seen anyone quite like the young woman before him. Used to seeing only court fashions, he looked away, embarrassed that he had stared at a woman in men's clothing. Her leather pants hugged her thighs and her large shirt was belted around her slender waist. He lowered his eyes to study her boots, which were covered in mud.

"Won't you look at me? Or am I too embarrassing?"

Jodathyn let his eyes slide up to study her curly, black hair which was plaited into a practical braid. Deep brown eyes bore into his. It took

Jodathyn a few moments to recognise her as the woman that Will had rescued at the ale house. She leant on a hefty staff, giving Jodathyn a few moments to recover himself.

"I thought you would have fled further west," Jodathyn blurted. "I'm glad to see you are looking well, Fydellah."

Her impenetrable eyes surveyed her unwanted guests. "They are still watching the roads. Will and I decided I should stay nearby until the spring."

"I am glad you are safe," Jodathyn said.

"Uncle, do you know this lady?" Carvelle asked, tugging on Jodathyn's tunic. "She has pretty hair."

A smile tugged on Jodathyn's lips as he shushed Carvelle. Kieryn had been quite a sensation with the ladies before he married Odelle; perhaps Carvelle would grow up to be a charmer just like his father.

"And I see you are in trouble again. Tell me, is the King going to exact revenge on your behalf, Jodathyn?"

"Oh, I hope he will," Carvelle murmured.

"Manners dictate you ought to introduce me, Jodathyn Pallarus. Who is this little man?"

"Carvelle Pallarus," Carvelle said, stepping around Jodathyn's legs before his uncle could hush him. "I'm the King's son."

Fydellah's eyes hardened. "What trouble have you brought to my door?"

"Some men kidnapped me," Carvelle continued, despite Jodathyn shaking his head in warning. It was as if all the time watching his kidnappers in silence had built up a well of talkativeness. "My uncle saved me. Now we're in hiding. Uncle Jodathyn says we need water, food and shelter. And we climbed up a big tree and we watched them go past ... it was a game you see ... they thought to trick us ... they had a man following behind ... but we won the game."

"Well, I won't leave a child in danger. I guess you have run into good fortune."

Relieved, Jodathyn nodded his thanks. He wrapped his arm around Carvelle as they watched Fydellah retrieve the rabbit from the trap and break its neck. Jodathyn flinched, thinking of the man he'd killed last night. Life seemed fragile.

"Will's hermit hole isn't too far. Come."

"I don't have coin to pay you," Jodathyn admitted.

"I know," Fydellah said. "I suppose you did try and save me. It was gallant of you."

"I failed miserably," Jodathyn muttered. "Kieryn is still punishing me for it."

"You don't seem to lie," Fydellah said. "Unusual for a highborn."

"You seem to have a poor opinion about highborns."

"I used to be one. They're vain, contemptuous creatures, the lot of them."

"Really?" Carvelle asked. "What was your family name?"

"I would rather forget."

"Can I call you Fydellah Nahilya? Royalborns have the right to give people new family names."

Fydellah stopped to stare at the Prince.

"In ancient times, many years before Arturyn and Vadroil, there lived a maid named Nahilya. It was said she dressed in dark leathers and made her home in the forests. She gave health and aid to travellers. The stories say she communed with dragons," Jodathyn said.

"I know the stories." Tilting her head to the side, Fydellah studied the Prince as if to see if he was teasing her. Carvelle stared back in earnest. "I will accept your gift, Prince Carvelle."

"I feel compelled to tell you we may be pursued."

"A truth," Fydellah murmured, her back stiffening. "Slavers?"

"As far as I know – no."

"Murderers," Carvelle added.

Fydellah relaxed a little. "We can handle murderers; slavers are more dangerous. Here we are."

Out of nowhere a hut seemed to emerge from the trees. Fydellah was right. Will's little hideaway wasn't far from the rabbit trap. Jodathyn could smell the powerful, sweet honeysuckle that grew on the hut's outer wall. The hut was like nothing he had ever seen before. The structure itself was built haphazardly from a combination of pieces of wood and mud bricks. Jodathyn tilted his head to the side, wondering if the hut was waterproof. He had expected something more structurally sound from Will.

Glancing down at his nephew, Jodathyn tried to convey with his eyes that the Prince should not say anything rude. Carvelle quirked a cheeky eyebrow at his uncle's silent warning.

"Uncle, I can hear the river! Water was on your list," Carvelle exclaimed.

"The settlement of Edisyn is only a few short miles away." Fydellah held the door open, ushering her guests inside.

Feeling awkward, Jodathyn stood to the side until Fydellah snapped at them both to sit down at the table. He whispered a word of thanks as two bowls of oats and honey were placed before them. Grateful for the food, Jodathyn took up his spoon and began to eat. It was simple fare, but that didn't bother him. He remembered what he ate with the servants at Lord Solan's summer house. This was better.

"Eat, Carvelle. You need your strength," Jodathyn admonished.

"Yes, Uncle," the child grumbled, looking at the food.

"Be glad of food, Carvelle. Little orphans don't eat so well."

"Little orphans like you?" Carvelle replied.

Jodathyn grimaced at the Prince's sass.

Fydellah laughed as she left the hut.

"Did you have to eat *rats*, Uncle?"

Jodathyn sighed in resignation.

A few minutes later, Fydellah returned with a pail filled with water. She ladled water into pewter mugs and placed them on the table. Jodathyn drank. He emptied two more cups before he was sated.

Coming to sit at the table, Fydellah regarded Jodathyn. "You don't act like a prince. You seem to lack something."

Annoyed, Jodathyn ceased his meal, glaring up at Fydellah. "I am not a prince. My father rejected me."

Fydellah's grin widened. "You have the makings of a good man, Jodathyn Pallarus, but do you have the characteristics of a great man? Do you know what they are?"

"I have a feeling you are going to tell me," Jodathyn remarked. Somewhere deep within him, anger was beginning to stir. The emotion uncurled like an unwholesome beast, ready to lunge at those that offended it. Jodathyn checked himself, gritting his teeth against the impulse to utter harsh words.

"A good man is bound by his honour. He is loyal and generous, but that is his weakness. A great man is more. A great man can make difficult decisions with confidence. A great man knows his own mind and uses it to wield power."

"I think Uncle Jod is great," Carvelle interjected. He pouted and placed his fists on his hips.

"Prince Carvelle seems to have what you lack, Jodathyn Pallarus. He will be a great king when he takes the throne."

Jodathyn looked Fydellah in the eye. "When that day comes, I will gladly kneel before him."

"*Gladly?*" Fydellah murmured. "Yes, I see that you believe that."

"I will kneel before my King with a glad heart." Jodathyn turned back to his meal in a silent declaration he was done with the conversation. "*A good man is loyal*, after all."

Fydellah studied Jodathyn with knowing eyes. "Loyalty is no small thing. Not all of us are born for greatness."

"Uncle, we've been walking all night. I'm tired," Carvelle said, snuggling close to Jodathyn's side.

Jodathyn wrapped his arms around the Prince, tugging him even closer. "You've been a brave boy. I'll get you home soon. You'll see."

The hard expression on Fydellah's face softened. When she pointed to the straw mattress, offering Jodathyn somewhere to sleep, he accepted. He lay down, Carvelle tucked under his arm. They were asleep within minutes.

CHAPTER FIFTEEN

Kieryn

The Citadel of Pallaryn

Kieryn's heavy footsteps echoed a warning for anyone foolish enough to linger in the palace corridors. Servants busy with pre-dawn tasks scuttled to hide in enclaves. Palace guards, unable to leave their posts, stared ahead. He knew word of his return to Pallaryn had spread like the sweating sickness.

Slamming the door behind him, Kieryn was disheartened by the silence that greeted him within his personal chambers. From a young age he had been taught that to be king, meant to be alone. Even his manservants, many who had served him from the time he was a prince, would never dare to comfort him. In many ways he was envious of Jodathyn's easy relationship with his servants.

Picking up a priceless vase, a gift from the Sionian King, Kieryn howled and threw it against the wall. The coloured glass shattered into dozens of tiny shards. With an irreverent curse, he flipped a chair of heavy oak. He was left with emptiness and rage.

One of his servants scurried forward to pick up the broken vase. He was careful to make himself small, eyes averted so as not to intrude upon the King's presence. The show of submissiveness only fuelled Kieryn's anger. A snarl twitched on his lips as he observed his servant.

"Kieryn?"

Shuddering, the King turned to face the one that made him feel like an ordinary man. Odelle was barefoot, and wore only her nightgown and robe. Her long golden mane had been divested of the festival berries.

From the moment they'd met, she had held his fascination. He fondly remembered her as a young northern lady, a stranger, daring to admonish him for berating a guard. He'd been incredulous, and had asked if she knew who he was – to which she'd replied she knew him to be the Crown Prince, and didn't he know how to behave himself?

Those who thought Queen Odelle was nothing more than sweetness to calm his storm were fools. She was a sharp sword wrapped up in silk skirts and a pleasant smile. And he loved her for it.

Exhausted, Kieryn dismissed his manservant with a murmured apology. The servant's face was neutral as he nodded in understanding. It was as if he didn't see his king's pain.

Kieryn collapsed in a chair with an oath, holding his head in his hands. "Oh, my boy!"

Odelle swept across the room, placing her hands on his shoulders. Reaching up, he curled his fingers around her slender wrist, guiding her so she stood before him. "I should be strong for you, my Queen."

"Why can't we be strong for one another?" Odelle asked. "I also made a marriage vow to uphold you in times of trouble."

"You should rest, sweets," Kieryn said, staring into the flames in the fireplace. His servants had anticipated he wouldn't want to sleep upon his return.

"As should you, my love," Queen Odelle replied. She sat herself upon his lap like she used to when they were newly wed. Leaning in closer, she pressed the soft skin of her cheek against his beard. Kieryn breathed in the floral perfume of Odelle's porcelain skin. She was much smaller than him, and fitted perfectly into his chest. He knew that Odelle revelled in the warmth of his skin and the powerful feeling of him encompassing her.

"I doubt either of us will sleep tonight."

Kieryn exhaled, running his hands down her hair, just the way she liked. "As you wish, wife."

Queen Odelle glanced into the flames as two tears trickled down her fair face. Kieryn knew she was thinking of their son, who meant everything to her. He tightened his embrace.

Before Carvelle she had birthed two tiny daughters. Both came into the world with no breath of life in them. When some of the older lords of the council dared to denounce her, Kieryn had flown into a grief-induced rage. He had roared for the court to hear his daughters were *born sleeping and beautiful.* He would hear no more nonsense about him abandoning his wife in her time of need.

"I do not wish to bury Carvelle," Queen Odelle gasped as great sobs shook her body.

"Be strong and courageous as a daughter of the north." Kieryn pulled her body closer to him, tucking her head under his chin as she sobbed.

"I want my baby back."

"Hush, we will find him." Despite his own overpowering fears, Kieryn did his best to sound confident. "Carvelle will need his mother calm."

"Jodathyn spoke to me. I took it for foolish fancy that he predicted a girl child born in the season of summer," the Queen whispered.

"What did Jodathyn say?"

"He was confused ... he said he saw me with two girls called Hasinah and Lavinah. That they followed me everywhere. We never told him their names."

Kieryn had ignored the southern tradition that considered it an ill omen to name a child who had died before they took their breath. It had been important to Odelle as a lady of the north that all her children had names. Their daughters' names were secret. Never to be spoken. It broke his heart all over again to think upon it.

Kieryn ghosted his hand over his wife's abdomen. He leant over to speak into her ear. "I already knew ... I was waiting for you to be ready to tell me."

Queen Odelle uncurled herself a little as Kieryn pressed his lips to her temple. "What are we to do? Three girls could be considered an ill omen. Will this one die too?"

"All this talk about omens is foolish. King Brantyn had three daughters ... so did King Tyburne. In fact, one of his daughters was a great queen when she ascended the throne."

Odelle wiped the tears from her face. "You only admire Queen Mavyah because she was said to be over six foot and had a reputation for sparring sense into her nobles."

"She was a strong woman," Kieryn agreed. "I also liked the story of her twin sisters, so sweet they were often underestimated. Their treaties with Sion have benefited generations of Ramians."

Odelle sniffled. "The nobles would prefer I give you a son."

"Those simpletons don't get a say," Kieryn scoffed. "I would welcome a daughter. We'll just have to make sure she doesn't get spoilt rotten by her big brother and her uncle."

A delicate cough behind the royal couple broke their moment of comfort. "Majesty, Lord Will Hartcurt is here."

Kieryn's jaw tightened. "Send him in. Then leave us."

The servant nodded. A moment later, Will slipped through the door. Kieryn could see by the young man's blank face that he already knew the Queen was with child. Will had once confessed that his ability to read minds was as natural to him as breathing. He had no control over what he heard in people's thoughts.

"Do you have news?" Kieryn saw no point in pleasantries. Will would not have risked coming to him without something to say.

"I will not speak of the child, Your Majesties." Will took in a deep breath. "My King, I believe Lord Whitoak may also benefit from what I have to say."

Kieryn tilted his head. "Indeed? Then by all means ask the servants to fetch him."

"My King, you know Whitoak makes me uneasy. Would you be gracious enough to convey the message to him?"

"Of course," Odelle soothed, before Kieryn could snap he wasn't a messenger boy. "What is it you have come to say?"

"Lady Illeanah was indeed the last person to see Jodathyn. She does not know anything of note about the disappearance of your son. To detain her would be a useless endeavour."

It came as no surprise to Kieryn that Will already knew of his intention to send the King's Guard to question Lady Illeanah.

Will's power to read minds had made him a commodity to his family. When his own father sold him to a more powerful lord, Will had ran away in a desperate attempt to escape his fate. With nowhere to hide he found himself living in a Pallaryn brothel with his older brother, who used his skills for his own gain. Unfortunately, Will's master had tracked him to Pallaryn, and he'd fled to the seclusion of the King's Orchards. That was how Kieryn came to find him, a sobbing boy, intent on hurting himself to escape the cruel world. Broken, Will had not recognised him and had told him the sordid tale.

Now Will's abilities served the Crown, and in return Kieryn provided him with an income and safety within the palace.

"How does this benefit Lord Whitoak?" Kieryn asked.

The pleasant smile on Will's face did not reach his intelligent eyes. "I thought Whitoak should know that Jodathyn broke his friendship with Illeanah as requested. Illeanah blames Jodathyn. Jodathyn would not want to come between Illeanah and the father she loves."

"Poor, sweet Jod." Odelle dabbed her eyes.

"Anything else of note?" Kieryn felt impatient. Will could have come to him in the morning with this information. He knew that Will had a strong dislike of Hallidyn. Will's words felt like another attempt at discrediting his favoured lord.

"Hallidyn's little stable spy is hoping to harm Jodathyn ... Lord Kamoore is increasingly difficult to read. Lord Solan's mind is ever on betrayal. The plan seems to be to get rid of Jodathyn."

Kieryn's face twitched. "Solan is behind this?"

"As far as Prince Carvelle's disappearance is concerned, Solan is baffled. Of late he has become wary of me. I can't get close enough to read his mind, Your Majesty." Will looked angry at his failure.

"Keep trying."

"Always, Your Majesty."

Will glanced about the room, his brow furrowed, as if debating with himself.

"Will ..." Kieryn had seen this look cross Will's face before. It was the expression he made when he was wrestling with whether or not to reveal a secret.

Will hung his head. "Jodathyn never spoke to you about who rescued him at the ale house."

"He said it was a stranger."

"That was a lie I asked him to tell."

"Were you out there that night, Will dear? Did you intervene on Jodathyn's behalf?"

"Yes, my Queen. I was also there to rescue the slave."

"Would they have ..."

The Queen did not need to finish her question before Will answered. "Yes, they meant to kill Jodathyn, my Queen. They were too dumb to realise who he was. Even after I revealed Jodathyn's identity, many were still in favour of slitting his throat."

"The point of this, Will?"

"I told Jodathyn that I had a safe house by the Paldera River, near Edisyn. If Jodathyn has any sense, he'll head there if he can't return to Pallaryn."

"What else aren't you saying?"

"The slave from that night. She's still there."

"Is she dangerous?"

Will's face split into a grin. "Only to liars and cheats. Fy will not hurt Jodathyn or the Prince."

Kieryn's lips quirked. He allowed a stirring of hope to enter his heart. Carvelle would be home safe soon.

Chapter Sixteen

Jodathyn

The Paldera River

He was alone. The night air was cool against his scales. The wind whispered as his leathery wings beat in a slow, glorious rhythm. Stretching out his elongated snout, he sniffed the air. Rainfall was coming.

Now strong enough to commune with his human, he had broken free of his prison of skin and bone. As his human slept, he flew the skies of Rama.

He knew he could not afford to spend too much time rejoicing. Danger was coming and it was his duty to strengthen himself so that soon he could manifest in the flesh. For now, he haunted his human's visions and thoughts.

He dipped his left wing, banking as he spiralled down in a lazy circle until he felt his claws touch the ground. Nearby a stream bubbled and gurgled.

Reaching out his long neck he took his first glimpse of himself in the reflective water. Large slitted eyes that gleamed silver stared back at him. At first glance his scales were white but as he moved, he could see iridescent hues of greens and blues. His claws and talons were like black spears.

Tornyth, Winter's Dragon, was free. Lifting his head, he bellowed.

A scaly smile lit Tornyth's face as he remembered the feel of a leather belt around an enemy's neck. The heady feeling of power and dominance as the man fought in vain for breath was invigorating.

There would be more reckonings to be made. Perhaps his human heart would allow him to chomp down on his enemies. One day soon, he would spill blood.

Tornyth felt dizzy with the thought.

Now it was time to win the human, Jodathyn's, trust.

A startled cry caught in Jodathyn's throat as his eyes snapped open. Images of the night sky and the cool breeze on his scales teased the edges of his memory. Beside him, Carvelle snored and snuggled down closer to his chest.

"He is getting stronger." Fydellah was watching him from where she was sitting at the table. There was a peculiar expression on her face.

"Who is getting stronger?" Jodathyn extracted himself from Carvelle's grasp as he sat up in bed.

"Once upon a time those with great talent and dragons were honoured on the Isle of Myryn."

Jodathyn blinked, confused. Why was Fydellah speaking in riddles? "Who is getting stronger?"

"You've stopped taking the herbal tonics, haven't you?"

Rolling his shoulders, he stumbled towards the table to sit opposite Fydellah. "My servant Donatein was once an apothecary. He has a remedy for any malady."

"Including a herb that suppresses your power."

"Donatein would never do that!" Jodathyn cried.

Carvelle stirred. Both he and Fydellah paused to watch the child roll over.

"Wouldn't he?" Fydellah's fierce, toothy grin indicated she did not believe Jodathyn. "You wouldn't have stopped taking your loyal servant's herbs, by any chance?"

Jodathyn refused to answer. He shifted in his seat, knowing that Fydellah's powers would have already told her the truth. Since discreetly refusing the tonics Donatein had given him, his visions had become clearer and frequent.

Fydellah grabbed a piece of bread and tore a hunk off it with her teeth. Seeing Jodathyn watching her, she offered it to him. When Jodathyn shook his head, she shrugged and took another bite.

"You are from Myryn?"

Turning her back to Jodathyn, Fydellah murmured, "Yes. I intend to go back."

"I hear it is a very beautiful island. With plenty of birds."

"Yes, Myryn is known for its birds and vast libraries stuffed full of ancient texts. From what Will told me about you, I think you might like it there."

"Will spoke about me?" Jodathyn was unsure how he felt about Will Hartcurt talking about him.

"We had to talk about something to pass the night."

"Will handed me a note warning me ..." Jodathyn pulled out the small piece of parchment and handed it to Fydellah.

She thumbed the corner as she read the perfunctory message. "I would trust Will. If he felt he needed to warn you ... We're digressing. Can you not tell he is getting stronger?"

"Again, who are you talking about?"

"The dragon."

Jodathyn felt a thrill of dread at the mention of the dragon. He wondered if it was his fault there was a dragon loose. Had he inherited a monster from his mother's bloodline?

"*Dragon?*" Jodathyn repeated, feeling wretched.

"You've begun to commune with him." There was no hint of accusation in Fydellah's voice.

"How did you know?"

"When I lived in Myryn, I read a good many dusty scrolls about dragons. As you strengthen your talent, your dragon also grows stronger. When he is ready, he will find a way to manifest."

"Manifest?" Jodathyn felt stupid, parroting Fydellah's words.

"Become flesh. A real dragon."

Jodathyn inhaled sharply before asking his next question. "My gift is the cause of the dragon? Do you have a dragon?"

"Yes; your gift is the catalyst for a new dragon to manifest. And no. Not all with powers have a dragon within them. Your power must be particularly strong."

Jodathyn considered his next words. He didn't want to make a miscalculation and ruin the tentative trust he had built with Fydellah. "They say I am Vadroil's heir."

Fydellah snorted. "Well, with your bloodline, I would assume it is likely you inherited it from the dread dragon."

"How do I stop the dragon?"

"You are the dragon," Fydellah sighed. "Only you can answer that."

"I'm afraid. Help me, please."

"I don't wish to, Jodathyn Pallarus," Fydellah answered, her voice a low hum. "Dragons are creatures of war. Where there are dragons, death inevitably follows. They are bloodthirsty beasts. Thousands of human Ramians' lives were lost even after Vadroil was vanquished. The only thing that stopped the killing was when the dragons took flight and left Rama. With those scaly monsters gone we have enjoyed peace."

The memory of the dragon's glee as he recollected the death of the kidnapper, surfaced in Jodathyn's thoughts. He remembered the dragon's hope that he would be allowed to kill. He shivered, despite the air about them not being cold.

"Don't listen," said a voice deep within Jodathyn. *"We are a strong royal son. A prince among dragons."*

Fydellah frowned at him. "He's speaking to you now, isn't he? Whispering how strong and wonderful he is?"

Jodathyn didn't see any point in lying. "How did you know?"

"Your eyes gave you away."

"My eyes?"

Humming in response, Fydellah turned towards the door. She picked up a bow with a quiver of arrows. "Your eyes become silver slits ... your dragon was staring back at me."

"A trick of the light," Jodathyn murmured. "Are you afraid of me?"

"Not when you are in control," Fydellah replied. "Once your dragon manifests ... look, I'm going hunting. You should go back to sleep."

Conflicted, Jodathyn watched Fydellah's back as she slipped out of the hut and into the pre-dawn light. Never in his life had he felt so hollow. It seemed some of the strange rumours about him held some truth. Inside of him lurked a monster, waiting to get free. He had stopped taking some of the herbal mixtures that Donatein had been giving him and now, he was a threat. If he lost control of the dragon, it would be his fault.

In his sleep, the young Prince rolled over with a contented sigh. Jodathyn turned to study him. He needed to get Carvelle back where he belonged first. Then he needed to decide what to do about the dragon. He hoped he wouldn't need to flee Rama's shores.

Heaving himself up, Jodathyn tumbled back into bed with Carvelle. He stared up at the ceiling and in his heart, he hoped he might dream of flying again. Sleep did not come and Jodathyn berated himself for his selfishness.

"His name is Tornyth," Jodathyn said as Fydellah walked through the door of the hut. At his feet, Carvelle was building awkward towers from all sorts of objects he had collected.

"You cannot control the dragon, Jodathyn." Fydellah crossed the space between the door and the table without looking at him. She placed two plump rabbits on the table. "Dragons are not meant to be controlled."

"You think I am doomed."

Fydellah held Jodathyn's gaze. "I believe in miracles. How could I not, after two highborns came to rescue me? But I don't intend to find out if you have another miracle within you."

Jodathyn's shoulders slumped.

"Take this rabbit. There's a pack with food and supplies you can take as well."

Jodathyn nodded.

"Where will you go?"

"I considered my options last night. If I can't get to Pallaryn, I thought I might head to Androssah. One of Kieryn's most loyal lords lives there. His household staff know me."

Carvelle jumped to his feet to protest. "I want to go home to Papa."

"I know," Jodathyn replied. "We need to be smart. If the road to Pallaryn is being watched we may need somewhere safe to wait for your Papa."

Muttering, Carvelle went back to his game.

"*The woman is in danger,*" the voice whispered.

Jodathyn flinched, and resolved not to listen.

"*She must leave now. The kidnappers will find the hut.*"

Fydellah was eyeing him. "What is it?"

"He says you are in danger and need to leave."

Fydellah didn't need to ask who 'he' was.

She grabbed a pack, indicating that Jodathyn should do the same. Jodathyn looked up at her, surprised.

"Your Sight is strong. Your dragon wants you to trust him ... so at this stage he won't lead you wrong."

Deciding he did not want to meet with the kidnappers again, Jodathyn picked up the pack and held out his hand for Carvelle. Annoyed, the little Prince left his game and came to his uncle's side.

The unwelcome presence seemed to purr and ripple. "*I'll show you where to hide.*"

Jodathyn slipped out into the woods, the small princeling trailing him. He could hear Fydellah's irritated sighs behind him. She was hesitant, unsure whether she could trust him.

With a firm hold on Carvelle's hand, Jodathyn let his instincts guide him. The sound of bubbling water piqued his interest.

"Is there a bridge nearby?"

Taking charge, Fydellah marched forwards, her gait choppy. The ground near the bridge was wet.

"*Hide, under the bridge. Wait.*"

"Tornyth wants us to hide under the bridge and wait," Jodathyn said.

Her eyes narrowing into slits, Fydellah moved towards the bank first. Jodathyn followed her, helping Carvelle down. He pressed himself against the stone bridge and drew Carvelle close to his body to hide them both in the shadows. Fydellah's appraising gaze continued to linger on him. Unused to such open scrutiny, Jodathyn jutted his chin out and pretended he didn't care.

"Do you know what the rough translation of the name Tornyth is?"

"I am palace educated," Jodathyn murmured. "Of course I do."

"What does it mean, Uncle?"

Jodathyn pursed his lips, not daring to let his eyes sweep over to Fydellah. "*Return to Glory.*"

"It's just a name," Jodathyn snapped.

Fydellah indicated to Carvelle with a nod. "Do you love him?"

"Of course, I do," Jodathyn gritted out.

"And when he is king?"

"The crown of Rama changes nothing."

Fydellah considered his response. "For now, that is a truth."

"What's that supposed to mean?"

"People's truth changes."

Jodathyn opened his mouth to argue his point of view, when Carvelle shook his hands. "Someone is coming!"

Carvelle was right. The steady rhythm of hooves was coming closer. Tensing, Jodathyn pulled Carvelle tighter into his body, so that the Prince squirmed. Carvelle's large eyes stared up into his face and his small hands took a hold of his tunic.

Men's voices rung above them. "This must be the bridge that leads to that abandoned hut."

Jodathyn counted at least five pairs of boots hitting the ground as the men above dismounted. His heart hammered in his chest as his pursuers crossed the bridge. They had left their horses tethered on the opposite bank. His hand fluttering over the dagger he had stolen, Jodathyn prayed under this breath that he would not end up in a fight. A man like Valt Axtin was better suited to circumstances such as this.

"Not time to fight, human. Count in your head until I tell you to stop. When I say go, run up the embankment, across the bridge and get to the horses ..."

Sucking in a deep breath, that was exactly what Jodathyn did. He counted to sixty-seven before the voice returned.

"Now."

Grasping onto Carvelle's hand, Jodathyn burst from underneath the bridge, scrambling up the bank. Wet foliage slipped from under him, but he pressed forward. "Quiet!" he hissed as Carvelle whined in complaint.

Beside Jodathyn, Fydellah also struggled towards the bridge, her face set with determination.

Not allowing Carvelle to rest, Jodathyn ushered them across the bridge towards the horses.

"Take the black mare. Give Fydellah the white stallion ... he suits her. Release the others."

Jodathyn didn't pause to think. He hurried forward and grabbed Carvelle around the waist to hoist him onto a strong, intelligent-looking mare. He slashed the other horses' reins, handing Fydellah the reins of a handsome white stallion.

"Here," he said. "May he protect you on your road ahead."

"Tell her the north road is safe."

Fydellah stopped to stare at Jodathyn. "I was expecting you to beg me to come with you."

Jodathyn hit the remaining horses' rumps, crying out loud like a wildman to scare them into a canter. Their loss would stall the kidnappers' pursuit. The black mare snorted, pawing the ground as she watched her companions flee. Jodathyn ran a soothing hand along her silky neck. Satisfied, he swung himself into the saddle, wheeling his horse around so that he could look down at Fydellah.

"I know you do not wish to linger in my presence. So, I will not ask that of you. It may be foolish, but I hope we meet again one day. The dragon says the north road is safe. Farewell."

"I wish you well," Fydellah whispered, as Jodathyn kicked his mare into a frantic gallop.

He did not look back.

CHAPTER SEVENTEEN

Jodathyn

Sant Burgundy Bridge

Crouched over the neck of the stolen mare, Jodathyn could almost forget his current circumstances. Under him the mare's muscles moved in perfect fluid motion. There was nothing quite like the ecstasy of racing the wind on the back of a horse.

Jodathyn laughed as the wind swept about his face. He thought of stretching his wings out wide to embrace the air and all her currents. No one could hunt Carvelle in the heavens. The Prince would be safe. All he had to do was break free of his human prison.

"Think of Carvelle," Jodathyn muttered between gritted teeth. He shook his head in an attempt to separate his strange dragon-like thoughts from his human ones. Carvelle's survival depended on him remaining in control.

Judging that the mare had put enough distance between them and the kidnappers, Jodathyn pulled her to a steady walk. It would not be wise to kill the horse in their haste to reach safety.

"Which way is Pallaryn?"

Jodathyn soothed Carvelle's hair down with his hand. They were alone on a grassy plain. In the distance, small cottages were dotted along the horizon.

"The road to the citadel is not safe. They are watching."

Jodathyn shivered.

"Uncle, are you well?"

"We need to find someone to help us."

"That shouldn't be hard. I'm the King's son." Carvelle turned in the saddle to look up at Jodathyn. There was a smear of mud on his nose. "What do you suppose the horse's name is?"

"I don't know," Jodathyn replied, thankful for a change in conversation. "I guess it's up to you, since we commandeered her for the Crown."

"We stole her," Carvelle pointed out. "Do you know what happens to horse thieves?"

Jodathyn chuckled. "Do you have any idea what your papa will do to any that raise a hand to hurt you?"

Carvelle leant into Jodathyn's chest. "They're in big trouble. Papa will chop off their heads. They won't want to get caught."

"All that's merciful and mighty," Jodathyn said. Carvelle was right. The kidnappers would be desperate to silence them now.

As if in answer, a warm wind blew about Jodathyn, buffeting his legs and whipping strands of his hair. He closed his eyes; the unnatural heat of the air felt like it was calling him home. The trees rustled about him, sounding uncannily like laughter.

"They are coming. Bolt."

Jodathyn's eyes snapped open. He tried to swallow but his mouth was dry. The image of Carvelle's broken body in the grass churned his stomach.

"There's a bridge at Sant Burgundy – head there."

The black mare stopped of her own accord. Flattening her ears to her head, without any cues from Jodathyn she galloped away in the direction of where they had come from.

The mare moved with such urgency that Jodathyn felt a stab of fear. He had heard Valt say that beasts had a keener sense of danger than a man.

The grassy plain sped past at an increasing rate. And still the horse continued her incredible gallop. She paid no attention to Jodathyn's commands to halt. Sweat had formed on her withers like silver rain, but the animal gave no sign of slowing.

"Uncle!" Carvelle cried.

He swore viciously, crouching lower over Prince Carvelle in an attempt to shield the youngster with his body.

About a half mile from a great stone bridge, the mare stopped. Jodathyn exhaled in relief. He dismounted, reaching to smooth his hand down the mare's glossy neck.

"Sant Burgundy Bridge," the voice gloated. He could almost hear it cackling. *"There's nothing quite like the Wind Song, is there?"*

"She's a very fast horse, Uncle," Carvelle saw fit to mention. "Father would love a horse like this in the palace stables. Perhaps we shall call her Zarine."

Jodathyn smiled in reply. Taking the horse's reins, he turned towards the bridge. If he walked, the power in his head was less likely to make their mount gallop.

"This is the bridge to Sant Burgundy."

"How do you know, Uncle?" Carvelle slipped his hand into Jodathyn's. Jodathyn wasn't sure how to explain the voice to himself, let alone another person.

"Maybe there is a kind–"

Twack!

Jodathyn jolted as an arrow flew past his ear, lodging in the stone bridge.

They had been found. The kidnappers were all mounted on fresh steeds. Jodathyn grabbed Carvelle around the waist and hoisted him back into the saddle. Clicking his tongue, he kicked the horse's sides. The mare leapt forward into a frantic gallop.

The horse tossed her head up in panic as another arrow narrowly missed them. She balked, taking a few steps backwards. Jodathyn kicked her sides, urging her on. The poor beast's stamina was almost depleted.

Jodathyn swore again. *"Ri rshon hanoch!"* He gripped Carvelle's hand and slowed the mare. Lowering Carvelle to the ground he yelled at him to run. He didn't wait to see if Carvelle had obeyed. Roaring, he whipped the horse around, charging at their pursuers.

Jodathyn locked his eyes on his would-be murderers, screaming as his mount careened towards them. The sound of the mare's hooves beat on the bridge like war drums. If he was going to perish, he would die giving Carvelle the time he needed to escape.

There was a moment where the kidnappers paused, stunned by Jodathyn's defiance. The leader laughed at the futile attempt to protect the Prince. Then, as one, the kidnappers hurtled towards Jodathyn.

With a flurry of screams, Jodathyn collided with his foes. The mare reared and he tumbled from the saddle. A sharp pain in his shoulder left him gasping. He lay stunned, unable to move.

Inhaling, Jodathyn could smell the heavy scent of horse, sweat and blood. A shadow passed over his prone body as his attackers came to stand over him. He could only hold onto the thread of hope that perhaps, in some way, he had made his brother, his king, proud.

"Fight," goaded the rumbling voice. *"Fight like a son of a dragon you are."*

Whether this phantom voice was meant for good or for ill, it was right. He was descended from a long line of Ramian monarchs. Their blood flowed in his veins. He wasn't going to let his proud lineage down. He was Pallarus.

Jodathyn squashed his feelings of dread as he unsheathed his stolen dagger. Firm footfalls approached and the mockery continued.

"That's it. Wait for him to come to you ... Then slash his face open."

Jodathyn snarled as a hand touched his shoulder to turn him over. Dagger in hand he thrust it into the man's face. He felt the blade connect with flesh. With a yell of triumph, he tore the blade free.

Grunting with effort, Jodathyn kicked at the injured man's knees, sending him crashing to the ground. Two others grabbed for his knife. His arms were wrenched behind him.

Jodathyn screamed and kicked as the assassins frogmarched him forward to the riverbank. They waded into the water a little way, forcing him to his knees. Helpless, he stared down at his reflection. The memory of the night where he had almost been drowned in the beer barrel resurfaced. Drowning was not a pleasant way to die.

The man whose face Jodathyn had slashed followed his men into the water. Jodathyn sneered and spat. "Traitor!"

The man swiped his face with his sleeve, pinning Jodathyn with a contemptuous gaze before backhanding him. Determined to show no weakness, Jodathyn did not react.

"Blood for blood," the man growled, pointing to the cut under his eye. Jodathyn raised his gaze to survey the wound. His lips puckered into a smile; the gash was deep and would cause significant discomfort.

"I imagine the sharp edge of the executioner's axe would do more damage," Jodathyn said, licking the blood from his lips.

The kidnapper took the proffered blade from one of his men. All thoughts of the injury that he had inflicted disappeared from Jodathyn's mind when the kidnapper grabbed his thigh. He struggled as the man's fingers pinched his flesh, and the other attackers gloated. Grinning, the kidnapper plunged the blade savagely into Jodathyn's thigh.

A bolt of pain tore through Jodathyn's leg. He roared, convulsing as the water about him ran red. The kidnapper wrenched the blade out, pausing to enjoy Jodathyn's screams.

"Blood for blood." The voice in his head echoed the kidnapper's words. *"I'll be tasting his blood."*

Without contemplating the consequences, Jodathyn lunged forward to headbutt the captor that stood in front of him. The impact of hitting his assailant with his skull left him dazed. In the confusion, his arms were released and he stumbled to his feet.

Jodathyn's bid for freedom was only brief. He was grabbed by the scruff of his neck and pushed back down into the river. Valt always did say headbutting in a fight was not the smartest strategy.

"Let me out ... let me kill," the voice cried.

Jodathyn roared in protest as he was pushed into the river. His head was held under; he continued to struggle. When he was lifted out of the water, he gasped, desperate for air. Even though it would prolong his own torture, he filled his lungs with as much air as he could.

A deafening whinny rent the air. Surprised, Jodathyn saw the black mare hurtling towards them at an alarming rate. There was fury in the beast's eyes as she plunged into the water.

For a frightening moment Jodathyn thought he would be trampled by the charging animal. However, the horse veered as she scattered the men. Whinnying, she reared, kicking and biting any that dared approach her.

In numb disbelief, Jodathyn watched as the horse continued to form a barrier of fearsome mare. He had never seen or heard of anything like this before.

Determined to survive, Jodathyn clenched his teeth and crawled from the river. He scrambled up the bank on his knees. If he could get to the bridge, he might be able to find help or hide.

"Someone, kill that horse!"

Lunging forward, a man grabbed at the trailing ends of the mare's reins. She reared and jerked her head. The man skidded and fell away. Another foolish man jumped onto her back, but she bucked him off. The remaining two tried to ambush her, but the enraged animal kicked herself free.

While the horse defended him, Jodathyn dragged his body to the bridge. He grasped at the stones as he reached what he hoped was salvation. He was aware that, because of his injury, he couldn't hope to get far.

Thwack!

He stumbled as an arrow flew from the far side of the bridge. It lodged into the stones between Jodathyn and his attackers. He fell to his knees as another arrow sailed overhead. *Thwack!*

This one nearly hit one of his pursuers.

Everyone seemed to freeze. Even the mare stilled, her ears pricked forwards. She pawed the ground and shook her mane.

"Leave this place at once before we sink an arrow in your gizzards," a voice cried out. "Troublemakers are not welcome in Sant Burgundy."

Jodathyn looked up to see the fuzzy silhouettes of a small company of men.

When no one moved to obey, another arrow was let loose, only missing the target by a thumb's width.

Jodathyn shuddered. "House Pallarus thanks you!"

"Leave this place at once," one of Jodathyn's liberators cried out.

Jodathyn scrambled to his feet. The mare came trotting up behind him. She stretched her neck and started to nibble on his curls.

Twisting about, Jodathyn saw his attackers fleeing in the other direction. It seemed that the cowards didn't want a fair fight

"My nephew, the Prince ..."

"The child is safe."

Jodathyn felt a surge of relief, knowing he would not be drowned. Carvelle was safe. He could no longer battle his fatigue. His legs collapsed from underneath him. He sat, sprawled, panting from exertion.

Chapter Eighteen

Orion

The Citadel of Pallaryn

The grief in Donatein's eyes was palpable. The outlook for Jodathyn didn't seem favourable. After mourning the loss of his parents, Orion understood Donatein's need for seclusion. Unable to provide any comfort, the kindest course of action was to give the old man some privacy.

Jodathyn's shocking disappearance had left Orion at a loose end. He wandered around the palace searching for something to do. Wherever he went, he was met with suspicion or outright hostility.

Before long, Orion had been chased out of the kitchens and the palace library. His offers to help in the stables had been met with excuses. He had very little hope of being welcomed in the tiltyards. Still, it would be a relief to have a bout or two.

Upon entering the tiltyards, Orion caught sight of Captain Tiernan. Over the last few weeks, he had become accustomed to the big man's gruff demeanour. He decided to ask the captain if he had a task for him. Anything to alleviate his boredom.

Orion was about to call out when he spotted two palace guards huddled in a corner. Creeping up behind them, he hid himself in an enclave to listen.

"Lord Whitoak's little stable spy is causing trouble again," one of the guards complained.

"He ain't just spying for Whitoak though, is he? He's singing mightily pretty for Solan too."

"Solan has already signed the arrest warrants ... soon as his spy told him that Jodathyn's servants were hiding something ... Poor buggers. Their necks are sure to stretch for this."

"Almost too easy," the other guard sniffed. "They hid the evidence under the mattress."

Oh, Pitiless Otherworlds. Orion bit his lip, suppressing the urge to duck his head out of his hiding place and look for Captain Tiernan. The captain seemed fond enough of Jodathyn, maybe he would be willing to help. But then, as a King's Guardsman, his loyalty was to the King. Would the captain be able to do anything, or would he renounce them and hand them over for judgement?

Backing away, Orion decided his destiny lay in his own hands. It was up to him to get Donatein and himself out of trouble. He didn't have much time. The guards had said the arrest warrant had already been signed.

Stiff backed, Orion turned around and walked in the opposite direction, his mind awhirl. Should he go to the King and beg for mercy? He dismissed that thought. The murmurs around the palace spoke of the King's reluctance to see anyone. As a servant, he wouldn't make it to the King's feet to plead for his life.

The only option was to warn Donatein and get out of the palace.

Orion wished he had stabbed the poor excuse for a stable hand the moment he had caught him spying. Poor Donatein had been rifling through Jodathyn's personal affects when Orion had disturbed him. In Donatein's hand was a stack of parchments. He was pale and trembling.

The old man had brushed past Orion, hiding the parchments under his mattress. They weren't alone.

A stable hand was standing in the open doorway. In his long bony fingers, he clutched a highborn's cloak. Suspicion was already stirring within Orion as he stepped forward and took it. When Orion had questioned where the dark grey cloak had come from, the stable hand had told him he'd found it at the Autumn Festival. In that moment, Orion knew it was a lie. Jodathyn was highborn, his cloak for the festival reflected the season and was a soft burnt orange, trimmed with bronze and gold threads.

"Keep your weapons at hand," Donatein had whispered as he closed the door behind their unwanted visitor. His hands were shaking. "We may need them yet."

Orion pulled himself out of his thoughts. If he was to escape the palace, he would need a clear mind. He rounded a corner and dipped his head as he strolled past two palace guards. Jodathyn had told him with a wink that if one walked submissively around the palace, no one paid attention.

"Merciful Otherworld! I miss my old life. Why couldn't I be in Silverdyne and not worrying about court intrigues and plotting?"

Turning into the last corridor, Orion saw that it was clear. He dashed the rest of the way. Without knocking he pushed open the door and shut it behind him with a deafening thud.

"Orion!" Donatein admonished.

"We've been betrayed," Orion said. "The guards are on their way to search under your mattress. *They know.*"

Donatein's eyes widened. Orion fancied he could hear heavy footsteps approaching.

Donatein took some steadying breaths. "Orion, go to the stables and leave. Find Jodathyn."

"The stables?"

"Use your head, boy. Steal a horse and take your damn weapons. You're a dead man if you stay here."

Orion could not imagine adding stealing a horse to the list of his 'crimes'. He stared in disbelief. The punishment for thieving from the King was death.

"As long as you look the part you won't be caught. Your riding boots and weapons are on the master's bed."

"What about you?"

"I'm too old. I'll stall them so you can get away."

A small voice whispered in the back of Orion's mind, that Donatein had planned for this. The old man had thought about how to get him to safety. "Thank you."

"You have your whole life ahead of you."

"My father–"

"Take it from an old man. Your father would want you to live. Go in peace, Orion."

The chamber door rattled. Then there was a heavy knock. "Donatein Manideep, open the door."

Both Donatein and Orion jumped.

"I should have silenced the fiend," Orion muttered.

"Quick – go through the servants' door."

Orion dashed over to the master's bed. Thrusting the heavy crimson curtains wide, he took up his sword and buckled it to his hip, then his bow with a full quiver. With one last look he glanced to his master's favourite servant.

"Tell Jodathyn I am proud of him," Donatein choked. Tears started to well in his aged eyes. "I love him dearly."

Nodding, Orion grabbed his boots and dashed to the servants' door. He let the darkness envelop him.

"Be safe, Orion Maysden."

"Donatein Manideep!" The knocking became more insistent.

"I'm coming, young man." Donatein's voice was muffled.

Orion held his breath as Donatein allowed the guards access to Jodathyn's chambers.

"We've got orders from the council to search Jodathyn Pallarus' rooms. Your rooms, sir, are of particular interest."

"Are they now, young man?" Donatein asked. Orion thought he sounded calm, as if he had resigned himself to his fate. What had his master written down that could have them all arrested?

"Perhaps I should show you the way then, gentlemen."

Orion listened as Donatein led the guards towards his own rooms. Kicking off his ordinary shoes, he rammed his feet into his riding boots. He laced them before taking up his bow. Then he was sprinting along the servant tunnels.

Although Jodathyn had detested the use of the tunnels, Donatein had insisted on showing Orion anyway. Orion thought Jodathyn would have been interested in the tunnels. When he mentioned his thoughts to Valt, the giant man had shaken his head with a long-suffering sigh. Apparently, Jodathyn got himself lost there as a boy. It had taken Donatein and Valt half a day to find him. Since then, Jodathyn had avoided the tunnels.

Since the tunnels had fallen out of use in this wing of the palace, Orion was confident he would not be interrupted. Donatein had shown him exactly where to go if the occasion called for it. He exited where he had expected, in a room directly below Jodathyn's.

Orion didn't waste any time; he ducked out of the room and made his way towards the laundry. Always keen to gather information, he had overheard Valt complaining that Jodathyn had used the laundry to escape the palace.

At the top of the steps, Orion took a deep breath. Dozens of maids were engaged at their work. Keeping his eyes ahead, he weaved through the workbenches. They were too busy gossiping to take any notice of him.

Orion took the time to say a quick prayer of thanks for Donatein as he left the laundry behind. Somewhere inside the impressive walls of the palace, the old man would be in the custody of the guards. He owed it to Donatein to commit to the plan.

Boots crunching on the gravel, Orion sauntered to the stables. With his attire and horseman's lock, any other servant would assume he was a stable boy. Due to the festival, there were plenty of extra servants in the palace.

More at home with the four-legged beasts than among people, Orion strolled past the horses in their stalls. He breathed in the scent of horses and hay. Closing his eyes, he reached down for his power that had laid dormant.

The one time his father caught him experimenting on a fierce stallion, he had wrenched him away from the animal. Orion would never forget the look of abject horror in his father's eyes or the sting of the riding crop against his backside. When his terrified father had asked him to swear an oath that he would never use his powers again, Orion had agreed.

The circumstances had changed. His parents were dead. He was alone in the world and he couldn't get the herbs he needed to dampen his talent without arousing suspicion. Without the tonics he had felt his power moving and growing within him.

Clutching at his power, Orion held out his hand and sensed each of the horses around him. He tested each strand until he came by a strong thread, which belonged to a magnificent dappled grey stallion with black legs and a thick black mane. He made his way over to the horse. Reaching up, he ran his hand down the beast's quivering neck.

"Come with me," Orion's power sang.

Big, intelligent brown eyes stared back at him. The great stallion snorted, pawing the ground.

"Come with me."

Lifting his head high, the stallion stamped his feet. It seemed he was eager to please.

Grinning, Orion grabbed the tack and saddle. From his limited experience he knew the horse had agreed to his request. He hefted an expensive leather saddle onto the stallion's back when a voice interrupted him from behind. "I hope you're aware that's my father's horse."

Orion jumped and spun around on his heel. He hoped his face conveyed a politely confused air.

"Forgive me, Milady," Orion stammered, his head bowed. "It seems I am confused."

Lifting his gaze, Orion studied the woman before him. He wished he hadn't. Realisation of whose horse he was about to steal washed over him like a bucket of icy water.

"You recognise me, boy?"

"I do, Lady Illeanah," Orion mumbled.

"I recognise you too," Illeanah announced. Her eyes narrowed "You're Jodathyn's servant."

Orion didn't answer.

"Come now, don't be shy," Lady Illeanah said. She stepped forward and stroked a gloved hand down the stallion's nose. "This stallion is a good pick. He will look after you."

Orion cocked his head to the side, wondering if he should pinch himself to make sure that he'd heard correctly.

"Jodathyn may have broken our friendship, but I love him still. You're going after him?"

"I am."

"Then go in peace."

Orion mounted the horse and glanced back down at the lady, as if challenging her to raise the alarm. Lady Illeanah stepped alongside him and patted Orion's leg. "The stable spy has betrayed you."

Orion nodded and stared out at the distance.

"There is nothing left for you here except death."

"Donatein?"

"King Kieryn, in his wisdom, will delay trial for as long as he can."

Orion took up the reins and Lady Illeanah opened the stall. "I can give you two hours before I raise the alarm that my father's prized stallion is gone."

CHAPTER NINETEEN

Jodathyn

Sant Burgundy

Jodathyn battled the temptation to fall asleep where he had collapsed upon the bridge. His eyes began to close. Exhausted, he pressed his forehead to the cold stones in attempt to stay upright.

Several pairs of boots marched across the bridge, convincing Jodathyn to open his eyes. His liberators stood over him, gawking at his helplessness.

"He said he was of the house Pallarus."

"He ain't no High King."

"King got a brother, don't he?"

"If it is Jodathyn, I would recognise him."

"Check for the scars."

A broad-shouldered man, not much older than Jodathyn, knelt down beside him. His large calloused hands touched his upper arm, brushing his curls away from his right ear.

"Help me ..." Jodathyn wasn't sure whether he had spoken aloud.

"Jod?" The man's face lit up with a pleasant grin. "It *is* you."

In confusion, Jodathyn could only stare into the stranger's face.

The man bent down, offering Jodathyn his hand, and pulled him upright. Jodathyn wavered, crawled to the edge of the bridge and vomited.

The bearded man followed Jodathyn, pulling him to his feet again. The stranger's ready smile tugged into a frown as he steadied Jodathyn and saw the blood. "He's hurt."

Jodathyn vomited again in reply. "I need help."

The man snorted, wrapping his arms about Jodathyn for support. "Obviously, my friend. Lean on me, I'll take you to the house."

"I don't know you." Jodathyn peered at his saviour again. His dark blond beard and pale face were dirty from manual work. Likewise, his pants were stained. Big brown eyes stared down at him, almost as if to tease his memory. "Can't say I've met too many ..."

"I've made my life as a farmer now. I didn't think I would ever see you again. Are you hungry?"

"Give 'im some time to gain his bearings, eh Rue?" An older man pushed his way forward. Grasping Jodathyn's arm the old man helped him to stand, bidding his younger counterpart to support Jodathyn on his other side. Jodathyn could feel the eyes of the remainder of the group following his every move.

"I didn't think I would ever see you again, old friend. I thought that ..."

Finding he could barely keep his eyes open, Jodathyn nodded his head, hoping his saviour would be content with his answer and be quiet. His head was throbbing.

"You do recognise me, Prince?" the young man asked.

Jodathyn stared up at his rescuer, flummoxed. It felt like the stranger was laughing at him. "Sir, I have no idea who you are. I'm not a prince and where is my nephew? You said he was safe."

"Noble little Jod, you were always a real prince to me."

Jodathyn blinked. "My nephew, do you have him?"

The blond stranger smiled, shaking his head. "He's safe in my farmhouse. You still don't know me?"

Jodathyn shook his head.

"I will admit I have grown somewhat. I'll grant it was a long time ago that we were children."

Long-buried memories were jolted awake. His rescuer's lopsided grin was familiar. "Ruevyn?" Jodathyn asked. "But – but I thought you were dead."

"So, you do remember, Jod?"

"I thought they killed you ... you were just gone one day ..."

Ruevyn's grip tightened on Jodathyn's side. "I was lucky. I left that house after Meena ... and, well, I ended up here. It's Ruevyn Kelvie these days. I'm a farmer."

Jodathyn looked at his friend, who was beaming down at him. "I can see that. Look I'm in real trouble ... those men ... they'll be back."

Ruevyn hummed. "First you need someone to look at that wound and get some rest."

"I feel obliged to tell you that by helping me, you are putting yourself at risk." Jodathyn sent a concern sideways glance at the old man on his other side.

Having nothing to contribute to the conversation, the old man stared back.

"Well, seems like it's my turn to do the noble thing and protect you, Jod. Not the other way round. Just tell me they aren't slavers."

Jodathyn's eyes flicked to the old man. "I don't know. I don't think so. I hope not. Maybe ... I upset Lord Solan ..."

As Ruevyn's smile twisted into a sour grimace, Jodathyn turned his attention to the small farm house. Beyond the modest, tended fields, the land abruptly sloped upwards into a thick dense forest. A lonely apple tree stood proud beyond a rickety gate. Ruevyn had certainly made a new life for himself.

"Malara Gorge. I am very fortunate here, as I have the beauty of Rama on my doorstep." Ruevyn pointed beyond the second gate. "The gorge will provide you with some safety. Horses cannot pass through the gorge."

Jodathyn gazed out again. Malara Gorge was well known to the people of the citadel. It had long been shrouded in myth and legend. Now it seemed it would play a part in his own adventure.

"That's some creature you have, Joddie," Ruevyn said, pointing. Jodathyn looked up to see the black mare trotting after them. "I would have thought the fighting would have scared her off."

"Take your friend inside. I'll tend to his mount." The old man patted Jodathyn's shoulder and took the mare's reins.

"You don't have to worry yourself about Old Vic, he's not going to be spreading word in the market place." Ruevyn pushed open the door to his farmhouse. "Little sir. I have your uncle. You can come out now."

Carvelle's dark head appeared from his hiding place. With a cry of delight, he rushed to Jodathyn, wrapping his arms about his uncle's legs.

"Your uncle is hurt, child, I will need to take a look." Ruevyn plucked up the little Prince with ease. He swung him around and set him on his feet, away from Jodathyn's wound.

Glaring up at Ruevyn as the farmer left the room, Carvelle frowned. Jodathyn sent his nephew a warning look to behave himself. He wasn't used to being told 'no', and certainly not by a lowborn. Carvelle poked out his tongue.

Gritting his teeth against the pain, Jodathyn lowered himself into a wooden chair. Ruevyn returned with some rags and a glinting needle.

"How much practice do you have with that?" Jodathyn asked, his eyes on the point of the needle.

"Don't you worry, Jod, you're in good hands," Ruevyn said. He knelt at Jodathyn's side, ripping open the fabric of his trousers to expose the wound. "I know you can handle a little pain."

"Papa calls Uncle 'Jod', all the time," Carvelle saw fit to interject.

As Ruevyn pressed the needle against his skin, Jodathyn looked away.

Jodathyn lay on the pallet bed with Carvelle tucked once more under his arm. Glancing down at the prince, he wished he could get word to Kieryn. Thus far he'd done a poor job of taking care of Carvelle.

Somewhere out there, the kidnappers were biding their time. He could only imagine what they might do if they managed to capture them. They would be making another attempt soon.

Overwhelmed, Jodathyn slipped out of bed. He covered Carvelle with the blanket and tiptoed downstairs.

"Did you sleep well?"

Jodathyn started as Ruevyn appeared behind him. Being early morning, he hadn't expected to see him up and about.

Observing him for a long moment, Ruevyn nodded to some work clothes folded neatly on a chair. "I found you some other clothes to change into. Those men are tracking two princes, not commoners. These might help disguise you for a time."

"I'm not a prince," Jodathyn mumbled. He suppressed a weary sigh, tugging off his tunic and shirt. "That's a wise suggestion."

Wincing at the scarring that ran down Jodathyn's back, Ruevyn chose his next words carefully. "I have always wondered what you told your brother about Aviah Valley."

Jodathyn twisted his body so that Ruevyn could not see the shame he felt. He dressed in the commoner's shirt, quickly hiding his disfigurement.

Jodathyn forced on his boots, gritting his teeth against the pain. He glanced up to see how his friend had taken his silence. Ruevyn leant over a bench, his dark eyes watching him struggle. His fingers traced the hilt of a familiar dagger.

"It was retrieved from the river."

Thanking him, Jodathyn took the dagger. Even though he was unaccustomed to carrying weapons, he felt reassured by its weight. He slipped it into his boots just as Carvelle bounded down the stairs.

"I should have a dagger too, Uncle," Carvelle said, holding out his hand.

"Uncle says a big resounding 'no'," Jodathyn replied with a shake of his head.

Pouting, Carvelle crossed his arms, glowering up at Jodathyn.

Jodathyn shared a smile with Ruevyn as his friend fumbled around for something to break their fast.

"I was wondering how you ended up here," Jodathyn murmured, as Ruevyn set bread and cheese on the table, along with some dried fruit. "Did you find yourself a family?"

Ruevyn broke the loaf to share. "I had a betrothed once."

"What happened?"

Rolling up his sleeve, Ruevyn revealed a small tattoo of an eye and a spear. Jodathyn's lips curled up at the sight. "Slavers. They found me out. I had to leave her behind. We were to wed this coming high spring."

"I'm sorry," Jodathyn murmured.

Ruevyn waved the apology away. When he looked back to Jodathyn, his eyes were hard. "I have always wondered what you told your brother."

For a long moment Jodathyn said nothing. "It was a year after I was taken from Aviah Valley before I saw Kieryn again. Assumptions were made ... we have never spoken about Lord Solan's summer house."

Snarling, Ruevyn thumped the table. "You could have made a real difference."

Carvelle made a strangled sound and ducked under the table.

"What power do I have? I'm the rejected son. My own father wanted me dead. No one would have listened to me," Jodathyn spat, feeling his temper rising. The beast inside lifted his head in agitation. "You have no idea what it's like knowing at any moment the King's council could vote to take your life away. I can't show weakness. Showing anyone a measure of trust is folly."

Ruevyn's brows furrowed. "Carvelle said something interesting when he came up to the farmhouse."

"Oh? He often has something interesting to say."

Even though Ruevyn's lips quirked, Jodathyn knew his friend was still angry. "Carvelle told me the men were after you, as a pre-emptive measure to silence you. Has *he* threatened you?"

"*He* told me if I ever spoke out, he would kill my family," Jodathyn whispered.

"Your family is the royal family ... how?"

"There're such things as assassins and poison," Jodathyn retorted. He leaned over to retrieve Carvelle from underneath the table. "Kieryn was right, I shouldn't have been so vocal about my wish to end the underground slave trade."

"At least someone is standing up for us," Ruevyn said.

"Well, if he thinks sending people to harm me and Carvelle is going to make me cower, he thought wrong. Even if I am banished, I will find a way to tear down his trading."

"Listening to you, Uncle, it goes to show, court life is half-truths, fantasies and a hint of dragon dung," Carvelle quoted primly.

Taken by surprise, Ruevyn looked down at the little prince. He seemed to have forgotten that there was a child listening in on their conversation. Raising an eyebrow, he turned to Jodathyn with a laugh. "He reminds me of you!"

Jodathyn smiled in response, unsure if Ruevyn's anger with him was spent.

"Who are you quoting, Your Highness?" Ruevyn enquired.

"Uncle Jodathyn," Prince Carvelle replied, grabbing Jodathyn's abandoned hunk of bread. "Occasionally, he says something very wise."

"But only very occasionally," Ruevyn added with a teasing smirk.

"Apparently," Jodathyn replied. "What have I told you about listening in on other people's conversations?"

"Papa says a clever king knows to listen," Carvelle replied. There was a little frown on his face. "Uncle ... you were talking about Lord Solan, weren't you?"

Before Jodathyn could answer, Carvelle turned to Ruevyn. "Uncle says that Lord Solan is the biggest dragon dung in the council."

Jodathyn's cheeks reddened as Ruevyn turned to him, a smirk upon his lips. "They weren't my actual words."

"But father disagrees. He says that Lord Kamoore is a bigger, weaker dragon dung, who expresses no desire to learn how to form his own opinion. He says Rama suffers due to his unendurable foolishness."

Ruevyn chuckled. "He is *very* much like you. I wonder how you didn't earn yourself more lashings."

"What do you mean *more* lashings?" Carvelle asked. "It was just the once with the dog whip, right? Papa says everyone in the kingdom knows *that* story."

Jodathyn sent a warning look in Ruevyn's direction. His friend stared up at him, a frown on his face.

"Was Lord Solan punished for what he did?"

Jodathyn sighed. "He claimed ignorance."

"Uncle," Carvelle said, his face set in a serious scowl. "If Lord Solan hurts you, I'll punish him."

After their breakfast, Ruevyn led them to his small barn. Against the wall was an old sword. Handing it to Jodathyn hilt first, he said, "I know you have your dagger but I would feel better if you also had a sword. Please take it."

"I'm not a swordsman."

Ruevyn pulled Jodathyn into a fierce embrace. "Take it anyway, Jod."

Jodathyn felt the weight of the sword in his hands as he took it.

A simple weapon. But sharp.

"Your help has been invaluable, thank you," Jodathyn replied. "What are you going to do?"

"I can't risk your pursuers finding me out. I will stay with friends in the village, then I will flee to a new life."

"Take the horse," Jodathyn breathed. "We can't take her through the gorge."

"Look after her, her name is Zarine," Carvelle added from behind his uncle's legs.

"My cloak. I left it upstairs. Sell it for what you can."

"Jodathyn, I can't. That cloak is worth a prince's ransom!"

"Exactly. It's the only way I can help you!"

Ruevyn crushed Jodathyn in another tight embrace. Finally, he stepped back, nodding. "I've packed some new supplies into your pack, including bandages, and herbs for the pain." Ruevyn smiled again, pulling an apple from his pocket. He placed the fruit into Jodathyn's hands and took his elbow to escort him back into the sunshine. "Do you remember the apple tree?"

"Of course," Jodathyn replied, his voice thick. His eyes never left the apple. "We made a solemn vow we would be friends for all eternity."

"Dragon Friend," the voice purred.

Jodathyn could tell whatever was inside of him was immensely pleased by the gift.

"I hold to my promise," Ruevyn said. "Come, I'll take you to the gate."

"Uncle Jod – an apple is a strange gift," Carvelle said, as they made their way across the farm.

"One day I'll tell you a story about the apple tree," Jodathyn said.

"If they are that special, perhaps you should plant one," Carvelle suggested.

Ruevyn turned to the Prince as they reached the gate. He gestured to the tree on the other side of the fence. "This is the tree I planted in memory of Aviah Valley. Wherever I settle in Rama, I plant an apple tree."

"Even though I have brought misfortune to your door, Rue. I'm glad I found you."

"The rain will have made the tracks through Malara slippery and difficult for anyone to track you. If you can get through the gorge, you'll reach the intersections of the great roads."

Jodathyn nodded; he had studied the maps of Rama for many years. He felt confident that if he could find the intersecting roads, he could work out directions to Lord Whitoak's summer house and help.

"Go through the gate, never mind the geese. They bite, but don't look back at them ... best to march straight through the middle."

"Why would you own geese if they are so much trouble?"

Ruevyn ignored Jodathyn's question. "Go up the hill, you'll find a little path. Look closely for it; most people miss it. Follow it, and when it forks, take the downhill route. Be careful – it's slippery. At the bottom of the slope, you will find Malara Gorge. The village of Belrah is near where the roads intersect."

"I'd better go."

"Yes, and hurry."

Jodathyn pulled out a slim gold chain from around his neck and handed it to Ruevyn, pressing the unexpected gift into his friend's hand. "I don't have an apple to offer you in return. If this all works out and if you are ever in need, find me."

"Travel fast. I won't forget you," Ruevyn murmured.

"Nor shall I forget you." Jodathyn studied Ruevyn's face, committing his features to memory.

CHAPTER TWENTY

Jodathyn

Malara Gorge

Fumbling with the rickety gate Jodathyn eyed the geese. In his opinion their intimidation tactics of hissing and flapping their wings worked.

"Uncle, I don't think the geese like us," Carvelle said. His voice wavered.

"As long as we don't bother them, they won't bother us," Jodathyn replied.

Carvelle looked doubtful and huddled closer to his legs, peering out at the birds.

Jodathyn nudged the boy through the gate and shut it. While his back was turned the geese rallied into a feathery throng and charged his feet.

"Ouch!" Jodathyn cried. He aimed a kick at the biggest goose, which had latched onto his trousers. "Get off!"

The geese did not listen. Retreating, Jodathyn eyed them in dismay. He pressed his back against the fence. Carvelle, meanwhile, had used the time to climb to safety. From the topmost rung he watched as the geese assaulted Jodathyn's boots.

"They don't like you at all, Uncle."

"Climb onto my back," Jodathyn commanded. Ruevyn had told him to walk through the middle of the geese. And so that was what he would do. Carvelle grinned in delight as he clambered onto Jodathyn's back.

Taking a deep breath, Jodathyn made sure he had a tight hold of his nephew and prepared for the geese to attack. The vicious flock watched him with beady eyes, honking and hissing. He stepped forward.

"Keep moving ..." Jodathyn muttered, striding forward, ignoring the twinge in his leg.

"Giddy-up!" Carvelle cried, kicking Jodathyn's sides.

"I'm not doing this when we get back to the palace," Jodathyn warned. He winced as his leg spasmed.

The geese and their discordant melody followed Jodathyn up the incline. He limped on, gritting his teeth against the pain. Halfway up the hill, the geese decided they had done an excellent job. They waddled back to their posts.

"Maybe we can ask the cook for roast goose when we get back," Carvelle suggested.

Jodathyn hummed in agreement, setting Carvelle on the ground. He pressed on towards the gate. The Prince poked out his tongue and began to sing an old traditional children's song.

Jodathyn listened to his nephew's high, shrill voice without comment. Finding the path, he was dismayed to see it was covered in wet foliage and thick, black mud. He was so busy making sure each step was cautious and measured, that he nearly missed the sudden fork.

Scowling, Jodathyn took the downward route. Halfway down, he lost his footing in the slippery mud and tumbled.

"Uncle?"

"Be careful, it's slippery," Jodathyn called from where he lay on his back. Panting, he willed the pain to subside so that he could stand. He watched as Carvelle clambered his way down to him.

"Uncle you need to get up." Little hands grabbed his elbow and attempted to lift him. "I can't carry you."

"A moment," Jodathyn gasped. He rallied all his Pallarus stubbornness and grabbed onto a tree branch. Counting to three he hoisted himself up. He glanced back at the track his body had made, wincing as he rubbed his sore backside.

Carvelle took a step and slid over. "It's slippery."

Jodathyn stepped out, his arms outstretched for a counterbalance. It was a slow, painful process, descending into the gorge. Carvelle attempted to help him each time he toppled over into the mud.

"Uncle, this is a little bit fun," Carvelle declared. He let go of the branch he was using to hold himself upright, and fell. "But only a little bit."

Jodathyn paused to make sure Carvelle was uninjured. Through the trees he spotted the river. Encouraged, he pressed forward, ignoring his pain. Beside him Carvelle whooped and slid the rest of the way on his bottom.

Grateful to reach the river, Jodathyn crouched to wash his face and hands. Carvelle contented himself painting his face with mud. Fumbling with the pack, Jodathyn found a small tin with Ruevyn's promised herbs. He uncapped it to study the light green powder. It smelt faintly of earth and home. Dipping his finger in, Jodathyn scooped up some powder and placed it onto his tongue.

While he waited for the pain to dull, Jodathyn studied their surroundings. The waters were high, almost spanning the width of the gorge. Large rocks formed a path along which they could pick their way through the running water and to the other side. The walls on both sides of the gorge towered above them, their banks dense with growth.

Jodathyn knew that the gorge offered plenty of places for them to hide. But it was also the perfect place for an ambush. Deciding it was foolish to stay in the open, he called for Carvelle. They needed to keep moving.

Stepping out, Jodathyn moved from one moss-covered rock to the next. His leg twinged as if to remind him that he was injured. If he caused further damage, he would not be able to signal for help.

Beside him, Carvelle scrambled every which way, relishing the rock pools and waterfalls hidden among the boulders. "Uncle, this place is more fun than the palace gardens!" he cried.

Jodathyn furrowed his brow, concentrating on each placement of his foot. By the time the sun was high in the sky, the air in the gorge was dense and sticky. Jodathyn's skin was slick with sweat and mud. His head ached.

Up ahead, Carvelle peered over his shoulder. "Uncle why don't we stop here for something to eat? You look pale."

Grimacing, Jodathyn looked back at how far they had come. Carvelle was right, he needed a rest. He collapsed down on a boulder.

Carvelle joined him and started digging through the pack. "I'm hungry. I'll get you something to eat, Uncle." He pulled out a few dry cakes, pushed them into Jodathyn's hands and took one for himself.

Jodathyn bit down into the cake. It was dense and floury. He took another bite. And then another, until it was gone.

"You should have a drink too," Carvelle said.

"I'm supposed to be looking after you, Carvelle," Jodathyn replied. He took the water canteen and drank. He felt like he was cooking from the inside. The water did little to cool him.

"Who says I can't also look after you, Uncle?"

Jodathyn had to admit, Carvelle had a point.

As the light faded into dusk, Jodathyn called a halt to their trek. From the river's edge he had spied a lone tree stump. He resorted to climbing up the bank on all fours in order to reach it.

Sidling up to the stump, Jodathyn swept his hand through it to remove unwanted spiders from their make-shift bed. The stump was blackened and charred from where it had been burnt. But it would do them for the night. Wrapping his cloak about them, Jodathyn wedged himself into the stump. They sat cramped inside their shelter. Jodathyn's chin rested on Carvelle's head.

"Uncle, tell me about the apple tree," Carvelle demanded.

Jodathyn cleared his throat, thinking of the rosy red apple in his pack. "In a faraway kingdom, long, long ago, there was a household where children were servants. The household was an unhappy one, but when the children were together, something magical happened ..."

"What, Uncle?"

"Hush. As I was saying, something magical happened. No matter how dreary or difficult life was, when the children were together, they found happiness. These children went on many adventures together."

"What did they do?"

"They stole coins and gave them to the poor."

"They did not!"

"They paddled in a magic stream with healing waters. However, the most special adventure was climbing trees that sheltered them from all harm."

"What do you mean, Uncle?"

"There was a special apple tree. When the children climbed it, the mean knights could not find them. They were always safe in the branches of that tree. One day, the children made a solemn promise. They didn't have any special trinkets to make their sacred vows, so they went to the apple tree and asked her to give some apples.

Under her branches the children exchanged their apples and promised they would always be friends and look out for one another, no matter what might happen."

"That's a nice story."

Jodathyn hummed.

"It was about you and Ruevyn, wasn't it? Did they hit him with the dog whips too? Does he have a scar just like yours?"

Jodathyn sucked in a deep breath as if he had been struck.

Carvelle was already onto his next question. "Did the stream really have magical healing properties?"

"It did."

Carvelle cuddled in closer to Jodathyn's chest. It seemed that all the exercise, jumping rock to rock, had worn the Prince out. Soon his gentle breathing became shallow as he drifted off to sleep.

Staring up into the night sky, Jodathyn tightened his grip around Carvelle. The sky rumbled, and then it began to rain.

His human heart was asleep. Tornyth was strong enough to break free and track those who dared hunt his human and prince. Their mothers should have taught them not to meddle in the affairs of dragons. Dragons were fierce adversaries. They would not see the dawn.

A wicked grin spread across Tornyth's scaly mouth. He might be confined to Jodathyn's dreams, but he would soon find a way to escape. The land of the living beckoned to him.

Tornyth unfurled his strong wings and leapt into the air with a roar of triumph. There would be no escape from his wrath.

The hunters had just become the helpless prey.

Tornyth caught the updraft, sailing into the night sky. He sniffed the cool air and caught the scent of the ones that meant harm. He flew high until he hovered over where the fools had camped.

Their fire was burning low. The men's horses were hobbled at the edge of the camp. All of the kidnappers were sound asleep. Soon they will be slumbering in the Otherworld. Tornyth's chest rumbled with a dragon's laugh of glee.

He brought his great horned head around to count his victims. It would be a dreadful shame to kill an innocent.

He banked, and landed in front of the horses, which screamed in fright. He cocked his head to the side and, with very careful movements, used his talons to cut the animals free. They galloped away in terror.

The commotion woke the men, and they tumbled from their beds. Grabbing their weapons, they fanned out. Tornyth could see the disbelief and horror in the whites of their eyes.

He laughed at their desperation and the futility of their weapons.

"What do you want, beast?"

Tornyth moved his head so that it was level with the leader. He smiled at the terrible-looking injury on the man's face. His human had done a good job.

"You hunt what is mine," Tornyth replied.

Without warning, Tornyth lashed out with his tail. Two men flew through the air and hit the ground with a heavy thump. They would never get up and walk this earth again. He grasped another third unfortunate with his great claws and squeezed him until his bones cracked. A fourth man he impaled with his horns. And then only the leader remained.

Tornyth paused to look at the human. The human stared back; his face ashen. He could smell sour urine as it dripped down the man's legs.

His chest rumbled in a chortle. "Not so tough now that you face a dragon."

Tornyth brought his powerful jaws down with a snap.

At first light, Jodathyn opened his gritty eyes. His hair, boots and clothes were drenched from last night's downpour. He stretched the sore muscles of his legs.

Carvelle tumbled out of his arms and rubbed his eyes. "That was not a good place to sleep."

"My apologies, oh Prince," Jodathyn replied.

"I'm sorry, Uncle. I'm tired and grumpy and I want my Mumma."

"We should keep moving." Jodathyn smiled down at the little boy. He stood, his stiff leg screaming in protest. Fearful of what he might see, he'd been avoiding checking the wound. Now was the time to change the dressing.

"How about a bath, Carvelle?"

"I bet I can stay in the cold water longer than you, Uncle!"

Jodathyn carefully made his way to the bank, dumping the pack on a dry rock. He knelt to trail his fingers through the fresh water. He stripped and stood shivering on the bank, wishing he'd asked Ruevyn for soap.

Jodathyn took a deep breath and slid into the frigid water. As his lower body submerged, he stifled a gasp. Goosebumps broke out on his skin. He wrapped his arms around his chest with a sigh and walked further into the depths.

"Is it cold, Uncle?" Carvelle grinned at him. With a gleeful whoop he jumped into the river, sending a wave of cold water over Jodathyn's head.

"Wash behind your ears," Jodathyn said as his cheeky nephew surfaced. Carvelle poked out his tongue and found his own space to wash. Jodathyn watched him, ensuring he was safe as he cupped his hands, capturing water to wash his torso. He rubbed away the dirt smears on his body and face, then ducked under the water, raking his fingers through his filthy hair.

Before his flesh could grow numb, Jodathyn returned to the bank and pulled himself out of the river. He used his cloak to pat himself dry. With one eye on the Prince, he found a place to lie in the sun. It was time to check his injury. Unwrapping the bandages on his thigh, Jodathyn winced as he saw the wound.

It was weeping. Thankfully, the gash did not look like it was re-opening; left to its own natural devices it would heal. From the top of the pack, he grabbed the herbal tin.

"I'm sorry you are hurt, Uncle." Carvelle waded in the shallows, watching him. "Ruevyn said he packed new bandages. Guardsman Jael once told me that keeping wounds clean was important."

"Guardsman Jael is correct." Rummaging through the pack, Jodathyn found the unused bandages. Wrapped among them was a strong-smelling ointment, which he applied to his wound. His skin tingled until it became numb. Jodathyn sighed in relief.

Carvelle continued to observe him. "Uncle, did you hear the roar last night?"

"Roar?"

"Yes, it was like a great beast bellowing. The ground shook."

"No."

"I tried to wake you, but you were fast asleep. I was very warm and safe with you."

A shiver crept up Jodathyn's spine. A memory of horses screaming, of bones crunching and the sharp, coppery tang of blood on his tongue flitted through his mind.

CHAPTER TWENTY-ONE

Orion

Outskirts of Sant Burgundy

I f he hadn't been fleeing for his life, Orion would have found being back in the saddle relaxing. Underneath his thighs the stallion was strong and sure-footed. He was confident that with this horse, he could travel long, hard distances with little hardship. He could only hope that Lady Illeanah was trustworthy and hadn't alerted the guards to his theft too early.

Orion was a horse thief now. He could almost see the creases in his father's forehead as he frowned in disappointment. His father would have a lot to say about his only surviving child losing his ancestral home and being lowered to a servant. Further adding to the shame, he was now a wanted criminal. The thought of his sins did not sit well with him, but Orion wanted to survive.

Growing up, Orion had dreamed of joining the King's Guardsmen. The idea that someday he might wear the black and silver was now impossible. While Jodathyn had been under Captain Tiernan's watchful eye, he had been hopeful he might be noticed. Now the best he could expect was a necklace of rope.

Thinking about his future only made Orion despondent. He sighed and decided he would make his way to the village of Sant Burgundy. He reasoned that if he listened to the village gossip, he would hear of anything unusual happening in the area. If Jodathyn was nearby, causing trouble, someone would know.

The stallion suddenly halted and refused to move forward.

"What now?"

The horse pinned his ears back to his skull in reply. Orion caught sight of black smoke curling up from the grassy plain. He tilted his head and sniffed. The stench on the wind was not wood smoke. The grey stallion's eyes had rolled back.

"Hush now," Orion murmured, running his hand down the frightened animal's neck. He let his power flow from his palms to calm the stallion. Becoming still, the horse stood unmoving, its leg muscles quivering.

Urging the horse into a gallop, Orion thought it would be best to investigate. Valt had often complained that Jodathyn had a special knack for getting into trouble. He needed to find out if the smoke was somehow connected to his master before the lawmen were called.

Reaching the place of the smoke's origin, Orion covered his mouth and nose. Burnt grass crackled under his boots as he dismounted. The smoke was billowing from the charred ruins of what appeared to be a campsite.

"Stay here ... peace ..."

Orion patted his stallion's nose. When he was sure the beast would not bolt, he approached the edge of the destruction.

Unnatural, twisted corpses greeted him. Their mouths were open in silent screams and their fingers reached out for salvation that would never come. Each blackened corpse held a sword in its hand. Whatever had killed them had easily overpowered them.

Orion shivered in revulsion; he couldn't imagine anyone surviving the onslaught.

Kneeling beside a tree, Orion saw the imprints of hooves. These men had horses. But while their human masters had fought and died, the horses had vanished. He could only surmise the horses had been taken.

"You!"

Jumping, Orion whipped around to see a small group approaching on horseback. To flee the scene would make him look guilty. He knew his best course of action would be to play the curious traveller. Although his hand itched for his sword, he waved in greeting.

"What are you doing out here?"

Forcing a smile on his face, Orion looked to the large woman who had barked the question. "I was travelling towards the village when I noticed the smoke. I headed out here to see if I could be of assistance." Orion turned to the body closest to him. "It seems they aren't needing any help."

"That's a nice animal you have," one of the men answered. His assessing gaze did not leave the horse. Orion didn't like the look of greed in his eyes.

"A last gift from my late father," Orion murmured, touching a hand to his horseman's lock. He had practised the lie, knowing his lock would give credence to the fib. Every Ramian knew of the horsemen of Silverdyne.

"Did you hear the roar last night?"

Orion shook his head. "I heard nothing. What did this?"

"Something nasty is lurking out there." The woman gestured over the plain.

"A great beast, they say, with the strength of a thousand men. It came from Malara Gorge."

"Seems these men lost their fight by their own campsite," Orion said with a shrug. "Their horses are gone."

One of the older men dismounted. He approached the closest body and peered down at it. "Reckon these are the same blokes that caused the ruckus. They deserved a violent end."

"How can you be sure they are the same troublemakers, Vic?"

"Same number of men that we run off. Now why would anyone camp near the gorge? It's best to find shelter in these parts. Unless you're up to no good."

"What sort of trouble did they cause you?" Orion asked. "You seem pleased by their demise."

"There was a disturbance near Sant Burgundy Bridge. These men nearly killed a young man and his child."

That doesn't sound good, Orion thought with a frown.

Vic sent a withering glare at the woman. "We agreed we weren't going to talk of the young man ... he's running."

"What's he running from?"

Vic's stare darkened. "You're asking too many questions. You should come with us. I'm sure the lawman would like to speak with you."

Orion held out his hand. "Please, I'm travelling through and have nothing to do with these men or their deaths."

"If that is the case, you won't be afraid of a little talk with the law, will you?"

Orion stepped backwards as they dismounted.

"Hello!" a voice called out. "What's happened here, Vic?"

Orion almost breathed a sigh of relief at the sight of a big, blond man on horseback. While her rider was wearing work-stained clothing, the mare was stunning.

He turned to Vic, who seemed to be the leader of the group, to gauge his reaction.

"Ho, Rue!" Vic called, waving. "Found some stiff bodies and this one poking his nose into local business."

The blond man brought his horse close, gazing down at first the bodies and then Orion. His eyebrows quirked. "Aren't you a little far from home, horseman?"

"I'm travelling."

"He never said where."

"I'm looking for someone."

"He never said who."

Snorting, Rue dismounted. He walked slowly around the campsite. "I think these are the same men."

"I said, that, didn't I?" Vic said, turning around to his group.

Rue regarded Orion. "I'm Ruevyn Kelvie, I own a farm nearby. You ought to know that Old Vic can *sense* troublemakers."

Orion shifted.

"He's not telling us everything. He's in trouble," Vic muttered.

Ruevyn smiled at Vic; it disappeared the moment he glanced back at Orion. "If you don't want a trip to the lawmen, I suggest you saying something that resembles the truth. The lawmen in Sant Burgundy trust Vic."

Orion's eyes darted towards Old Vic. He held up his hand. "I mean no harm to anyone. I'm tracking someone who's in danger."

Ruevyn eyes slid over to Vic to gauge his reaction to this statement. Much to Orion's relief, Vic nodded. "More details."

Orion licked his lips. "My master went missing, along with his nephew …"

"You're looking for Jodathyn Pallarus," the large woman said.

"Hush, woman. That's secret in these parts."

"Please!" Orion burst. "If you have seen him, tell me where. He's in more danger than he knows."

Ruevyn considered him for a moment. "If Jodathyn is truly your master, tell us something about him."

Orion didn't pause. "When he's nervous, he murmurs the ancient alphabet backwards; he's taught me to swear in the ancient language; his closest confident is Lady Illeanah Whitoak; his favourite text is *Ancient Mythology of the Four Isles* and as a boy he got stuck in the servant passages and wasn't found for hours."

Ruevyn nodded along. "Sounds like our Jod."

Vic glared. "He seems genuine enough. Can't verify it though, can we?"

"He also used to steal coins off a knight in Aviah Valley to feed servants," Orion continued. He had heard Captain Tiernan and Valt guffawing over Jodathyn's confession to Lady Illeanah. Valt had said Jodathyn's audacity had not surprised him.

Ruevyn froze. "I can verify that Jodathyn did steal coins to feed servants."

Orion blinked, his brain catching up to his mouth. "You knew Jodathyn?"

"Once upon a time."

"Please, he's in grave danger."

"Well," Ruevyn said at length. "You'll be glad to know I sent Jodathyn and the Prince into Malara Gorge. If you hurry you can meet them where the great roads intersect."

Relieved, Orion bobbed his head in understanding. "Thank you. If anyone else comes from the palace, please be careful what you reveal to them."

"Who do we trust?" The woman crossed her arms under her bosom.

"If at all possible, demand to be taken to the King. If not, a captain of the King's Guard. Be sure to stress Jodathyn is *protecting* the Prince."

Ruevyn smiled and pressed an apple and a hunk of cheese into Orion's hand. "Farewell, horseman of Silverdyne, servant of Jodathyn."

The small group of villagers parted, allowing Orion access to his stallion. He mounted and looked down at each of them.

"House Pallarus thanks you."

Kicking the sides of the stallion, Orion urged him into a canter. He was relieved to be leaving the charred campsite behind. And hopefully, with Ruevyn's information, he would be the first one to reach Jodathyn.

After that, they needed a plan.

Chapter Twenty-Two

Kieryn

The Citadel of Pallaryn

Kieryn glared in disgust at the signatures scrawled on the bottom of the parchment laid out before him. He slammed his half-empty goblet down on the table, causing some of the tart wine to splash onto the document. The droplets formed red beads that looked like the blood the council was after.

His palms flat against the wood, Kieryn dragged in a deep breath. His council was growing bolder. While it was encouraged for the King's council to vote on matters as their consciences dictated, they were not permitted to make final judgements. As High King, that burden was his and his alone.

"How did this happen?" Kieryn hissed. He swiped the goblet from the table.

"Perhaps while we were indisposed, my King," Lord Whitoak said. He stepped over the goblet and wine, which had spilled over his plush carpets. His tone was placatory.

It didn't work. Kieryn felt a spike of fury.

Drawing another breath, Kieryn filled his lungs with air until they burned. He sighed, releasing his breath. A king should not be a slave to his anger. He could almost see his late father's stern face studying him bitterly. Before his mother's death Kieryn had been a happy child. His grief had left him angry and discontented. Once he had been his father's golden child; without his mother, Kieryn was a source of frustration and disappointment.

Reining in his rage, Kieryn leant against the table. He didn't have the luxury of breaking. He was the lord and master of Rama. It was his duty to be strong for his nation in all circumstances.

"I cannot stay here doing nothing while my son is out there." Kieryn peered over at Lord Whitoak, who had been his constant companion since his son's disappearance. It hurt to see the look of concern on his normally impassive face.

"I know, my King," Lord Whitoak said in a low, gravelly voice. "I can attempt to keep the council busy, if that is what you wish."

"It is what I need," Kieryn admitted. "That and someone I trust with my wife."

Kieryn knew he was being selfish. A king must protect all those of the Pallarus bloodline; his own needs came second. Odelle needed peace and calm. She needed her son back in her arms. It hurt that he wasn't able to provide his Queen with what she needed.

Odelle had been a perfect choice for his Queen. Even now she held herself with poise. But as a mother, in private, she was heartbroken. When he wasn't pacing the floor, Kieryn lay by her side as she wept for her missing child. He couldn't bear to see her in so much pain.

Kieryn discarded his robe and picked up his heavier ceremonial garments. He let the black velvet settle about his shoulders. One of his manservants materialised apparently from thin air to assist. Used to such fawning, Kieryn shooed the servant to go fetch his crown. This was the armour he wore against the schemes of those who sought his ruin.

"We shall see what the king's council has to say to their lord and master."

Kieryn ignored the appraising gaze of Lord Whitoak as the servant returned with his crown. He may have started his reign as an underaged boy; now he was a formidable man. The king's council had made a grave misstep.

Perhaps they thought their actions would go unnoticed. Or that he would be apathetic. Or they had simply underestimated him. Fools.

"Come." Kieryn swept out of his personal quarters without a backward glance. Lord Whitoak followed in his infuriated wake as a frightened hush fell over the corridors.

When the heavy doors of the audience chamber loomed before them, two servants rushed forward. Kieryn did not hesitate. He stormed through the open doorway to stand before the King's council. Several lords and ladies looked up at the interruption and quaked at his palpable rage. *Good.*

"What is the meaning of this, my lords?" Kieryn's voice boomed across the expanse of the chamber. Striding forward, he glared in Lord Solan's direction as he ascended his throne. He paused to arrange his robes about him to give his council time to answer. When none of the members attempted to respond, he barked, "Well, what do you have to say for yourselves?"

"Perhaps if Your Majesty would kindly let us know what you are asking," Lord Solan injected, sounding confused by his King's ire.

"What I am asking you, Lord Solan," Kieryn continued, his voice soft. "My command was to detain Donatein Manideep to await my pleasure. So why did my council think it was permissible to sign a death warrant in my stead?"

"Your Majesty, the man in question was a commoner," Lord Kamoore replied. His tone conveyed he thought the council's action was more than reasonable. "We need only a vote of three within the council ..."

"The last time I checked, Lord Kamoore, the burden of final judgement is on my shoulders. The crown of Rama sits on *my* head."

"Majesty, we meant no disrespect," Lord Frayn said. His eyes, darting over to Solan, belied how nervous he was. "The prisoner had withheld information that could help us with the search for Prince Carvelle."

"Yet, Lord Frayn, I have not seen this information. One must wonder why?"

"My apologies, my King," Lord Solan murmured, producing a sheath of parchments with a flourish. He approached the King with measured strides, holding them out. "I trust you will find these documents enlightening."

Kieryn resisted the urge to snatch the parchment from Solan. Instead, he took and inspected the documents covered in his brother's elegant handwriting.

"We have apologised, Your Majesty."

"I am not a child for you to chastise! I am your High King," Kieryn snapped. "I have more important things to worry about than woollen cloaks from Sion, Lord Kamoore."

Wrapping his magenta cloak about his shoulders, Lord Kamoore slumped in his chair, bristling at the insult.

"Those journal entries are in your brother's handwriting," Lord Solan said. "They indicate numerous facts which are a concern not only to your crown but also to our nation."

Kieryn pierced his least-favourite council member with a hard stare. With every passing moment the crown felt heavier.

"Firstly, Jodathyn was clearly able to predict Prince Carvelle's kidnapping and murder. As far as I am aware, the council was not told about Jodathyn's visions. Secondly, Jodathyn stopped taking the herbs to suppress the dragon within him – a deliberate act of rebellion."

"How could it be deliberate if Jodathyn didn't know we were drugging him?" Whitoak snarled.

Kieryn sent him a grateful glance. He hoped that Lord Whitoak's heart was softening towards his brother.

"Thirdly ..." Lord Kamoore paused, fiddling with a heavy golden clasp on his cloak. He looked around the chamber for support.

"*Yes?*" Kieryn prompted, his voice thick with sarcasm.

"He predicts the rise of a dragon coming from a great house," Lord Solan replied. "He even illustrated the beast. The king of dragons."

Kieryn looked down at the last parchment and willed his hands to stop shaking. Jodathyn had illustrated a great winged beast, with strong claws and talons. Its right foreleg was crushing the throne. Under the illustration, Jodathyn had written, *A dragon born from a great house is coming to take the throne.*

"What house in Rama is more powerful than your own, Your Majesty?" Lord Frayn said.

"It says *a great house*," Kieryn said.

"That points to more than one family," a lady added.

"Well," Lord Solan said. He paused and pursed his lips, trying to look as if what he wanted to say pained him. Kieryn wasn't fooled. His cold eyes spoke of how much he enjoyed creating havoc. "There's more news, Your Majesty."

"What news?" Kieryn's voice was tight. He clenched his fists on the armrest of his throne and ground his teeth.

"My men, who I graciously offered to aid Your Majesty in your search, have recovered a body."

Kieryn shot upright. "A body!" he exclaimed. "*Carvelle? Jodathyn?* Why wasn't I informed?"

"No," Lord Solan replied. A feral grin of victory lit his pointed face. "A common man."

Annoyed that Lord Solan had flustered him, Kieryn leant back in his golden throne and scrutinised the lord. "That's hardly news, my Lord Solan."

"It's news when the man was murdered."

Kieryn grunted.

"The murder weapon." Lord Solan held up a leather belt with a dramatic flourish. At first the belt seemed unremarkable. Then Lord Solan approached, ascended the steps, and, with a bow left the belt at Kieryn's feet. Kieryn stared down at the alleged murder weapon, his stomach plummeting.

"As you can see, Your Majesty, the leather of the belt is clearly inlaid with the royal family insignia – you can see the flaming crown and sword. Yourself and Jodathyn are the only men alive to whom the belt could belong."

"Where was this found?" Kieryn could only gawk down at the belt with rising horror.

"The belt belonging to Jodathyn was found around a man's neck."

"Do not provoke me, Solan! I am the High King of Rama."

Lord Solan merely dipped his head in reply.

"The area has been searched," Lord Frayn said, glancing between the King and Lord Solan.

"What is concerning is that Jodathyn is a murderer," Lord Kamoore commented.

"Nonsense," Lord Whitoak scoffed, "All we know is, Jodathyn's belt was used to kill a man. We don't know what happened or why it happened. You are jumping to conclusions."

Kieryn pinched the bridge of his nose and listened to his council argue. He was the most powerful man in all of Rama, and he was powerless.

"Jodathyn's man you had sentenced to death – bring him to me," Kieryn commanded.

A hush fell over the council before Frayn said, his voice quivering, "Majesty, I am afraid we cannot."

Kieryn closed his eyes. He was certain he already knew the answer to his next question. "Why ever not?"

"The sentence was carried out this dawn," Lord Kamoore said. "Donatein Manideep is dead."

Defeated, Kieryn returned to his personal quarters and removed his robes. The king's council thought him so blind that he would not see that some members were plotting against him.

He was torn. He wanted to forget his duty as the reigning king and go find his son. On the other hand, he knew that in order to safeguard his family, he had to find a way to topple Solan from his seat of power.

Jodathyn's life wasn't the only one at stake. A loyal servant had been executed and another had been forced to flee Pallaryn. He had delayed Donatein's trial, stating he was too unwell, in a bid to save the old man's life. When he had been told of the young horseman's escape, Kieryn had refused to allow guards or lawmen to pursue him. If the boy was smart, he would run to a port city and leave Rama's shores.

Lord Solan had smirked as he told the council of Donatein's defiance. On the gallows, Donatein confessed that he loved Jodathyn as a son and would gladly lay his life down for him. Even though the old man's devotion to Jodathyn was forbidden, Kieryn had encouraged his closeness to his brother. Donatein had been good for Jodathyn.

With a tired, desperate sob, Kieryn hung his head. He had been out manoeuvred. The harsh reality was that his son was missing and the council was plotting to remove Jodathyn.

They now knew that the dragon within Jodathyn was stirring. Jodathyn's relationship to him would not be enough to stay the executioner's axe. His brother's only hope for survival was if someone smuggled him out of the country.

Feeling a surge of determination to find a way to help Jodathyn, he returned to his desk to start further correspondence with his neighbour. The Sionian people were fond of adoption. The King of Sion had been quite taken with his younger brother. If Jodathyn gave up his Pallarus bloodline and was adopted into a Sionian household, he could not be persecuted by the council.

His eyes flicked up to a mirror and caught sight of a reflection.

Will Hartcurt was standing the shadows, waiting for Kieryn to notice him.

"What have you found?"

"Jodathyn has been at my safehouse, my King."

"Jodathyn? Carvelle?"

Will stepped forward, a tiny piece of parchment between his fingers. "This was left on the table. It was a message I handed Jodathyn at the Autumn Festival. There is evidence of several men ransacking the safehouse. I can only hope that Fy and Jodathyn fled."

"What message did you give my brother?"

"I warned him of danger, and that Solan was a threat to him." Will's face was inscrutable in the reflection. He stepped forward and placed the slip of parchment by the King's hand.

"Solan is convinced that Jodathyn killed a man."

"It's possible, my King," Will murmured. "When cornered, a man is capable of many things."

"That worries me."

"Betraying you has never crossed Jodathyn's mind," Will said. "He longs to make you proud. He loves Carvelle. He adores the Queen. My King, Jodathyn wouldn't willingly do something to harm your family."

"I am proud of him."

"If I may, Majesty. Whitoak's stable spy who started this vendetta against Jodathyn is gone. I don't like it. The worm was also in the pay of Lord Solan and he hated Jodathyn. Furthermore, Whitoak may have sent a rider, but I would hesitate to put my trust fully on him."

"Whitoak is loyal," Kieryn growled. He had tried to convince Will of Whitoak's worth, but Will despised his favourite. He was aware of Will's efforts to undermine Whitoak, but he did not involve himself in the squabbling of his courtiers.

"Whitoak is not always truthful, my King," Will cautioned. "He himself is full of deceit."

"Yet you have brought me no proof."

"Walk the streets of Pallaryn, Majesty, with your mind open and your ears ready to listen to the lowest born. That should be the only proof you need," Will muttered. A half-hearted sneer tugged on his lips as Kieryn raised his eyebrows at his daring outburst.

Kieryn considered his next words carefully. Only two years older than Jodathyn, Will was a source he trusted. If Will's words held only a speck of truth, perhaps they were worth investigating for himself, without relying on Hallidyn Whitoak. "If something happens to me, I will be relying on you to keep Odelle safe."

Will's lips parted, he sucked in a breath to speak and then thought better of it. He considered Kieryn with his brown, intelligent eyes. "You saved my life, Your Majesty. I am forever loyal."

"I didn't save you for your gifts, Will," Kieryn sighed.

"I know, my King. I will fight for House Pallarus to my dying day."

Kieryn's fingers played with the parchment. "Find me something to justify removing Solan's treacherous head from his neck."

CHAPTER TWENTY-THREE

Jodathyn

The Intersecting Roads

J odathyn felt immense relief when he scrambled out of the thick undergrowth. Thankful they had made it through Malara Gorge, he stepped out onto the road. He could see where the roads intersected. Travelling would now be less of a strain on his leg.

"Look, Uncle, we did it!" Carvelle shouted. He bounded past with a cry of delight.

Jodathyn stretched and cracked his back. He wasn't sure where Carvelle got his endless energy from. "Uncle needs a rest. Don't go far, Carvelle."

Too exhausted to care, Jodathyn sat down on the dusty road. He searched through their belongings for something to drink, only to find the canteen empty.

"*Rshon hanoch!*" Jodathyn resisted the urge to throw the canteen. He closed his eyes, ignoring his throbbing leg. Carvelle was quiet – he would rest for a minute.

Jodathyn let the whisper of the wind and the sighing of the rustling trees lull him. When his head suddenly jerked forward, he realised he had dozed. His eyes snapped open. He had been relying on Carvelle's inability to stay still to keep him alert. He hadn't heard a peep from his nephew. He was too quiet.

"Carvelle!"

Jodathyn stood, feeling a fluttering of panic.

"Uncle!"

Turning towards Carvelle's small cry, Jodathyn was shocked to see his nephew being restrained by a vaguely familiar face. An ugly dagger was pressed under Carvelle's chin. His nephew's lips quivered. Jodathyn cursed. How long had he been asleep?

"Don't do anything reckless, *rshon hanoch.*" Jodathyn unsheathed the sword he was carrying, raising it. He forced a fearsome sneer onto his lips. "I've killed a man for less."

"I've seen you fight, Jodathyn. You don't have it in you to spill blood."

"You're the stable hand that got me the cloak, then betrayed me?" Jodathyn felt a flicker of recognition at the man's voice.

"Aye."

"You stole my grey cloak."

"Aye."

"Rip his throat out!"

"What do you want?" Jodathyn demanded. He took another step forward.

"I'm going back to Pallaryn. I will be hailed a hero."

Jodathyn snarled. "What about Prince Carvelle?"

"I will tell Papa the truth – that you are an awful, lying simpleton."

The stable hand sneered at them, his eyes hardening in malicious glee. "I guess I don't have to return the princeling alive to be a hero. Drop your weapon."

Jodathyn wished Valt had taught him how to free a hostage. He raised his sword. "Your greed will be your own doom."

The stable hand laughed. "I'm not the one about to die."

"Are you sure about that?"

If Jodathyn was surprised to see the stable boy out on the road, he was astonished to see Orion, mounted on Lord Whitoak's prized stallion. His manservant had his bow notched and ready.

Jodathyn wondered if the stable hand knew of the legendary skills of the horsemen of Silverdyne. He had heard Orion telling Valt his preferred weapon was his bow. There was no doubt that Orion was already on his way to mastering the sword that was belted to his hip.

The stable hand pressed the dagger a little higher under Carvelle's chin, until he nicked the skin. A drop of blood dripped onto the dusty road.

"Rain fire down on him," the voice in his head snarled. *"He has our Prince."*

"Are you going to risk it, horse boy?" said the stable hand, gloating.

Jodathyn knew by the hard look on Orion's face that the stable hand had signed his own death warrant. He should have taken his opportunity to turn tail and flee into the forest. Orion didn't bother to reply to the jibe. He loosed his arrow. The stable hand tumbled to the ground, dead, the arrow wedged between his eyes. Shrieking in horror, Carvelle leapt away from his captor and into Jodathyn's waiting arms.

"Yes, I'll risk it." Orion lowered his bow, surveying his handiwork. His brown eyes swept over the tearful Prince, wrapped in Jodathyn's embrace.

Murmuring soothing words, Jodathyn turned his body in an attempt to spare Carvelle the sight of the dead man lying on the dusty road. Grateful, he nodded in his manservant's direction.

"I'm sorry if I upset the Prince," Orion said. "I didn't want to give the knave time to harm him."

"I'm not upset. I think you might be my hero." Sniffling, Carvelle wiped his face on Jodathyn's tunic. He turned adoring eyes onto Orion as he pointed to the body. "I think he might be dead."

"He is not getting up after that shot, my Prince." Orion's lips twitched with dark humour as he dismounted and marched over to the body on the road. He knelt, then in one swift motion wrenched the arrow from the corpse's skull. Inspecting the arrow, Orion cursed and tossed it to the side. He stared down the road, his eyes glassy and unseeing. Jodathyn noticed a slight tremble in his manservant's hands.

"Are you well?" Jodathyn asked.

Orion refused to make eye contact. "I should be fine. No one will miss him ... I'm fine."

"First kill?" There was a note of curiosity in Jodathyn's voice.

Rubbing his hands on his trousers, Orion looked over his shoulder.

"As you said, no one will miss him ... Try to dismiss it from your mind," Jodathyn said, shuddering at the memory of his own kill.

Orion gave a jerky nod.

"How did you find me?" Jodathyn wasn't sure he wanted to know the answer. But he needed to say something to distract Orion. "And why do you have Lord Whitoak's horse? I can't imagine he let you borrow him."

"I stole the horse," Orion admitted, his eyes shifting away. "Lady Illeanah allowed me to escape. She said she loved you still."

Remembering his poor behaviour at the Autumn Festival, Jodathyn felt something crumble inside of him.

"As to how I found you?" Orion continued. "I met a man called Ruevyn."

"Where's my Papa?" Prince Carvelle demanded, stamping his little foot. "I want Papa. Take me to him!"

"Your Highness," Orion murmured with a slight, clumsy bow; he glanced at Jodathyn from under his fringe.

"Stop bowing. Where's Papa?"

Orion glanced between the young Prince and his master, biting his lip. "I apologise, my Prince, but I had to leave the palace quite suddenly."

"Come, Carvelle, why don't you take my pack and find somewhere nice for us to have a rest and something to eat?"

"You just had a rest," Carvelle said.

"My servant hasn't," Jodathyn replied, with a wink in Orion's direction.

Jodathyn and Orion watched the little Prince take the pack and walk away, muttering to himself. As soon as he was out of earshot, Jodathyn rounded onto Orion. "I can tell something terrible has happened. Tell me."

Orion bit his lip, turning his face away before whispering, "Valt was found dead."

Jodathyn exhaled, his shoulders slumping. Considering he'd seen no sign of his personal guard, he wasn't shocked by Orion's news. In the back of his mind he had been preparing himself to hear confirmation of Valt's death.

"He told me to run. Was it ... bad?"

"Master, dying by sword is not a kind way to die. Valt did his duty in allowing you time to escape with your life," Orion replied. "He wouldn't want you to fret over his death."

Although Orion's statement was true, the thought of Valt's demise brought a strange taste to Jodathyn's mouth. He couldn't help but feel some responsibility for the manner in which he'd died.

"The palace also suspects you as the chief conspirator."

"*What?*"

Orion nodded his head in confirmation. "I caught Donatein looking through your papers. He found something that concerned him. He hid the paper ..." Orion shivered. "We should have slipped out of the palace that night."

"*And ...?*"

Orion shifted. "We were betrayed. I had only moments to warn Donatein that the guards were coming to search your rooms. He was arrested."

Jodathyn swore and ran a hand through his unkempt hair. "And you fled with the horse."

Orion grunted. "Lady Illeanah let me escape with him. Is that still stealing?"

"Yes. She can never admit allowing you to flee."

"If either of us return to the capital, we're dead men," Orion said. "I tried to get Donatein to come. He wouldn't ... he wanted me to find you and let you know you were in danger."

Jodathyn gestured about them with an air of helplessness. "I had gathered that."

He led Orion over to where Carvelle had set up a picnic. Sitting beside his nephew, Jodathyn took the food Carvelle offered and began to eat. He raised an eyebrow when Orion ignored the food and tended to the horse nearby. Sighing, he retrieved his tin of herbs from the pack. His servant looked to him and then the tin in his hands.

"Are you hurt, Master?" Orion asked. He was more alert than Jodathyn had thought.

"Just a nick," Jodathyn mumbled.

"There was so much blood," Carvelle said, waving his hands about. "Ruevyn sewed Uncle Jodathyn up with a needle. Ruevyn said Uncle was very brave but I think Mumma's sewing is neater."

Orion tilted his head to the side. "This afternoon you should ride. To take some weight off your leg."

"I'm fine."

"Master, a wise man would get on the horse," Orion replied.

"You're good with horses," Carvelle said with a mouthful of food.

"Aye," Orion replied, returning his gaze resolutely to the stallion.

"Lord Whitoak's horse suits you very well," Carvelle stated. "I'm Carvelle, what's your name?"

"Orion, Highness."

"Come, sit, I will not begrudge you a rest." Carvelle patted the ground next to him. "Talk to me – I don't speak to common folk very often."

Orion glanced down at his hands as he sunk down to sit next to the Prince. He stole a look at Jodathyn, as if he was expecting to be chastised. Content to listen to Carvelle's chatter, Jodathyn smiled and returned to his food.

"Aren't you hungry? Here, have some nuts." Carvelle took a handful of nuts and dried fruit, dumping them unceremoniously on Orion's lap. "How old are you?"

"Sixteen," Orion muttered. He regarded the food Carvelle had given him in confusion.

"If my lessons are correct, you are from Silverdyne. The braided horseman's lock on the left-hand side of your temple tells me you haven't killed before."

"That would be correct."

"You killed today. When Papa finds us, I will have to tell him that you should now braid on the right-hand side of the temple," Carvelle said, in his serious, no-nonsense tone.

Orion blinked.

"Right-hand side means that you have killed for the Crown or have shown some great feat of loyalty to the Crown, no?"

"That is correct, my Prince."

"I should order you to change it now," Carvelle said. He stood to reach out to touch Orion's braid. "Here I'll help you."

"I think there would be a great deal of people unhappy about that, Your Highness," Orion replied stiffly.

The young prince froze, an expression of puzzlement on his young face. "But you saved me."

"It's your father's decision, Carvelle, and his alone." Jodathyn finally spoke up, thinking perhaps he should rescue his helpless manservant from his nephew's enthusiasm.

"Well, when we get back to Pallaryn, I'm going to drag you in front of Papa and tell him that you shot a man dead on the road to save me. Papa will have no choice in the matter but to decree that you change your lock."

Jodathyn had reluctantly agreed to ride, after Orion insisted he mount the stallion. He hadn't realised how obstinate his manservant could be. When Orion served him back at the palace, his subservience had annoyed Jodathyn.

With few courtiers willing to befriend him, Jodathyn liked to be on friendly terms with those that served him. Many of the rich and powerful looked down upon him because of his relationship with Donatein and Valt, but he'd never cared.

"It was suggested that we make our escape to Belrah. Then move on to Androssah, to Lord Whitoak's estate. We can be sure to get help there," Jodathyn said as Orion helped Carvelle into the saddle. He settled his nephew before him, wrapping his arm around his slim waist.

"Are you sure we can trust Lord Whitoak, Master?" Orion turned to fiddle with his bow, refusing to look at Jodathyn as he spoke.

"He is my brother's favourite," Jodathyn said, shrugging. "I have no one else to turn to. Would you suggest going to Silverdyne to your people?"

Orion's head dipped further. "Only trouble awaits me in Silverdyne. I didn't leave on good terms."

"Androssah then," Jodathyn said.

"I only have a little coin." Orion grabbed the reins. "If we are still out in the elements when the weather turns, we are going to need it."

Jodathyn grunted, and they made their way into Belrah in relative silence. He had never had to sleep outdoors in the elements before now. He hoped Orion had more experience with such things.

Jodathyn felt a sense of wonderment as they entered Belrah. It was a small settlement. No more than eighty huts were grouped together to make the town. Although Jodathyn had only seen illustrations of villages in books, he recognised the stylised layout of the ancient Ramians, who preferred their towns to have a circular pattern.

"There should be a market square where we can take a rest," Orion said.

"We've only been walking a few hours," Jodathyn replied. Part of him wanted nothing more than to spend the night in the village in a bed. But he couldn't ask Orion to part with his coin to pay for a luxury.

"We should rest before we head out again to the next village. It's only common sense."

Jodathyn sat in the saddle, enjoying the hustle and bustle of village life. From his vantage point mounted on the horse, he could hear a baker yelling over the milling crowds about his fresh meat pies. To his left a barmaid was chasing one of the tavern's small serving boys with a raised broom.

"Stay here," Orion warned as they entered the market square.

Jodathyn swung awkwardly from the saddle. Orion came to his side, gripping his elbow to steady him as he stumbled.

"You're in pain, Master. Do you need a healer?"

Shaking his head, Jodathyn helped Carvelle from the saddle. "My leg is healing. I wouldn't waste your coin unnecessarily."

Orion frowned at him. "Rest here, I'll take a look around."

Grateful for the chance to stretch his legs, Jodathyn decided that taking too much of the herbs would be unwise. Instead, he took Ruevyn's apple from his pocket. With a smile he bit down into the fruit, enjoying the fresh, sweet juice as it dripped down his chin.

"Uncle, that was a gift from Ruevyn!"

"Friendship and loyalty are meant to be partaken of," Jodathyn replied with a wink, offering Carvelle the second half of the apple.

The Prince took a great big bite. "It's good."

Jodathyn felt the burden of Orion's and Carvelle's safety settle upon his shoulders as he watched his manservant weaving among the common folk. In a cruel twist of fate, it would be his doom if he returned to Pallaryn. This sure knowledge that he couldn't go home unsettled the beast inside of him. His only real option was to flee the council's anger. He couldn't take Carvelle with him.

If only he hadn't set foot in the forest that day ...

"Ah," replied the traitorous voice in his head. *"If you hadn't followed Carvelle, our nephew would be dead."*

Head in his hands, Jodathyn whispered a prayer for Valt. It felt pointless. There was no bringing Valt back from the dead.

Trying to push Valt from his mind only made Jodathyn think of Donatein. He hoped the old man was being treated well.

When he was a child, Jodathyn had had an unpleasant stint in the dungeons. Lord Kamoore had heard the crazed cook yelling at him when he'd investigated the kitchens. Grabbing Jodathyn by the scruff of the neck, Kamoore had marched him to the cool bowels of the dungeons.

"This is what becomes of naughty boys," Kamoore had told him, throwing a tearful Jodathyn into a dark cell.

For hours, Jodathyn had cried himself hoarse, until one curious jailor decided to see what the fuss was about. The astounded man had released and returned him to Donatein.

Apparently, after putting an emotional Jodathyn to bed, Donatein had accosted Kieryn's manservants, demanding to see the King. When Donatein was told he wasn't allowed to, the old man erupted. News of the disagreement reached Kieryn's ears.

It was said that when Kieryn heard Donatein's complaints, he summoned his council and flew into a terrible rage. The furious King had thrown a full goblet of wine at the stunned Lord Kamoore.

Since that day, the dungeons had featured heavily in Jodathyn's nightmares. He hated the thought of the old man alone in a dark cell, awaiting judgement.

"Do you have a plan, Master?" Orion had returned. He seemed worried as he studied Jodathyn's face.

Jodathyn looked down at Carvelle, who was enjoying rummaging through the pack.

"The little boy's life is more important than our own."

"Carvelle needs to get back home," Jodathyn murmured, trying to quash the voice in his head, even though he agreed with it. "That's more important than my own safety. We continue onto Androssah."

"But nor do we want to needlessly throw our lives away," Orion said. "I quite like my head where it is!"

Jodathyn snorted back laughter. "Even if we sent a message ahead to the King, we couldn't be certain he'd get it."

"We need to try to get a message through anyway."

"We should keep moving," Orion suggested.

Jodathyn shrugged on the pack, taking Carvelle's hand in his own as they stood. He followed Orion as his servant began to lead him to the far side of the town.

"We need to try and get a message to Pallaryn, even if we have doubts it would get to my brother," Jodathyn said, wishing his visions could give him a clearer picture of what to do.

They rounded a corner and found themselves pressed into a crowd. They had no choice but to pause their trek.

"You can't do this to us!" someone shrieked. The frightened voice sent a chill up Jodathyn's spine. Craning his neck, he caught sight of a small line of prisoners being forced into a transport cart. Jodathyn watched with a mix of confusion and pity.

"Go drown yourselves in a cesspool!" the prisoner screamed.

Orion touched Jodathyn's sleeve. "It's best not to get involved."

Jodathyn continued to stare after the prisoner. He was shocked to realise it was a young woman, wearing men's trousers. Her strange ashen hair was cropped to just below her ears. Her pale face was gaunt, as if she had been recently ill.

The voice in Jodathyn's head rumbled with laughter. *"Oh! I like! Get her."*

"My brother didn't do it! He didn't do it! You mangled clay-brained codpiece! He didn't do it!" The woman fought against the guards holding her. When one slapped her, she halted, before lunging at him with her teeth. Her hazel eyes were cold with fury.

Entranced by the scene, Jodathyn looked for her brother. A dark-haired boy was pushed to the ground. Where his sister was muscular, he was willowy. One of the guards booted him in the stomach, telling him to get up. A whoosh of air left his lungs as he collapsed.

"Theo!" the girl screamed, kicking the guard in the shin. "Leave him alone. Theo!"

"She's fierce. She would be good for our team."

The guards laughed and kicked her brother again. She howled in outrage.

"This isn't right," Jodathyn muttered, feeling sorrow for the prisoners. He pushed through the jeering crowd until he was standing before the spectacle. Crouching before Theo, Jodathyn grasped his elbow and helped him to his feet. Jodathyn could feel the creature in him move beneath the surface of his skin as he touched the prisoner. The other boy's eyes widened as he took in his rescuer's features.

"This one is smart. He sees me."

What do you mean he sees you? Jodathyn asked the voice in his head.

The creature within seemed to ripple in pleasure. *"You speak, human heart. I thought you never would. This one before us can see the dragon. He sees me. Yes, I like this one too!"*

Jodathyn bit back a curse. His dragon wanted him to rescue criminals.

"Move!" One of the guards pushed Jodathyn to the side. He didn't understand the guard's intention, until he wrapped his fingers around a silver earring in the prisoner's ear. Horrified, the prisoner cried out, realising the guard intended to rip his earring from his flesh.

"No!" Jodathyn cried. "Don't touch him!"

"Payment," the guard grunted.

Orion barged forward, grabbing onto Jodathyn's elbow. He felt his servant's fingers dig into his skin. "Take these two silver coins!" Orion spat. "Leave him alone, you coward."

The guard took the offered coins, shoving them into his coat. He hauled Theo to his feet and didn't look back as he marched his prisoners away.

Jodathyn returned to where Carvelle was playing with the grey stallion's reins, blissfully unaware of what was happening around him.

Orion followed, shaking his head. "We don't want to be making a fuss, Master. I only have one coin left."

"Why did you pay the man?"

"Didn't want you to cause a bigger scene. Not that it's going to make too much difference to them."

Unimpressed, Jodathyn stared back.

"They are bound for Artroth. They're good as slaves now," Orion said in a low voice.

"But Kieryn halted the prison ships ..."

"Looks like Solan and Kamoore don't care."

"Why would you say that?"

"In this part of the country, Lord Solan or Kamoore would benefit from their sale to the prison ships." Orion stared after the unfortunate men and women. "Poor sods."

Since meeting Fydellah that night in Pallaryn, a fire had been stoked in Jodathyn's belly. It was anger for men like Solan who profited from other people's pain. Why not hurt the great lords while he still had freedom? If he was to die because of those who plotted against him, at least he could die honourably. He had told the council and the King he would end things

...

Would freeing two prisoners hurt Solan?

"We have to start somewhere," the voice inside purred. *"Two lives saved is better than two lives lost."*

"When I was a child, I played with the servants," Jodathyn said out loud to Orion.

"I heard rumours of that," Orion replied.

"I freed a few of them," Jodathyn confessed.

Orion raised his eyebrows.

"We could be heroes today," Jodathyn said. "We could free some souls and start my revenge on Solan's purse strings."

"And tomorrow we could be swinging on the gallows," Orion muttered.

Chapter Twenty-Four

Jodathyn

The Village of Belrah

"Are you deranged, Master?" Orion exploded in disbelief. He lowered his voice. "That's outright dangerous."

"I like the idea," Carvelle said.

"We don't even know their crimes," Orion ground out. "They could be murderers or kidnappers. I would have thought you'd have had your fill of those."

"One way to find out," Jodathyn replied. He grinned at Orion, who stared at him as if he wanted to say something but was afraid. Before his servant could gather his courage and form an argument, Jodathyn pushed his way through the crowds.

"Master ..."

Without checking over his shoulder, Jodathyn knew Orion was positioning himself close by in case he was needed. Finding a lawman, he approached, his chin downcast, in case his eyes gave him away. He tapped the man on the shoulder.

The lawman turned, studied and dismissed Jodathyn as a threat in seconds. "Yes," he drawled. "What do you want?"

"What crimes did those prisoners commit?"

"They're thieves, every single one," the lawman grunted, spitting on the ground. "Good riddance, I say."

Grimacing, Jodathyn thanked the man and stepped cautiously away. Feeling victorious, Jodathyn sauntered back to where Orion and Carvelle were waiting for him.

"They're thieves," he said.

"How exactly are thieves going to help us?" Orion huffed. "For that matter, how are we going to rescue them?"

Jodathyn didn't answer. Instead, he lifted Carvelle back onto the horse and without a word started walking out of the village. Moments later he could hear Orion's footsteps and his cursing. Jodathyn grinned.

"You are becoming braver," Jodathyn commented as they left the front gate of the village. "I like this version of you better than the submissive servant."

"Rural villages are where I am comfortable." Orion glanced around as if expecting to be sprung by a lawman at any moment. "If I'm going to die, I might as well take the opportunity to give you lip."

Jodathyn snorted.

"Have you never wanted to tell someone in a higher position exactly what you are thinking?"

"Frequently," Jodathyn replied. "Much to my brother's annoyance ..."

"Someone needs to be honest with those lordly types."

"Father says Kamoore is Dragon Dung," Carvelle said, keen to add his own perspective.

Jodathyn exchanged an amused glance with Orion and laughed. "*Rshon mahthyt* in the ancient tongue."

They followed the prison cart, watching for an opportunity. Jodathyn hoped the voice within him would come up with some ideas on how to rescue the thieves. Orion was the only one in their group who was any good with weapons.

"I would prefer not to have to shoot anyone today," Orion said.

Jodathyn wasn't listening. He was watching the guards. They had halted the carts and had wandered off as a group to relieve themselves. A hazy plan was starting to form in his head. The guards were clearly poorly trained and they weren't in a hurry to finish their business to attend to their prisoners.

"Did you notice?"

"Notice what, Master?"

"When the guards relieve themselves, they take their time. They spent a good time with their backs turned, drinking, eating and er ... pissing. No one is watching the prisoners."

"I never wanted to go to court and be placed in the middle of a conspiracy." Orion sighed. "What's the plan?"

"When they stop again, what is to stop us from taking the prisoners? They won't notice."

"It could work," Orion admitted. "It also means I don't have to shoot anyone."

"It's brilliant," Carvelle declared. "My uncle is a genius."

While they were still at an inconspicuous distance, Jodathyn left the road to follow the cart. Orion remained with Carvelle, falling behind with the horse, so that they wouldn't appear to be a threat. In the shadows of the trees Jodathyn tracked the cart, waiting for the moment to stage the escape.

The guards quarrelled among themselves, drinking and shouting, while their prisoners glared out of their cage with expressions that varied between angry and resigned. As one of their number taunted the prisoners, the woman his dragon liked rushed at the bars with a curse, clutching at them with strong fingers as she snarled and snapped. "What are you looking at, you lumpish dog-hearted clotpole?"

"We can give that brother of yours another beating, my ash-haired harpy." The woman stepped back in defeat and slumped down beside her brother. Delighted, the guards made fun of her distress.

"Soon dragoness..."

The guards stopped a short while later, needing to relieve themselves after drinking copious amounts of beer. Jodathyn crept towards the cart, careful to keep his body close to the ground. A finger to his lips, he shushed the prisoners as he emerged from the bushes. With impossible ease he slid the bolt from the cart and the door swung open. The prisoners tumbled out.

Jodathyn wasn't interested in most of them – he let them pass, waiting for his targets. Grabbing the arm of the boy with the earring, Jodathyn looked around for his sister. She was only a few paces away, glaring at him.

"Follow me." Jodathyn let go of the prisoner and darted into the undergrowth. In the split second the young man studied him, Jodathyn knew his dragon had been recognised for what he was.

"I'm Theo and this is Nym. And you are?"

Jodathyn shook his head. This wasn't the time for introductions.

"Theo!" Nym hissed stamping after them. "Come back here!"

"Hush, Nym!" Theo hissed. "We don't want the guards to hear us!"

Jodathyn paused at the base of a tree. "Climb. As long as you are quiet the guards won't look up."

The young woman opened her mouth to argue.

"Climb." Jodathyn smiled, flashing his perfect white teeth and shoved her forward.

Jaw tight, she obeyed. Her brother scuttled after her. Waiting until the prisoners were hidden, Jodathyn slipped through the trees and back to the road to join Orion and Carvelle.

Taking the horse's reins, Jodathyn struggled to keep a straight face as the guards up ahead discovered the empty cart. There was lots of shouting and waving of hands before the guards decided to approach the 'travellers' behind them.

"Good day, gentlemen." Jodathyn greeted them with a raised eyebrow. "Problem?"

"We've lost prisoners."

"Most unfortunate. Don't mind us. We're camping here."

"Your prisoners looked like such a motley crew," Orion said, strumming his fingers along his bow. He pulled the string tight and let it go with a *twang*. "I wonder what sounds they would make if I stuck them with an arrow or two?"

Chuckling, Jodathyn watched the guards as they crashed, grunting, through the undergrowth. They swung their blades, cursing as they went.

"Make camp," Jodathyn hissed to Orion. "I'll keep our new friends company."

Orion ushered Carvelle to the base of the tree where they had hidden the prisoners. They would keep watch until the guards gave up and left the area. Jodathyn gripped the trunk, and climbed.

"Uncouth louts," the woman muttered, as Jodathyn settled himself in the branches. Her hard hazel eyes were fixated on where the guards had disappeared. Jodathyn could only assume she had good cause to be so angry.

"You look quite comfortable in a tree," the young man said. "I am Theo Torkelle born of Korkalie, and this is my sister Nym. I should thank you for not allowing them to rip out my earring. I'm quite fond of it."

"You two are interesting."

"You're are a rich man," Theo continued, a large grin split his fair face.

"His clothes are not stained, Theo. Any fool can see that," Nym griped.

"I like to wash," Jodathyn replied. "Is that a crime?"

"It's his teeth that give him away," Theo said, shrugging. He chuckled as Jodathyn ran his tongue along his teeth. "You haven't told us who you are."

"There hasn't been time for introductions. We plan to camp here tonight. The guards will move on once they capture most of their wayward thieves. I am Jodathyn."

Theo froze. *"Jodathyn?"*

"Pallarus?" Nym added.

Jodathyn flushed. "I've run into some trouble. I need to get my nephew back to my brother."

"Hold on," Theo interrupted. "If you are Jodathyn Pallarus, your nephew is the Crown Prince and your brother is the High King?"

Jodathyn smiled at them winningly. "Yes."

"So that little boy is Prince Carvelle?" Nym repeated, pointing to where Carvelle was dancing about the firepit Orion was busy building. They could hear the strands of a popular children's song as the youngster sang and spun about.

"Yes."

"His father, the great and powerful High King of Rama is looking for him?"

"Yes."

"I'm guessing that since you haven't gone to a lawman, something horrible has happened?"

"Hmmm." Jodathyn wanted to avoid that question.

"Could we die if you bring us into this plot?"

Jodathyn's grey eyes darkened. "Most definitely."

"If we don't join you?" Theo pushed. He looked towards his sister, fidgeting.

Jodathyn felt a stab of disappointment. "Then you are free to go and do as you wish."

"I'm in," Nym declared.

Theo looked at her in askance. "People like us do not have happy endings when they tangle with royalty."

"If we help the High King's son, will he show us favour and hear our complaint?" Nym asked.

Jodathyn tilted his head again and smiled at them. "The King does not like whining, but if you tell me your story, I could tell you his likely reaction. I may be able to push for a pardon."

"A royal pardon?" Nym muttered. "You could do that?"

"Possibly, I do have very little power," Jodathyn replied. He sensed it was best to be honest. "Kieryn does try to be a good and fair king."

"We're thieves," Theo began. "But we weren't always thieves. Our parents owned a small plot of land."

"We had an understanding with our pathetic flea-bitten neighbours. All was well until ... until ..."

"They accused our brother of stealing from them. There was no trial. Our brother was carted off. In compensation the magistrate awarded our small plot of land to our complaining neighbours. Our parents were devastated."

"I found them hanging by their necks ... dead. The lawman threw us out on our rear ends with nothing but our clothes," Nym complained. "We've got nothing. I enter fighting bouts to win coin but we rely on Theo's thievery for our day-to-day needs."

"I used to be an apprentice stonemason. I spent my days creating works of art. When my master heard that I had lost everything, he tossed me out." Theo sent Nym a withering glare. "To shorten the story. Someone became impatient and got herself in trouble ..."

"If we could get a fair hearing," Nym insisted, "I know I can prove those maggoty mange-ridden rodents liars."

Jodathyn exhaled. "I am very sorry to hear of your misfortunes. Do you have physical proof of your brother's innocence? Kieryn prefers to have evidence before he judges."

"We have no proof," Theo said.

"If you have no proof, make friends with Carvelle. Kieryn will listen to his son's opinions."

"That is helpful advice."

But Jodathyn was shaking his head.

"Guards returning. Quiet."

"Your eyes!" Theo gasped. "They're silver ... I haven't seen anything like this before ... I can see the dragon."

"Shh," Jodathyn whispered, unaware of the dragon stirring beneath his skin. "The guards are coming back."

Sure enough, as Jodathyn spoke the guards reappeared under them.

"Did you find them?" Orion asked from the base of the tree.

"Five; missing two," grunted a guard. "They'll do. We're not running around in the forest more than we have to. Strange things have been happening. Hold on. Where's your companion?"

A breath caught in Jodathyn's throat. But Orion was ready with an answer. "Foraging," he said, shrugging his shoulders. "He has visions of a nice plump rabbit for our dinner. He's useless, though. Best we can hope for is a wild mushroom or two."

"Be careful."

"Oh, we will," Carvelle chirruped.

Jodathyn watched, a satisfied smirk on his face, as the guards lumbered off with their prisoners. When he asked Theo and Nym to wait another half an hour before climbing down, Nym growled at him, mumbling unflattering comments. Jodathyn contented himself with listening to her complaints. When he thought enough time had lapsed, he climbed down without a word.

"Useless, am I?" Jodathyn walked up to the campfire to warm himself. Theo and Nym followed in his wake.

Orion shrugged, eyeing their new members. "Occasionally."

"This is Nym and Theo Torkelle, they will be joining us," Jodathyn announced. He wrapped his arms around a giggling Carvelle. "This little charmer is Carvelle and my other companion is Orion Maysden."

"How exactly do you think we're going to be able to help a royal Dragon Lord?" Theo asked. "Couldn't you just fly Carvelle back and rip out whoever's throats?"

"We could fly if you would just let me out!"

Jodathyn dropped his hands to his sides and glanced at Theo in confusion. "I don't understand."

"You're a dragon," Theo said. "I saw him move within you before. Your eyes changed."

"I ... I ... am not ... I can't be a dragon," Jodathyn stammered.

"You'll be safer if you let me out. I could protect you."

How many people would you eat?

"Dragons don't eat people ... mostly."

How would you get out?

"Honestly, I don't know. That's for you to work out."

Theo made himself at home next to the fire. Stretching his hands towards the flames he raised his eyebrows. "How often do you fight with your dragon? It's fascinating to watch war wage across your face."

CHAPTER TWENTY-FIVE

Jodathyn

Westgate Road

Carvelle always had the talent to entertain. That night around the campfire the Prince regaled their guests with tales of 'Uncle Jod'. Jodathyn made his excuses and fled when his nephew began the tale of the Apple Tree Prince. It was not a story he wanted to hear.

Standing alone in the shadow of the tree line, Jodathyn could still hear the murmurs of voices. To distract himself he tilted his head skywards to study the stars. If he was a dragon, would he be able to touch the celestial bodies?

A soft rustling announced Orion's presence. "Master, are you alright? Is your leg aching?"

"A little. The wound is healing and the herbs numb my flesh."

"I'm afraid I was never talented with the healing arts," Orion murmured. "For that I am sorry."

"I have always had a high tolerance for pain," Jodathyn said, waving away Orion's apology. "I don't like hearing about my past."

"One day it won't seem like a festering wound, Master."

Flinching, Jodathyn was quick to change the subject. "I should thank you for leaving Pallaryn and coming to me."

Orion sighed. He stepped closer to Jodathyn and laid a hand on his shoulder. "Donatein had a message for you."

Jodathyn froze. Orion took his lack of reaction as permission to continue. "He said he wanted you to know that he loves you and he's proud."

Jodathyn nodded, not sure what he should say. As a child, when he had declared his love for Donatein, his servant had hushed him. He swallowed past the lump in his throat. Orion seemed to understand. "You should know I have some terrible secrets."

"You aren't the only one with secrets." Orion smiled in the dark. "I think in another life we might have been friends."

Jodathyn was silent for a long while, his arms crossed against his chest. Orion exhaled and withdrew his hand.

"I would like to think, Orion, that in this life you and I are friends." Jodathyn's voice was quiet. "Come, we should get back to the campfire. It doesn't take this long to relieve oneself."

"Unless you're a useless guard."

They sniggered at their own jibe as they returned to the campfire. Carvelle's prattling halted the moment he noticed Jodathyn. "It's time to sleep," Jodathyn said, beckoning to his nephew.

"Goodnight, everyone!" Scampering around the campfire, Carvelle joined Jodathyn on his bedroll. He nestled close to his uncle's chest. Before long he was asleep, snoozing in Jodathyn's protective embrace.

"I'll take first watch," Theo offered. He indicated they should all take the opportunity to rest.

Jodathyn lay awake, listening as Nym then Orion fell asleep. He pressed Carvelle closer to his side. Staring into the dying embers of their campfire, Jodathyn resisted the urge to roll over. He didn't want to disturb Carvelle.

When Jodathyn was younger, night terrors had often disrupted his sleep. Having no parents, he'd relied on Donatein's reassuring touch to calm him. He learnt to love the warm, safe scent of Donatein's nightshirt and the sound of the old man's voice in his ear.

Huffing at the memory of his past, he pressed his lips to his nephew's head. He lifted his gaze beyond the fire. Theo sat still as stone with his back to the flames.

"I'm sorry if what I said earlier upset you," Theo said, speaking to the dark.

"How did you know I was awake?"

"The power of observation." Theo turned to look at him. "You should sleep."

"Do you know about the Dragon Lords?"

"A little bit," Theo admitted. "Stonemasons need to know the legends and Ramian culture if they are going to carve something meaningful."

"What can you tell me?"

"Don't fight your dragon, let him manifest. It's the only way you'll ever feel whole."

"Manifest?"

"Do you hear his voice or see with his eyes?"

"No," Jodathyn lied. He remembered Fydellah saying something similar to him.

"Next you will become one with the dragon that lives within you." Theo didn't seem bothered by his lie. "I know what I saw. You can't ignore him forever."

Choosing to overlook Theo's remark, Jodathyn closed his eyes, stilling his body to meditate. He allowed himself to drift into unconsciousness.

Tornyth flew above the great citadel of Pallaryn. Tonight was the night he had decided to look for his human heart's father. The old one was special. Jodathyn had chosen this man as his family.

Tornyth could feel Jodathyn's fear as he surrendered to sleep. He was afraid that something might happen to Donatein. It was reasonable to assume that if he could ensure the old one's safety, Jodathyn would be calmer. A calm human was more likely to release their dragon.

Tornyth dipped his wing and flew over the palace making soft calling noises. He spiralled down to get a closer look at the human home. He made another pass, his keen silver eyes using his Sight to see if he could find any answers.

His dragon sight shimmered and he caught sight of Donatein's face. Tornyth felt a thrill of excitement. The old man would be so pleased to see him. With some confusion, Tornyth watched as his vision showed him Donatein walking along the outer wall of the palace. The servant's face was grim. The poor man missed his Jodathyn too!

Eager, Tornyth turned his horned head to study the area of the outer wall. He hoped Donatein was close by. Seconds later, Tornyth's hope was stripped from him. In horror, he hovered in place.

His dragon heart erupted with a sharp pain he had never experienced before. Bellowing, he lifted his head, so that all of Pallaryn could hear his grief. He beat his wings and reached out with his talons to grip on the thick stones of the palace wall.

He had found Donatein. Lifeless.

Crying out again, Tornyth raked his claws against the stones. Brittle shards of stone and rock crumbled, plummeting to the ground below.

Red hot rage built in his chest. He turned his snout towards the wall to breathe dragon fire upon the stones. The wall blackened under his fury.

Tornyth was not surprised by the sudden commotion of palace guards approaching. He heard their frantic footsteps and yells. They came for him, spears down and poised. Their mouths were wide with astonishment. As

Tornyth turned his crowned head to roar his anger at them, they stepped back in fright. Some even dropped their spears.

Tornyth wanted to scoff at the audacity. They recoiled from him as if he was the monster. Look what they had done to his kind, wise Donatein. The harmless old man was dead.

Carefully, Tornyth reached out a clawed talon and plucked Donatein from the wall. In disgust he looked back at the palace guards and leapt into the air with his powerful hind legs.

There was only one thing a dragon could do. He needed to take Donatein home. Flying west he headed to the fields of Habron where his loyal servant had been born.

Time all but stopped for Tornyth. He was alone in the sky with his heavy heart and tired wings. Before long he flew over a small hamlet. He decided it was best that he land nearby on a grassy hill that overlooked Habron. It would not do to unduly upset the humans that lived there.

He lay Donatein on the ground, pausing to give him an inquiring nudge, only to feel his heart break all over again when the servant did not respond to his touch.

Turning away from the shell of the man he once loved, Tornyth grasped at any stones that he could find. With each new stone he began to build a wall around Donatein. He kept with his task until Donatein was hidden from view.

Waving his head back and forth Tornyth breathed over the stones. The stones melted, becoming soft until they were liquid. They intertwined before fusing together into a black, shiny tomb.

Tornyth lay down beside the tomb as he cried dragon tears for a man who had shown him nothing but kindness. Oh, he knew he had been suppressing his dragon half and it was a horrible thing to do. But Tornyth forgave him.

Nose to tail, Tornyth curled himself around the tomb. He stayed wrapped around Donatein, rumbling.

Believing he was alone in his grief, Tornyth was astonished to hear another deeper rumbling that replied to his own. The sound seemed to be a command telling him to stay where he was. Something was coming for him.

Tornyth shifted uncomfortably as a shadow flew overhead. He did not want to leave Donatein alone. He growled. Satisfied that he had sufficiently warned away anyone foolish enough to disturb him, Tornyth closed his eyes.

The beating of strong wings and a thud interrupted Tornyth's soft keening. Shocked that his warning had gone unheeded, Tornyth's eyes shot open as he raised his head. He stood, his movements sluggish as he sought the intruder.

A dragon with glistening emerald scales stood before him. Tornyth had thought he was a large dragon, but this newcomer was colossal. Amber eyes that glittered with centuries of wisdom studied him.

With the unworried gait of one who was larger and mightier, the green dragon approached. Reeling back, Tornyth snarled.

"That's quite enough of that, hatchling," the green dragon rumbled.

Tornyth lowered his head to the ground, slinking further away. He swished his tail back and forth, growling low in his throat.

"Enough," the green dragon commanded.

Tornyth wearily backed himself further around Donatein's tomb. His claws dug into the soft earth beneath him, gauging deep rivets into the ground.

The green dragon eyed the tomb with amusement. "That is an interesting use of your dragon talents."

Tornyth lowered himself and prepared to leap into the air to fly away.

"Stay," the green dragon commanded.

Tornyth reared in horror when he realised that at the green dragon's word he could not fly away.

"Are you afraid of me, little white scales?"

Tornyth didn't reply, but quaked in the great dragon's presence. If the green dragon wished to end him, he wouldn't have a chance to defend himself.

"Who are you?" Tornyth demanded.

The green dragon studied him once more. "You truly don't know? I am Mandros the Deliverer, the Father of this Land. I am Flame and Fury."

"You're not very humble."

"Hatchling, when you're my age you don't need to be humble." Mandros took a further step forward. He sniffed the wind. "You are Tornyth, Winter's Dragon. You are the Return of Glory for dragonkind."

Tornyth lowered himself to the ground and swayed his head back and forth. "You're teasing. Me, glorious?"

Mandros tilted his head to one side; his luminous amber eyes softened. "Yes, you are rather on the small side for a dragon. I have never seen a grown male so…" the green dragon lifted a claw, searching for the word, "petite… as you."

Tornyth rumbled at the gall of being called 'petite'. The green dragon laughed in response; the sound was comforting.

"Your vision gifting is powerful," Mandros continued. "Only to be expected. If you were not strong you would not have been able to emerge in your human's dreams and affect the world about you. But here you are and you have built a … a …"

"Crypt," Tornyth supplied. "My human heart won't accept me."

The green dragon laid himself on the grassy plain and curled his long scaly tail around his body. "He will in time. You are dragonkind and you will endure. You and he are one and the same. He will have no choice but to let you manifest and take flight. Take heart – the time for you to be born of man is close."

"Why did you come?"

The green dragon failed to hide his amusement. "You invited me here."

"I did not."

"You called for your papa like a little hatchling."

If it had been at all possible for a dragon to blush, Tornyth would have been crimson. He turned his head again to look at his handiwork with Donatein's tomb.

"Ah, so it's a dear one's resting place?" Mandros reached out and nudged Tornyth.

Tornyth nearly stumbled at the great dragon's power. "Your heart will heal in time, Tornyth."

"How do you know that?"

Mandros stood and stretched his wings. "One doesn't become 'Father of this Land' without losing many that one held dear."

"Who are you, really?"

The emerald dragon leapt into the air and hovered a few feet above the ground.

"Mandros, the Green, the Deliverer, the Father of this Land, the dragon of Flame and Fury. I will see you again I am sure, Tornyth, Winter's Dragon. Peace fly with you, elt Mynrell."

Jodathyn startled awake, shocked to feel his face wet with tears. Trembling, he ignored Carvelle's cries of protest at being woken and stumbled into the woods.

His knees buckled, hitting the ground. He took a great gasping sob. Donatein was lost to him. His dream had been real.

"Master." Orion reached out a quivering hand to squeeze Jodathyn's shoulder. "Are you well? Can I get you something?"

Jodathyn turned to Orion and saw that beyond him, the rest of the camp was awake.

"I had a dream," Jodathyn whispered.

"Oh, it had to be a mad one," Nym groused.

Theo hushed his sister. His eyes glittered in the dark as if he had been expecting something like this to happen.

"A vision," Jodathyn clarified.

"What did you see?"

"Tornyth ..." Jodathyn said. "Tornyth wanted to find Donatein."

"Who's Tornyth?" Orion sunk to his knees beside Jodathyn.

Jodathyn blinked, wiping away the tears threatening to spill down his cheeks.

Nym shook her head in disgust, laying back down on her bed roll. She turned her back on the boys, muttering.

"The dragon is Tornyth," Theo said. "Isn't he?"

Jodathyn nodded. "You were right. He's within me. Waiting to come out."

"Perhaps he should hurry," Nym grumbled. "We could use a dragon."

"You'll have to forgive my sister. She's a bit grumpy when she doesn't get her sleep."

"Master, what did your dragon do?" Orion coaxed.

"They executed Donatein ... Donatein is dead!"

"You need to be calm if I am ever to get out!"

Orion swallowed, refusing to look in Jodathyn's direction. "Is that all?"

"No, Tornyth took Donatein's body and created a tomb for him."

"That's nice," Carvelle said. "Wouldn't it be awesome to have a grave made by a dragon!"

Jodathyn looked in disbelief at his nephew.

"Anything else?"

"No," Jodathyn lied. He remembered the power he felt from the dragon, Mandros. He felt sick, thinking about Mandros' belief that he would have no choice but to accept the dragon. He couldn't bear to think about what would happen if he lost control.

The emerald dragon had also called him something in the ancient tongue. It was a word he had never seen in any of the ancient texts he was permitted to study. Perhaps that word held a key to his survival.

CHAPTER TWENTY-SIX

Jodathyn

Westgate Road

Jodathyn dried his tears as his companions returned to their beds. Orion lingered a moment longer. Shifting his weight and averting his eyes, Orion whispered, "Is there anything I can do, Master?"

Touched by his servant's concern, Jodathyn shook his head. "I shall seek rest."

Orion moved past Theo. "I'll take the next watch."

Carvelle was already snoozing on their shared bedroll. Jodathyn lowered himself beside his nephew, wrapping his arms around the sleeping child. Too restless to sleep, he lay rigid on his bedroll. While his merry band slept, his thoughts were consumed with Donatein. He could only imagine his servant's final moments of terror. Jodathyn wanted to fight the reality of Donatein's demise. He was a harmless old man, why would Kieryn order his death?

Confused and ashamed by the depth of his grief, Jodathyn choked back a sob. He didn't realise he was weeping again until Orion crept behind him. Kneeling in the dirt beside his master, Orion reached out and grasped Jodathyn's upper shoulder.

"Nym and Theo are asleep," Orion whispered. "I'll sit with you until dawn so that you're not alone."

A terrible lump lodged in Jodathyn's throat. He wanted nothing more than to scream and cry, but he kept as silent as he could.

Withdrawing his hand, Orion didn't speak another word but remained sitting beside Jodathyn until the sun rose, heralding a new dawn. When Theo began to stir, he moved away. Jodathyn was grateful for his discretion.

Laying still on his bedroll, Jodathyn pretended to sleep as the camp awoke. He didn't bother to listen to the hushed conversation, which was no doubt about him. Even Carvelle was subdued this morning.

"Master." Orion touched his shoulder. "We should pack up camp and move."

Blinking away the tears that threatened to fall, Jodathyn rolled to his knees and forced himself to stand. It would be no good for his companions to see and know how weak he was. He ignored the stares, walking into the tree line to relieve himself. He took his time.

When Jodathyn made his way back to the campsite, it was silent. They were waiting for him.

"Prince Jodathyn, I was just–" Theo started.

Jodathyn held up a hand. "It's Jodathyn. I am a rejected son of the house Pallarus."

Theo winced. "I was just trying to explain to the others what you experienced last night."

"I'm fine," Jodathyn protested. He went to his bedroll and proceeded to pack it up. He ruffled Carvelle's hair as the Prince joined him to help.

"Your dragon has been able to make himself known to you. What you saw last night happened. Your dragon flew over the capital and stole that man's body," Theo said, ignoring the pained look on his sister's face.

Jodathyn glared. "I thought I made it clear I didn't want to talk about dragons."

"It must have been quite a shock, Master," Orion offered. "We all understand if you feel ... conflicted."

Jodathyn wiped at his eyes and forced back the urge to roar. "I don't think you understand. Donatein was the man who raised me ... and he is gone."

Nym clucked her tongue. "Get yourself together, man. You're not the only one who knows grief. Theo and I are both orphans, so is your servant."

Jodathyn clenched his jaw. A furious blush heated his olive skin. "You're right. I'm sorry."

Theo threw a dirty look in Nym's direction. "Give him some grace to grieve, sister."

"I'm fine." Jodathyn stood up and took Carvelle's hand in his own. He marched towards the road without glancing back.

"Perhaps you could apologise to him," Jodathyn heard Orion hiss to Nym. "The old man loved Jodathyn enough to die for him."

The small group walked in silence for the first few hours. Jodathyn stalked up ahead, his chin raised. He only stopped to rest when Carvelle dramatically slipped his hand away, plonking himself on the side of the road.

"Uncle, I'm hungry."

In answer to Carvelle's complaints Jodathyn rummaged through the pack until he found some suitable food. Carvelle started to nibble like a half-starved squirrel. Jodathyn stood over him, his glassy eyes staring down the dirt road. The others might think him oblivious, but he was well aware of furious glances between Theo, Orion and Nym.

It was Theo who broke the silence first. Stepping forward, the thief lay a hand on Jodathyn's arm. "Nym and I found an abandoned house on our travels. It's a few more miles down the road. It would be a good place to stay."

At the sound of her name, Nym glanced up. Jodathyn imagined he saw a little sliver of guilt in her eyes. "Jodathyn. You need to forgive my bitter tongue."

Jodathyn didn't move, he heard Nym grinding her teeth together. He felt his back stiffen and the hackles of the dragon within him rise. The dragon was suspiciously quiet this morning.

"I believe I may have been overly harsh."

Jodathyn regarded her for a moment longer. He felt the dragon huff. The creature was upset with Nym but didn't have the energy to hold a grudge. Jodathyn nodded regally. "You're forgiven. Next time try asking for forgiveness rather than demanding it."

"We should stay at the house that Theo mentioned, Uncle," Carvelle said between bites, unaffected by the tension between the older members of the group.

"Yes," Jodathyn agreed. "We should."

Theo's abandoned house was a fair distance off the main road. The front of the house was shrouded with trees. Its garden may once have been a pleasant place to relax. Now it was overgrown with weeds.

"We're near the village of Corlyn, but we're isolated here. There's not another dwelling nearby," Theo said as they entered through the front door. "I scouted the area last time we stayed here."

Without ceremony each of them found their own corner in which to dump their belongings. Jodathyn hoped they could rest for a few days before making their way to Androssah.

Eager to be alone, Jodathyn left the main group and walked through the house. He was disappointed to find the dwelling only had three rooms. At the back door he stared, dumbfounded by the vastness of a large flat area.

"This place must have been a farmhouse at one stage. You can still see evidence the ground has been cleared ready for crops to be planted." Orion stood behind him, watching him with a concerned expression.

"Did you once live in a farmhouse like this? It's small."

"My father's house was a little bigger and we had stables," Orion answered. "This is a comfortable-sized house for a lowborn."

Jodathyn nodded. "It must seem strange to you that sometimes I dream of being a lowborn. Foolish, even."

"Being born to the house Pallarus did not make you immune to suffering ... It's just different to what I or the others have faced." Orion tilted his head to the side. "I'm going with Theo to see if there's anything of use that can be salvaged. You should rest, Master. I know you didn't sleep last night."

Orion didn't wait for Jodathyn to answer. With a few quick strides he was heading out the front door. Blinking, Jodathyn stared after him, his lips quirking into a bemused smile. Orion's tone had been a command.

Jodathyn conceded the wisdom of Orion's suggestion. He needed to rest. He returned to the main room and sat on the floor. Carvelle came to sit beside him and began to draw his letters in the dust. Lifting his gaze to Nym, he half expected another scolding. She stared back at him with lidded eyes.

"You look terrible," Nym said.

Leaning forward, Jodathyn corrected some of Carvelle's letters. He had thought Nym would be bored watching Carvelle's impromptu lesson, but she stayed, her hard hazel eyes observing them.

"Do you wish me to teach you?" Jodathyn glanced up.

"I don't know my letters," Nym admitted, scowling, as if daring either Jodathyn or Carvelle to laugh.

Jodathyn smiled. "I can show you. I like teaching."

"Theo is the intelligent one. My parents sent him to be educated and he had an apprenticeship as a stonemason. I was only good enough to help around the farm."

Jodathyn felt a stirring of pity for Nym's jealousy of her brother. He understood too well the feeling of being overshadowed by a sibling. "I think you're as intelligent as Theo."

Carvelle nodded enthusiastically. "Uncle has taught me so much! His maps are the best!"

Nym walked forward. Jodathyn bent down and wrote something on the floor. "These are the letters for your name ..."

Jodathyn wasn't sure how long he worked with Nym, teaching her the letters of the common alphabet. It wasn't until Theo and Orion returned, barging through the front door, that he looked up.

"What luck! We found some wine," Theo announced. "It's probably a bit old ..." He trailed off, staring at Nym on the floor working with Jodathyn.

Jodathyn smiled up at them. This was good news indeed. "Wine sounds fantastic. Nothing better than wine and words."

Nym snorted in playful disgust.

"While other young lords boast of their great physical strength, Jodathyn is known for his academic prowess," Orion said. He winked at Jodathyn. "Let's uncork a bottle, shall we?"

"Uncle Jod is the best climber too!" Carvelle cried. "His climbing skills are famous."

"Why don't we play a drinking game?"

"How do you play a drinking game?" Jodathyn asked the room.

Jodathyn soon learnt that the drinking game demanded a daring feat be executed. If the unfortunate soul who had been dared failed, they had to drink and tell the group a secret. There was also drinking in between the dares so everyone was well and truly giddy with drink.

"Alright, Orion ... dare you to shoot an arrow into Theo's behind." Jodathyn giggled, feeling delighted, silly and a little too relaxed at the same time. He took an extra swig of wine.

Theo made a noise of protest, fearful his backside might become a potential target for one of Orion's sharp arrows.

"Shoot the window!" Nym cried.

Orion did a drunken little bow and grabbed his weapons. He notched an arrow, shooting it through the glass. The glass shattered, much to the delighted shouts of his audience.

"Now Lady Nym. Fetch!" Orion yelled, gulping down his wine.

Nym scowled and got to her feet swaying from side to side. She tripped on something solid and fell face first onto the floor. The boys roared with laughter as she kicked the obstacle.

"Who puts a metal ring in the middle of the floor?" Nym asked.

"It's a trap door! How marvellous!" Jodathyn exclaimed, as he jumped up from his seat.

"And why is the palace brat still graceful when he is so obviously drunk?"

"Plenty of practice, dear Nym." Jodathyn winked at her and executed a bow. Laughing he grasped the metal ring and pulled. The trap door creaked and opened. Jodathyn could see stairs descending into a dark cellar.

"That's interesting," Theo said.

"I'm going to have a look," Carvelle remarked. He had been watching them with accusing eyes since the game had begun. He hadn't said a word.

"I'm coming too!" Jodathyn cried.

"Uncle," Prince Carvelle said. "You're drunk. Do you really think this is a good idea?"

"I can do stairs," Jodathyn protested. "I'm much older than you."

"I'm a prince," Carvelle added, his nose in the air. "You're not."

Jodathyn stepped back, stung by the remark. He brushed past Carvelle, slipping down into the black hole. He fell to the bottom with a curse. Several more curses flew from his mouth as he crashed and bashed about below. Eventually he returned to the house, where everyone was waiting for him.

"It takes you back to the forest," Jodathyn announced as he struggled to climb up.

Prince Carvelle took the opportunity to jump down the hole and have a look around himself.

"There's more wine down here," Carvelle said. "But I don't think any of you should be drinking any more."

"We're going to have sore heads in the morning," Theo groaned.

"Serves us right," Nym muttered.

"Jodathyn, I dare you to turn into a dragon," Orion said with a giggle. He took another a drink.

Jodathyn glared. "You know I can't," he whined.

"Rules are rules," Nym said in a sing-song voice. "Drink up and spit out a truth."

Jodathyn took a delicate sip from his cup and examined its contents. "One time I told a girl that I was fond of that I loved mathematics. I was trying to impress her."

"Illeanah Whitoak," Prince Carvelle commented from downstairs. "Everyone knows you're sweet on her."

"Well, one of Kieryn's servants overheard us talking that day and told my brother," Jodathyn said. "Kieryn thought it would be a lovely surprise to get me one of the most renowned mathematics tutors in the country for my fifteenth birthday. I hate mathematics! Kieryn was so pleased with his surprise; I didn't have the heart to tell him ... I worked so hard under that man too, without complaint."

The company roared with laughter.

"The next year father got you a science tutor," Prince Carvelle remarked, popping his head back up through the trap door.

Orion bent down and helped him up.

Jodathyn grimaced at the memory. "I worked hard under that tutor too! He was a tyrant."

"So, Miss Illeanah, eh?" Nym teased. "The pretty maid that our Jodathyn is destined to woo."

"Her father hates me," Jodathyn complained, staring at his hands in his lap. "He doesn't even want me speaking to her. The last time we spoke we had a terrible fight."

Nym tilted her head to study Jodathyn. "You don't have to speak to woo a woman."

"Then how ...." Incredulous, Jodathyn glared up at the gathered group. They were sniggering at his reddening cheeks. "Her father said ..."

"Pfft. You just need plenty of practice."

"*Practice?*"

Wobbling to her feet, Nym stumbled towards Jodathyn. Before he could reel back, she took his face in her hands. Jodathyn could feel the warmth of her fingertips as she raked her nails down his jawline. He wasn't able to contain a shiver of excitement at her closeness.

Nym grinned. "You've got the slightest hint of stubble ... not necessarily a bad thing on a man."

Jodathyn swallowed thickly. He was tempted to pull away but also curious as to what she intended to do with him. A moment later her lips were pressed firmly against his own. Bewildered, Jodathyn froze. He didn't move away as Nym's fingers found their way into his curls. She gave his hair a playful tug.

"Hmm ..." Nym murmured against him.

Jodathyn took Nym's slender hands in his own, and moved out from under her reach. "I apologise ... I shouldn't ... I'd never ..."

Nym winked. "It was just a chaste kiss, Jod."

"What's an unchaste kiss?" Jodathyn's cheeks flushed. Kissing Nym was more pleasant than he would have expected.

Nym's hands were in his curls again, tugging him closer. Jodathyn lost his footing and was almost nose to nose with Nym. Up close he realised how pretty her hazel eyes were. "Are you hungry for more, Prince?"

"I'm not ..." Jodathyn's reply was muffled by Nym's lips crushing down onto his own. Her hands released his hair and trailed down his chest.

"Relax," Nym murmured pulling away.

"I ..."

Nym returned, her tongue running along the seam of his lips. He opened his mouth as Nym deepened the kiss. His eyes fluttered closed when her hands found their way back into his curls. She playfully nipped Jodathyn's lips as she pulled away.

"Physically you are a fine specimen, for a weedy flea-bitten runt. A little too innocent for my tastes ... but I'm sure you'll appeal to many maids."

Concerned at what the others might think of him, Jodathyn's eyes darted towards Theo and Orion. The thief looked like he was trying not to laugh. Orion was rolling his eyes.

"Papa won't be pleased about you going and kissing women all around the country side," Carvelle chirruped. "You are the son of a royal house."

"I'm just one woman." Licking her lips, Nym looked every part the she-wolf to Jodathyn. He was confused as to why she would kiss him if she had no affection for him. The more he thought about it, the more Jodathyn was baffled.

CHAPTER TWENTY-SEVEN

Kieryn

The Citadel of Pallaryn

At first light, King Kieryn left his chambers to inspect the damage done by the dragon. He would have preferred to view the destruction alone. Unfortunately, the King's council felt that the palace's defence concerned them, so they accompanied him to the outer wall.

Kieryn kept Captain Tiernan and Guardsman Carew close by to serve as a buffer between him and his council. It wasn't the first time he had used the King's Guard in this manner. The slight twitch of Tiernan's lips was the only indication of how humorous the captain found the situation. Guardsman Carew had not yet mastered his father's characteristic guarded expression.

Kieryn turned his gaze to survey the carnage before him. Last night's scaly visitor had been furious. When he had been alerted of a white dragon descending upon Pallaryn, he had wanted to confront the beast himself. Tiernan had not been in favour of it. Had it not been for Odelle's stern criticism, he would not have heeded his captain's advice.

Studying where the dragon had scorched the wall, and where his claws had gouged the stone, Kieryn saw the wisdom in Tiernan's pleas for him to remain inside.

For all the chaos, no human lives were lost. It was as if the formidable beast had a tantrum.

"This beast should be hunted," Lord Frayn said, gesturing wildly to the wall. "He's out of control."

"Yet no injuries or deaths among our people. That would suggest the beast had some measure of control," Carew replied. His hushed words were overheard by the council. A smile threatened to tug at Kieryn's lips. He was becoming more like his father; saying whatever he thought with little respect for what the council might say. Kieryn liked that about Tiernan.

"The dragon took a body to desecrate," Lord Solan said. His malicious eyes were studying the sky as if he could see the white dragon.

"Is there any proof of that?" Lord Whitoak replied. "It was only the body of a commoner you had discarded."

"He was Jodathyn's servant," Kamoore hissed. "Maybe the dragon came back for his co-conspirator."

"My Lords believe the dragon is Jodathyn?"

"We know it is so, Your Majesty," Lord Solan said. "I know you hold some familial tenderness towards Jodathyn, but you must show your loyalty to your realm and protect your people."

"Jodathyn hasn't harmed anyone," Kieryn replied.

"With all due respect, Your Majesty, that is incorrect. He killed a man in the forest."

"Circumstantial at best."

"Your Majesty, a dragon must not be permitted to fly over the skies of Rama."

"What would you have me do, Lord Solan?"

"Send out the mighty men of Rama. Hunt the beast and remove him."

"You mean to murder my brother," Kieryn hissed in agitation.

"Execute is perhaps a better word. The dragon wouldn't think twice about murdering you," Kamoore replied. His smug look was enough to make Kieryn's blood boil.

"The dragon hasn't manifested yet," Kieryn murmured, biting his tongue. It would not do to alienate his council when his brother's life was in the balance. "The reports say the dragon's scales were still iridescent. He can only move in my brother's dreams and visions."

"What happens if he does manifest? It would be too late then."

"Can dragons speak?" Tiernan wondered aloud. The critical stares of the council turned upon him. "If indeed the dragon can speak, like in the ancient tales, perhaps it would be wise to reason with him?"

"You cannot control a dragon." Lord Frayn frowned, deep in thought. "Although the idea may have some merit."

"I wasn't suggesting controlling the dragon," Tiernan said. "That would be foolish. If we can figure out what the dragon wants, maybe we can soothe his temper and find a safer place for him. It is said that the great dragons of ancient times are still out there somewhere."

"It would be best to come to an agreement without bloodshed," Lord Whitoak said.

"Not all the dragons that flew over the Ramian skies were of evil intent," Guardsman Carew continued. "Before dragons were expelled from the country, they were our friends and protectors ... that is, of course, according to the ancient tales."

"Are we a believer of ancient stories told by nursemaids, guardsman?"

"Well, if you can believe that Jodathyn is cursed because of three ill omens upon his birth ... I suppose I can believe in the Dragon Lords of old."

Kieryn had to bite his lip upon hearing Lord Solan put in his place by a much younger man. A son of a guardsman, no less. The glare Tiernan shot at Carew was only half-hearted, and it had no affect on his son. For his part, Carew looked well pleased with himself as he stood confidently to attention. If it came to sending his brother to a foreign power, Carew Candyde would be a good man to accompany Jodathyn until he was settled.

"Dragon society is said to have been brutal. Have you forgotten how many human lives were lost?"

"No more brutal than taking an old man and executing him without a king's judgement," Kieryn said, looking back to where the body should have been. "I gave orders for Donatein's body to be removed and treated with respect. I'm disappointed to hear that my will was not done."

"The dragon probably showed the old man more respect," Tiernan said.

"Their lordships should also consider how many dragons' lives were lost, along with their human kin," Carew grumbled.

Drained from dealing with the whims of the council, Kieryn turned his back. As he stalked away, they continued to bicker among themselves like a pack of discontent children. He was tired. In his state of worry for his family and country, Kieryn could not find any measure of peace. Lack of sleep and food, along with his obsessive pacing, did not help his temper.

"Majesty."

Kieryn paused long enough to let Captain Tiernan know he had heard him. Not wanting to be overheard, he changed direction, heading towards his chambers. He'd established the practice of using his private rooms as a place where those he trusted could speak openly to him.

At the door to his quarters, one of Kieryn's manservants greeted him. Kieryn paused and frowned at the servant.

"The Queen is unwell, but will not see a physician," the man whispered. "Shall I send for one, my King?"

Pregnancy was always difficult for Odelle, and the burden of her missing child weighed heavily on her mind. Concerned, Kieryn inclined his head towards his guardsmen. "Carew, please send for Guardsman Jael."

Clinking his heels together Carew left the King's side to find his troop healer.

"My King, a guardsman? What shall I tell Her Majesty?"

"My Queen trusts Jael. Tell her to dismiss her ladies and I will come to her side shortly."

The servant was bold enough to raise his eyebrows at the suggestion. Nevertheless, he turned to do the King's bidding.

Entering his chamber, Kieryn dismissed his other servants with a wave of his hand. Those who served Kieryn Pallarus learnt quickly that the King required absolute secrecy. It did not bode well for a servant to be found gossiping about their king.

Kieryn loosened the ties on his shirt, slumping into one of his plush chairs to stare up at Captain Tiernan.

"I am a man of action, my King. We need to make our move if we are to save Jodathyn."

"What do you suggest, Captain? Odelle's father is a good man, he would protect Jodathyn if he could ... I've sent a messenger to the King of Sion."

"Majesty, I am here to petition you to allow Carew and me to see if we can find out where the dragon flew to last night. If we can find a way to help the dragon ..."

"Go," Kieryn said. "There have already been rumours of the dragon being sighted in the west."

"Habron."

Kieryn started upon hearing Odelle's voice. She stood by the edge of his bed, pale, her eyes red from weeping. The manservant had been right, Odelle did not look well. Kieryn leapt from his chair, taking her into his arms.

"My sweet, you must rest," Kieryn murmured in her ear.

"I cannot."

"You must ..."

"I took the liberty of finding out where Donatein was born," Odelle said, trying to push herself upright. "Habron."

Kieryn's hands hovered protectively over her waist.

"Any mother would have heard it in the poor creature's roars that he was mourning. Jodathyn would have taken Donatein home for his eternal rest."

Kieryn nodded and turned back to Tiernan, who was waiting. "Upon your return, speak to no one but me."

A father to three sons, Tiernan was no fool. Kieryn could tell from the set of the captain's jawline, that he had concluded that Odelle was pregnant with another precious royal child. The captain's lips parted to speak; he was moments away from suggesting tightening the security around himself and his Queen.

"Go, please. Speak not of our unborn child. Not even to Carew."

"My King, be assured of my silence in the matter."

CHAPTER TWENTY-EIGHT

Jodathyn

The Abandoned House, Corlyn

Raising his head, Jodathyn took in the thick smoke that was filling the house. A shock of alarm snaked up his spine as he realised Carvelle was missing from his arms. Gagging, he crawled over to Orion. He reached out and turned the servant over. Orion's eyes stared up at him, wide and glassy in death. His lips were parted in a silent scream. His olive skin was already clammy in death as grey specks of ash drifted down, covering him.

"Carvelle," Jodathyn croaked, looking away from the grisly sight of Orion's corpse. The smoke stung the back of his throat. "Carvelle, where are you?"

Gasping for breath, he tried to stand. The smoke was a shroud of suffocation. Nearby, death was waiting as the world was set on fire.

The shadows moved; the ceiling of the abandoned house erupted into flame. He was trapped in an inferno. The abandoned house creaked and groaned under the assault of the flames. The heat was unbearable.

Above Jodathyn a great crimson dragon with cruel black eyes watched him. His scaly mouth was pulled back into a twisted smile.

Screaming Tornyth's name, Jodathyn fell back. He scooted himself away from the terrible creature.

"Winter's Dragon won't save you now," the red dragon purred. "I am the great dragon of Death and Despair. I am Galgothmeg. The supreme general of Vadroil."

"Tell me, Galgothmeg, what is it you want?" Jodathyn demanded, feeling brave as he felt Tornyth stirring beneath his flesh.

"I have come to kill, steal and destroy. The royal house of Pallarus shall crumble beneath my claws. All shall behold me and fall to their doom."

The crimson dragon called Death and Despair lunged at Jodathyn, his razor-sharp teeth snapping.

Jodathyn screamed.

Bolting upright, Jodathyn glanced about, looking for the source of what had awoken him. On the floor, Orion lay crumpled, rubbing his hip. He was glaring at a table of solid timber.

"Sorry, Master," Orion muttered, holding up his hand. He pushed himself off the floor. "I didn't mean to wake you. Seems like I drank more than I thought."

Carvelle murmured in his sleep and rolled over. Neither Nym or Theo moved. Their drunkenness had made them deaf to everything about them.

"I think we all did," Jodathyn sighed and flopped down onto his bedroll. His head twinged. "Are you hurt?"

"No. Bloody table."

Since lying down, Jodathyn hadn't been able to think of anything other than the kiss he had shared with Nym. "So... the kiss."

Orion's cough sounded suspiciously like a laugh. "Master, you are held to different standards than the common man. You didn't do anything wrong. Nym shouldn't ..."

"I think I enjoyed it," Jodathyn confessed, rolling onto his side. "Have you ever kissed anyone?"

"Haven't you seen your brother with his queen? Kissing is perfectly natural and, well yes, enjoyable," Orion murmured. "I did have a lass in Silverdyne before I lost my inheritance."

"I'm sorry, Orion. I really am."

Orion waved Jodathyn's concern away. "It's not your fault. Truth be told, none of my misfortunes are."

"This is happening because of what I said in front of the King's council that night I got caught sneaking out. It's all my fault." Jodathyn gripped his fringe with his hand, nearly tearing out hair at the roots. The blossoming pain made him forget. "Donatein and Valt would be alive if not for me. Carvelle would be home safe ... You wouldn't be–"

"Jodathyn, stop," Orion said. "If what you say is true, that the lords were challenged by what you said that night, they are the ones responsible for this chaos. I may just be a servant, but I do not believe you said anything wrong."

"Kieryn did ..."

Orion sniffed. "You're taking other people's blame and placing it on your shoulders. The King was trying to be a good big brother and protect you."

Jodathyn fell silent.

"Orion," Jodathyn whispered, when the silence became too stifling. "If something happens to me, can you get Carvelle back to the King?"

"Nothing is going–"

"You can't promise that," Jodathyn interrupted. "The truth is, we don't know what tomorrow might bring. All we can do is our best with the circumstances we are given."

"Our circumstances are pretty dire," Orion replied, his voice sounding tight. "I'll do what needs to be done."

"You would have made a fine King's Guardsman."

"Am I that obvious?"

Jodathyn smiled, peering into Orion's face in the dim light. "Everyone could see how you adored Captain Tiernan. He only had to look in your direction and you'd preen."

Orion flushed. "I did not!"

"You most certainly did. Valt thought it was amusing."

"Do you think the captain knew?"

"Orion, all of the King's Guardsmen knew."

"Well, I'm a criminal now. I'll never wear the black and silver," Orion said. "That future is gone."

"It may be selfish to say it, but I'm glad you're helping me despite my *dire circumstances*."

"You should sleep, Master. Theo will take the next watch."

"*Araae helphelwyn. Terini gorthorawyn.*"

"*Wake up. He's coming…*"

It was just before dawn. Jodathyn knew with a certainty that the great red dragon called Death and Despair would be upon them soon. They were running out of time.

The trap door! It led to the forest.

Stumbling over his friends, Jodathyn shook them all awake. Sleepy eyes glowered at him. Ignoring them and all their protests, he took them down the trap door.

Each of them walked through the grey light of the cellar in complete silence. Jodathyn led the way, his hand feeling for the soft earth of the tunnel. He painstakingly led them to the bottom of the stairs. Then they climbed.

He stepped into the light of day and came face to face with Galgothmeg, the dragon of Death and Despair.

Galgothmeg studied the group with a curled lip. He lifted his serpentine head, snarling and snapping. His mouth opened. Jodathyn and all who were with him were bathed in fire.

Jodathyn's eyes snapped open. In the pre-dawn light, he could see all his companions were accounted for. They were safe. For now.

"He's coming," the voice inside his head whispered. There was a note of urgency. *"Get up. He's coming."*

Jodathyn didn't need to ask who was coming. There was another dragon in Rama, who wished them ill. To stay in the abandoned house would be certain death. If they left via the trap door they would perish. Jodathyn's instincts were telling him it was imperative he should heed his vision's warnings.

"He's coming."

Jodathyn rolled himself to a stand, casting a glance at Theo, who was on watch. Shaking the remainder of his band awake he ignored the thief's smirk and the complaints he knew were coming.

"Quiet," Jodathyn commanded, his voice cracking like a whip. "We're in danger. We need to go."

"This is ridiculous," Nym whined. "My head hurts."

"Your belly aching is ridiculous," Jodathyn snapped. "We don't have time. He's coming."

"Who's coming?" Orion asked, rubbing his eyes.

"Galgothmeg, and he isn't a dragon we want to meet."

Theo froze, gesturing frantically about. "We definitely do not want to be here when Galgothmeg comes."

"Oh, those old stories."

"Do *you* really want to be here to see if he comes, Nym? There's a very good reason his name means *Death and Despair*!"

Theo was already opening the trap door, shimmying his way into the dark hole.

Jodathyn watched him disappear with a look of satisfaction.

"We can't go down there"

No, Jodathyn thought. *If I go with them, they will perish. Galgothmeg is interested in us. He will not concern himself with a small boy and thieves.*

There was a rumbling inside his gut. Jodathyn didn't know how, but he was sure Galgothmeg wanted him out of the way. Sacrificing himself would give the others an opportunity to escape. Carvelle would survive.

"Quick," Jodathyn said, taking Carvelle's hand and propelling him forward. "You next, my Prince."

Carvelle stared up at him, uncertainty in his eyes. "I don't like what is happening here."

"I need you to be brave, Your Highness," Jodathyn said, kneeling down so he was level with Carvelle. He imprinted his nephew's face into his memory. As long as he had the image of Carvelle in his mind he could do what needed to be done. "I am proud of you, Carvelle. No matter what happens today, be brave."

Carvelle tilted his head to the side to study Jodathyn's face. "You're acting strange, Uncle."

"I'll see you soon," Jodathyn said.

Reaching up, Carvelle touched Jodathyn's cheek. "You're my favourite, Uncle Jod."

Jodathyn grasped the small boy's hand and blinked back tears. "Take him," Jodathyn said to Orion. "I'll come from behind to make sure we aren't followed."

Orion nodded and took the Prince. Nym followed, her face screwed up with a puzzled expression as she too stepped into the darkness.

Jodathyn was left alone in the hut with his dragon. He sat at the table staring at the hole in the floor. He was tempted to follow his friends but he knew if he did, there would be no survivors. Galgothmeg would find them.

"We will not survive the confrontation with Galgothmeg."

I know. Jodathyn closed his eyes in defeat. He never imagined in his last moments he would be alone.

"You are not alone. I am here."

Jodathyn stood, brushing his hands on his trousers as he made his way over to the trap door. He bent down to close it, but his forehead smashed into something hard. Stars exploded behind his eyes as he reeled back.

"Clumsy vain hedge-born flap-dragon!"

Nym clambered up out of the hole.

"Nym!" the voice in his head crowed. It seemed the dragon within was pleased to see her.

Nym turned pertly on her heel and closed the trap door. She stomped over to a woven mat, pulling it over the trap door to conceal the escape route. She then picked up a chair, dumping it on top of the mat.

"You weren't going to follow us," Nym stated, after she had clattered about. Her hazel eyes shone in accusation. Jodathyn thought he saw a glimmer of admiration, which sent a thrill up his spine.

"She's pleased with us."

"No," Jodathyn confirmed in a low voice.

"You plan to sacrifice yourself?"

"Galgothmeg hunts for Tornyth, not for a tiny prince. They will be safe for now." Jodathyn turned his back. "He'll be here soon. You should go too."

"No."

"*No?*" Jodathyn turned back around, surprised. Nym hadn't exactly kept it secret she thought he was weak.

"You're going to need someone if you are going to survive this insanity," Nym said. The freckles stood out on her pale face.

"*You see, she's good for our team. Perhaps if we get lucky, a good mate.*"

"Do the others know you are here?" Jodathyn asked, ignoring his dragon. He did not want a mate. He wanted to survive.

"No," Nym replied. "I pretended I dropped something and told Theo to run. He trusts me. He would have hurried Orion along the tunnel."

Jodathyn nodded as he left the house to meet his doom. He walked in the opposite direction to the tunnel's exit, moving like a man being escorted to his execution. Lifting his chin, he slowed his breath.

Nym followed.

'*Our death will likely be quick and relatively painless. Dragons don't have a lot of patience when they kill.*"

Jodathyn wished he could stop the quaking in his limbs. He hated to appear so weak in front of Nym, especially now she seemed to have found something to like about him.

"*Donatein would be proud of us.*"

Jodathyn wasn't so sure.

In the air they could hear the triumphant roar of a beast. Galgothmeg would be arriving soon.

"Can you call your dragon?" Nym whispered.

"No." Jodathyn lifted his face to the sky, preparing himself for the sight of Galgothmeg. "I don't know how."

Very soon they could both hear the rhythmic beating of wings. The dark silhouette of the red dragon cast a shadow across the land. Wishing he wasn't such a coward, Jodathyn planted himself to the ground. His hands were trembling.

Galgothmeg spotted Jodathyn waiting for him and roared in victory. He circled the abandoned house twice. His flight seemed almost graceful and unhurried. If his tactic was to scare Jodathyn, it was working.

Nym sucked in a deep breath as the monster landed before them. Malicious dark orbs regarded Jodathyn and scaly lips puckered into an ugly leer. Determined to show fortitude in his moment of terror, Jodathyn stared back.

While Galgothmeg and Jodathyn engaged in a battle of wills, three armed men scrambled from the red dragon's back. Surprised, Jodathyn was the first to break eye contact.

"I hadn't thought you to be a packhorse, Galgothmeg," Jodathyn commented. The other humans sidled away from Galgothmeg's range. Their swords were drawn but their eyes were trained upon the dragon.

"Tell me," Jodathyn demanded, turning to the leader, a tall man with a black wiry beard. "How many of your companions did this one eat?"

Galgothmeg swept his haughty gaze over Jodathyn. "Can't you face me as a dragon, Jodathyn Pallarus? Bring out Tornyth, Winter's Dragon." He stretched out, turning his terrible eyes onto Nym. "Who is this tasty morsel?"

"Nym Torkelle, born of Korkalie," Nym stated. "Are you going to give us a fair fight or not?"

The red dragon smirked and lay on the grass before them. Jodathyn felt a rumbling of anger in his belly as Golgothmeg wrapped his tail about himself and grinned at them with malevolent glee.

"I like her, she's strong," Galgothmeg remarked. He waved a spiked claw in her direction. "I tell you what, human. I'll allow my men to sell you to the prison ships instead of killing you."

Galgothmeg raised his head and sniffed. "You see, I can be merciful." He waved his head around again and studied Jodathyn. "Where is your dragon? I want to see Tornyth before I kill him."

Jodathyn squared his shoulders, wishing Galgothmeg would kill him quickly. "You're out of luck, Galgothmeg," he said. "Tornyth is in my head."

"Pathetic," Galgothmeg said sneering. "Disappointing ... Weak. Your dragon has not manifested himself."

The red dragon stood, peering loftily at Jodathyn. "You're not a real dragon if you can't manifest. I shall not waste my time in killing you. These men can kill you slowly and painfully. They'll let you scream yourself raw. Once you're dead, I won't have to worry about Tornyth ruining my plans."

The dragon gave them one last contemptuous sneer as he leapt into the air, leaving the men behind.

"So much for a quick death."

The dragon's men leered as they pressed in closer, the blades of their swords flashing in the autumn sunlight. Jodathyn groaned, remembering he'd left Ruevyn's sword inside the house. He felt better when he realised Nym hadn't thought to take up the sword either.

Relieved he'd kept his dagger inside his boot, Jodathyn slid it out and thrust it into Nym's hands. She spluttered in surprise as he turned upon his heel and ran towards the house. Behind him, Jodathyn could hear the mocking laughter.

"Jod!" Nym yelled.

"Cover me! The sword!" Jodathyn hollered. Nym had made it known she was a talented fighter. He needed to get the sword into her hands. "We need the sword!"

Jodathyn resisted the urge to check over his shoulder to see how Nym was faring. As he reached the door, one of the men intercepted him, grabbing his arm. Jodathyn was wrenched backwards so that he slammed into the ground. The man with the black beard loomed over him. Jodathyn waited for him to come closer, then he kicked his kneecap with as much force as he could muster. Howling, the man stumbled, allowing Jodathyn to roll to his feet.

"Thank you, Carew!"

Nym's cries of attack were abruptly cut off. Unable to resist, Jodathyn searched for her. One of their attackers was holding her around her throat and was squeezing.

"No!" Jodathyn cried. "Take your hands off her!"

"You don't command me, boy."

"Let her go!" Jodathyn yelled. "I'll surrender – just let my friend go."

A fist connected to Jodathyn's face and pain exploded behind his eyes. He was aware that he had fallen onto the grass; his attacker was straddling him. He could hear the sound of blood pumping through his body as pain blossomed in his skull. The sounds of the fight were muted, like he was underwater. There was a second, then a third blow. Blackness overpowered him as he lost consciousness.

CHAPTER TWENTY-NINE

Orion

The Abandoned House, Corlyn

Orion had seen the glint in Jodathyn's eyes the moment his master had shaken him awake. He recognised the look of a man who was determined to do his duty, even though he was afraid. Jodathyn's farewell to Prince Carvelle only confirmed his suspicions.

"We left the horse behind," Orion said, trying to dismiss the thought of his master facing the dragon alone. There was a part of him that wished he could turn back. But Jodathyn had given him charge over the Crown Prince. He wondered if Jodathyn had staged the conversation last night in preparation for this moment.

"Forget the horse," Theo snapped. His stumbling footsteps sent pebbles ricocheting along the tunnel.

"He's a good horse," Orion argued. "It can be the difference between life and death."

"What would you know?"

Orion scoffed. "I've trained under my father since toddlerhood."

"We should go back for the horse," Prince Carvelle added. "And Uncle."

"Also, Nym."

Orion had to bite his tongue. He had heard Nym leaving them and had guessed what she was up to. In order not to scare Prince Carvelle, he remained silent. He felt a stab of guilt as he pushed past Theo and Carvelle. To cover his unease, he started to climb up the steps at the end of the tunnel. He bent to help Prince Carvelle, then Theo, into the open.

"We should find shelter in the trees nearby," Orion suggested, glancing around. His first reaction was to look for any signs of danger. It's what any good solider would do. Satisfied it was safe to do so, Orion turned to the Prince. "Prince Carvelle, why don't you find a place to hide."

Eager to be of use, the Prince scampered off. Orion grabbed Theo's sleeve to stop him from moving away. The thief crossed his arms against his chest and cocked his head to the side.

Waiting for the Prince to be out of earshot, Orion whispered to Theo, "Jodathyn and Nym aren't coming back."

"Excuse me?"

"Jodathyn doesn't believe he will be joining us," Orion explained. "His look was of a man trying to be brave when he knows he is doomed."

"You don't know that."

"He farewelled Prince Carvelle. He doesn't expect to see him again."

"No." Theo shook his head in disbelief. "Why didn't you stop him? Why didn't you stop Nym?"

Orion ignored the accusation in Theo's tone. "Everyone inside the palace has a rank and a duty. If necessary, it is Jodathyn's duty to sacrifice himself in order to save the Prince."

Theo stared at Orion in silent reprimand.

"There would have been no convincing him," Orion continued. "He wouldn't want us preventing Prince Carvelle reaching safety."

Theo opened his mouth, he paused then clicked his jaw shut.

"Last night Jodathyn asked me to get Carvelle back to his father in Pallaryn," Orion said. "I mean to do exactly that. Whether you come with us is up to you."

Theo scowled. "I'll come with you. Only because Nym is missing. Once my sister returns, I'm leaving."

"She went back for Jodathyn."

"I'll wait for my sister."

Prince Carvelle returned, interrupting the conversation. He grasped Orion's hand in his own, dragging the older boy over to the cover of the trees. "I found a hiding spot. Come and see, horse boy."

Orion let Carvelle lead him away, glancing back at Theo, who grumbled and followed. Carvelle led him to a thicket.

"I think we'll all fit," the Prince said.

"It'll be cosy. Well done, my Prince," Orion replied.

Grinning, Carvelle disappeared into the thicket, which would provide them with some camouflage. Orion shrugged and got down on his knees to squeeze himself into the tight space. With a dramatic sigh, Theo joined them.

The air about them thrummed with the sound of gigantic wings. Orion shared a significant glance with Theo. They had hidden themselves just in time. He tried not to think about Jodathyn facing one of the most infamous dragons of Ramian myth.

When he had been appointed as the Son of the Crown's manservant, Orion had prepared himself to dislike his master and fellow servants. He had come into Jodathyn's service as a bumbling country boy who was clueless about palace life. Patient and kind, Jodathyn had never scolded Orion or embarrassed him. There had even been a few instances where he had covered up Orion's mistakes. Maybe Jodathyn was right. Maybe, in some strange way, they were already friends.

"What do we do now?" Theo's voice was tight.

"We wait."

"No." Theo indicated the Prince with a sharp nod of his head. "We can only hope we don't lose our heads in the meantime."

"My master did warn you that you could die," Orion reminded him.

Prince Carvelle eyed the two older boys and then hushed them. To distract Carvelle from the argument, Orion let the small prince huddle closer to him as they listened to the sounds of the dragon. Carvelle shivered and inched closer.

Theo's eyes gleamed as he studied Carvelle and Orion.

"Didn't think servants were permitted to cuddle royalty," Theo whispered.

"Uncle Jod always slept in Donatein's bed," Carvelle said. "And sometimes, Papa said that when Uncle Jodathyn was really scared he snuck into bed with his giant guard. We're not to discuss it though."

Orion tried to imagine a younger Jodathyn climbing in Valt's bed. He failed.

"I don't think dragons sound fun anymore," Carvelle said. "Where's Uncle Jod?"

"It is going to be alright, Your Highness," Orion murmured.

"Yes, but where is Uncle Jod? I want him right now."

"Your uncle will meet us a little later on," Theo invented. "He's just making sure you stay safe."

Carvelle sniffled. "I still want him."

When the sounds of the dragon ceased, Orion had them all wait a little longer. He had seen Jodathyn do the same thing when they rescued Theo and Nym. It seemed like a wise tactic.

Eventually Orion nodded, giving Carvelle a little nudge and they all crawled out of the thicket.

"We should check." Theo's attention was in the direction of the abandoned house.

Orion raised his eyebrows. "Are you sure that's a good idea?"

"The horse will be helpful. There might be some supplies left behind. Not to mention some clues about what had ..." Theo trailed off.

"I'm sorry about your sister," Orion said. "I do understand. We go quietly."

"I can scout ahead," Theo offered. "My skills as a thief are useful after all. Wait here."

Drawing Prince Carvelle close to his side, Orion nodded, watching as Theo slipped through the trees.

"Orion," Carvelle said. "The dragon scared me."

"It scared me too," Orion assured him. His eyes were fixed on where Theo had disappeared from view.

"Uncle said we were going to Androssah. Are we still going there?"

"We will go wherever we can find safety," Orion answered.

Moments later, Theo returned. "No one is there. They've left the horse."

Exhaling, Orion decided this was the moment to let Theo know he was taking charge. "Theo, I need you to gather whatever supplies you think will be of use. I'll have a look and see what tracking marks I can find."

"You're a tracker?"

"I've had some experience," Orion said, with a frown. "My grandfather taught me a few tricks."

Theo looked displeased as he led them towards the house.

Once they reached the front gate, Orion guided Carvelle over to the thief. "Stay with Theo."

He didn't let the Prince or the thief argue with him. Instead, Orion slipped around the perimeter of the house and out to the flat ground out the back.

It didn't take the skills of a tracker to see the obvious signs of a fight. It seemed that Jodathyn and Nym hadn't gone down easily. Orion could also see the patch of grass that had been flattened by the dragon, Galgothmeg.

Orion swallowed, thinking about the terror Jodathyn must have felt when he faced the dragon known as Death and Despair. He scanned the land, looking for more clues.

There was very little blood and no bodies. Hopefully that was a sign that Jodathyn and Nym hadn't perished on their foolhardy mission.

The discovery of multiple men's boot prints startled and worried him.

Re-entering the house, Orion saw that Theo and Carvelle had found the pack. It seemed whoever had attacked Jodathyn and Nym hadn't bothered to search the area. Jodathyn's borrowed sword was still on the table.

"Take the sword," Orion said to Theo. "I have my own."

"I guess the dragon had no use for the horse or weapons." Theo eyed the sword. He touched the blade before taking it up. "Never thought to own one of these."

"Let's hope we don't have to use it," Orion said.

Grabbing two bottles of wine, Theo met Orion's blank stare. "I need a good stiff drink and I don't think taking Prince Carvelle to an ale house is a good idea."

Orion conceded to Theo's point and made his way to where they had tied up the stallion. Even though Theo had said he was still there, Orion was still surprised the horse hadn't been stolen. The beast greeted Orion with a frightened snort, pulling his ears back in warning.

Lifting his hand, Orion grasped for his beast magic.

"Peace, four-legged friend ... Calm ..."

"I think they are still alive," Orion said that night around the campfire, after Prince Carvelle had chatted himself to sleep. "No bodies, not much blood and boot prints. Something heavy was dragged along the grass."

Theo looked up.

"It looks as though someone dragged unconscious bodies along the ground," Orion explained.

Theo's eyes flashed. "Why didn't you say anything?"

"Think about this logically. The King is our only real hope to helping Jodathyn and Nym."

"Why do you think someone so high and mighty might help us?" Theo scoffed. He stood abruptly, grabbed kindling and threw it into the fire. "How can you be sure that the King will even want to help Jodathyn?"

"The King is more attentive to him than Jodathyn knows."

"How can you know that?"

"Because I'm a spy."

"*A spy?* For the King?"

Orion shook his head. "For the King's favourite, Lord Whitoak. I can only assume what I tell Whitoak is told to the King."

"You're *spying* on your master?"

Orion shifted, grabbing a branch as he poked at the fire. He watched the fierce yellow glow of the flames. "Whitoak appointed me to watch Jodathyn. If I fail the Lord, I will lose everything. I only revealed the inconsequential things, such as which passages he read over and over and which tonics Donatein gave him. And, then to my eternal shame, how much Jod admired his daughter Illeanah. I hadn't expected Jodathyn to be a kind master."

"You're spying for Illeanah's father? The man who doesn't like Jodathyn?"

Orion exhaled. "Everyone's afraid of Jodathyn."

Theo snorted. It was hard to miss the sarcasm in his tone when he spoke. "Because he's *so dangerous.*"

"Anyway, the point is, I only gave Lord Whitoak information that he probably knew already. But we're off topic ... this Galgothmeg dragon is a real concern," Orion said.

Theo sniffed.

"The King needs to know about Galgothmeg. Your reaction to his name was enough to tell me there's a big problem if he is in Rama."

Theo threw some more kindling into the fire and watched the flames sputter.

"What do you know about Galgothmeg?"

Theo didn't answer.

"Theo?"

"Galgothmeg is an ancient dragon, second in command to Vadroil."

"The *Vadroil*?"

"Yes. Legend states that Arturyn killed Vadroil in a great victory but was severely injured. Galgothmeg was able to escape. Arturyn was unable to follow. Instead, he banished Galgothmeg and the Grey Shadows along with him."

"Grey Shadows?"

"Grey dragons that served Vadroil. They were all said to be mad."

"If Galgothmeg was banished ... then how – ?"

"How is he in Rama?" Theo considered the fire before him. "Someone let him in."

"Pardon?"

"Magic has kept Galgothmeg out of Rama's skies. Someone has found the key and let him in."

Orion stood and thought about the matter. What could a simple horse boy do about a great dragon of old returning? Patting the stallion's velvety nose, Orion finally said, "We need to warn the King. Rama is depending on us."

"We're not following Nym's trail, are we?"

"No," Orion admitted. "Sometimes the good of the realm comes before our own needs. We're going to need help if we are going to rescue Nym and Jod."

Theo stared out into the bleak darkness. Orion knew he was thinking of his sister. He thought Theo would turn to him with a rebuke.

"Belrah is a bad place for us to go," Theo said, his shoulders drooping. "It might be the quickest route back but it comes with too much risk."

"Agreed. Where do you think we should go? Androssah, like Jodathyn intended?"

"A little further east there is another small settlement. We can restock supplies there. And there's also a lesser-known road to the capital."

Orion nodded. "I don't have much coin."

"I wasn't suggesting we pay for things," Theo replied.

"Thieving comes with risks."

Theo shook his head and turned back to the campfire. "I'm not going to get caught. We should sleep. I'll take first watch."

CHAPTER THIRTY

Jodathyn

The Road to Thrangul

"Prop him up."

Gruff, muffled voices and a terrible throbbing in his head were the first things Jodathyn became aware of. Cruel fingers pressed into his flesh as he was jolted into an uncomfortable upright position. Every muscle in his body screamed in protest.

He opened his eyes, ignoring the blinding pain in the back of his skull. He blinked once, then twice, to force his sight into focus, and failed. In defeat he closed his eyes and slumped.

"Up, I say!" A hand pushed him back up into position. His head was wrenched back.

Jodathyn cried out in protest as a cup was brought to his lips. The familiar smell of bitter herbs registered in his subconsciousness. It reminded him of Donatein and home. His instincts were bellowing in warning.

"Don't swallow! Fight! Fight!"

Jodathyn knew he should have been able to recognise the voice. It was low, urgent and came from deep within.

The cup was pressed harder against his chapped lips, insisting he drink. Jodathyn swallowed past the painful lump in his throat. The liquid was tipped into his mouth. He spat it out.

The hand that was holding him released him for a blessed moment. Then the fingers were back, pulling Jodathyn's face upwards. The cup was refilled and pressed against his lips. Moaning in protest, he tried to spit but his chin was held up. He was forced to swallow so he could breathe. Gasping, Jodathyn heaved and battled the hands holding him.

"There's more medicine where that came from."

Jodathyn cursed once more, blinking his eyes. A cruel face came into sharp focus.

"You're quite a handsome specimen, my young friend," the man said. A feral grin lit up his face. Jodathyn recognised him as one of the men he'd fought with at the abandoned house.

Gathering saliva in his mouth, Jodathyn spat in the man's face. He watched with malicious glee as his spittle hit his black, wiry beard.

"You're a dead man," Jodathyn whispered.

Scowling, Jodathyn's captor stood to his full height. He kicked Jodathyn in the ribs. Jodathyn hunched over as the wind was knocked out of him.

"Your brother, the High King, shall not be King for much longer."

"Nor will your head be on your shoulders for long." Jodathyn forced himself to glare up at the man. To show him the pain did not bother him.

"Brave words for a prisoner."

Jodathyn struggled, finding his hands were bound. He glanced around. The abandoned hut was nowhere to be seen; he was perched inside a cage in a wooden cart. Nym was watching the exchange from the opposite corner. To Jodathyn's distinct lack of surprise, her mouth was gagged.

"Who are you?" Jodathyn demanded trying to lurch forward.

"Atek Rytter. And you are going to fetch me quite a bit of gold, Master Pallarus."

"Who says I'm going down without a fight?"

"Again, reckless words for a humbled boy."

Jodathyn growled deep in this throat. His threat didn't have the desired effect. Atek threw his head back and laughed.

"Do you know how much an enslaved dragon is worth in Artroth?"

Jodathyn kicked the man's heels and missed. For this folly, Atek slapped him. As Jodathyn's world tilted, his ears rung with a whirling, high-pitched sound. In his peripheral vision he saw Nym shaking her head. She was a fine one to talk. They had gagged her. He wondered what she had said.

"We'll be giving you the tonic to repress the dragon. I suggest you cooperate or you will soon find your situation far from accommodating."

Jodathyn snarled and lashed out again, earning himself another slap. Exhausted and angry he lay slumped on the floor of the cart.

"You are a slow learner, aren't you pup?" Atek sneered.

"What good am I if the dragon is suppressed?" Jodathyn muttered, nursing his wounded pride.

"Not to worry. Once you are paid for, your new masters will be able to extract the dragon. There are ways to safely force a dragon into submission. You'll lose your wits, of course," Atek told him. "And your soul. Your dragon will be nothing but a mindless beast."

"No ..." Jodathyn felt himself paling. That fate sounded worse than death. "Please, there must be something I can offer you."

"Submission is all I require," Atek said.

Strutting away, Atek stopped to chat with his other companions. From the glow of their campfire and the smell of roasting meat, it seemed they had stopped to camp for the night. Jodathyn eyed Nym who was glaring at him. He wondered how long she had been conscious. If they were to survive this experience with their sanity intact, they needed to support one another.

Groaning, he lay down on the wooden base of the cart. He wriggled his way over to Nym. He was bruised all over, and it was a slow process but he made it to her side as the men started to unpack their bedrolls.

Once Jodathyn was sure the men had retired for the night, he leaned close to Nym's face. She stared back at him, looking afraid of what he was planning. "I can try and get this gag out, if you wish? I'll have to use my teeth."

Tilting her head at him, Nym nodded. With a smile, Jodathyn pressed his body closer to her and delicately bit the dirty cloth. It tasted foul but he shook his head side to side until he had worked it loose. It hadn't been tied tight.

"Are you hurt?"

"My throat hurts," Nym whispered.

"Did you say mean things?" Jodathyn teased. "Is that why they gagged you?"

Nym snorted. "They weren't treating you gently … I told them what I thought of their parentage."

Jodathyn chortled quietly.

"Would you have really surrendered to save me?"

Jodathyn raised an elegant eyebrow. "Of course."

Nym brushed her lips lightly against Jodathyn's. "If you want to court this Illeanah girl, kiss her like this. Gentle, sweet and swift. If you are the man she wants, she'll come back for more."

Jodathyn sat back dumbfounded. He could not help but imagine what kissing Illeanah Whitoak might be like, even though her father didn't approve. "If I'm not the man she wants?"

"She'll probably run away and never speak to you again." Nym looked pleased. "I know very little about highborn ladies."

Leaning back, Jodathyn stared up into the night sky. The stars seemed dimmer tonight. He hoped that wherever Carvelle was, he was safe and Orion was looking after him.

"Are you okay?" he whispered after Nym remained silent.

Nym nodded shakily. "You need to stop letting them give you the tonics."

"I don't think there's much I can do about that." Jodathyn lay himself down, feeling strangely fatigued. "How long have I been out?"

"Two days."

"Two days!" Jodathyn cried.

"Quiet, you mewling fool-born dewberry!" Nym hushed him. With what seemed a great effort, she softened her tone. "They are taking us to Thrangul."

Jodathyn withheld a shudder of dread. Whatever these men had planned for them in Thrangul, it was going to be unpleasant.

"It's the port where they load the prison ships. Once we are boarded that's it, we're doomed."

"I don't plan on going quietly," Jodathyn said.

"You can't exactly fight your way out," Nym replied.

"I thought you would have approved of my fighting spirit. We'll just have to watch for an opportunity to present itself."

"You sound like Theo," Nym said bitterly. "No one has ever escaped."

"There's a first time for everything." Jodathyn closed his eyes, feeling himself drifting off again. "I'm so sleepy."

"They've added something to the tonics to subdue you," he heard Nym say. "They make you lethargic as well as keep your dragon at bay."

The sun was high in the sky when Jodathyn regained consciousness. The ragged sway of the cart as the poor horses pulled them along made him sick to his stomach. Keeping his eyes squeezed shut, he tried to ignore the hunger in his belly. He felt rather than saw Nym make her way over to him.

She held a small canteen of water to his lips. "You need to drink, Jod."

So Jodathyn drank. It was just plain water.

"He's awake."

The cart stopped swaying. Jodathyn heard the heavy footfalls of men approaching the cart. The door was unlocked, swinging open to allow Atek to enter.

"Time for some medicine, lad."

Jodathyn shook his head. "Please, no!"

"He's had enough!" Nym cried. "Leave him alone you rank pox-marked harpy!"

"Mind your tongue, girl, or we'll cut it out!" Atek turned to regard Jodathyn. "Are you going to behave yourself?"

Jodathyn glared defiantly back.

"No. Very well. So be it," Atek turned. "You two, looks like he wants to play tough. Get in here."

Paralysed with fright, Jodathyn could only watch as Atek's two companions joined him. They took their places either side of him and grabbed his arms. The larger of the two took a fistful of his hair to force his head up. Glowering, Jodathyn clenched his jaw shut.

"Open his mouth. I would love to play, but we don't have all day."

The smaller man nodded and brought his hand either side of Jodathyn's cheeks. His fingers searched for where his jaw bones met. He pressed, forcing Jodathyn's mouth wide. The bitter mixture was brought to his lips and poured down his throat.

Jodathyn struggled as a second cup was forced on him.

Then they left him, alone, spluttering and cursing as they continued their journey.

"It's been another day," Nym whispered. "We're nearly at Thrangul."

"We've got a stop before then, my pretty," one of the men chuckled.

"I don't think the young dragon is going to enjoy it," his companion replied.

Jodathyn blinked and looked towards Nym for answers. She shook her head and offered him a hunk of stale bread. Taking it, Jodathyn nibbled on the dry crust. He knew he had to keep up his strength. There wasn't going to be better offer of food.

His nerves rattled, Jodathyn could only wait to see what their captors planned to do with him. Mid-morning melted into the afternoon. Jodathyn sat in silent trepidation as a port city came into view.

Atek looked over his shoulder, leering at his prisoners. "We have a surprise for you."

Nym glared back at the brute, while Jodathyn lolled his head to the side. His voice was laced with venomous sarcasm. "It wouldn't be a decent meal by any chance?"

"I can see the Artist's dwelling now."

Whoever the Artist was, Jodathyn was certain he did not wish to meet him.

A short time later, the cart was halted. Unsure of what he was expecting, Jodathyn was surprised by the humble dwelling they had stopped at. One of his captors swaggered to the door of their prison. He felt numb as the man grabbed the crook of his elbow and hurled him from the cart. Nym was left behind.

Jodathyn tried to struggle out of Atek's harsh grip, but he was forced through the dark opening of the doorway.

"Sit him right here." The Artist was a tall, scrawny man who stank of stale sweat. Around his waist he wore a leather apron, spattered with inks and something else.

Atek escorted Jodathyn to a wooden seat.

"Where do you want it?"

"He's right-handed, so right wrist."

"Crime?"

"No crime," Atek replied. "He's got a dragon in him."

The Artist's eyes glimmered with greed. "Marking a dragon is a double fee."

"Done," Atek agreed without blinking. He turned to Jodathyn. "Enjoy, sweet Prince."

"I'm not a prince," Jodathyn grumbled.

The Artist studied Jodathyn's face and brushed his thumb along his cheek. "His cheek is another option."

Disgusted by the man's touch, Jodathyn wrenched his face away.

"We're not wanting to mark his pretty face," Atek said.

The Artist shrugged unconcerned. "And the girl?"

"Leave her unmarked, we haven't got all day."

"Well, two runes, that'll be ten gold coins. Then double that for a dragon, gentleman."

Atek fished out a leather purse and threw it in the direction of the Artist. He deftly caught the purse, weighing it in his clawed hands. Satisfied, he turned to Jodathyn with a grin. "Let's get started then, shall we?"

"Please ..." Jodathyn murmured. He didn't understand what was happening but he was afraid.

"Release his right arm so I can work."

Atek's two underlings worked as a team to untie Jodathyn. They grabbed him before he could make a swing in an attempt to punch one of them. With ridiculous ease they were able to bind him back to the chair with his right arm free. They had done this before.

Jodathyn struggled but his elbow was pinned down. He could barely move.

The Artist rummaged around and dropped a heavy chest onto his worktable. He opened it and pulled out a bottle of clear liquid. Wetting a cloth, which he pulled from his leather apron, the Artist hummed as he washed Jodathyn's right arm. To Jodathyn's nose it smelt of a strong soap.

"This is for your masters; we wouldn't want a nasty infection, would we?"

"I have no master but my brother, the High King of Rama."

"Jodathyn Pallarus, you are about to learn the hard way that life isn't always predictable or fair."

"Any particular colour?"

"The standard green."

The Artist smiled and picked up a vicious-looking object. It was white, long and sharp. Jodathyn suspected it was made from bone. "I suggest you look away."

The horrid object was brought to Jodathyn's wrist and pressed down until it punctured his skin.

Jodathyn yelped. "What are you doing?"

"You, my lucky lad, are receiving a slave's tattoo. This is so your masters in the new land will know what you are. It will help with your sale. Stay still."

"Stop this at once!" Jodathyn's words came out in a tumble of panic. He didn't expect the men to listen to him.

"It's easier for you if you stop moving," the Artist said. "The job will be completed either way."

The men held Jodathyn down firmly as the Artist bent his head over his arm. Jodathyn only half watched, biting his lips to stop his whimpers as the Artist painstakingly traced a pattern with his bone needle. He wouldn't give them the satisfaction of hearing his distress. Biting harder, Jodathyn could taste his own blood. He concentrated on his bleeding lip to avoid acknowledging his current predicament.

Jodathyn closed his eyes, trying to still his panicking mind. His thoughts were a jumbled mess. Mentally he called out to his dragon half ... anything to stop the sharp sting of disfigurement. Tornyth was not to be found.

Panting, Jodathyn looked up into Atek's inscrutable face. "Why?"

"It's just profit, boy."

After what seemed a long period of time, the Artist stood and cracked his back. He washed down Jodathyn's arm.

Jodathyn looked down at the tattoo now gracing his right wrist.

"*Wirahli Sais-Levly*," Jodathyn groaned, swallowing a mouthful of bile. Try as he might, he couldn't tear his eyes away from the two ancient runes that read *enslaved flying lizard.* Above the runes was a small eye with a spear.

"Vadroil's crest," the Artist told him, wiping Jodathyn's arm again with a strong-smelling rag. "The mark of the enslaved."

Jodathyn couldn't imagine what Kieryn would say if he was to learn that he had been mutilated. Some highborns held onto the belief that a tattoo, especially the mark of a slave or criminal, brought eternal shame on the bearer's bloodline.

"Why?"

The Artist didn't answer him. He grabbed a bandage and started to tightly bind Jodathyn's arm. When he looked up, he avoided eye contact with Jodathyn. "Keep it clean, gentlemen."

"When I fly free," Jodathyn murmured, knowing that he was speaking the truth, "you will regret marking one of Pallarus bloodline. The enemies of house Pallarus will be forced to kneel."

CHAPTER THIRTY-ONE

Jodathyn

The Port of Thrangul

The idea of visiting the coastline of Rama had been a fanciful daydream of Jodathyn's. Born into the status of Son of the Crown meant his opportunities to travel was limited. The lure of the forbidden only intensified his curiosity. As the cart lumbered into the busy port of Thrangul, he languished in his prison. His great sadness left him no energy to care for his surroundings.

His freedom had been stolen from him. And now Tornyth was gone. He had never realised how much he relied on his elusive dragon half. Even though he was terrified of the dragon, it had always been a part of him.

Wriggling up into a seated position, Jodathyn rested his head against the bars of the cart. The strong smells of salt and fish were heavy in the air. Filthy children ran along the cobblestones, shrieking, jumping and leaping. Fishermen called out to each other about their catch. Merchants and sailors mingled in the mass of the crowd.

Jodathyn wanted to scream at them. Instead, he hung his head in despair and stared once more in horror at his bandaged wrist. He clenched his teeth as his treacherous mind replayed the sting of his branding. He was forever defiled and shamed.

When Jodathyn had heard Orion's ill news of what was transpiring in Pallaryn, he had still held onto a sliver of hope. Now that he knew he would never see the great walls of the palace again, he wished he had never left.

"Do you still hurt?"

Jodathyn glanced over to Nym, who had mellowed over the last day. "It's itchy."

"If you don't know what it says, it's fetching."

Jodathyn scoffed. Nym's words rang false. If she was trying to be encouraging, she was failing. Who would want a damaged Son of the Crown?

"Think of them as battle scars."

Jodathyn shook his head. With the tattoos, his life looked grim.

"You took on a dragon and lived," Nym said.

"Look where I am now, Nym. I'm better off dead."

"We're not sold yet," Nym argued.

"Oh, don't you fret, my pretty." One of their captors skulked around the cart like a predator. "There's plenty of time for that. Atek is looking for a ship's captain to take you off his hands. It won't take long."

Jodathyn scowled at the man's retreating back. "I always dreamed of sailing on the ocean."

Their captor was correct, it didn't take Atek long at all to find a ship's captain willing to take them. He returned a short hour later with his customer, who was keen to survey his purchases. Indicating to his lackeys to retrieve his prisoners, Atek returned to his conversation with the captain.

As his tormentors opened the back of the cart, Jodathyn glared at them. They laughed and, infuriated, Jodathyn spat into their faces as they bent to grab him. When one of Atek's men raised his hand to strike Jodathyn, the captain interrupted.

"Stay your hand. He's mine now to punish. On your feet, scum."

At the captain's command, Jodathyn was shoved from the cart. He stared at the captain as he was forced to stand before him.

"You should not look at your betters directly, boy."

Jodathyn studied the captain, refusing to avert his gaze. The captain would have been approaching his middle-life. His skin was weather-beaten and he smelt distinctly of wind and salt.

"I am your new master. I will be your host and owner while you travel the seas."

Jodathyn raised an unconcerned eyebrow. He sneered as Nym was dragged to join him. "I am Jodathyn Pallarus."

"Not anymore," the captain said. He smirked, showing two rows of yellowing teeth. "You are lot 568432 *wirahli sais-levly.*"

"That does not change who I am."

The captain turned to Atek's men. "Take lot 568431 *sharp tongue girl* to my ship and settle her in. Lot 568432 needs a lesson in manners before he is shown his new accommodations."

Jodathyn watched, helpless, as Nym was dragged away.

"Shall we?" Atek took Jodathyn's upper arm and marched him behind the captain. The crowds melted before them like snow in the springtime.

"I can hardly wait," Jodathyn groused.

"Your tongue will get you into trouble, prisoner."

"Just think on what my tongue might whisper in my brother's ear, Captain. I trust you've heard of him?"

"Silence!" the captain barked.

Seeing the annoyance in the captain's stance, Jodathyn felt a small thrill of victory. He threw his head back and laughed. "My brother has a temper. Do you know what happens to someone who harms a royalborn? They end up very, very dead."

Atek jerked on Jodathyn's arm to force him up the gangplank. "Be quiet."

Despite the awfulness of his situation, Jodathyn stared in wonder at his first sight of the ocean. It was crystal blue and beautiful. He longed to test the cool water with his fingertips.

His moment of serenity was shattered by the approach of a hard-faced man.

"First mate, this one has earned himself a lesson in manners."

Atek threw Jodathyn into the first mate's waiting hands. The first mate grabbed him, thrusting him forward. "Get moving, scum."

Jodathyn turned his head in time to see the captain and Atek continue a hushed conversation. A purse of gold was handed over. He narrowed his eyes. The purse looked heavy. Atek would be repaid in more than gold for what he had done.

"You're an expensive one," the first mate snorted. "Hope you're worth it. You don't look like much."

"Looks can be deceiving," Jodathyn replied.

The first mate snickered, pressing his palm between Jodathyn's shoulder blades and pushing him forwards. "You won't be proud for much longer."

"You won't be alive for much longer!" Jodathyn snarled.

The crew of the ship had stopped to see what the commotion was about. The first mate grabbed Jodathyn's wrists and secured him to the mast. His ears were met with mocking laughter as his shirt was ripped from his body. He stood with his bare back on display for all to see his scars of his childhood.

Jodathyn knew when the captain had concluded his business with Atek by the clipped footsteps of the man's boots on the wooden deck.

"Do you feel exposed, Jodathyn Pallarus?" The captain ran his hands down Jodathyn's back in a parody of a comforting touch.

Jodathyn swallowed bile as gooseflesh rose on his skin. He would not show his fear. "Off to the Otherworld with you."

The captain tsked and turned in a tight circle as he spoke to his crew. "Come, who would like to see Jodathyn of house Pallarus stripped of his dignity?"

Jodathyn closed his ears to the hoots of laughter from the sailors about him.

"This is going to be the last time you hear your name spoken – you are now 568432. On *The Tribulation* we use the cane on disrespectful prisoners."

"My name is Jodathyn Pallarus, the second-born son of King Hadryn."

"An unwanted son ... and now you are my prisoner."

The cane whistled through the air and slammed into Jodathyn's back with a resounding crack. He cried out in shock at the flaring pain. It was like nothing he had ever felt before. The crew held their breath as the captain paused, allowing Jodathyn to feel the full force of the blow before he struck again.

"Say your number," the captain commanded.

"No," gasped Jodathyn. "I am Jodathyn Pallarus."

The cane came down against his back in three swift strikes. "Your number."

"I am Jodathyn Pallarus."

"You're a stubborn one. Never mind, we have broken stronger wills than yours before."

By the time the ship's crew had finished with him, Jodathyn's world was on fire. His ears rang with their mocking taunts and his howls. The caning felt like it had lasted an eternity. When his wrists were released, he fell, sobbing, into a boneless heap. The captain had no mercy. He was hurled to his feet by his hair and dragged along the deck. He had no idea how he made it below the deck. His legs felt like they were shaking more than a newborn foal's.

A door to a cell was opened and Jodathyn, unable to stand, fell face first. He lifted his head to glare at the sailor in the doorway. "I *am* Jodathyn Pallarus."

The sailor's eyes hardened as he booted Jodathyn's side. "Tomorrow you should utter your number."

Jodathyn dragged himself to his knees; his stance was unstable. "I wouldn't bet on it. You haven't met a more stubborn son of a king than me."

The man snarled. "We'll be back in a few hours with your medicine. Be in a more respectful mood."

Jodathyn curled his lip and let himself go limp on the floor. Disgusted, the sailor left.

"Are you hurt?"

Jodathyn opened one eye. Even though the cell was pathetically small, he hadn't realised he was with Nym. "Didn't you hear my delicate screams?"

Nym winced. "Sorry. That was a silly question."

"I think I have deafened myself."

Nym slid down the back wall of the ship and hugged her knees to her chest. She looked upon Jodathyn's naked torso with something akin to horror. He could see her take in his hideous childhood scars as well as his newer, fresher welts.

"They're ghastly, I know."

"What I find ghastly is the mangy boil-brained weasel that did this to you. All over a puppy!"

Jodathyn snorted and shuffled his back around so that Nym couldn't see his disfigurement.

"They're not remotely ugly or repulsive."

"They're unsightly."

"They're a mark of your courage," Nym growled. "But honestly, Jod, give the slavers what they want. You need to be in good shape if we're going to figure out how to escape."

"They want my name," Jodathyn muttered.

"When has the name Pallarus ever treated you fairly? You don't owe anyone your loyalty."

"I am Jodathyn Pallarus."

"The ship moves more than I suspected it would," Jodathyn murmured from his corner of the cell. He had the vague sense he might have slept. He lay listening for Nym's next colourful phrase. "Is it day or night?"

Nym crawled over to him. "How do you fare?"

"Sore. Hurt. Hungry and so very cold."

"I would lay beside you to warm you but ..."

Flushing, Jodathyn tried to imagine what Nym's body pressing against his might feel like. Would she be muscular and sinewy, or soft and warm?

"Oh, don't be so embarrassed by the thought!" Nym scoffed.

Jodathyn was glad that Nym had taken his silence as shyness. "I'm not ... just ..."

"Well, I won't lay beside you ... I would be worried that it would hurt you more. Otherworld, Jod, you should have heard your screams."

"I did," Jodathyn replied.

"They left us something to eat."

Part of Jodathyn wanted to reject the hard piece of bread that Nym offered. Instead, he reached out and took it. His eyes were half lidded with fatigue as he nibbled the hard crust.

"I think they are giving you a high dose of herbs."

"Do you think it will always be like this?"

"Life isn't going to be pleasant, Jod. We're not bound for the palace in Pallaryn."

"Life in the palace isn't pleasant."

"Surely you lived with enough to eat, drink and somewhere to lay your head. What more could you want? You're a right palace brat, Jod."

Rolling onto his side, Jodathyn didn't reply. How could he possibly explain to Nym that although there was a part of him that missed his home, he had always longed for something else? While his brother could provide him with material comforts, Jodathyn had been isolated. "We have to get out of here," he muttered.

"How do you plan on that?"

"Keys. The first mate keeps them around his waist."

"Do you know what the punishment is for an escaped slave?" Nym asked, her tone of voice severe. "*Death.* They probably won't kill you but they wouldn't hesitate to kill me."

"You're not tattooed yet. If you escape before they mark you ..."

Jodathyn took Nym's silence to mean she was considering the merit of his words. He knew she would risk everything to be free and for the chance to reunite with Theo. Slavery was no life at all. They couldn't give up. If they were going to escape, they needed each other.

CHAPTER THIRTY-TWO

Jodathyn

Aboard the Tribulation

It had taken Jodathyn and Nym a few days to piece together a plausible plan. Each time Jodathyn was dragged up on deck to be punished for his insubordination, his determination to escape grew. He would not be the victim of fate; he was going to forge his own destiny. Slavery was not an option.

"Here they come. Are you ready, Jod?"

In the dim light, Jodathyn could see that Nym's face was as ashen as her hair. She didn't like the first part of their plan. He hoped it was because she didn't like to see him hurt.

The key turned in the lock, and Jodathyn stood on shaking legs. He sucked in a deep breath to prepare himself for what he knew must happen. Nym grasped his hand, and Jodathyn gave her a grateful smile.

"Courage, Jod. I would take your place if I could."

The first mate and his companion entered the cell. His cold eyes took in Nym's hands clutching onto Jodathyn and he smirked. Refusing to be cowed, Jodathyn met their malicious sneers with a cool expression. "You're earlier than I expected, gentlemen."

The first mate didn't speak as he reached for Jodathyn to escort him onto the deck. Jodathyn gave Nym one last glance and a nod. He would not fail her.

"I'll see you soon."

Jodathyn had realised that his unconcerned air frustrated the captain and his crew. There was power in that. They wanted to see him grovel and beg. But Jodathyn would never yield. He wasn't about to become some poor, broken plaything.

Determined to force Jodathyn to submit to his authority, the captain had created a ritual of beating him. For his part, Jodathyn continued to be stubborn. He would not give up his name.

Nym thought a name a minor thing, but he was a royalborn. His whole identity was wrapped up in his bloodline. Without it he would only be a husk of a man.

"Who might you be?" the captain asked, twirling the cane in his hand.

Jodathyn lifted his chin, his grey eyes flashing in a silent dare as he eyed the captain's instrument of torture. "I am Jodathyn Pallarus, the second-born son of Hadryn; the brother of the High King of Rama and Son of the Crown."

"Very well, proceed," the captain said. He handed the cane to a nearby sailor. Since the captain couldn't break Jodathyn he had given different crew members the opportunity to do so. Jodathyn had heard the reward for breaking him was an extra day's rations.

Jodathyn was ready for the first mate to spin him around. This was the opportunity he had been waiting for. His days of stealing when he lived in Aviah Valley had taught him the art of stealth. Without the first mate realising it, he was able to steal one of his daggers and pocket it. Nym had been unbelieving when Jodathyn revealed this skill.

Breathing in through his nose, Jodathyn readied himself for the harsh whoosh of the cane as it cracked against his back. Then exhaling, he began to draw the map of Rama in his mind. He labelled as many towns, rivers and roads as he could. He thought of the dagger he had stolen and the plan to win his freedom. When he believed he could no longer bear the suffering, the beating ceased.

Sick and dizzy from the pain, Jodathyn felt himself being led away. The first mate took him down below alone. The fool was confident that the beating had been enough to subdue his captive. Obviously he had not been up against Pallarus stubbornness before.

The first mate dropped his hold on Jodathyn with one hand as he fumbled with the lock. Jodathyn's fingers slipped around the hilt of the dagger. He knew Nym would be waiting in her spot, as they had practised. She had been adamant they should rehearse how they could take the first mate by surprise.

The first mate swung the cell door open. Unresisting, Jodathyn stepped into his prison. Not wanting to lose an opportunity to make Jodathyn's life miserable, the first mate followed him into the cell. Jodathyn pressed the hilt of the dagger into Nym's waiting hands. She was efficient. There was no time for the first mate to open his mouth to sound the alarm. She slashed his throat open in one powerful slice.

Rich, red blood sprayed from the man's wound. Nym had cut deep, and Jodathyn thought he could see bone. The first mate dropped to the deck, gargling and writhing before he became still. Jodathyn swore. Nym rolled her eyes and grabbed the man's ankles, dragging him into their cell.

"There was so much blood," Jodathyn murmured. His face looked a little green as he took in the splatter on Nym's face.

"What were you expecting?"

Jodathyn ran his hands through his hair; they were shaking. "I could do with a bath."

"Palace Brat. I thought some herbs for the pain would be higher on your needs." Nym shook her head and crept past. Jodathyn thought he heard a note of fondness in her voice. "This only works if we have the element of surprise."

Together they skulked forward. The plan was simple and it hinged on getting onto deck unnoticed, and stealing a longboat.

Jodathyn wasn't sure where they were ... hopefully they would row in the direction of land. Nym had declared that she had impeccable sense of direction. He wasn't sure if that particular skill was transferrable when one was at sea.

They made it to the deck unhindered. Crouching in the shadows, Jodathyn watched the workings of the sailors. He had hopes of reaching a boat without being spied. Finally, he saw a break and indicated to Nym to follow him.

They tiptoed onto the deck.

"Escaped prisoners! The first mate is dead!"

Nym swore and took off running along the deck. Her sudden flight meant she was instantly spotted. Two men pounced on her. She went down screaming insults.

Jodathyn took two steps backwards, ducking behind a barrel. It seemed it was up to him to rescue Nym and himself. He wasn't sure how he was going to go about that. Sailors were running all over the deck. If he moved, he would be spotted. If he stayed, he would be found.

With a sinking heart he watched as Nym was bound and forced to her knees. Her keen eyes were on the spot where she and Jodathyn had last been hiding. He growled under his breath. Her heated gaze showed the sailors exactly where he had been.

"High and mighty fish thought to hide."

Jodathyn stood and spun on his heels, punching the man behind him. It happened to be the captain. Snarling, the captain reached up to hold his nose. Jodathyn realised with a spark of victory it was bleeding. The captain's feral grin promised retribution. He waved for his crew to take hold of Jodathyn. He was seized and dragged along the deck to join Nym.

"Tell me, which one of you sliced open my mate's throat?"

"I did," Jodathyn said. Remembering what Nym had told him about escaped slaves, he decided he did not want her taking credit. "I pocketed his knife and waited until we were alone."

"*You?*" The captain didn't look like he believed Jodathyn's tale.

"I'm a dragon. I have a violent streak."

"Bring all the other prisoners on deck."

"Yes, Captain."

Nym and Jodathyn were forced to wait on their knees for the other prisoners to be brought up. They were lined up, one by one. Jodathyn watched the proceedings from underneath his fringe. From the interesting body smells, some of them had been captive for a long time.

"Bring forth the canes."

Jodathyn bit back a groan. He was getting tired of being punished.

"These miscreants 568431 and 568432 killed the first mate and made an escape attempt. The rules aboard *The Tribulation* are clear."

Jodathyn was met with the furious gazes of the other prisoners. He wondered what unwritten rule the captain was talking about. Beside him, Nym was shivering.

"Everyone shall be punished for their transgressions. Mr highborn 568432 will receive double."

"Death to 568432! Kill him! Death to 568432!"

Jodathyn barely raised his head to listen to the yelling of the other prisoners. Their chant had started the moment he was dragged down the ladder and thrown back into the cell.

When the jail door slammed shut behind him, Jodathyn noticed he had landed on top of the cooling body. With horror, he realised the crew had intended to leave the first mate where he had fallen – they meant for them to share the cell with a dead man. He couldn't look at the corpse. He felt sick.

This was the second death Jodathyn had been responsible for since this misadventure had begun. Nym had been the knife he had wielded. He felt no pride, only hollow shame and fear. A man was dead and he was no closer to freedom.

"Give us his head. Give us 568432!"

"How do you endure it?" Nym's voice was quiet in the dark.

Jodathyn's eyes fluttered open. They were sticky with clotting blood from his victim. "The pain or the chanting?"

Nym sniffed.

"I have lived with scorn all my life. And pain is becoming my friend, I fear."

"I'm serious."

Jodathyn lay down his head again in utter exhaustion. "I think about something complicated that I know well and I concentrate on only that. For me I can lay out the entire palace or draw maps ..."

"I'm not educated like you," Nym replied.

"No. But you fight well. Make up a fight with an opponent in your head. Plan out the moves ... I find that if you use something suited to your own gifts it is easier to manage."

Nym was quiet for some time. Jodathyn found he was able to drift into a daze to escape his agony and the corpse. He envisioned his home at the palace, imagining seeing Donatein again. He could almost smell Donatein's herbs as he lined them up to create a remedy. The smell of the spiced wine which Kieryn favoured followed. Upon his cheek he could feel his soft feather pillow as Carvelle's lithe body snuggled close to him.

"I think it's working," Nym whispered.

"Death to 568432!"

Abruptly, Nym stood, slamming her fists on the door. "Shut your flapping traps, you boorish fool-born maggot pies!"

Jodathyn cracked one eye open. "The trick is to stay calm."

Nym turned to look at him. She looked like she wanted to claw her way out of their prison with her bare hands. Resting her head against the door she lowered her voice. "Why did you say you killed the man?"

Jodathyn shifted his shoulder. "I didn't want to lose a friend."

Nym sat down beside Jodathyn. "Let's talk about something more pleasant. What is His Majesty, King Kieryn, really, truly like?"

With some effort, Jodathyn forced himself to sit up. He regarded Nym's face in the dark. "He's my brother. I'm loyal to him. Being fourteen summers older than me he can be terribly bossy. Then he is High King so I guess he's doubly bossy ..."

Nym stifled a laugh.

"Kieryn knows he is regal and magnificent. He uses that to his advantage. The King is also quite stern and commanding. Don't make him angry. Once in a fit of anger he threw a goblet of wine at Lord Kamoore."

"The people of Rama love their King."

"I am glad," Jodathyn said. "Kieryn is a good man. I had hoped to be like him one day."

Nym reached forward, grabbing Jodathyn's hands in her own. "Today you made your brother proud."

Jodathyn turned his face away. "We're sharing a cell with a dead man."

"Kieryn sounds like a man who would fight," Nym replied. Her grip on Jodathyn's hand tightened. "He wouldn't want you to give up. We need to keep fighting, for both of our brothers."

Jodathyn blinked and shook his head. "And if we fail?"

"Then we fail," Nym said. "It's better than not trying."

Jodathyn closed his eyes. Where had his resolve to fight gone? His courage was exchanged for a sense of dread and helplessness. If they could get off the ship, then what? What did either of them know about survival on the seas?

"Jod, think on this, something from home you can't wait to see or do," Nym whispered.

Jodathyn shook his head and lay himself back down. He felt tears dripping down his nose. "I know you think I'm weak and foolish. I can't take any more of this ... I want to die. Oh, please Otherworld ... let me die."

"You don't want to die," Nym said, brushing her hand through Jodathyn's curls. "It's going to be alright, Jod."

Jodathyn shivered.

"Think of Prince Carvelle," Nym insisted. "Fight for him. If Kieryn is toppled as King, what do you think will become of your nephew?"

"Did your mother brush her hand through your hair?"

Nym's ministrations stopped. "Has a woman never mothered you?"

Jodathyn shook his head. "When my wet-nurse finished weaning me, my father sent her away. I know I shouldn't, but I have always wondered what having a mother was like."

Nym made an odd sound in the back of her throat.

"I know my father could not accept me. Sometimes I thought about asking Kieryn whether my mother might have loved me if she had lived. If I had never been born ..."

"Then we wouldn't have met," Nym replied. "And Carvelle wouldn't have a loving uncle who would do anything for him, including taking on a dragon."

Jodathyn stirred, feeling uncomfortable talking about things he would never have before.

"What about your dragon?"

"Tornyth? He's silent."

"Have you tried to reach him?" Nym asked.

"I haven't tried since the first day," Jodathyn confessed. "It's pointless. I am afraid of him."

"Well, with all the commotion I'm sure you may have skipped a dose or two of those herbs ... maybe..."

"Did you not hear me when I said I was afraid? The dragon ... he ... he can make me do things ... terrible things."

"Jod," Nym sighed. "We need something terrible to get out of this situation."

Jodathyn shook his head. "You have no idea of the evil inside of me. I am not a good man."

Nym scoffed. "Jod, you have to be one of the most innocent young men I have ever met ... Other than a dragon, what secret could you possibly be hiding?"

"I planned to murder a man in cold blood when I was a boy."

"You're jesting?"

"I wish I was. My Sight warned me someone was going to hurt Odelle ... Something inside of me was angry. Knowing what I do now, I think the dragon stirred then. There was enough time to steal some of my servant's herbs and mix a poison. From there I concocted a plan. I bribed a woman my guard was fond of to tempt him away. Unfortunately, the lord's spies found me out. They forced the poison down my throat and broke my arm. I was left with a warning that I should never speak of the incident. I should have died ..."

"Did you not go for help?"

"I was so ashamed ..."

"You wanted to punish yourself," Nym replied. "Oh Jod, we have a name for what you tried to do where I am from."

"Murder ..."

"Execution." Nym's fingers wound around Jodathyn's upper shoulder. Jodathyn could feel the warmth of her skin on his bare arms. "Tell me, your big brother you are so fond of ... what would he have done if he had known of this lord's ill intent for his wife?"

Jodathyn shivered, envisioning the fury his brother would have displayed. "It was Kieryn's unborn child he was after ... Carvelle ... Kieryn would have him taken to the palace walls and ..."

"Hung them up for all Pallaryn to see?"

Jodathyn nodded.

"See," Nym declared. "Exactly the same. How did the Queen stay safe from her would-be assassins?"

"The lord intended for me to die alone. But Donatein got worried and I was found by some King's Guardsmen. Kieryn was away on matters of state so they called for their own troop medic who recognised the symptoms of poisoning. They roused me and questioned me. I told them that I had snuck to the kitchens and had drunk the Queen's wine. My personal guard had already been dismissed and I may have had a cheeky reputation so the lie was believed. The poisoner didn't get another opportunity to poison the Queen. Kieryn was terribly angry when he arrived in Pallaryn ..."

Nym stood from her crouched position and stumbled to the other side of the cell. Jodathyn noticed she was careful to side-step the body. His head felt like it was stuffed full of duck down. He closed his eyes.

"Please, Jod," Nym whispered. "Please try for me."

Jodathyn nodded reluctantly. The truth was, he was afraid of Tornyth and what he might be capable of. But he was more scared about what would happen if Tornyth was enslaved. From the snippets of conversation he'd heard while he was being beaten, an enslaved dragon lost their sanity.

What was the better outcome? Tornyth with his own mind and will to make decisions, or an enslaved dragon at the mercy of a master's bidding?

"Tornyth has come to me most often when I am asleep," Jodathyn sighed.

"I'll watch over you," Nym said.

Jodathyn took a deep breath and started to practise some of the exercises Donatein had taught him to calm his body. He wasn't sure how to reach his dragon, but he remembered Tornyth mentioned being calm.

"And thank you for what you did for me today." Nym's words seemed to be coming from far away.

CHAPTER THIRTY-THREE

Jodathyn

Aboard the Tribulation

Though many had shunned Jodathyn for his visions, he had always cherished his gifting. His power was what had made him special. As a child he had believed his power was the key for him to unlock his purpose in life.

But no matter how hard Jodathyn strained, he couldn't call Tornyth's presence forward. His white dragon was lost to him. It was time to change tactic.

Tornyth wasn't the only dragon Jodathyn had met in his visions. There was another dragon who was older, wiser and more powerful. What if he could reach into those realms in his human state and call another dragon?

Jodathyn's memory of his encounter with the emerald dragon was hazy. Mandros had called himself 'Father of this Land' and had insisted Tornyth had called for him 'like a little hatchling'. From what the emerald dragon had said, he'd heard Tornyth's cries and had come to investigate. The way the ancient one had looked upon him gave Jodathyn hope that he would come if called.

If Tornyth had unintentionally called for Mandros, was it possible for Jodathyn to intentionally reach him?

Shaking with cold and fatigue, Jodathyn opened his eyes to check on Nym. She went quiet every time he closed his eyes. He knew she was holding on to hope for any sign he had managed something. He knew he was disappointing her.

Jodathyn licked his dry lips. "I want to try something else."

"Be my guest," Nym replied.

Jodathyn closed his eyes again and put Nym's foul mood from his mind. She was scared, he told himself; she was scared, hungry and cold, just like he was.

Taking in a deep breath, Jodathyn held it and then very slowly released it. He took a few more deep breaths and tried to relax his mind. When he felt himself in a meditative state, he tried to project his thoughts outwards.

Mandros ... Mandros ... Father of this Land ... please ...

His mind stayed blank. He was alone in his own consciousness. It was bleak and depressing. Jodathyn didn't want to open his eyes and have to admit to Nym that he had failed. Her disappointment in him was hard to bear. He stayed in the black nothingness, surrounded by his misery.

Flame and Fury ... I need you ... help us ...

The sea of black deepened and Jodathyn felt himself sinking. His thoughts stilled and became silent as his mind gave away to slumber.

He had a vague sensation of a rumbling sound, of something warm and rough against his cheeks. There was a ripple of green within the blackness.

And so, Jodathyn slept.

Jodathyn came to when his arms were grabbed and he was dragged from his cell. He could hear Nym making her displeasure known. Her voice echoed behind him as he was forced onto the ladder. Today they planned for her to join him for his beating.

"Leave her alone." Jodathyn wasn't entirely sure if he had spoken. He was dropped onto the deck at the captain's feet. "Water ... please ..."

The captain kicked him over. "Give me your number."

Jodathyn licked his lips, glancing to where they had dumped Nym onto the deck. He closed his eyes in defeat. "I have been many things in my life ... but never a number."

The captain leered down at him. "Give him his drink."

Jodathyn didn't have the energy to care. They propped him up and forced him to drink the cursed herbs. His world was pain and loneliness. He tried to think of his young nephew, Carvelle and his brother, but his memory of them was fading. Hope died, leaving him with only the dark terrors that thrived in his thoughts.

A sudden groan and lurching from the ship shattered Jodathyn's dazed state. All around him the sailors shouted as an explosion lifted the vessel. It rose into the air and then came down with a mighty roar of water. Men began running for their weapons, abandoning Jodathyn where he lay prone.

Confused, Jodathyn stayed sprawled along the deck. Nym crawled over to his side. She seemed to be screaming something at him.

"This is our chance ... Jod. The lifeboats!"

Jodathyn blinked with understanding and stumbled to his feet. He wobbled before falling over. Nym was at his side, grabbing him and almost dragging him across the deck.

"I know you're in pain, Jod! But dragon dung, help me!"

A second explosion sent them reeling across the deck. Jodathyn forced himself to his knees, ignoring his spasming muscles and the blood pounding in his ears. Gathering up what little courage he had left he grabbed the railing. Before he could change his mind, he swung himself into a lifeboat. A heartbeat later, Nym joined him.

"DRAGON!"

Her face paling, Nym lowered the lifeboat. When the wooden deck burst into flames, she cursed and pulled out a knife to cut the ropes.

The boat was falling. It hit the surface, sending a cascade of cold water over Jodathyn. He sucked in a lungful of air as the impact capsized their lifeboat. Before he could open his mouth to scream, he was plunged into freezing water. Almost immediately he began to sink. He struggled. He shouldn't have been so coy about his disfigurement. When Valt had offered to teach him to swim, he should have accepted. No doubt his personal guard would have a few things to say about his pride when they met in the Otherworld.

By some miracle Jodathyn forced himself to the surface. Around him the water was on fire. Screams rent the air and reverberated in Jodathyn's ears. He trembled with fear. Perhaps it was to be his fate to drown.

"Nym!" Jodathyn cried, rallying what was left of his Pallarus stubbornness. "Nym!"

A giant shadow loomed over Jodathyn as his head went under another wave. He clawed at the water in a frenzy, desperate to reach the surface once more. He screamed and breathed in salty water. As his eyes began to slide shut, a strong scaly claw reached down and plucked him from the watery depths. In the next moment he was being lifted up high and fast. In a panic he struggled, panting and coughing.

His feeble movements captured the attention of his rescuer. The green claw brought him closer to an elongated snout. Bemused amber eyes blinked at him. The dragon beat his wings so that he hovered in the air.

"Enough of that, human." The voice that came from the dragon was deep and stern.

"Please – my friend Nym."

The dragon lifted his other forearm and in his clutches was a scowling Nym. Her arms crossed against her chest, she looked half drowned and unimpressed by their rescue.

"Are you looking for this human? She seemed to be trying to escape with you so I rescued her too."

"Jod, tell this ill-begotten beast to put us down."

Glancing at the churning waves far below them the dragon cocked his head to the side. "To drop you now would be indeed unfortunate."

Jodathyn lifted his face to the wind, a laugh of surprising joy filled his belly. If the dragon were to drop him, he knew he would die happy. Unable to stop, Jodathyn laughed harder.

"You're enjoying this, aren't you, you rat-brained bastard."

"No need to be so surly, female human. Your friend is merely experiencing Wind Song for the first time."

Screaming, Nym struggled in Mandros' grip. The dragon made a hushing sound and soared upwards. The speed the dragon could travel was incredible. Jodathyn shivered as the cold wind whipped about him. In response the dragon tucked him closer to his chest, where his scales were warm. Jodathyn's shivering ceased.

"You're not going to eat us?" Nym asked. Her voice cracked with uncertainty.

The dragon's chest rumbled in a chortle. "I am not that kind of dragon."

"What kind of dragon are you, then?" Jodathyn muttered. His eyes darted around, fascinated by the fog of the clouds and the sea beneath them.

"Do you truly not remember, little white dragon? I am the Father of this Land. I am Flame and Fury. I am Mandros the Deliverer."

"That tells us nothing," Nym complained.

"The white dragon called for me." Mandros shook his great head. "I am Mandros the Deliverer. Did I not deliver you?"

"Land!" Nym sighed in relief. Below them was an island, thick with wild vegetation and vast beaches. Mandros drifted down and landed on his back legs. He released Nym from his mighty grasp. She fell to her knees, her hands clawing into the sand as if it would keep her grounded.

Mandros did not release Jodathyn. "If you beg my intrusion, Lady Nym. Your companion and I are overdue for a long conversation. I thoroughly look forward to seeing you tomorrow night when you find us."

"No!" Jodathyn cried.

But Mandros had already taken off with him, leaving Nym a tiny, angry speck on the beach.

"Fine! Keep him!" Jodathyn heard Nym yell. "He wasn't much use to me anyway! Useless muddled-brained lout!"

"Where are you taking me?" Jodathyn demanded, craning his neck to see if he could still spot Nym on the beach.

"Somewhere safe," Mandros replied. "Young dragons like places that are safe and warm."

CHAPTER THIRTY-FOUR

Kieryn

The Citadel of Pallaryn

Sweet Odelle was suffering; Kieryn could see it in the deep lines of worry on her face. Guardsman Jael had assured him that the sickness and stress his queen was experiencing was not unexpected. She was a devoted mother; it was only natural that she would pine for her child.

Kieryn felt conflicting emotions every time he looked at his wife. He was scared for her; her pregnancies were always difficult. When Jael had confided to him that their unborn child was female and thriving, Kieryn was excited. That Jael's healing powers could determine the sex of an unborn child fascinated him. After Odelle's loss of two daughters, Kieryn was looking forward to holding his living, breathing princess.

And then ... there was another part of him that was preparing itself for the grief of losing the child. Guilt over his worry and excitement gnawed at him. Then there was his constant, crushing fear that he might lose his clever little Carvelle.

"What are you thinking, sweets?" Odelle looked up from her needlework. Kieryn could see she was stitching the little yellow flowers that were native to the northern region of Rama. They were the same flowers that were placed on their lost daughters' graves. When she was afraid, Odelle tended to stitch yellow flowers.

Feeling remorse for even thinking about his daughter dying before her first breath, he blurted out the first thing that came to mind: "We should name her after your mother."

Odelle dropped the needlework onto her lap, screwing up her nose. *"Gytullah?* My mother hated her name."

Kieryn stifled a laugh. It seemed wrong to find a moment of amusement while his son was still missing.

"Let's find a different name to honour my family, if that is what you wish, my love."

A servant at the door cleared their throat. "Captain Tiernan begs an audience, my King."

Kieryn exchanged a glance with Odelle. "Let him in. No one is to disturb me."

Captain Tiernan and Guardsman Carew entered a few minutes later. They saluted, Carew standing a few strides behind his father. Kieryn took Odelle's hands in his own as she abandoned her needlework. It almost hurt to see the hope glistening in his wife's eyes.

"Pray, what have you found out, Captain?"

"My Queen was right," Tiernan replied. "The dragon indeed took Donatein's body to honour him. There's now a crypt for him on the hills of Habron."

"This should indeed be a relief for us," Odelle murmured. She ran her hand up Kieryn's arm. "The dragon isn't a beast if he honours the dead."

"That is true, Your Majesty," Carew said. "There was something else that we learnt."

"What is that, guardsman?"

"While the white dragon was mourning, a much larger dragon approached him."

Odelle gasped in horror, bringing her hands to her mouth. "Was the white dragon hurt?"

"No," Tiernan answered. "The dragons did not fight. They seemed to be speaking."

"Your Majesty, no dragon has been seen in Rama for centuries and suddenly there are two."

"We can theorise that there are more than these two around."

"Or hope that dragonkind can protect Jod, where I cannot," Kieryn murmured, brushing his fingers through his beard.

"It also muddies the meaning of Consort Ammerie's words," Queen Odelle said. Kieryn could feel her trembling from fatigue as she lay her hand over his again. She should be resting.

"Odelle, my sweet, perhaps you should go with your ladies."

"Kieryn, I will stay. Carvelle is our son and I'll hear what needs to be said." The Queen's voice came with quiet confidence. She brought her hands to her lap.

Reaching out to take her hand, Kieryn lifted it to his lips, kissing her knuckles.

Tiernan coughed, as if to remind his sovereign he was in his presence. Kieryn lifted an eyebrow, amused. His captain was one of the few men who saw him in moments when he was able to behave like an ordinary man. Tiernan knew his depth of affection for his wife.

"Is it worth going over what we know Ammerie saw and remove any assumptions, Your Majesty?" Tiernan queried, his voice soft. "Her gifting with the Sight was not strong. There were those who felt her predictions were inaccurate."

Kieryn shifted, feeling the fatigue in his bones. Tiernan's suggestion had merit. "She knew she would birth a son in winter who was of both Pallarus and Vadroil bloodlines. The fact she was already pregnant with Jodathyn when she revealed this vision doesn't exactly give credence that she was accurate."

"She saw a child with silver eyes and dragon white of scale," the Queen sighed. "This points to Jodathyn, if we have assumed correctly the dragon is indeed your brother."

"A herald for the dragon king to return. Possibly ruination of the Pallarus family. She mentioned 'Vadroil's heir' a number of times."

"Vadroil is an ancient line, how can we be sure that Jodathyn is the last of Vadroil's blood even if royal historians have confirmed it?"

"That is a reasonable question, my sweet, with another dragon ..."

"Also," Carew interrupted. "From the little that has been passed down to us from ancient times, dragon culture has different ideas on what qualifies as an heir."

Kieryn looked up sharply. He hadn't heard that before. "What do you mean?"

"While most dragons do consider their offspring their heirs, Your Majesty," Carew replied, "the primary requirement for dragons is an heir must be found *worthy*. Bloodlines are a secondary concern to dragons. Some dragons found bloodlines an unimportant nuisance in the acquisition of heirs."

"*Acquisition of heirs?*"

"Dragons are said to be fiercely competitive when they seek heirs, my Queen," Tiernan replied.

"I thought dragons hoarded gold and jewels."

Carew sniffed. "Not Ramian dragons ... their clan system was their greatest treasure. Older dragons like to have strong, worthy heirs to build their families."

Kieryn considered this point. "If we can offer Jodathyn to a dragon ... never mind ... I am still troubled by the notion that Jodathyn will be bathed thrice in royal blood." This was the prediction that Ammerie had frequently tormented him with. "Perhaps it's time we looked more closely at Consort Ammerie. Carew, please go to my personal library. Upon the highest shelf you will find a locked wooden box. Bring it to me."

"My King." Carew bowed deeply and left the room without a backward glance.

Each occupant was left to ponder their own thoughts in the silence of the King's private rooms. It wasn't until Carew returned with the requested box that Kieryn stood, indicating that the guardsman should leave the box on a hardwood table.

The Queen puzzled over the box. "What is this, Kieryn?"

"Ammerie was a cruel woman. She was unkind and spiteful. It is ironic that her words could destroy the son she would have used to depose me. Ammerie I hated, but her son ... I care deeply for Jodathyn."

His dark eyes studying the box before him, Kieryn held out his hand for Tiernan's sword. The captain handed it to him hilt first. Wrapping his fingers around the leather grip, Kieryn ignored his sweaty palms as he approached the box.

"Ammerie recorded what she saw with her Sight with pictures and words. Much like Jodathyn has done. Upon her death, my father, in his *wisdom*, locked up all her records."

"You have never looked through them, Your Majesty?"

"No, never. Now is the time."

It was a bitter thought to Kieryn that he had allowed this box to haunt him as a young king. He realised his hesitation to open the box had been because he was afraid of what he might find.

After grieving for an appropriate amount of time for his first wife, King Hadryn was enamoured by Ammerie. Kieryn had been angry that his father had remarried and he had responded to his new step-mother with childish dislike. In turn, Ammerie relished in tormenting him.

King Hadryn had been displeased with Kieryn and Ammerie when he heard of their conflict. Kieryn would never forget the day that his father had struck his heavily pregnant consort and the public declaration that followed, stating he would not claim his unborn child.

Ammerie had been left deserted and distressed. Jodathyn was born days later, dangerously early.

Swaddled in the bed sheets his mother had birthed him on, Jodathyn was brought before the king's council. Upon laying his eyes on Jodathyn for the first time, Kieryn could not bring himself to hate his tiny half-brother. He knew he could not allow the squalling little pink creature to perish at their father's whim. And so, he made his oath to protect Jodathyn.

It was time that the secrets that bound his family came to light. Regarding the box full of Consort Ammerie's mysteries, Kieryn swung the sword. His anger fuelled the impact of the blade. The box splintered and fell apart.

Kieryn pushed aside the remains of the box, and removed the leather-bound journals that had once belonged to his step-mother. He flicked through the books, feeling the age of the parchment on his fingertips. The journals were made from the finest Ramian leather; he could almost smell the inks that Ammerie had used. She had been quite a talented artist.

Kieryn felt his heart skip a beat as a beautiful sketch caught his attention. He turned to it and ran his fingers over the artwork. In a tidy script Ammerie had written, *My son and his child.*

Gasping, Kieryn brought his hand to his mouth, trying to hold back his cries. Exhaustion and anxiety had been his constant companions since Carvelle's disappearance. His anger left him feeling raw.

"Kieryn?" Odelle's voice was soft.

"I want my son home."

"Kieryn? May I?" Odelle took the journal from Kieryn's lap where he had dropped it. She stared down at the illustration.

"Kieryn," Odelle said, her voice rising in excitement. "This is good news ... this is confirmation that a few days ago Carvelle was alive. Ammerie has misunderstood ... this ..."

"It's Jodathyn, a fully manifested white dragon and Carvelle," Kieryn finished.

The Queen stared down at the sketch; a few tears dripped down her flushed cheeks. "Look at the way the dragon is with our Carvelle. He's protective. Carvelle is embracing his snout." The Queen handed the journal back to Kieryn. "This means that wherever Carvelle is, Jodathyn is protecting him. Our boy isn't alone. He has a dragon."

Kieryn chuckled in disbelief and continued to flick through the book. Most of the sketches were of minor everyday events. He paid them no mind. It wasn't until he came upon Jodathyn's unmistakable stormy grey eyes that he stopped.

Horrified, Kieryn took in the face of his brother. In the painting Jodathyn could be no more than six summers. Tears ran tracks down his face. His small fingers were clutching a dirty rag doll. His nightgown was too large and hung from his shoulders. He was saturated in blood.

"This painting is labelled, *my son bathed thrice in royal blood.*"

Kieryn wanted to rip the parchment and feel the satisfying tear of destruction. He desired to throw Ammerie's journal in the fireplace and watch it burn until there was nothing left but ash. Two things stayed his hand. He had hoped that Ammerie's journals might hold some speck of crucial information. His second reason was that he wished to find something of Ammerie that he could give Jodathyn. His brother deserved to know his mother, even if he hated her.

The journal tumbled from Kieryn's lap and Guardsmen Carew stepped forward to pick it up. Kieryn heard the guardsman's hitched breath the moment he spotted the tiny detail no one had ever known about.

"Oh Jod, I'm so sorry," Kieryn whispered shaking his head. "You were just a little boy."

"Kieryn?"

"My son bathed thrice in *his* royal blood," Carew muttered. "Otherworlds!"

Kieryn hung his head with shame and horror of what Jodathyn had endured. Never had the burden of the crown felt so heavy. "Not my blood. Not Carvelle's. But *his* own blood. Oh, he was so young."

"It says thrice," Carew commented, earning a reprimanding glare from his father.

"Oh!" Kieryn couldn't form any other words. He could not bear thinking about what this prediction might mean for his brother.

Captain Tiernan stared over his son's shoulder at the horrific picture of a bloody Jodathyn. "Perhaps Carew can look through the journal and see if there's any further clues."

Kieryn nodded and took a deep, steadying breath. "I am going after Carvelle and Jodathyn. Tonight. I will take a few good men to search for my boys myself."

Tiernan's steely gaze held onto Kieryn's. Kieryn knew his captain had expected him to come to this decision. He closed his eyes, leaning against his chair, feeling his wife's tentative grip on his hands. He brushed his finger along hers relishing the silky smoothness of her skin.

"Take Jael."

"Odelle ..."

"Kieryn, please. I am safe cloistered here in the palace. But out there ... please, you may need Jael's expertise."

"Your Majesties," Carew said, interrupting the royal couple's conversation. "I think I know where to look for Jodathyn."

Carew held up a picture. It showed Jodathyn huddled in a cave, two companions by his side. Ammerie had captioned it, *Kudah mines.*

CHAPTER THIRTY-FIVE

Orion

The Village of Yanyima

Orion was sick with dread. It had been three days since Jodathyn and Nym had been taken. Theo did not seem inclined to make himself useful. So, out of necessity he had taken responsibility for both Theo and Carvelle. From a young age, Orion's father had taught him that leadership was an honour. Now Orion wasn't so sure.

No matter how Orion tried, he couldn't draw Prince Carvelle out of his misery. He struggled to remind himself that Carvelle was only a small child and it was natural that he would be melancholy.

Theo's moods were not much better. The thief had only agreed to stay in the hope his sister might return. Each afternoon Orion sent Theo out to see what food he could forage; it had the added benefit of giving him a break from the other boy's frayed temper.

"A half-starved rabbit!" Theo came stomping back into their makeshift camp. "That's all I've got."

Orion frowned, studying the gaunt rabbit. It would be a meagre meal tonight. As leader he would, of course, take the smallest portion.

"Is there *anything* I can do to help?" Carvelle broke his silence. "Can I go hunt with Theo tomorrow?"

"You can help me look after the stallion. I'm sure when you're older you will have your own horse. It would be useful for you to learn how to look after him." Orion took the rabbit from Theo's clutches to skin it ready for cooking. He wanted to avoid having Carvelle accompany Theo on a hunt. The thief didn't need the distraction of the Prince.

"I have two ponies already," Carvelle announced. "Can't you show me something useful?"

"Do you have a suggestion?" Theo asked, stretching out his legs.

"Can you teach me to build a fire? Princes don't get to do that. And Uncle Jod didn't know how to cook."

Orion considered the Prince's ideas. From his brief time serving at the palace, he knew there were some ordinary tasks that royalty did not do. Commoners were taught from a young age how to build a fire and prepare a meal. Surely there was no harm in teaching a royalborn some essential life skills.

"I was six summers old when I learnt to build a proper fire," Theo said. "How old were you, Orion?"

"Four. Carvelle, how about you go with Theo and get us some firewood."

Excited, Carvelle jumped up and took Theo's hand and tugged him towards the trees. "I'll be the best firewood collector in the whole of Rama!"

Theo glared at Orion as he passed. Orion knew that the other boy wasn't comfortable being alone with the Prince. But the thief needed to take some responsibility. Impatient, Carvelle tugged on Theo's arm and the thief had no choice but to stumble after him. It was the happiest Orion had seen the Prince in the last few days.

"Don't go too far!" Orion called after their retreating forms.

"Yes, Mother!" Theo shouted over his shoulder.

Grinning at the irritation in the other boy's tone, Orion turned back to his task of skinning the rabbit. When he finished, Theo and Carvelle hadn't returned, so he brushed the stallion's coat. He had already seen to the stallion when they made camp. But he was fidgety and it was something he could do. He was beginning to panic that something untoward had happened, when Carvelle came skipping into the campsite. Theo trudged behind him carrying a bundle of firewood.

"Prince Carvelle would only pick the best kindling," Theo said by way of explanation. "Royalborns have to have the best of everything."

"If you are going to do something, you do it well," Carvelle replied. "That's what Uncle Jod says."

"Sometimes your uncle is wise." Orion invited Carvelle to come by him, so that he might demonstrate how to build a fire. Carvelle watched everything with rapt attention.

Theo, Orion noticed, didn't attempt to help. He sat on his log daydreaming as Orion finished preparing and cooking dinner. Exasperated, Orion served Carvelle first, then Theo and himself.

"Why do you serve yourself last?" Carvelle asked, picking at the meat he had been given. "And why don't you eat much?"

Orion bent his head over his meal so that he could avoid eye contact. "It's the manners my father taught me."

Theo's hand stopped halfway to his mouth. It seemed as if Orion's comment had upset him. Orion didn't understand why.

"We need more food," Carvelle said, nibbling his dinner to make it last longer.

"A blanket or two would be beneficial. The nights are getting colder."

Theo smirked, peeling off the burnt edges off his meat. "We are near the village of Yanyima. Tomorrow I'll see about getting us some more supplies."

"You mean to *steal* them?"

Theo scowled at Orion, tearing the flesh off his rabbit with his teeth. Orion thought the display was completely unnecessary. "You can be a self-righteous idiot sometimes, Orion Maysden."

According to Theo, early morning was the best time to pilfer supplies from unsuspecting victims. The vendors would be busy setting up their wares and gossiping. So as dawn broke, Theo led them into the village of Yanyima.

Orion estimated the village was twice the size of Belrah. He held on to Carvelle as the Prince gawked at the villagers passing him. Rural life seemed to hold a strange fascination for Carvelle and Jodathyn. The royalborns seemed to react to village life as if they were visiting a foreign country.

"Wait here." Theo nodded to the alleyway beside the tavern. Without waiting for a reply, the thief slipped into the street and into the market square. Orion could only assume he was looking for easy targets as he wove in and out of stores. He had expected Theo to grab food and make his escape. Instead, he strolled through the market, nodding greetings. Ushering the Prince into a laneway, Orion tried to ignore the tantalising smell of fresh bread. His stomach cramped.

"You're hungry," Carvelle said. "You should eat my dinner tonight."

Smiling, Orion patted Carvelle's head. He turned away from the temptation of the bakery, only to eye the stall holders setting up crates of autumn fruits. Orion's mouth watered. "Don't you worry about me."

"There's Theo!"

Orion glanced up to see what their resident thief was up to. Without breaking his stride, Theo swiped a ripe apple from a vendor's cart as she turned to gossip with the farrier's wife. Orion couldn't help but shake his head as Theo strolled past.

"Stay here, I've made my marks," Theo said, ruffling Carvelle's hair. He glared up at Orion. "I won't be long."

Orion frowned. The prospect of stealing from hardworking people stirred unwelcome feelings of guilt. In the Otherworld his father would be ashamed of him. He couldn't understand how thieves could be pleased with such a dishonest trade.

Unconcerned, Carvelle turned to Orion as Theo made his way to a cheese merchant. "Do you suppose stealing things is easy?" he asked.

"Hush," Orion said, his eyes staying on Theo. "We don't want to be overheard, do we?"

"Do your feet hurt? You've been walking a lot."

"A little," Orion admitted.

"We should share the horse."

Orion smiled down at Carvelle. "That's kind, but not necessary."

"If we share, you and Theo won't be so sore. Maybe Theo would be less cranky in the afternoons … or maybe it's the hunting that makes Theo cranky."

Orion grinned. Peel away all the trappings and finery of court, the Crown Prince was still just a boy.

"What will you do when we get back to Pallaryn?"

"Hopefully," Orion muttered, "go back to Silverdyne where I belong."

Carvelle asked the question that Orion had been dreading. "Can you go back to Sion?"

"No, my mother was a part of the Sionian community in Silverdyne. I have never been to Sion."

Carvelle's attention was already elsewhere. He jumped up, pointing at a crowd of gathered children. "Oh look! I wonder what they are up to!"

Before Orion could grab at Carvelle's hand, the boy had scampered out from the shadows. He pushed his way through a group of gathered children. Groaning, Orion stood to follow.

Unpredictability must be a trait belonging to the Pallarus bloodline, he thought with some irreverence.

Wading through a sea of excitable children, Orion found himself surprised by a puppet show. He caught sight of Carvelle who had placed himself right at the puppet master's feet.

Orion remembered the travelling minstrels visiting Silverdyne when he was small. He had sat proudly on the spearmaster's lap, while his older siblings had stayed with their mother. Once upon a time he too had been entertained by the simple shows. Hanging back, Orion decided to let Carvelle be entranced by the puppets. No harm ever came from watching a puppet show.

He studied the puppets, patched together with colourful fabrics, with some amusement. The first was made to resemble King Kieryn, complete with a small golden crown. Orion could see the smile of wonderment on Carvelle's face as he gazed upon his father's likeness. The second puppet was a dragon.

"Come, dragon, the house Pallarus welcomes you to Rama. Come and gobble up the children."

The children around the puppet master shrieked and clapped.

Carvelle's face twisted into a confused frown. Orion shifted from foot to foot.

"Children are delicious," said the dragon puppet. "I have just finished devouring your little prince."

"Yum! Yum!" the children chorused.

Orion had a terrible feeling about the puppet show. It was unlike any puppet show he'd seen before. His eyes darted about, looking for Theo. If they needed to make a quick escape, he couldn't leave the thief behind.

"I, King Kieryn, release you, dragon, to go burn the fields. None shall protect my people."

"This is ridiculous," Carvelle shouted.

"Shhh ..." snarled an older girl with wisps of fly-away hair escaping her bonnet. "We're trying to learn about the King and his evil brother Jodathyn."

Carvelle placed his fists on his hips. Orion could have groaned. Knowing the cleverness of the Pallarus tongue, it wouldn't be long before the Prince said something to put himself in danger. Orion started to push his way through the crowd. He needed to silence Carvelle.

"This play is silly. Uncle Jod doesn't eat children!"

"Ah, so we have a sceptic in the crowd," the puppet master cried out. "Do you have something to say, young sir?"

"No!" Orion yelled, ignoring the looks of disgust he was receiving as he jostled through the children in his attempt to reach Carvelle.

"Yes!" cried Carvelle. He stood up before the puppet master. There was something reminiscent of his father, the King, in that moment. "What do you think you are doing saying such horrible things about the King? That's treason."

"If a king does not defend his people, then he betrays his own nation. King Kieryn has committed treason against all of Rama. He has allowed a dragon into our country."

Carvelle pulled a face. "What dragon?"

"His brother, the conniving, scheming Jodathyn. He wants the throne for himself and his kind. He'll burn the country to the ground ... King Kieryn is helping him."

"That's the most stupidest story I have ever heard," Carvelle declared. "The only dragon I've met is a–"

Orion managed to clamp his hand over Carvelle's mouth. He pressed the Prince against his legs, trying to draw him out of the crowd, ignoring his furious stare. He might be the Crown Prince of Rama, but he was also a little boy out of his depth. It was up to Orion to shut Carvelle up and get him out of the village, before he stirred up trouble.

"Forgive my cousin, he's a passionate boy. He never stops talking."

Wriggling free, Carvelle stomped on Orion's toe and turned glaring at the puppet master. "Your story makes as much sense as a silken gown on a sow."

"There's no room in Yanyima for those who sympathise with dragons."

The crowd jeered.

"Come," Orion hissed between clenched teeth into Carvelle's ear. He started to drag the Prince back to the place where Theo had left them. "Move."

Carvelle followed, moping. Anytime he went to open his mouth, Orion shushed him.

"I am a prince!" Carvelle stomped his foot.

"Be quiet!" Orion hissed, slapping his hand over Carvelle's mouth again. "Or it will be our heads."

"Why didn't you let me say something?" Carvelle demanded, as Orion brought him alongside the tavern and released him.

"Crowds can be dangerous," Orion cautioned. He glanced around, looking for Theo. Where was that thief?

"I don't understand," Carvelle said.

"That was the sound of uprising," Orion replied. "From now on we need to watch everything we say."

"I still don't understand."

"Sometimes when a large group of people get angry, they can end up doing terrible things. We don't want to get caught in the middle of a mob," Orion explained, reminding himself to be patient with the Prince. He wished Jodathyn was with him. His master would know what to say.

Carvelle blinked. "If I'd told them who I was they would have calmed down."

"Carvelle, listen to me. It is best you keep your name secret from now on. When a crowd speaks ill of your Papa or Uncle Jod, say nothing. Under no circumstances tell anyone who you are."

"I don't like the way they spoke of Uncle Jod. It wasn't fair."

"I didn't like that either," Orion said. He stopped as Theo joined them. "But your Uncle Jod would want you to act wisely. I need you to promise that you'll listen to what I have to say so I can keep you safe."

His arms laden with an assortment of breads and cheeses, Theo looked between Carvelle and Orion. Judging that something was wrong, the thief didn't say a word; he jerked his head to the side indicating they should move from their place. Orion and Carvelle followed him.

In disbelief, Orion stared at one item that wasn't on the list of things they needed.

"Why do you have a lute?"

Theo ignored him, stuffing the pack full of his pilfered goods. Satisfied with his haul, he stood. "Are you going to tell me what is happening, horse boy? Or are you going to make me guess?"

"They were being nasty about my Papa and Uncle Jod!" Carvelle said.

Orion could tell the Prince was hoping Theo would take his side of the argument. "Orion says I have to keep my name secret and be quiet."

"Dissension is brewing," Orion explained as Theo lifted an eyebrow at the Prince's pouting face. "It's not safe to linger here."

"I hate Yanyima!" Carvelle snarled.

Orion patted his head.

"Are you suggesting there's rebellion against the High King?" Theo winced. He too looked down at the young Prince. "Carvelle, I think horse boy is right. We keep quiet."

"We have the Prince," Orion continued. "If anyone rebelling against the King finds us with him, it won't end well for us."

Theo bit his lip. Orion could tell he was thinking about the possible grisly fates they might suffer. "We could keep moving or we can go to ground."

"You're the criminal."

Theo sent Orion a disgruntled look. "Is that you asking me for my opinion?"

Sighing, Orion shook his head. "I guess so. Father never taught me what to do in this situation."

Theo snorted. He considered their options, then replied, "We need to get some distance between us and Yanyima. My suggestion, if you are really asking for it, is to find somewhere safe and lie low. If rebellion is happening, we don't want to be on the road."

"I want to go home," Carvelle wailed. "I miss Papa and Mumma!"

"I know. We'll find another way." Theo knelt so that he was eye level with the Prince. "Let's find somewhere safe and learn what is happening first. Maybe we can get word to the King."

CHAPTER THIRTY-SIX

Fydellah

The Citadel of Pallaryn

Fydellah had thought Jodathyn a rich, over-indulgent fool as she watched him gallop away. Even then her powers had whispered that her assumptions were untrue. Jodathyn Pallarus had thirsted for something more than glory. Determined not to be dragged into a mess created by highborns, she turned a deaf ear to her inner judgement.

Highborns tended to coat their words with falsehoods and double meanings. Jodathyn was an enigma. When he had pressed his golden ring into her palm, she knew he didn't want anything in return. Now the ring weighed heavily around her neck. He might not have needed anything from her on the night of her liberation, but his circumstances had changed. He had been too afraid to ask her for what he wanted.

"Royalborn miscreant."

It wasn't unreasonable for Jodathyn to seek help to safeguard his young nephew.

After nearly three days heading westward, Fydellah turned her horse around. Even if Jodathyn had been born into the lap of luxury, he deserved the chance to live; after all, she had also been born into a prestigious family. She reasoned that Prince Carvelle might remember her act of mercy when it came time for him to take the throne. When the crown of Rama rested upon his head, he might be inclined to show clemency to people like her.

Fydellah returned to Pallaryn, exhausted. The citadel would forever haunt her dreams. When she'd left with Willyrd Hartcurt, she'd vowed she would never willingly return. Yet here she was.

Hiding her stolen horse near the northern gates, she entered the citadel unhindered. She tugged on her tunic and kept her head low so as not to attract attention. It would not do for her to be captured again by the guild. Even though the High King had punished her captors harshly, she was sure he had done that for Jodathyn's sake. No doubt there was a new guild master in Pallaryn. There was always another willing to risk their life for gold.

Talking to no one, Fydellah slipped down cobblestone lanes, making her way to the palace. She didn't yet have a plan, but she needed one soon. How could she, once a highborn lady and now an ex-slave, get the attention of anyone of importance?

"A pretty flower for the lady."

Fydellah jumped back, staring dumbfounded at a flower seller who proffered a yellow rose. She shook her head at the merchant and went to step around him.

"Come come, girl just a copper for old Garryt."

Fydellah pushed the flower away with a scowl. "Leave me alone."

The merchant pulled back his spindly flower to his chest as if it were a precious child. Turning away, he spotted another potential customer to annoy. As the merchant waddled away, Fydellah breathed a sigh of relief.

Finding her way to the palace wasn't difficult. It towered over the citadel like a beacon of stone. Every now and then she would dart a cursory glance over her shoulder as she wound her way through the streets.

Before long, Fydellah found herself in the shadow of the palace. It was as imposing as she remembered. She approached the guards' gate. Will had told her this gate was useful for nobles wanting to leave without close scrutiny. It paid to be friendly with the guards.

Fydellah tucked herself beside the palace wall to observe the pair of guards stationed at the outer gate, hoping she might hear something of use. They were arguing with a bearded man, whose clothes were stained with dirt.

"Please! Listen to me. Take me to the King," the bearded stranger demanded.

"Look here. You can't just come up to the palace and request an audience," a guard replied. The tone of his voice was bored.

"I told you – I have information."

"And if you have information of use we will send for Lord Solan."

The man grunted. "I don't wish to speak to Lord Solan. I wish to speak with His Majesty."

"No one is seeing the King."

"I'm not just anyone."

The guards scoffed, looking at the young man's worn clothing smudged with dirt.

The man shifted, his shoulders tense. The lines of his jaw were tight as if he was stopping himself from saying something he would regret. "Then send for Lord Hallidyn Whitoak. Tell him *Whisperer* has returned and needs to speak with him about an urgent matter."

"Whisperer is not a name we're familiar with, I'm afraid." The guards exchanged bemused smirks, which seemed to infuriate the young man. He took a few steps forward and leaned in close. Fydellah strained her ears so she might hear what he was about to say.

"I have a token from Jodathyn. He's doing his best to protect the Prince, but he's hurt and he needs help that I can't give him."

A shock tingled up Fydellah's spine. This stranger had also seen Jodathyn. She frowned. His words about Jodathyn being injured rang with concern and worry.

"Show us the token."

The young man hesitated before taking a gold chain from around his neck. Jodathyn was generous with his jewellery. As the man's fingers brushed against the guard, his wrist was grabbed and his sleeve shoved up to his elbow.

"Ah, a mark of a criminal – thought so. Who's the unlucky bastard you stole off? Thought to deceive us and get a reward, did ya?"

The young man struggled, his yells of protest gathering attention. Fydellah craned her neck. From her awkward position she could see the guild's mark on the stranger's wrist. He had been a slave too, at one time. Not that the uneducated fools on the palace gates would know what the symbol meant.

"Stop this!"

The man and his captors ceased their struggle as a young woman stepped out from the guards' gate. Fydellah eyed her gown with some envy. It was navy blue, trimmed with cream lace which accented her coppery braids beautifully.

"Lady ..."

"This man has committed no crime."

"My Lady."

The slow curl on the woman's lips froze, her eyes travelled the height of the stranger. There was a glimmer of recognition in her expression. Fydellah had to wonder how a highborn lady would know of a lowborn man. "His name is Whisperer ..." She turned towards the man, her eyes at once were cold and hard. "Come now, what is it this time you have to whisper in my father's ear, and for what price?"

"Jodathyn ..."

"You abandoned him. Don't speak his name."

"Lady Whitoak, Joddie needs help."

It seemed so strange that this man would use Jodathyn's moniker, but Lady Whitoak stepped back as if she had been slapped.

"He speaks of you; he misses you." Lady Whitoak lowered her voice and asked, "What is it you want?"

"I need to speak to the King."

"The King has left Pallaryn, I am afraid."

"Left? What do you mean left? I must be brought before the King!"

"He's gone." Lady Whitoak sighed. "You shouldn't have left the village where Father placed you, Ruevyn."

"I had no choice."

Lady Whitoak's face twitched into a frown. "Lord Solan has taken it upon himself to look after the King's affairs while he is absent."

"That's not satisfactory," Ruevyn snarled.

"Then I suggest you leave."

Growling, Ruevyn turned upon his heel and marched away.

Fydellah watched his tall frame parting the curious onlookers.

Lady Whitoak held her hand out to the guards. "Give me the chain. I'll take it to Jodathyn's rooms."

"Begging your pardon, Jodathyn Pallarus is under suspicion of murder and kidnapping. He's to be killed on sight."

"On whose orders?"

"Lord Solan's ..."

"Then not His Majesty's command." The expression on Lady Whitoak's face was one of extreme frustration. Grumbling, the guard gave her the chain. She closed her fingers around it, bringing it to her chest. Fydellah saw the briefest of sighs leave her lips before she slipped back through the gate and disappeared from view.

While the guards watched Lady Whitoak's retreat, Fydellah slipped away to chase after Ruevyn. He was easy enough to find in the crowds with his broad shoulders and angry stomping. She kept a few paces behind, careful to keep two or three people between them.

As he disappeared around a sharp corner, Fydellah followed. She didn't expect to barrel into his broad chest and come face to face with him. He had led her to a dead-end alley.

"Who are you?" he growled; his fingers dug into Fydellah's shoulder. Although his grasp was tight, she could feel him shaking. She understood his fear, he would think she was from the guild, tracking him.

"I'm not a slaver," Fydellah murmured. "Hear my voice and know my truth."

Ruevyn's eyes went glassy, his harsh grip loosened and he nodded. Fydellah never liked this part of her gifting but it had got her out of one or two scrapes.

"My name is Fydellah Nahilya. I am not from the slaver's guild." To prove her point, Fydellah rolled up her sleeve to show him her matching tattoo. She hated looking at the eye and spear. It made her sick to think about what other human beings would do to one another for profit.

Ruevyn's eyes softened, his lips forming a soft oh of surprise. "Do you need help, miss?"

"That's very kind, Ruevyn. No. I've also seen Jodathyn – I have a horse outside the north gate waiting for me. I want to help you find the King and convince him of Jodathyn's innocence."

Ruevyn swayed from side to side. "I don't know how I am going to achieve that. I'm indeed fortunate that Lady Whitoak didn't tell the guards what she knows about me. She might still ..."

"I'm sure you felt my power. It will be useful in revealing to the King the truth. What's your power?"

Ruevyn's hand brushed through his beard. "I don't have a power."

His statement rung true. If Lady Whitoak didn't have knowledge of a power, what else could he be hiding that had him so scared?

"Do you trust me?"

Fydellah scoffed. "You're concealing something."

Shrugging his shoulders, Ruevyn refused to look in Fydellah's direction. "So are you." It wasn't a denial.

"How can I know if I can trust you?"

"You're the one who approached me," Ruevyn reminded her. "I have a horse at an inn not far from here. I can meet you at the north gate in two hours. If you're not there, I'll assume you've decided to go your own way and leave without you."

Later that evening, Fydellah curled her feet underneath herself as she stared past the campfire at Ruevyn. He had exited the north gate of Pallaryn an hour earlier than he'd said. When he saw Fydellah he merely grunted, mounted his horse and kicked her into a gallop.

Speechless, Fydellah had stared after him. She knew that he'd seen Jodathyn, but she was still surprised to see him mounted upon the horse that Jodathyn had stolen. She dreaded asking why Jodathyn no longer needed the black mare.

Ruevyn led the way south, only breaking the silence to tell her curtly that he had gathered gossip before leaving the citadel. A few of the servers where he had stayed had told him the direction in which the King's party had been heading.

As the sun began to set, Ruevyn claimed he was tired. Fydellah had protested, but Ruevyn had ignored her and dismounted. While she built a fire, Ruevyn had seen to the horses.

Now Ruevyn sat in sullen silence, staring into the flames as if he had a heavy burden upon his shoulders.

"How do you know Jodathyn?"

Ruevyn's eyes glinted at Fydellah's question. His lips were pursed shut. He didn't want to answer her.

"In Pallaryn, what the lady said to you suggested you knew Jodathyn prior to this mess."

"So, you were eavesdropping," Ruevyn replied, stretching out his long, muscular legs. "We knew each other as children. He was my friend."

Fydellah sniffed. "Highborns aren't friends with slaves."

"He was the best friend a boy could have." Ruevyn sighed, hanging his head. "And I left him behind."

Fydellah let the silence lengthen between them. She took a deep breath and asked the question that had been bothering her all afternoon. "If you don't have any powers, how did you become a ..."

"Slave?" Ruevyn tilted his head to stare into the fire. "Poverty, starvation and desperation. My mother couldn't feed all her children. She sold me to a village magistrate so that she and my younger siblings might live."

"That's terrible."

"People do terrible things when they're desperate." Ruevyn sighed again. He was speaking from experience. "I can't imagine having to choose a child to give up. What my mother would have gone through ..."

Fydellah couldn't help it. She laughed at the stupidity of that statement. "She sold you!"

"So that my siblings could live. I can't find it in my heart to hate her for it. Sometimes I find myself wondering what happened to her." Ruevyn's assessing gaze caught her through the flames. "How do you know our sweet little Joddie?"

Fydellah sighed. "He saved me in Pallaryn – he tried to buy me from the slavers and it didn't end well for him."

"He's a good friend to have, Jodathyn Pallarus."

Leaning back onto the soft grass, Fydellah looked up. Away from the hustle of Pallaryn, the night's sky was alight with thousands of stars. "Wherever he is, I hope he is safe."

Ruevyn muttered, "I should have stayed with him. You get some sleep."

"How do I know I'm safe with you?"

A strange expression flitted across Ruevyn's face. "I have never murdered a woman."

Fydellah hoped the horror blossoming on her face wasn't visible to Ruevyn. He had chosen his words carefully, but in doing so had revealed another side to him. She could almost hear his deep tenor confessing.

"I have murdered men ..."

There would be little sleep for her tonight.

CHAPTER THIRTY-SEVEN

Jodathyn

The Isle of Torqui

The anguished cries of the sailors as they perished echoed in Jodathyn's mind. He could not decide if he was troubled or smugly pleased by their gruesome demise. Living in Pallaryn, he had seen harsh justice handed down before, but he'd never felt so unsettled by his dark thoughts. This time the deaths had seemed personal. Uncomfortable, he squirmed in Mandros' mighty grip.

Above him Mandros thrummed deep in his throat. With two powerful beats of his wings, the great dragon soared higher. "It is perfectly normal to feel anger, *vehyl*. Be angry but do not be a prisoner of your anger."

"I will never be the same again," Jodathyn grumbled. He sucked in a deep breath, bracing his hands along the scaly ridges of Mandros' claws. Flying through the clouds, clutched in a dragon's firm grasp was both invigorating and terrifying.

"That is true. In life we do not choose our suffering. Do not be dismayed, you are in control of how your suffering changes you. Let it be that your harsh experiences teach you to grow into a man of great strength."

Jodathyn closed his eyes. The sensation of the cold air caressing his cheeks and tussling his hair brought him unexpected pleasure. "Why did you help me?"

"You are not a man who's easily swayed into bitterness," Mandros replied. "You are strong. I can help you become stronger. The Isle of Torqui is the perfect place for you to find rest and peace."

Not wanting to mull over the fate of the ship's crew any longer, Jodathyn fell silent, staring in wonder at the Isle of Torqui. From the sky the island shimmered like an emerald jewel set in silk. It was the most wild and beautiful sight he had ever beheld. Raising his eyes to the horizon, he caught sight of the coastline of Rama. His excitement melted into a flutter of fear as he thought about Carvelle.

"Shouldn't you take me back to Rama?"

"In due course. The Isle of Torqui is a place of safety for dragons." Mandros' voice rumbled with pride. "The ancients say this paradise was the birthplace of our kind."

"And was it necessary to leave Nym stranded?" Jodathyn could not help but recall the shocked outrage on Nym's face as Mandros had taken off without her.

"There is no need to be so alarmed. Your friend will find us. It is best a dragon is born away from prying humans."

Jodathyn felt his breathing hitch. "What if I do not wish for the dragon to be born?"

Mandros dipped his wing, beginning a gentle descent as they skirted around the island. For a long moment, Jodathyn thought the emerald dragon had not taken heed of his question. However, as he landed on a rocky outcrop, Mandros placed Jodathyn on his feet and replied steadily,

"Come, *vehyl*, no more denying yourself. Here in this ancient home your dragon can finally win his freedom."

"*Vehyl?*"

"When dragons ruled the skies of Rama, the *vehyl* were humans that were to be respected under dragon law. It's almost an affectionate term. On the other hand, *rokun* is a wicked human, not worthy of the respect of dragonkind."

Jodathyn stared in astonishment at the size of the yawning mouth of what Mandros had called an ancient dragon home. The emerald dragon seemed unimpressed by the cave as he ambled into the dark opening. Jodathyn watched, shocked, as Mandros' tail slithered into the darkness and disappeared.

Although he was curious as to the cave's true size, Jodathyn wandered over to the edge of the outcrop. They were miles above sea level. From his vantage point he could see a long way out to sea. Straining his eyes, Jodathyn thought he spied a small spark in the distance. He wondered if it was the prison ship, still burning.

His swift investigation of the surrounding area gave him little hope of escape. Even with his climbing skills, he knew it was too dangerous to contemplate scaling down the cliff to safety. The only way to leave the solitude of the dragon home would be to fly.

Jodathyn was at Mandros' mercy. Although the dragon had not threatened him, and had rescued him from his tormentors, he was conflicted. He was aware of his ignorance with regards to dragons, and he didn't know how much trust he should grant Mandros.

"Come *vehyl*." Mandros' deep voice echoed from the cave. His tone left no room for argument. The green dragon was used to obedience.

Stepping into the cave, Jodathyn felt a sense of peace he could not understand. Mandros had curled himself along one of the cave walls, the empty space dwarfing his hulking frame.

Exhaling, Mandros breathed a small ball of fire into being. At first, Jodathyn was alarmed. But fear gave way to curiosity as it floated before the green dragon, casting flickering shadows along the walls. He stepped forward to peer at the strange ball.

"We call it Dragon's Lantern, *vehyl*. It is used for light and will not burn or consume."

Jodathyn reached out to touch the wall of the cave, which had become more visible. His fingertips brushed the unnaturally smooth rock.

"Do you remember creating your loved one's tomb?"

Jodathyn winced in remembrance of Donatein. "Dragon fire did this?"

"Yes. Dragon fire made this home," Mandros replied. He blew on the dragon's lantern so that the bright orb floated closer to Jodathyn. He was so entranced by the orb, he didn't see what the ball of light had lit up for his human eyes to see. "*Vehyl* hands painted the story."

Jodathyn sucked in a breath, surprised that he hadn't noticed the paintings in the dim light earlier. Before him was a picture showing a small human boy riding a blue dragon. "Did humans ride dragons?"

"Only *vehyl* that were deemed worthy and honourable." The great dragon blinked his wise amber eyes, tracking Jodathyn's movements as he studied the painted walls.

"Was this your home?"

"For a brief time, yes, Torqui was home." Mandros lifted his head, surveying the picture Jodathyn was studying with a soft smile. "It's only polite that you give me your *vehyl* name so that I may address you correctly."

"I wouldn't have thought dragons held manners in high esteem."

Mandros tilted his head with an air of impatience. "That was most impertinent of you, *elt Mynrell*."

"Apologies ... I didn't mean ..."

Mandros huffed.

"My name is Jodathyn Pallarus, born of Pallaryn." Jodathyn's fingers brushed over a green dragon flying over a ship. It was burning. Small human figures were jumping overboard. He shivered, recalling the sounds of screams as men burned alive.

"Ah, a royal *mynrell* for me, with a princely name. It is about time we see a dragon born from that line. Welcome, Jodathyn Pallarus." Mandros seemed pleased by Jodathyn's revelation.

"Is this you?" Jodathyn tucked away yet another foreign word to ask about later. He nodded towards the scene of the dragon and the ship. He felt ignorant with all the questions surfacing to his mind.

Mandros smiled. "I was a fierce battle dragon when I was young."

"You've sunk prison ships before?"

"Plenty," Mandros assured him with a feral grin. "When you are an old cantankerous dragon like me, you find you don't have a lot of patience for *rokun* evil."

"What is old to a dragon? How many summers have you seen exactly?"

"Too many to count, Jodathyn," Mandros chuckled. "How does a prince of the house Pallarus find himself enslaved?"

Jodathyn sighed, wrapping his arms around his chest. "I'm not a prince. I am the Son of the Crown."

"*Son of the Crown?* Sounds like *rokun* foolishness."

"My mother was only a consort and my father did not wish to acknowledge me." Even now the knowledge of his father's rejection stung.

"Did not wish to ...?" Mandros looked baffled, as if the King's decision made no sense to him. "A legitimate son of a king is a prince. Why would he not lay claim to a son?"

"My mother was of Vadroil's bloodline," Jodathyn whispered as if speaking of a secret shame.

Mandros' tail flicked back and forth. "Vadroil was but one dragon in our long and proud history."

"Vadroil was *really* a dragon?"

"Ancient One's Talons! Of course, Vadroil was a dragon."

"Mother had said that I was Vadroil's Heir ... they say I will be the ruination of Rama."

Mandros' scaly lips quirked into a smile as his belly erupted with dragon laughter. A pleasant sound, Jodathyn reflected, not at all frightening. "It is notoriously easy to manipulate the power of Sight to create your own meaning. It is impossible for you to be Vadroil's heir."

"How so?"

"Vadroil is dead."

"My mother was the last of the bloodline."

Mandros lay his head on the floor and fixated his gaze on the fidgety human. "Dragons choose their worthy *mynrell* – their heirs. While most dragon parents will protect their own blood and claim them, it is never guaranteed. A little dragon that built a crypt for a human is something that Vadroil would not have tolerated. Even if he was alive, he would have found you unworthy."

"That seems strange."

"Does it?" Mandros smiled sadly. "I myself chose each of my children by blood to be my heirs. In cases of the young and vulnerable, older dragons take them under their wing when it is time for them to manifest."

"Did this happen often?"

"Dragons are fierce protectors and creatures of war. Too many of our young are orphaned during conflict. Then there are those like you. Born of an ancient line with only *vehyl* parents." Mandros' voice was low, he cocked his head to the side to spear Jodathyn with his unblinking gaze. "It is past the time that you allow Tornyth, your dragon, to manifest."

Jodathyn swallowed, lacing his fingers together so they would not tremble. "I've been told dragons cannot be controlled. What if Tornyth becomes like Vadroil?"

Mandros stared at him. "Jodathyn, consider this painting behind me."

Obediently, Jodathyn stood. The wall behind Mandros depicted a man who towered over cowering slaves. Even in the ancient work, Jodathyn could tell this man was evil. His hand was outstretched, grasping a weeping woman's hair. At the woman's feet was her dead child. Jodathyn's eyes moved upwards. A dark blue dragon with talons of red flew above, his maw opened in an eternal snarl. His eyes were grey.

"Vadroil!"

"Below Vadroil is his human heart, Soren Monster-Blade. He was an evil man. In turn, his dragon was heinous and twisted. He betrayed his own kind."

"The woman and child?"

"They were dear ones to me. Soren murdered them to injure me."

"I have Vadroil's eyes ..." Jodathyn couldn't tear his eyes from the depiction of the ancient evil one.

"Nonsense! You have the silver eyes of a dragon born in the depths of winter. Now, come by my side. Let me call to Tornyth."

Jodathyn considered Mandros' words. "They drugged me. Tornyth is gone."

"The power of those accursed herbal tonics was not enough to murder your dragon. Come lie down beside me, my side is warm ... Come sleep. I'll not harm you."

"They say a forced dragon loses their wits."

"There will be no coercion. I will not force you to submit."

Mandros' words were tempting. Jodathyn's feet shuffled forward until he was standing right underneath the snout of the green dragon. For a brief moment he thought he was being controlled against his will. The need to become what he was born to be resonated deep within him. Even if Tornyth was gone, the instinct for freedom was strong. He wanted this.

"May I touch you?"

Mandros sniffed at Jodathyn with his snout. "Of course."

With shaking hands Jodathyn reached up to stroke the scales of Mandros' lower jaw. Mandros purred and the air around Jodathyn became warm and thick. It wrapped around his body like a curling blanket. The pain of the daily beatings and his stab wound faded away to almost nothing. Sighing, Jodathyn's legs gave way.

"Dragon breath will ease your body's suffering."

"Thank you," Jodathyn mumbled. His eyes slid shut. Unconsciousness claimed him.

Jodathyn felt himself tumbling into a deep slumber. In this place there was no room for fear nor pain. He was cocooned in safety and peace. He never wanted to leave.

After what may have been an eternity in the hushed blackness, Jodathyn became aware of Mandros' scales pressing along his back. He could feel the dragon's muscles rippling as he curled around him. If the green dragon was able to penetrate this place, where was Tornyth? Why hadn't Tornyth come?

Mandros thrummed a low noise, sending shivers of anticipation through Jodathyn. He could feel the vibrations, but felt helpless to answer the call.

"Tornyth is resilient. Unlike many others, he will not perish under the suppression herbs. Bring him to me."

Jodathyn should not have been surprised that Mandros was able to speak directly into his mind. Confusion warred within him. He was a swirling storm of uncertainty, unease and homesickness. A discordant melody ran through Jodathyn's brain. No matter what he tried, he would never be brave enough or strong enough to grasp his destiny.

"You are enough. I have chosen you, elt vehyl." Mandros spoke right to Jodathyn's chaos. *"I lay claim to Tornyth, Winter's Dragon."*

At the mention of Tornyth's name, Jodathyn felt a pang of despair.

"Be at peace; terrible things can happen to a dragon who manifests under duress. Rshon-Aluel is here."

Jodathyn stirred, unconsciously sidling closer to the warmth of Mandros' belly. Unbidden, he shared with Mandros previously buried images of his childhood. Before them was a blossoming apple tree. Under the protection of the tree's branches sat Jodathyn as a child. His lap was full of wriggling pups. He could hear his childish giggles as they licked his hands and face. When the ground tilted beneath him, his cries of delight turned into cries of pain. Small Jodathyn was sprawled on the sticky, red grass. The puppies were gone. He was alone and afraid.

In his own mind, Jodathyn struggled and screamed.

"Tornyth – shed your past. It can't hurt you unless you grant it permission. It is time to bask in the glory of what you were born to be."

"I can't do this!" Jodathyn cried.

"You can and you will," Mandros assured him. His voice was still calm. *"It took great courage to show me that memory. Now you need just a little bit more to push past it and into the light. You are not a helpless little boy anymore. You are a son of a dragon."*

"I am afraid ..."

"Come to Rshon-Aluel. I will show you how to harness your fear into something greater."

"You use words I don't understand."

"I am your Rshon-Aluel. Your dragon-father. Your protector. Your guide. Come forth little white scales ..."

"Please ..." A voice that was not Jodathyn's answered.

Jodathyn came back to awareness with a start. Struggling to stand, his limbs flailed underneath him. His vision cleared so that he could see Mandros' face peering into his own. His bones creaked and groaned; his muscles stretched. A burning in his shoulder blades made him roll onto his belly. His skin and muscles spasmed as his soft human skin formed into hard dragon scales. Jodathyn would have thought manifesting was a painful experience. To his amazement, even as his body contorted, he felt nothing more than a slight discomfort.

"Tornyth, as long as the sun warms my scales, I am your *Rshon-Aluel*."

Bewildered, Tornyth blinked – he had transformed into a dragon.

Mandros' grin broadened, showing rows of sharp teeth. "Welcome, *elt mynrell*. You are a fully manifested dragon."

Tornyth could hardly believe it, he had conquered the damnable tonics that had sought to kill him. He had survived.

"Sleep," Mandros commanded, laying down his crowned head. "Once you are well rested, we'll stretch those handsome wings of yours."

A surge of pride caused Tornyth's wings to flutter, as Mandros' warm breath tickled him along the sides of his face.

"Hush now," Mandros said. "Your *Rshon-Aluel* is an ancient one among dragonkind. Sleep now, prince of dragons."

"I am free?" Tornyth stretched out his snout to whiff the air. He could smell the salt of the ocean and the dampness saying rain was not far away. "Might we fly over the ocean tomorrow?"

"Sleep, scaled prince," Mandros rumbled.

With a sigh of contentment, Tornyth rested his head along the cave's floor. *Rshon-Aluel* was pleased with him. And at last, he was free of his human prison. The promise of ruling the skies of Rama brought him great joy and for the first time in his life, hope.

This was the destiny he had been born to fulfil.

Love it? Hate it? Either way please consider leaving a review on either Goodreads or Amazon. All reviews are helpful.

Psst ... it the back. There's a QR Code for an exclusive missed scene! Go check it out!

a amazon.com/author/kjburrage

g goodreads.com/author/show/22623993.K_J_Burrage

List of Characters

Ammerie – (AM – ma – ree) – Jodathyn's late mother

Arturyn Pallarus – (AH – tur – en PA – la – rus) – The first King of Rama

Atek Rytter – (AY – tek RY-ter) – A man in service of Galgothmeg

Bear – (B – air) – Jodathyn's dog

Carew Candyde – (CA – roo CAN – dy – d) – Guardsman of the King's Guard

Carvelle Pallarus – (CA – vell PA – la – rus) – the Crown Prince of Rama, the son of Kieryn and the nephew of Jodathyn

Donatein Manideep – (DON – a – teen MAN – i – deep) – Jodathyn's oldest manservant

Frayn (Lord) – (FR – ain) – A great lord of the King's council

Fydellah Nahilya – (FI – del –ah NA – hil – ya) – An ex-slave, she was once a free woman

Galgothmeg – (GAL – goth – meg) – A red dragon known as Death and Despair

Hadryn Pallarus – (HAD – ren PA – la – rus) – the late King of Rama. The father of Kieryn and Jodathyn

Hallidyn Whitoak (Lord) – **(HAL – i – din WIT – oak)** – A great lord of the King's council. The King's favourite Lord

Illeanah Whitoak (Lady) – **(ILL– len – nah WIT – oak)** – Hallidyn Whitoak's daughter and childhood friend of Jodathyn

Jael Aryk (JAY – el AY – rick) – Guardsman of the King's Guard and Troop Medic and Healer

Jodathyn Pallarus - **(JOD – ath – en PA – la – rus)** – the Son of the Crown, the brother to the High King of Rama

Kamoore (Lord) – **(KA – more)** – A great lord of the King's council

Kieryn Pallarus – **(KEER – ren PA – la – rus)** – the High King of Rama

Mandros (Mand- roz) – An emerald dragon with many titles, including Flame and Fury, Deliverer, Father of this Land, the Green

Nym Torkelle (N-im Tor-kel) – A rescued thief

Odelle Pallarus – **(O – Del Pa-la-rus)** – the Queen of Rama, Kieryn's wife

Orion Maysden (O – ri -an Mays-den) – Jodathyn's servant, a horseman of Silverdyne

Parrie (Par-re) – Jodathyn's dog

Ruevyn Kelvie (ROO -Ven Kel-vee) – A childhood friend of Jodathyn

Solan (Lord) – **(SO-Lan)** – A great lord of the King's council

Soren Monster-Blade (S-or-en) – A human counterpart to Vadroil

Theo Torkelle (TH -e-o Tok-kel) – A rescued thief

Tiernan Candyde (TIER-nan Can-dy-d) – Captain of the King's Guard

Tornyth (TOR-N-eth) – Winter's Dragon

Vadroil (VAD – roy – el) – a dragon of myth and legend who

Valt Axtin (V – al – t AX – tin) – Jodathyn's personal guard

Lord Will (Willyrd) Hartcurt (WIL – lard HART –curt) – A young lord at court with a bad reputation

Zarine (ZA – reen) – A stolen mare

Language Guide

Araae helphelwyn. Terini gorthorawyn - (AH-ay HEL-fel-win TE-ree-ne GOR-thor- A-win) – Famous words of the King's Guard. Live Valiantly. Die Honourably.

Elt Mynrell – (EL-t MIN-rel) – My Heir (dragon use only)

Ri Rshon hanoch - (RI R-ish-on HAN-ock) – Considered coarse language – Old Dragon's Genitals

Rokun – (ROO-k-un) – Word for a human not worthy of dragon respect. Also used for a wicked person.

Rshon Aluel –(R-ish-on AY-lool) – Dragon Father. The title given to an older male dragon who adopts a vulnerable dragon. Note dragon adoption does not supersede human parentage. A dragon would refer to their acquired heir's father as Vehyl-Aluel (human father) or Vehyl-Lullah (human mother)

Rshon mahthyt – (R-ish-on MA-th-at) – Dragon Dung

Vehyl (V-hay-el) – Word for a human that is worthy of dragon respect. Often used affectionately.

Wirahli Sais-levly – (WER-ah-lee S-ace - LEV-lee) Enslaved Flying Lizard

Location Guide

Adavan Fields (AD-a-van)

Androssah (AN-dr-os-a)

Arah (AH-rah)

Arelle Forest (AH-el)

Artroth (ART-r-oth)

Aviah Valley (AY-vee-ah)

Belrah (BEL-rah)

Corlyn (COR-lin)

Farholm (FAH-hol-m)

Habron (HA-bron)

Haven Bay (HAY-ven)

Korkalie (KOR-ka-lee)

Malara Gorge (MA-la-rah)

Myryn (MY-rin)

Paldera (PAL-deer-ah)

Pallaryn (PA-la-ren)

Rama (RAH-ma)

Sant Burgundy (S-an-t BUR-gun-dee)

Silverdyne (SIL-va di-n)

Sion (SI-on)
Thrangul (THR-an-gool)
Torryn (TOR-ren)
Torqui (TOR-key)
Yanyima (YAN-yim-ah)

Acknowledgments

I would like to take the time to first thank you, the reader. Without a reader interested in reading my words, there would be no book. If you enjoyed the tale of Jodathyn and his struggles please consider leaving a review on Amazon or Goodreads.

Thank you to my alpha and beta readers: Janine, Kaye, Peej, Stephanie and Ronda. Thank you for taking your time to give me your honest thoughts.

To those who have always supported me. To my mother who was my first editor ... and edited pages, upon pages upon pages of my childish attempts to be like Mr CS Lewis. To my sister Janine, who has been my beta reader since she was eight years old!

To my loving husband who always believed the day would come when I would have a published piece of work. Thank you for believing in me more than I believed in myself. To my daughters who had enduring patience as Mumma started writing once more.

To my amazing friend Peej, who convinced me it was possible to take up writing and get published. Thanks for the nudge!

Thank you to the professionals I have hired who have made this project possible. To my editor, Sue Copsey, thank you for your patience with all my questions. I think you will all agree the team at MiblArt have done an amazing job on my cover. I can't wait to see what they come up with for the sequels! Thank you to the help from @thatdudemax on Fiverr, who helped me fix my maps and bring them to life!

KJ Burrage
AUTHOR

About KJ Burrage

KJ Burrage currently calls tropical North Queensland, Australia, home. She has been developing her craft since she was ten years old. Alas, the original floppy discs from 1995 have disappeared!

She lives with her three young daughters, an exuberant pug-cross and a cheeky blue parrot.

Growing up she had grand visions of becoming CS Lewis. When she grew up a little more, she decided she was going to be JRR Tolkien. Now, she's learnt to be proud of her own voice and the pen name KJ Burrage is perfect for her.

She has a Bachelor Degree in Primary Education with a major in literacy and worked as a primary school teacher. She has also been a co-owner of a laser engraving business.

Life can be unpredictable (and unfair). After the sudden and tragic death of her husband, she returned to her passion of the written word.

You can read more at www.kjburrage.com.

f   facebook.com/profile.php?id=100071328683512

⦿   instagram.com/kjburrage_author/

♪   tiktok.com/@kjburrage_writes

g   goodreads.com/author/show/22623993.K_J_Burrage

a   amazon.com/author/kjburrage

🐦   https://twitter.com/KJBurrage

KJ BURRAGE

THE ISLE ETERNAL SUMMER

Exclusive for readers of 'Son of the Crown' comes a missing scene just for you! Meet with Mandros as he returns home to the Isle of Eternal Summer to tell his kin that there is a new dragon of Rama. The password to access is SotC2022

SCAN ME

KJ BURRAGE

THE PATH TO PALLARYN

Discover more about some of your favourite side characters in this collection of short stories. Learn more about the tragic circumstances that Fydellah, Orion and Will face and how they find themselves in the Citadel of Pallaryn.

SCAN ME